DAMNED GROUNDS

Terry L. Vinson

DAMNED GROUNDS

A DOUBLE DRAGON PAPERBACK

© Copyright 2020
Terry L. Vinson

The right of Terry L. Vinson to be identified as author of this work has been asserted in accordance with the Copyright, Designs and Patents Act 1988

All Rights Reserved

No reproduction, copy or transmission of the publication may be made without written permission. No paragraph of this publication may be reproduced, copied or transmitted save with the written permission of the publisher, or in accordance with the provisions of the Copyright Act 1956 (as amended).

Any person who does any unauthorised act in relation to this publication may be liable to criminal prosecution and civil claims for damages.

ISBN 978-1-78695-397-1

Double Dragon
is an imprint of
Fiction4All

Published 2020
Fiction4All
www.fiction4all.com

Cover art by Deron Douglas
www.derondouglas.ca

Prologue, Part I

Gil and Buck at the Edge of the Abyss

April 15th, 1948
Red Bridge, Mississippi

Attempting in vain to wipe away the thick tendrils of smoke filling his eyes and nostrils, Buck Lomax hacked like a man choking on a mouthful of marbles.

“Holy smoke, Gil. I said only use enough of them firesticks a’yours to crease the mountainside, not blow a hole big enough to drive a mobile home through,” he blurted between coughs, backing up slowly from the massive hole he had been peering down into.

Treading carefully down the hillside, which was now coated in freshly crushed rubble, Buck resembled a man exiting a burning building, deep pools of tears propped at the corners of his squinting eyes.

He was met at the bottom of the hill by a man literally twice his size in both height and girth. Wiping his eyes vigorously, Buck came dangerously close to running into the other man before his forward momentum finally halted.

“Sorry ‘bout that, Buck. I just figured there was a lotta rock...” Gil Brock began, trying without much success to keep from breaking into an uncontrollable giggling fit.

Buck coughed harshly one last time, sending a thumb-sized chunk of phlegm onto his own dusty left work boot, then glared at the other man through a face engulfed in layers of dust.

“Damn it, Gil, your blast happy and you know it! I feel like I’ve been dipped in gravel, and I was supposed to be a safe distance away. Good thing I wasn’t twenty feet closer, ain’t it? I’d be pluckin’ granite from my balls!” He railed, his frail, thin frame trembling with rage.

Gil Brock, whose ample gut was now shaking like a half-settled bowl of pudding from semi-restrained laughter, turned away from the smaller man’s gaze and instead concentrated on the damage he’d inflicted, which at the moment resembled some sort of lava-less volcanic eruption.

“I said sorry, Buck. ‘Sides, you know as well as me they’ll want more room for the highway shoulder than that state blueprint shows. They always underestimate that stuff, am I right?”

Pointing a bony finger upwards and shaking it like a schoolteacher scolding an unruly pupil, Buck spat a small rock from the left corner of his mouth before speaking.

“That ain’t the point, Gil. Yer supposed to follow the blueprint, just like I am. This is about the third job you’ve showered my butt with rock. I’m getting sick and tired of finding burnt grub worms in my undies when I get ho...”

Both men instantly tensed, although later neither could recall exactly what instigated such a reaction.

A split-second later they felt the breeze first make contact with the slightly moist, exposed skin on their arms, neck and face.

“What the? Damn, that’s hot...” Gil blurted, his teeth ground tightly together.

Despite the sudden burst of heat, which both

would agree later had felt like steam escaping a punctured hot water heater; Buck Lomax rubbed his upper arms like a man fighting a sudden chill.

"I don't smell gas or nothin'..." he whispered through badly chapped, dust coated lips.

In the single blink of an eye, the breeze transformed into a stout gust of wind that threatened to topple the smaller man from his feet, while bending the larger of the two back on his heels like an ancient oak caught in a typhoon.

Gil regained his balance and leaned up just in time to reach out and prevent Buck from tripping over onto the loose gravel, his massive left arm wrapped around the other man's narrow shoulders.

The searing heat increased as the gust grew stronger, Gil later recounting to anyone who would listen that 'it felt like we was being baked from the inside.'

Then, just as quickly it had come, the gust halted, leaving both men posed in a comical two-step, their eyes closed tightly as if avoiding the scariest scene from a horror film.

All was as it had been moments earlier, only the smallest of breezes apparent, and without the unbearable heat of seconds earlier.

Gil backed away slowly, his thickly muscled arm leaving Buck's frail shoulders in a single jerk, his hands instantly moving to his badly itching eyes.

Moments later, both men leaned on Buck's ancient, battered back hoe, which had been parked a good one hundred yards from the blast site, it's front end protruding from two ancient oaks like some prehistoric dinosaur.

"Gil, what the hell you think caused that?"

Buck muttered, casually picking his nose through a stained handkerchief he had pulled from his coveralls.

Gil Brock alternated taking long sips of water from a clear plastic bottle and scratching his semi-balding head. He noticed with no small amount of confusion and irritation that his own clothes were still overly warm from the wind tunnel from hell they had just emerged from.

"Never felt anything like it, Buck old buddy. You sure you didn't fart? I saw ya munchin' on those sausage biscuits this morning at Mage's café."

Buck attempted a smile, but it came out a pained grimace.

"Cut the bull-crap, Gil. What would cause…something like that? I've been clearing land for over twenty years and never caught a belch of hot air like that 'fore."

"It did come from the damned hole I blew in the mountain, didn't it?" Gil asked somewhat timidly before gulping more water.

"A-yep. Came from that general direction, fer sure. Ya wanna go check it out? Seems like most of the smoke has blown itself out."

Shrugging his massive, hair coated shoulders, Gil smiled thinly.

"Why not? Don't think we can expect another sneak attack at this point, huh?"

It took the two men ten full minutes to cover the football field length of loose rocks and soft, slick dirt that led to the battered mountainside that Buck had so hastily departed half an hour earlier.

The black chasm they peered into was a mere six to seven feet wide and perfectly circular. It looked as though it had literally been cut out with the sharpest of slicing tools, the edges not the least bit jagged, but smooth as if seared away by a round object containing immense heat.

Gil grunted indifferently, running his fingers through his dirty, moist hair. “Ya see anything down there, Buck?”

“It’s a deep ‘un, all right. Maybe we’re diggin’ over an old coal mine or something,” Buck replied blandly. Both men stood with their leg’s spread, as if they were about to relieve themselves into the pitch-black abyss.

“Well, we gotta call in the boys and get this covered over with a plate. They might even have to shift the plans a bit. I… wha-…” Gil began, first rubbing then pinching his nostrils tightly with this right hand.

“Gil? What’s the ma-...” Buck began, then practically leaped back from the opening, waving his hands out in front of his own nose like a man warding off a swarm of bees.

“Damn, w-what in blue blazes is that s-*stench*?” Gil managed, performing an impromptu dance jig while backing spastically away.

Buck was about to attempt a garbled reply just before his boots slid back on a pile of loose gravel and he lurched back, his thin arms pin-wheeling madly. His narrow, bony rear end taking most of the burnt, he landed with a loud huff escaping his parched lips.

“Son of a... dog gone! Won’t be ridin’ the range anytime soon, that’s for sure...” he bellowed as both men finally began to breathe somewhat normally, their spastic reactions slowly ceasing the more distance they put between themselves and the opening.

Now a good twenty yards from the hole, both men stood with their hands propped on their hips, sucking in air as if just rescued from a cramped cave.

"Gil, I ain't sniffed anything that rank since my Marge had that bout with a stomach virus last year. She was pootin' and crappin' every five minutes for a week. I thought I was gonna hafta dig out my old WWI gas mask," Buck said through a weak, somewhat grisly smile.

Despite the happenings of the last hour, Gil couldn't help but guffaw loudly, his entire torso racked with rolling tremors.

It took a full minute for him to regain a semblance of control.

He then raised his right hand in a gesture of surrender to the other man. "No more toilet stories, Buck, I beg ya. I gotta agree, though. I've sniffed dead animal carcasses roastin' in the sun that smelled better. I think it sunk into my damn clothes to boot. Kinda like being sprayed by a skunk, ain't it?"

Buck pulled his shirt collar close with one callused hand and took a quick sniff, his mouth slightly agape in a comical grimace.

"Yep. My shirt smells like a fresh dog turd, alright. Susie's gonna half ta wash these in bleach fore I can wear 'em in public again."

Gil giggled and gave the smaller man a light nudge.

"Just stash 'em in the closet and wear 'em to preachin' next week, Buck. You'll have a whole pew to yourself."

Buck, displaying a smile void of the majority of his bottom row of teeth, gave his large co-worker a playful tap on the shoulder.

As they descended the hill back towards the heavy equipment campsite, both began to experience a slight throbbing at the back of their respective skulls.

Prologue Part II

Gil Peels Out

Gil arrived at his cabin around six o'clock that evening. A bit worn and in desperate need of some roofing work, the cabin stood at the edge of a dirt one lane some twelve miles from the city limits of Red Bridge. He had no neighbors to speak of, and the cabin itself was cloaked in such thick foliage it looked as if it had actually sprouted from the ground it sat upon.

Gil was almost forty and had never married, although he had made a habit of running the bars and juke joints of Tupelo since his late teens for occasional, however temporary, female companionship. Having never spent a single minute outside the borders of his home state, he found absolute contentment in a life uncomplicated by the pressures of city living. His father had built the cabin he now occupied some thirty years before, and he had long since accepted the fact that when his time was up, he would be buried alongside his folks in the nearby Red Bridge cemetery.

Gil was the proud owner of two full-blooded blue tick hounds, one male and one female. He subsidized his income by selling the pups they bred, and filled his cooler with the Opossums and squirrels they sniffed out on frequent hunting jaunts into the nearby forest.

The following morning, and for the first time in his twelve years of employment with Bowen Excavating Company, Gil Brock was a no-show at morning roll call.

He had awakened around three am; coated in

fresh, cool sweat, the back of his skull pounding as if someone was tapping the base with a ball-peen hammer. The skin of his face, arms and neck were hot to the touch, and stung with even the lightest contact with his probing fingers.

After washing his face with the partially cooled water pulled from a back yard well the night before, he peered into the partially cracked mirror mounted in his tiny bathroom and performed a flawlessly staged double take. Reaching up with one shaky hand, Gil peeled thick layers of dry, dead skin from his jawline and forehead. It looked as if he had fallen asleep in a blazing mid-morning sun and remained in such a pose until sunset. Gil was a man accustomed to the sun's burning rays, his complexion comparative to the leather straps that hung in the adjoining barn at the rear of the cabin.

That said, it was a vastly different, undeniably gruesome looking strain of skin burn that Gil bore witness to this particular night.

Rummaging through kitchen cabinets filled with ancient cob and spider webs alike, Gil managed on badly shaking legs, to discover the cloth-encased poultice his grandmother, long since deceased, had given him countless years before.

Gil eventually fell into a nightmarish slumber, the skin peeling from his moist frame like that of a shedding snake with each toss or turn of his body.

He awoke at noon, his entire being a raw, pulsating wound. Gil could briefly sympathize with all the fish and small game he had skinned over the decades. He filled the bathroom tub with a mix of cool and boiling water, then lied in its murky, slightly grimy contents for a full two hours, sporadically fading in and out of a bleary daze.

The tub's water, which had been a greenish color initially, was a light shade of crimson upon Gil's eventual departure, a fact he was hopelessly oblivious to due to the unbearable pain occupying his every move. As he attempted to dress, his mind debating a trip into town to visit the local Red Bridge sawbones, Gil noticed a pungent metallic smell filling his nostrils. It reminded him of a job he once held in town welding heavy metal frames together for trailers, the same scent of the smoke that filled his welding mask at the conclusion of each completed bead.

Thinking that it would improve his overall well-being, which at the time was relatively comparable to a dog in the final stages of rabies, lying with its neck lapped over the edge of a railroad track, Gil attempted to eat a slice of bread and chase it with fresh well-water. After heaving a moist chunk of bread halfway across the kitchen and watching in tickled amazement as it literally stuck to a far cabin wall like a glob of muddy clay, Gil quickly dismissed such notions. Instead, he began searching frantically for the keys to his old Ford pick-up, which he had nicknamed 'The Black Funnel' not long after purchase. On any given trip, 'The Funnel' was known for leaving a trail of remarkably thick, black smoke for miles in its wake. Gil realized it's days were numbered, but for the forty dollars he had slapped down for its services, deduced he would squeeze every last mile out of her worn out engine before finding a spot in the pasture for the vehicles everlasting resting place.

Gil passed out on the cabin floor long before

his search concluded, a flurry of ants scurrying in and out of his occasionally flaring nostrils where he had earlier spilled a glass of warm milk.

When he awoke, spitting various insects and even a rather fat caterpillar from his mouth as he painstakingly arose, the cabin was cloaked in darkness.

Stumbling from the cabin's only useable door, the back one had long since been boarded shut and a wood burning stove placed at her threshold, Gil suddenly realized with great self-embarrassment that the truck's keys would be found where he *always* left them, tucked securely within the ignition switch. He chalked up his earlier confusion about their whereabouts to the pain that had, after that last involuntary nap, subsided quite a bit. Thoughts of allowing old Doc Krane (a man he described to others as 'old Doc Undertaker', since the man never seemed to actually cure anybody of anything, instead just assisted in placing them into whatever wooden box the grieving family could afford at the time) to poke around on his person was not high on his 'things to do 'fore I croak' list.

No, Gil had decided he felt miraculously better, so much so in fact that he completely ignored the grisly apparition that glared back at him from 'The Black Funnel's' rear view mirror as he fired up the engine and prepared to head towards Red Bridge.

The man's face was flushed blood red, even the whites of his eyes engulfed by a thick coating of what looked (and would have smelled to anyone with normally functioning nostrils) like layers of fresh pus. The fingers that grasped and slowly turned the old Ford's scarred steering wheel were a dark shade of blue at the fingertips, the nails themselves tugging free from their hosts with each forceful pull of the wheel.

Despite the fog that entrenched his inner mind, Gil knew exactly where he was going. That much, at least, was crystal clear, though exactly why or how such a plan had been mapped out were *anything* but.

As he rumbled towards the city limits of Red Bridge, Mississippi, population seven-hundred sixteen, the truck's one working head lamp carving a thin line through the sweeping darkness of the narrow two lane it occupied, Gil glared down at his crotch and grinned. His coveralls could barely contain the massive erection held there, one he had not witnessed the likes of since that red- headed bar maid in T-Town soaped him up with hot oil a few years back. Gil's grin grew larger as he turned his concentration back to the bumpy, isolated stretch of road ahead. He was beyond all caring as two of his front teeth ever so gently dislodged from their gum-slots and dropped into his open shirt.

Gil couldn't recall a single action taken between the time he awoke and lunging into the musty cab of his badly rusted but usually reliable ride.

If asked, he would have vehemently denied strolling casually out to his small, pathetically over-stuffed barn and retrieving the oak-handled axe that had been leaning just inside the open front entrance.

Nor would he have recalled taking said axe and systematically slaughtering his two prize hounds while they slept peacefully atop his trash- strewn back porch, splitting each one's skull with a single, perfectly calculated swing.

Bounding joyously down the road with his barely concealed boner leading the way, Gil's memory of placing the blood-soaked axe behind the truck's seat would also be sketchy at best, although its very presence would invariably prove to be horrifically useful later that evening.

Prologue, Part III

Buck Springs a Leak

Marge Lomax met her husband at the front door of their modest two- bedroom home at exactly six-thirteen the previous evening.

Admittedly feeling a bit flushed, Buck began to cough lightly just as his wife was placing dinner on the table. While furiously blowing his nose, his narrow rear end parked on the far edge of the living room couch, Buck stared long and hard at his better half as she maneuvered so ungraciously around the square oak table.

Marge had been nothing short of pixie-like when they had first met some twenty-threes earlier, tiny enough for him to carry on his less-than-husky shoulders without a hint of strain. Taking in the present version, the wide girth of her massive rear end and the extra chin that jiggled freely underneath her once gaunt jaw line, he couldn't help but grunt in sour disbelief.

"Miserable lard-ass. How much of my hard-earned dollar has been spent keeping her trough full?" He whispered while bending to unlace his boots, which, were coated in a veritable Kaleidoscope of color born from dust, clay and spilled motor oil.

Marge peered in from the kitchen, her rotund face made all the more massive by the flat, oily clumps of hair that clung to her scalp like seaweed to the hull of a boat.

"Supper's on the table, Buck, whenever you're proper to eat," she said in a voice both weary and apathetic.

"Why don't you kiss my proper ass, you miserable blimp," Buck responded, a bit louder than he had intended.

"What was that?" Marge asked while standing prone over the steaming plate of cabbage she was toting from the kitchen hot plate.

"Nothin'. I'm just tired is all. Don't feel too spry, neither."

"Well, get in here and eat. That'll perk ya up," Marge answered, again with a tone of complete indifference.

Buck felt his teeth grind together just before the initial round of hacking coughs set in, the intensity of which proceeded to practically drive him to his knees in the center of the living room floor.

While washing up a few moments later, Buck felt the tips of his fingers begin to tingle madly at the touch of the lye soap he was lathering with.

He was still coughing, but not as harshly, the itch at his Adam's apple just a minor irritant compared to the pain now shooting through his fingers and slowly into his knuckles and wrists.

By the time he made it to the kitchen table some ten minutes later, the skin on his neck, arms, and hands no longer tingled as if falling asleep, but instead radiating immense heat from a horrid fever that seemed to be swallowing him whole.

Staring down at the warm, soggy cabbage and sliced portions of dried pork, Buck felt a wave of nausea slap his mid-section like a physical blow.

"Don't feel too good, Marge. Not s-sure I wanna eat right now..." he managed, desperately fighting the urge to heave onto the already full plate parked below his chin.

Marge barely acknowledged him, her mouth packed with cabbage, her face a mask of disgust.

"I spent all evenin' on this meal, Buck Lomax. The least you could do is try to eat at least some of it. *Go* on. More than likely all ya need is some warm food in your gut anyhow."

As Buck watched with eerie fascination as his wife of over two decades shoveled in bite after bite, the fork she held in one chubby hand unable to hold the majority of each load before reaching her wide maw, he found the strength to temporarily dismiss the unsettled rumbling at his midsection.

Five minutes later, his plate was spotless save a light coating of oil from the huge mound of cabbage he had ingested. The large portion of pork, along with two biscuits loaded with butter and molasses, had all been washed down with two tall mugs of cool apple cider.

Buck turned to Marge as she loomed over him while scooping up the dishes. Her melon sized breasts hung from inside the loose-fitting housedress she wore like twin church bells. As was normally the case when such a site filled his eyes, Buck's mind reacted with instant repulsion. However, as she reached to retrieve his drinking mug, Buck quickly discovered a vastly different emotion overtaking the first. This time, the tingling he felt wasn't in his fingers or hands. Grinning at his own shocked response, Buck couldn't help but release a low, muffled giggle.

Marge, her hands filled with dishes, gave him a strange look as she strolled over to the sink.

"What's so funny, Buck? Let me in on the joke. I could sure use one, I tell ya. Spendin' my days doing nothin' but cleanin' and cookin' leaves little time for laughter, you know?"

Waving her off, as he was apt to do in order to cut off further conversation between the two of them, Buck pushed away from the table and turned to exit the kitchen, the need to pee suddenly overwhelming.

"Nothin', Margy. Just work stuff. Back in a minute, I gotta..." he began, his feet halting suddenly as he reached the halfway point of the tiny living room, as if he had spotted a poisonous snake in his path.

Buck heard Marge babble something in reply, but found his powers of concentration no longer able to focus on anything other than the scorching shock waves pummeling his lower extremities.

"Oh *shit...*" He mumbled, unhitching his jeans while half-trotting in the general direction of the bathroom.

As he tripped forward, barely avoiding whacking his forehead against the metal sink before managing to straighten up, Buck was given two very specific commands by whomever was at the controls of his personal Department of Bodily Functions. Number one was to relieve himself via urination before his bladder imploded. Number two was to open his mouth as wide as his jaw muscles and the skin of his ragged, leathery mug would allow to spew forth the meal he had just so heartily consumed.

His pants wrapped around his ankles like thickly bound ropes, Buck was able to tug his shockingly rigid manhood forward just in time to avoid spraying the forward wall and the picture window framed there. Within the past few years, Buck had noticed the plumbing going a bit south in both potency of the stream emitted, as well as distance traveled of said waste. On this night, however, he wondered in stark fear whether it was his own body part he was grasping or a runaway firehose. There was a dull ache evident in his crotch as he urinated, one that was gradually making a b-line up his spine.

Marge rushed into the bathroom just as Buck turned his head and faced her direction while barely managing to avoid flooding the room with the sour-smelling remnants spilling forth like Niagara Falls from his battered bladder.

"Buck! What's the mat-..." his beloved spat just a split-second before a sharp scream finished her sentence.

Her loving husband of more years than she hardly cared to remember looked to be coming utterly unhinged right before her very eyes.

His mouth was opened so high and wide she first thought it to be some kind of mirage possibly induced by the pork they had both eaten (she had let it warm a bit too long that afternoon while napping). Once Marge accepted the indisputable fact that it was *indeed* Bucks mouth that seemed to be reaching to swallow her whole, she cringed back as if gut punched, another tiny wail escaping the back of her throat like that of a wounded animal.

"What's got into…w-what's *wrong...*?" She mumbled, stepping back into the narrow hallway just as Buck's upper body heaved forward in a spastic lurch.

Years before, when she had been fifty pounds

lighter and much quicker on her feet, Marge might have been able to easily duck the glut of barely digested, sickeningly melded together food items that sailed towards her resembling a wave of dark sewage gushing forth from an undersized pipe.

As it was, the heftier, more ponderous version of Marge was barely able to lift one blubber-encased forearm to ward off a tiny portion of the moist, doughy substance.

The majority struck her just above her massive breasts, just underneath her multi-layered neck. The sound it made upon contact was similar to a ripe tomato being tossed against a stone wall. Chewed portions of pork, cabbage, and bread flew into Marge's open mouth and into her flared nostrils, causing her to gag uncontrollably while falling back against the near wall with a muffled thud.

"Oh... gawd… it's in m-my nose… ughhh," she cried after spitting out most of what had landed in her mouth onto the badly worn hallway carpet.

Completely forgetting the source of her discomfort, Marge was just beginning to wipe the brownish sludge from her upper chest when the shadow fell across her face like a storm cloud passing overhead.

"B-Buck, are y-you okay? I guess the p-pork might h-have been ruined…" she began, only halting when the expression on her husband's face came clearly into view.

Despite the fact that his wife's weight that evening would have easily tipped the scales at upwards of two-hundred twenty pounds, Buck Lomax discovered that dragging her the short distance from the hall into their nearby bedroom by her chubby ankles an amazingly easy task.

Once the projectile urination and vomiting had ceased, Buck had experienced a feeling of euphoric relief he never considered imaginable, as if a truckload of cement had been unloaded from his slender shoulders.

Additionally, he had peered down to find his sexual excitement from earlier hadn't abated a single iota. Realizing that such unique arousal wasn't a permanent condition by any stretch of his fevered imagination, Buck deduced he had little time to lose, thus the rough and tumble tactics utilized with his beloved would have to simply be excused.

With a single right cross to her left temple, Buck had ended Marge's very vocal objections to the unexpected romantic interlude he had planned.

Once the deed was done, the first such activity witnessed by the surrounding walls in over three months, Buck hitched his jeans high upon his thin waist and simply turned and walked away, stopping only to pull his always loaded twelve-gauge shotgun from the bedroom closet.

As he pulled hastily away from the structure he had called home for all but two years of his adult life (two years spent in the service of Uncle Sam's Army the only exception), his bruised and unconscious wife lying spread eagle atop their bedroom mattress, Buck Lomax grinned like the lunatic he most certainly *was*. A thin line of brownish-white spittle ran onto his chin from the left corner of his open mouth. Buck never bothered to acknowledge the skin peeling so freely away from the fingers that held the steering wheel of his

Ford Wagon. He could almost feel the blood cursing through the veins at his temples, flowing like hot lava through a freshly dug passageway. He defined the pain as both excruciating and exhilarating at the same time, although neither state would detour him from the mission his mind had abruptly snapped upon like a steel trap on a deer's hind leg mere moments before.

Buck had a definite location in mind, and a certain person to address on topics such as respect for one's elders.

Prologue, Part IV

Separate But Equal Meltdowns

In the twenty-one minutes it had taken Gil to reach the Carlyle homestead on the far west side of the Red Bridge city limits, three more of his upper teeth now lay in the truck's moldy floorboard and the large majority of his fingers were mostly skinless.

He had cut the truck's engine a few hundred feet before gliding to a silent stop directly in front of a large, slightly dented metal mailbox with the inscription '*D. Carlyle*' painted on its left side in badly faded white paint.

Departing the cab of the truck with all the speed of a three-toed sloth hopped up on tranquilizers, Gil left the driver's door somewhat agape after removing a single item from behind the seat.

He recalled Marvin Carlyle having at least one dog, possibly two, but couldn't for the life of him remember what particular breed or if they were apt to treat his unannounced visit as an act of aggression.

Walking in a permanent crouch like a foot soldier assigned night patrol, Gil held the axe blade snugly against his bare chest, the skin of which was as oily slick as the hands that held the weapon's handle.

Avoiding the graveled one lane that led to the homestead, Gil instead stepped cautiously onto the grassy hillside just to its left; his boots sinking noiselessly into its padded contents. The house itself wasn't viewable from the road, blocked by a thick line of pines on either side, the steep hill its foundation rested upon cresting some seventy-five yards from where his truck sat parked.

Around mid-way to his ultimate destination, Gil felt the bottom end of the axe handle brush faintly against his groin, momentarily increasing the intense burning sensation that had refused to subside since departing his cabin.

"Easy, boy. Relief is almost in sight," he muttered through lips so chapped their outer layers seemed coated in rapidly peeling paint.

The first series of barks filled his ears a moment later, originating from the direction of the still blocked homestead. His step never wavering, Gil nonchalantly propped the axe atop his left shoulder as his boots made initial contact with the graveled drive.

Rounding the winding, increasingly steep hill, Gil caught a glimpse of the wide brick well he knew to be just a few scant feet to the left of the Carlyle's two- story home.

The dog's barks were growing increasingly clearer and a bit more intense in nature, although Gil did feel a sense of relief that they hadn't been accompanied by howls of a similar nature within the surrounding countryside. Country canines were infamous for barking at stout breezes in the night when the mood hit them, just as their owners were accustomed to hearing and in-turn ignoring such irritating melodies.

Gil heard the patter of paws on loose gravel to his left, just as the barking quickly transformed into a series of guttural growls.

Less than three full minutes later, Gil stood on the solid wooden porch of the Carlyle home, propped upon the axe handle like a distinguished gentleman about town, leaning on his trusty cane.

Upon viewing and more importantly *sniffing* the partially hunched over intruder to his everyday stomping grounds, the Carlyle family dog had wisely decided to take the road less traveled, sprinting into the nearby woods like a fox attempting to outdistance an army of blood-lusting hounds. Gil had found the mutt's hasty, cowardly retreat somewhat of a disappointment, but quickly dismissed such trivialities to focus on the mission ahead.

Eyeballing the metal screen door entrance to the home with an icy, emotionless gaze, Gil took a single deep breath and reached for the handle with fingers encased in his own increasingly rank bodily fluids.

After witnessing the derailing freight train snores of Marvin Carlyle first-hand, Gil realized that a pack of howling dogs positioned outside the bedroom window would have been easily drowned out. Gil had known Marvin since their grade school days, when Marvin had been known as 'Knuckles' and had spent every waking moment bullying the kids around him. Marvin Carlyle had grown older with the same temperament intact, a man known for his lightning-fast temper and fists to match. He had spent most of the past twenty years employed at the Graves Lumber yard in Red Bridge, having been fired and re-hired countless times, the former due to the aforementioned short fuse, the latter due to his unlimited tolerance for hard, physical labor.

Marvin's wife of the past seventeen years, Sandra, had been a homemaker and occasional pie and cake baker (whenever Marvin was between jobs at the yard) for Wheeler's grocery store.

A slim woman with a pleasant yet shy demeanor, Sandra Carlyle slept with her body turned away from her husband's, her bent frame curled under the thin covers in a young child's fetal position.

Despite his initial instincts to impose such, Gil truly wished no undue suffering upon such a woman, whom he figured had endured quite enough punishment over the past years with such a cruel, overbearing husband to tolerate on a daily basis.

He had quietly laid the axe down upon a pile of unfolded clothing that fronted the foot of the bed and removed his ever-trusty straight razor from his left boot, then proceeded to cut her throat just below her sharply pointed chin. Sandra had hardly moved as the life had drained from her, only the slightest twitch of her left leg indicating the subtlest of reactions.

Despite a fine mist of his deceased wife's blood spattering onto his exposed arms, shoulders and neck, Marvin Carlyle's thundering snorts had never missed a single beat.

Retrieving the axe with a singular glee only recognizable in the confines of the criminally insane mind, Gil Brock then proceeded to first remove the slumbering man's left arm with a single wild hack before inflicting similar damage to this right foot just above the ankle with a similar swing. Resembling a life- sized toy soldier devoid of certain limbs, long since broken or pulled free, Marvin had jerked up into the center of the loudly creaking bed just as the axe blade had shattered his leg like dried kindling.

Gil Brock stood back for just a split-second and observed the man, obviously savoring the grisly results of his handy work.

Carlyle had winked comically, his right eyelid in the midst of an uncontrollable spasm.

"*Mama*?" Marvin had whispered in a harsh, dreamy tone, just as the shadow standing before him again raised the object of his impending demise.

"Not quite, jackass" Gil had replied cheerily, the recently sharpened blade whooshing forward in a direct arc toward the prone man's forehead.

Two rooms down, Melissa Carlyle awakened with a start, her shoulder length blond hair wrapped around her face like a self-sewn cocoon.

Melissa was seventeen, a high school Senior at Red Bridge High, and only two months away from beginning a new era in her young life on the campus of Mississippi State University in Starkville, where she hoped to receive a Masters Degree in the social sciences. She was to be the first female from Red Bridge to attend such a school, complete with a scholarship that included free room and board. Melissa had been voted Red Bridge's Most Attractive Student two years running, and had been the target of countless suitors, both fellow student and otherwise, since her early teens.

Large boned but sleek of body, she stood a statuesque five-nine, her breasts round and firm, her lengthy legs twin ladders of beauty that many local men fantasized of taking a leisurely climb upon.

Melissa had long since decided that playing homemaker in such a one- horse town was not her idea of a blissful life, and had managed to ignore lustful temptation (*unlike* a number of her peers) in lieu of mapping out her life beyond the forested borders of Red Bridge.

Rubbing her bleary eyes vigorously, Melissa heard nothing other than the high-pitched croaking of a bullfrog somewhere outside of her opened bedroom window. Debating a quick trip to drain her lightly throbbing bladder, Melissa eventually chose to collapse sideways back into her ruffled bed, groaning a bit as her right foot attempted in vain to conceal itself in the rolled-up blanket she lay upon.

Gil tip-toed through the half-ajar bedroom door mere seconds later, the axe lain carefully against a hallway table lamp just as Melissa had been wrestling with her blanket.

Unzipping his pants as her neared her position; Gil realized without a shadow of a doubt that he had never experienced such an overwhelming rush of sexual euphoria in all his born days. His engorged penis standing out like a insect's probing antenna, he leaped forward with a graceful yet deadly quickness he had most certainly not been equipped with earlier that day.

Once she had been penetrated, it had taken him only three roughly executed strokes to achieve mission compliance. Gil released his death grip on her mouth, leaving behind a large portion of his rotted left palm dangling between her gritted teeth in the process.

He then reared back and proceeded to punch Melissa with a series of short but forceful jabs, most landing solidly on her lower chin, but one of which landed directly on her upper plate of teeth. Three were instantly dislodged and two subsequently swallowed.

Satisfied that young Miss Carlyle wasn't fatally injured but nonetheless temporarily incapacitated, Gil rolled from the suddenly sagging mattress and placed his still moderately erect manhood back into hiding with a quick shove.

"Sorry 'bout skippin' the candlelight dinner, sweetie. Maybe next time," he rattled through a mostly toothless maw, ignoring the searing pain shooting from his tattered, bloody hand.

The full moon that shone at his back illuminating the gravel path that led back to his waiting chariot, Gil held the still dripping axe over his shoulder like a marching infantryman's long rifle. The combination smile/grimace frozen upon his face was one no longer recognizable as anything remotely human.

As he haphazardly tossed the tool in the truck's flat bed, the thudding sound that followed muffled by the layer of moist leaves that had accumulated there over the years, Gil heard the distance echo of a canine's pained howls. It was the Carlyle's pooch, no doubt, returned to the scene of its greatest failure. Gil felt the briefest of guilty twinges at the thought, although not for the family unit he had just systematically obliterated, but instead for the mangy, cowardly canine he had just left master-less.

Pulling back onto the dusty two-lane would land him dead center on the main street of Red Bridge in less than half an hour, Gil nodded to himself in silent congratulations. His task was complete, his end of the bargain having passed without a single hitch. Knowing he would more than likely never see his personal sacrifices be given their due in the ultimate scheme of things didn't hamper his sense of accomplishment. As he cut through the pitch-black night towards the mundane yet somehow absolutely necessary fate awaiting him through the rolling hills ahead, Gil Brock smiled one last time, emitting just the briefest of giggles.

***

Balanced precariously on knees that threatened to buckle without significant warning, Buck Lomax stared without blinking at the mangled form lying only inches from the tips of his dusty, blood-crusted work boots.

"Should'a treated me with more respect, Alan old man. Callin' a man an ignorant horses' ass behind his back ain't the way ya show respect, *no* sir. Disrespecting his old lady ain't on that particular list neither. Marge ain't no beauty queen, I'll admit, but only I got the right to say such. I *had* to choose somebody. Got no choice in the matter. You came to mind first, that's all. Luck of the draw, old buddy old pal," he whispered, totally dismissing the thick brown blob of snot-like goo that flew from his mouth as he spoke.

The discharge landed atop the stilled right shoulder of the body at his feet, then dripped slowly into pool of liquid crimson that was quickly expanding onto the light-colored tile floor. In the darkness of the kitchen, illuminated only by the moonlight shining through a tiny window over his shoulder, Buck thought the flow resembled a wave of spilled molasses, only a bit thinner in substance.

Buck had been calmly sitting at the oak kitchen table, stroking his twelve gauge like a wounded pet, just as Alan Carter had entered the room with the sheepish, drowsy look of a man only partially awake.

The back door had been unlocked, and had opened without a single creak to warn the inhabitants of an unauthorized visit.

Buck had considered simply searching out the bedroom Alan and his wife were occupying in the relatively small three-bedroom home, but had decided instead to take a quick respite before proceeding. His head had been pounding like a jackhammer since leaving his own homestead, and he feared he might eventually pass out without a break from the constant strain.

He figured Alan had come in for a glass of water from the cooler, or possibly a midnight snack of some kind. Buck had noticed a pile of neatly stacked homemade biscuits covered with napkins sitting on a far kitchen counter. Just the thought of ingesting such an item made him feel instantly faint.

The recoil from the shot slid the oak chair back a few feet on the slick tile flooring, and Buck came dangerously close to flipping head over heels into a far brick wall before regaining his balance.

Buck didn't think his old nemesis had neither the time or clear enough view to recognize his killer before his head was sheared off just above the bridge of his nose, and he regretted he hadn't done a better job of identifying himself beforehand.

Leaning up, his knees popping like Fourth of July fireworks, Buck sighed heavily and strolled back into the back, left bedroom for a final glimpse at Martha. A plain woman with long, stringy hair, Buck had never given Martha Carter a second look if they met on the street. She had wide hips, broad shoulders, and legs that resembled warped toothpicks, her bowlegged walk adding even less to her overall attractiveness.

Still, on this night Buck found the old saying that 'looks were only skin deep' to be truly as right as rain. Martha Carter, beak-like nose, prominent wart on the end of her chin and all, could have easily been wearing the crown of either Miss Mississippi or The Ugliest Female Alive for all his libido cared.

She had jogged into the kitchen wearing only an ankle-length, thin as cob webbing robe, and upon entry had immediately slipped on a stream of her recently deceased husband's blood, subsequently smacking her head with a reverberating thud on the hard floor below.

Buck had thought this particular series of events extremely comical, laughing so long and hard he seriously thought he was going to heave up a lung.

Not evening bothering to move her rigid form, Buck then proceeded to kneel down and take her as she lay. Her hair and upper back matted in the bodily fluids of the man she had spent the past eight years with, Martha's only passing reaction to the violation of her lower extremities was a low, drawn out moan that sounded like equal parts pleasure and disgust.

Buck arose from the cool, wet tile wearing a mask of demented contentment, his fishing pole thin arms shaking spastically from the night's exertions.

"Martha my dear, you are a true lady in every sense of the word. Me and Old John Henry down there certainly appreciate your unknowin' yet damned polite participation in these here events," he mumbled through a mouth now void the majority of its chewing prowess. Before regaining possession of his shotgun, the barrel of which still emitted the aroma of a recent firing, Buck leaned down onto one knee and addressed his practically headless former co-worker with a final, faintly somber gaze.

"Old Doc Krane is gonna need a truckload of aspirin to even begin treatin' that ailment 'a yours, Alan old salt. Ya shouldn't have ragged me so, *shouldn't* have" Buck paused, his pus and dried saliva coated lips frozen in mid contortion. For a full thirty seconds he brooded, a trembling statue posed in the center of a slaughterhouse of his own making, his delirious mind attempting without success to pinpoint a solid conclusion as to exactly why he had just murdered Alan Carter. True, he had disliked the man, considering him nothing more than a loudmouth asshole whose only goal in the company was to climb the ladder regardless of who he was forced to boot off a step in the process. He had known for years of the man's belittling of him behind his back, but had long since brushed it off as the behavior of a sour, envious man with a small mind and extremely low self- esteem. Why then, had he chosen to scatter the man's brains all over and *around* his own kitchen at twenty past midnight on a muggy summer night no different than the previous sixty before it?

A low squeaking noise broke Buck from his self-imposed trance, but he quickly realized the source of the interruption before allowing the initial pangs of panic to set in.

The former Alan Carter Jr., ex-employee of Bowen Excavating Company and one-time All-County quarterback for the Red Bridge High Warriors, had released his final contribution to the world he had recently inhabited in the form of a highly aromatic, possibly a bit toxic, squealing stink bomb of a fart. Even in the traumatic state of mind-numbing shock his entire system had endured over the past eight hours, Buck felt his gorge rise at the scent of his victim's pathetically feeble attempt at retribution.

Snatching the shotgun in a sudden rush of energy, Buck departed the eerily silent confines of the Carter home in a trot, leaving the back door he had originally entered standing wide open. His bloodied boot prints marked a clear trail to his mode of transportation, which he had parked on a wide, grassy shoulder a few hundred feet down the deeply grooved dirt driveway.

Steering with hands and fingers that looked to have been shoved through a hay feeder, even the pupils of his eyes beginning to seep miniscule droplets of hot yellow liquid, Buck Lomax began to hum a tune that had been stuck in his mind all evening. He wasn't sure of the exact title, but knew the opening line by heart. Veering through a curved portion of the roadway, a sign that clearly read *'R. Bridge-2 miles'* flashing in his bleary orbs a moment later, Buck mumbled the few words of the ditty that he clearly recalled from past hearings.

"puppets on a string…we're all just puppets on a string..."

Prologue Part V
Brothers in Sin

At exactly one AM on the same muggy summer night in Central Mississippi, Buck Lomax and Gil Brock met alongside either lane of the Red Bridge Crossing, the rushing waters of Edgewater Creek passing beneath their quietly idling vehicles.

Both reached through the respective driver's windows and clasped hands like two long-lost relatives at a surprise reunion. Buck tried to initiate the conversation and instead coughed so harshly one of his few remaining teeth sailed from his mouth into the greasy patch of disheveled hair hanging across Gil's forehead, falling away only when Gil nodded amiably at its former owner.

"Funny how I knew you'd be here, Buck-O. You been as busy as me on this here night?" Gil finally managed in between frantically licking his raw, blistered lips.

"I was just contemplatin' along those same lines, Gil. You feel as bad as you look, old buddy?" Buck replied sheepishly, his scorched eye lids only half open.

Gil rubbed his right cheek softly, inducing a barely audible popping sound, like that of a ripe pimple being burst between two tightly squeezed fingers.

"Fixin' to ask you a similar question, old friend. Let's just say I feel...a might different than earlier this morning."

Both men stared at each other in eerie silence for a few seconds through hazy, unblinking eyes.

Studying the back of his raw, ravaged hands

with a wry expression, Buck's breathing became unusually labored as he spoke, as if he had just run a series of uphill sprints.

"You… uh… spread the seed, Gil?"

Gil winced a bit as he glanced out the passenger window at the rusty, badly warped bridge railing on the far side.

"A-yep. Buck, it was almost like…it wasn't me doin' it, y'know? I mean, there wasn't any controllin' it. Even now, sittin' here..." Gil paused while adjusting his side mirror until his mangled reflection came clearly, horrifically into view. "..are we *us*, anymore? I don't feel like the Captain of my own ship anymore, Buck."

Buck first grunted apathetically, then leaned his head from the cab and spat a thick line of greenish fluid onto the bridge's dark, rotting planks.

"Why even question it, Gil? I think we both know that answer, anyhow. You ready for the last step, are ya?"

Nodding trance-like, Gil grew instantly morose. With worn gears grinding loudly, the 'Black Funnel' began to slowly pull away.

"Meet ya there, Buck," he mumbled as the bridge groaned from the vehicles sudden lurching movement.

Buck waited until the other vehicle's taillights vanished past a thick tree line a few hundred feet ahead before departing his own vehicle in order to stand stoically on the edge of the rickety bridge.

Peering down into the fast flowing, shallow waters some twenty feet below, he caught a faint, shadowy image staring upwards. Cocking his head a bit to the left, as if to disprove the image indeed was his own, Buck then forced a sad, grisly smile.

"No doubt about it, Buck my man. You have definitely turned over a new leaf, I reckon. A leaf that's about the most poisonous som'bitch ever to sprout from God's green earth."

He considered a free-fall leap onto the jagged rocks below, one that would have certainly left him broken beyond repair. The thought passed like a weak fart in a funnel cloud, and Buck soon found himself tooling down the highway in the same direction as his former friend and present brother-in-arms had traveled just minutes before. He passed the Miller homestead a few miles up the road, slowing his progress a bit as he sailed by.

It had been a tantalizing temptation to stop by for a quick visit to the old couple that inhabited the old farmhouse and put an end to their insufferable existence, but a greater calling presently gripped his desolate soul. Buck felt sweet relief engulf his entire being as he neared the construction site. He recalled a similar emotion the day he had been baptized by Reverend James as a young teen near the same bridge he had just departed.

After ditching his vehicle a full hundred yards east of the site, he met Gil at the cusp of the crater, a veritable symphony provided by nature's chorus line sounding off almost in unison in the thick forest encircling them.

They stood at the chasm's edge, holding hands like man and wife strolling down an isolated stretch of beach line. Both peered wearily into the wide opening, as the volume of Mother Nature's insect minion's cries seemed to be inexplicably decreasing.

Looking as physically ill and mentally drained as humanly possible while still possessing a heartbeat, Gil didn't avert his gaze as he spoke.

"We have to go now, Buck? I mean… is it over for us now?"

Buck snorted a bit sarcastically, his breath again dramatically labored despite lack of actual exertion.

"Gil old friend, I do believe it's been over for us ever since the *first* time we stood over this damned hole. We just didn't know it at the time. We're just the humble beginnin' of a looong, drawn out breedin' process."

Gil slowly peered up at the larger man, his horribly dilated pupils coated in a clear gel that under normal circumstances would have been pools of fresh teardrops, and proceeded to nod weakly.

"Let's go meet daddy, what do ya say?" Buck asked in a voice tinged with more than just a hint of primal fear, despite the front of false bravado that disguised it.

Neither man leaped forward as if jumping into a pool of cool, clear water on a scorching summer day, but instead both simply took a single step into the center of the opening, their descent into the dark passage remarkably silent and without even the faintest of screams.

***

As the morning sun peeked out over the distant hillside a scant few hours later, a curious Bobcat cautiously sniffed the outlines of two separate and distinctly different sized boot prints along the edge of the circular crack. A brief but stout breeze shot from the chasm unexpectedly, causing the 'Cat to reel back on its short but muscular hind legs. As it sprinted away from the spot and into a nearby briar thicket, the 'Cat began to sneeze and cough uncontrollably, the putrid stench emitted from its mangy fur spreading a cloud of misty poison in its wake.

By the time the creature crawled weakly into its enclosed den a full hour later, the claws on its right paw had all but completely dislodged, and a fine line of discarded fur surrounded its fevered, trembling form.

CHAPTER ONE
One Man's Island

August 19th, 2003

Oak Mountain Campsite, four miles outside Red Bridge

The final tent stake firmly hammered into place, the man wiped the fresh sweat from his exposed brow and stared towards the sun through the thick, full oak limbs dangling overhead.

"Paradise, day one. Weather report from WMBG, that being 'My Best Guess', speculates temperatures basically hot enough to boil a man's brain through his skull plate and a darn good chance for afternoon thunder bummers. Well, what more should one expect from central Mississippi in late August, my man? Falling autumn leaves and light snowflakes to catch on one's outstretched tongue? Dream on, McDuff," he mumbled, pausing long enough to sip from a nearby canteen before turning to the trio of stuffed duffel bags lying just to the left of the clearing he was presently occupying.

Rubbing his callused hands together as if chilled, Jimmy Rollins grinned cheerily, although anyone who witnessed such a smile would have considered him borderline psychotic.

"Done and *done*. Tent designed for eight but housing only one is in place, single cot lying in the prone position, along with Yaffa designer shelving for everyday goodies. All that remains is the daunting task of unpacking and then properly decorating the ol' pad. However..." he paused, one chubby finger pointing into the air as if to make a vital point to an invisible audience of on- lookers.

"I do believe a little mid-morning snack is in order here. I mean; the weight will come off eventually, I'm sure. No need to *rush* things, my man."

The camouflage designed, metal-framed chair screaming its disapproval beneath him, Jimmy parked his rotund, two hundred fifty-pound plus frame down a few feet from the front entrance of the tent and began rummaging through an obviously overtaxed brown knapsack.

A few moments later, as he savored the first of what he deduced would soon be countless (possibly infinite) servings of well-preserved beef jerky, Jimmy sighed heavily and surveyed his new, albeit somewhat temporary, stomping grounds.

Despite their comical bulkiness, his mind contained an accurate mental inventory of what lay inside the duffels. The majority of the stuffing consisted of canned soups and meat, a varied collection of dried fruits, and an ample supply of various crackers, the whole of which could easily choke the most ravenous of armies. His nineteen-ninety-two model Jeep Cherokee, the vehicle he had chosen over the ninety-three Probe and the ninety-five F150 Ford pick-up before selling each, picked mostly due to its versatility and unmatched reliability, sat parked a few dozen feet to the right. It held a portable hot plate that had yet to be unwrapped since purchase, as well as a one-hundred twenty-watt boom box (actually it had been Jakes, but he no longer had use for it after sentencing), and a collection of enough A, double-A, and triple-A batteries to mechanize a small country. Three separate battery-operated lamps and two separate boxes of various CD's and paperback books finalized the supply count other than the sparse clothing items he had dragged along.

Forty-three years taking up space on Mother Earth, and everything I own lays before me in a space roughly the size of your everyday gas station bathroom. Jimmy my man, one name they'll never call you is pack rat.

Later that afternoon, as the sun's blazing rays fell below the tree line to the right of the campsite, Jimmy sat atop his Cherokee's cooled hood, his short, stubby legs propped on the front bumper's edge, and surveyed his makeshift kingdom.

The tent itself still held sufficient elbowroom within its confines, with only the folding chair, his tackle box and fishing rods sitting outside her nylon walls.

Not bad, Amigo. Got ample food to stay alive, but not enough to prevent losing a few layers of blubber over time. Saw that market just outside town if I need supplies. Like dear old pop used to say, 'son, all you need is something to wipe 'tween your cheeks and drinking water that don't taste like beaver pee. As far as campsites go, the rest is pure gray.'

Tuning in the boom box to the local Red Bridge station (which was really all that would pick up other than waves of blaring static), Jimmy went about the task of setting up the hot plate in preparation for a meal consisting of Campbell's Soup and saltine crackers.

Pleasantly surprised to find the local station's

play list consisted mostly of old classic light rock and pop tunes, Jimmy hummed along with a tune he instantly recognized as 'Band on the Run', something from the mid-seventies or possibly earlier. He had never considered himself a big Beatles fan, although he did recall warming up quite well to McCartney's later incarnation along the same vein named 'Wings.' Tapping his size ten Wolverines to the beat, Jimmy was acutely aware of the buzzing at his midsection. A hollow ache that had absolutely nothing to do with the lack of nourishment held there. It wasn't as prevalent now, not even touching the scale compared to around 5 AM that morning, when he had awoke to begin the trek from a Holiday Inn on the outskirts of Birmingham to the thick forest outside Red Bridge, Mississippi.

Then it had been more like a small crew of construction workers were attempting to drill their way through his abdomen. This particular malady coupled with the constant pounding at his temples and the occasional tidal wave of nausea brought back long dead memories of some of the horrendous hangovers he had experienced in college decades before.

A rented mountainside that was for all practical purposes completely isolated from the presence of his own kind, the nearest hint of civilization (according to the less-than-jovial old man he had rented the space from weeks ago) was a state prison site a full three miles to the north. To reach that location (other than driving back to the main highway and making a ten-mile plus circle) would constitute a trek through rocky, snake-infested hills and forest terrain as thick as fishnet webbing. It was not a jaunt Jimmy had the faintest notion of undertaking, no matter *how* pegged out his boredom meter might get.

The last thing he desired was contact with anything possessing working vocal cords. After months of careful planning and organizing, the numbers associated with calendars, alarm clocks and newspaper headlines meant less than nothing. How long they remained in such a state of indifference was something he accepted as being presently out of his control, just as everything in his life had been for the past five years.

Certain things, the obvious outer layers of what his existence had become; the ten-hour workdays and fifty-hour work weeks; the daily one to two-hour commute to the location where he plied his trade, such trivialities were easily cast aside. It took no effort to discard the mundane, the disposable portions of one's life that were once thought to be anything but. Jimmy didn't mind work. He had earned a weekly paycheck since the age of sixteen (packing groceries after school and in the summer months) and had never been forced to even consider state or federal aid such as unemployment or welfare. It wasn't the daily grind or monotony either. He could sit aboard a forklift all day (in fact had on countless occasions), loading and unloading semis. He could inventory a warehouse full of items, big or small, low or high quantities, as quickly and proficiently as anyone on the planet. He didn't despise such work or even find it overly annoying, despite a full two decades of languishing within its admittedly limiting field. Jimmy Rollins had never been the supervisor type, unlike his father. He was a man who, when inquired about through co-workers, had been labeled as 'quiet, unassuming, reliable or other such bland, ordinary descriptions. A classic loner he was, a man his brother in law had once remarked had been 'damned lucky to find a woman who has a thing for mummies', hinting marriage would have otherwise been an impossibility in his life span.

Patricia had passed away three years earlier, a burst blood vessel in her brain ending their blissful eighteen-year marriage in a matter of mere seconds. Jake was currently in the fourth month of a ten-year sentence (without parole) for armed robbery with intent to kidnap. Jake, their second born would be just short of his twenty-eighth birthday upon his release back into society. Kassandra, their first born, had married a man well known around Birmingham as a gang-affiliated drug dealer and subsequently moved to Hawthorne, California, presumably to allow him to better ply his trade. She had just turned the ripe age of seventeen a few days before the wedding, a ceremony that her father neither attended nor was even invited to view. Jimmy hadn't heard from his barely eighteen-year-old daughter since, despite many long and winding efforts to do so.

Bart Carnes had simply chosen the wrong day to whisper 'Lard Ass' within Jimmy's earshot on the fateful day his way of living was unceremoniously ended. In the end, the cords of loyalty to the company for which he had toiled for over a decade were cut free without fanfare, severed much like his non-relationship with the two children he had sired as a young, albeit somewhat naive and undeniably overwrought father.

Never an individual prone to confrontations, much less of the physical variety, Jimmy discovered on one particular muggy June afternoon some weeks earlier that, indeed, even the most mild-mannered of the species had a breaking point.

A simple left hook to the jaw had transformed sixteen years of hard, sometimes back-breaking work into a meaningless mirage no longer significant in the grand scheme of things, at least by management's standard. No matter that Carnes had belittled and insulted him since becoming his supervisor, taking credit for both ideas and completed tasks that Jimmy alone had been responsible for. Jimmy hadn't mourned the loss in the least. In fact, he had welcomed it with a genuine sigh of relief, never quite understanding why he had bothered to hold onto it after Patty's life insurance settlement had come through two years before.

He had no friends to speak of at work or otherwise, having placed all his eggs in one basket in that department the day he met and confirmed the identity of his one true soulmate. He had invited no thoughts of dating after Patty's death, although his family had begun badgering him about such matters for years. Jimmy knew and accepted what type of being he was. His brother in law, pompous and ignorant as he was, had been correct. Jimmy Rollins had been fortunate enough to find and love the one person he was meant to have. He was the male wolf disguised in human form. There would be no other such chance meeting.

Patty's insurance settlement had come to just

over two hundred thousand dollars, plus the twenty-thousand-dollar policy she had set up through her job at the car lot where she had worked as receptionist.

Jimmy had systematically sold (or donated) all their furniture, the two extra vehicles, and most of Patty's belongings within the past twelve months, just as the initial outline of the plan was forming at the edges of his frazzled mind. Two days before the punching incident that ended his days as a blue-collar employee, Jimmy had been forced onto the slick shoulder of the interstate at nearly sixty miles per hour as a police chase involving authorities from three counties ensued during morning rush hour. The subsequent eighteen car, two semi-truck pile up a few miles down the same stretch of road forced him to endure four-plus hours of excruciating *non*-movement (the Cherokee had no air conditioning), sitting under a blazing mid-morning sun with temperatures nearing ninety-five degrees. By the time he endured a subtle yet still undeniable dressing down from one Mr. Carnes about the 'importance of being on time', Jimmy had known the time for permanent change of location and lifestyle wasn't looming too far on the distant horizon.

The night of his firing, Jimmy sat in his mostly empty two-bedroom apartment (he and Patty had never seriously marketed for a permanent homestead, a fact for which he was remarkably grateful after her passing) and wrote up two separate lists by hand.

The first was titled '*Pros to Continue*' and the second '*Cons to Persevere*'. Both had been written out with a black-ink ballpoint pen with his former employer's logo scribbled down its center.

The first list was pathetically short and void of any substantial merit, the second breathtakingly long and sharply detailed.

The first merely stated:

Things will get better eventually.

Pop always said that 'each time you quit something it's like a series of little deaths that pile up like rotted bodies over time'.

That was all he could muster, despite considerable deliberation. Comparatively, list number two's contents flowed easily and without pause, and stated the following:

Work stress - nil.

Bills to pay - nil.

Financial Obligations - nil.

Traffic jams (rude factor number one) to wade through - nil.

Loud, obnoxious, unruly neighbors (rude factor number two) to listen to through painfully thin apartment walls - nil.

Blaring, glass-shattering, teeth-jarring rap music for ear drums to endure - nil.

News of fresh homicides, rapes and muggings every half-hour, thievery and every form of human debauchery to swarm the senses via TV, the internet and newspapers - nil.

Said Internet garbage to wallow through - nil.

Crappy television to be hypnotized by on a daily basis - nil.

Arrogant, unsympathetic, down right Jackass to

the bone people to deal with - nil (final rude factor).

The list concluded with detailed annoyances that flew from his pen in spastic waves, as if his arm and adjoining hand were being telepathically controlled by an inner, subconscious being bent on hammering home the point he had already accepted as truth.

Such topics as 'surprise terrorist attacks', 'unused busy signals and red lights', 'idiots on cell phones', 'pop music's porn divas' and 'kiddie bands' sailed forth, along with old school favorites such as 'junk mail', 'cancer causing prescription medicines' and 'the government's constant trial of lies'. At the bottom of the page, where room barely allowed, were the six words that summed up all the rest in a neat, tidy little package of inner loathing and unbridled vileness. Jimmy had to stare long and hard at the words, written in his unmistakably tidy handwriting but penned with such force that the bond paper itself was actually punctured at certain junctures along the writing trail.

The words were simply stated, concise and directly to the point. They read: '*The HELL with this SHIT. I've had my share."*

A man not prone to using profanity unless at the brink of immense rage, Jimmy nonetheless accepted that in this particular scenario, nothing *less* would have sufficed.

A single trip to the nearest Wal-Mart had provided the provisions necessary to begin the transition. Jimmy had spent less than two thousand dollars on said provisions, placing the remainder of the rather bulky nest egg in a local Birmingham

Savings and Loan (he had long since closed his checking and savings accounts) for future use.

He gave his apartment complex only two weeks' notice before departing, gladly paying the two-hundred dollar fine imposed for not allowing the full thirty days specified in his lease. Jimmy had paid his six hundred fifty-dollar a month rent on time (usually a day or two early in fact) for the full three-and-a-half-year stay, but was treated with nothing less than contempt upon departure. In a complex with more than its share of welfare and unemployment participants, he felt a bit angered at being treated with such obvious disdain, but simply chalked it up to the rude factors listed earlier. Simply more fuel to feed the fire of his disgust with society in general.

Having been a Birmingham native since birth, Jimmy used a local library computer to scan the Internet for a suitable spot to vegetate outside the bustling, increasingly noisy city limits. After hours of wading through countless web pages dedicated to 'Local Camp Sites', he ran across a small page dedicated to Red Bridge, Mississippi, a town he mapped as being only one-hundred thirty miles to the west of his hometown. The page listed 'Red Bridge Oak Mountain RV and Camping Rentals' as being a 'year-round trek back to the best nature has to offer'. After only a short mulling period, Jimmy decided the location was perfect; out of the state but not *too* far in case he suddenly awoke with a different perspective on things. He figured the scorching summer days kept the camper population at a bare minimum, plus the town itself was painstakingly small, a population listed at around seven hundred, with no surrounding metropolis in site.

As the pop-up ad (another annoying element of modern society Jimmy quickly decided he most definitely wouldn't miss) had spouted, '*Eight Thousand Acres of Blissful Peace and Quiet* (plus some of the best fishing around!)'.

At a mind-numbingly low cost of thirty dollars per week (the price to rent day to day had been a tad higher), Jimmy had an entire thirty-acre spread to himself. The package included a nearby private stream supposedly 'packed' with bass and brim, and scenic 'mountain' views on either side of the campsite, although the 'mountains' themselves were little more than rolling, rock-infested hills.

Just what a fatigued psyche needed to regain a semblance of normalcy, and allowed frazzled, shell-shocked nerves to at least begin the process of healing.

Jimmy's dad, a forty-five-year veteran of the Birmingham steel mills, had been an avid fisherman and hunter, and stressed the need for at least semi-annual camping treks with the family. Learning to create, place, and correctly time the running of trout-lines became second nature, as did the tracking of deer and techniques for bagging squirrel. Although he had given up hunting since a teen, referring to such activities as 'a coward's sport' to anyone willing to listen, Jimmy did gain a measure of satisfaction from the occasional afternoon spent baiting hooks and lounging on a soft, grassy bank. Patty had been mentally allergic to such proceedings, the idea of even touching Catfish bait or Crayfish to place on a metal hook inducing a comical grimace that Jimmy secretly relished viewing from time to time. He hadn't been fishing since her death, finding no inner motivation to do so. It was one of the few hobbies he had decided was worth re-visiting, and now he had the most golden of opportunities to do so.

Time is no longer the enemy. Not many get to ditch life and re-focus like this. I guess that's why a lot of them end up swallowing gun barrels. Not this boy, no way no how. All I need is time to plot and plan, scheme and re-tool. Call me Robinson Crusoe Rollins of Red Bridge.

Just as dusk began to overtake the landscape and the crickets began their nightly opera, Jimmy Rollins lay atop his padded cot and drifted in and out of consciousness, a slight tremor causing his hands to spasm periodically.

***

Patty slept in a cot on inches from his own, the soapy smell of her freshly bathed skin filling his flaring nostrils. Silently, he leaned up and over to kiss her exposed forehead, her bright red hair pushed atop her head and flowing back over the edge of the cot like crimson ocean waves.

Becoming aware of the constant throbbing sensation in his hands, Jimmy raised them up and held them to his face, the darkness of the night unable to conceal the pulpy mass of moistness they had somehow become. He noticed the thumb and forefinger were mysteriously nail-less, a yellowed liquid with the texture of syrup filling the spaces they once occupied.

Sensing movement before being able to actually visualize it, Jimmy noticed his wife's feet begin to tremble beneath the thin, lily-white sheet concealing them.

His lips peeled apart with a slight tearing sound, as if they had been matted together for days and sealed with Elmers Glue, the words escaping his parched throat in a low, harsh whisper.

"P-Patty? Are you awake, hon? There's something w-wrong with my… hands."

Emerging from the tangled sheet as if sprung from tightly wound bonds, the form halted its spastic, blurred movement mere inches from Jimmy, who was sitting upright with his moist, fevered hands raised as if awaiting an impending assault.

He suddenly felt as if he were frozen into position, only his rapidly blinking eyelids and badly trembling hands able to accept and carry out his mental commands. Just as he began to lower his guard, the figure he had obviously mistaken for his deceased better half began to speak, the tone strangely muffled initially and then crystal clear, like the words were being transmitted through a partially connected stereo speaker.

"I miss your touch, lover...so *very* badly." It croaked somewhat cautiously, followed by the sound of something being spat out onto the ground beside Jimmy's cot; tiny, solid objects that sounded not unlike someone had split a handful of Tic-Tacs onto a tile floor.

Jimmy first peeked between his outstretched fingers, then dropped them to the side in order to get a full picture of whom or what was addressing him in the midst of such a dark, foreboding dreamscape.

The thing had Patty's hair, as wonderfully full-bodied and wavy as the day he had met and fell hopelessly into lust with her.

The forehead that protruded below the wavy hairline was a barren landscape of torn flesh, grooved, bloodless ridges creating a pattern of spider- web efficiency. Her bulging, pupil-less eyes were spinning like pinwheels, a long, grayish colored lump of flesh hanging from her toothless mouth like an overripe slug. Jimmy peered down towards his boots and instantly understood the origin of the earlier noise. Jagged, reddish colored teeth of various sizes lay atop the grass like spilled Red Hot's candy.

"...your hands are just the beginning, lover… something is unnatural here...something from deep inside... and nearby… closer than it seems." The thing muttered, the snake-like tongue lolling back and forth like a pendulum made of human flesh.

Jimmy began to punch his right knee in panic, hoping with every fiber of his being it would force him back into consciousness.

Just as the grisly apparition disguised as his former wife leaped forward, it's decay-ridden maw opened wide as if to swallow his entire soul, Jimmy landed with a loud thud on the hard ground beneath his cot, the air departing his lungs in a huffed groan.

***

Leaning against the tent's solid center pole with his upper back, his badly shaking lower body still propped atop the grass, Jimmy wiped the sour smelling sweat from his moist forehead.

Holy crow, man. What the hell was that all about? Not exactly the sweet, easy dreams of a newly crowned man of leisure, to say the very least.

Sitting upright on the edge of the cot a moment later, Jimmy heard an obviously distant yet somehow distinctively clear howl. Rubbing his hands together as if chilled, despite the muggy temperatures of the still, breezeless night, he giggled to himself briefly. He halted almost instantly, the sound of his own cackling less than comforting after such a vivid, horrific dream.

Gingerly, as if nursing a battered torso as well as mind, Jimmy lay back down and released a lengthy sigh filled with a longing he someday hoped would at least subside a notch.

I miss you, girl. Damn, do I miss you.

Outside the sturdy, stiff walls of the tent, the howling first faded, then ceased altogether.

Inside those same walls, one man fell into a dark, somber haze, his eyeballs flicking madly underneath their moistened lids.

CHAPTER TWO
Uneasy Ranks

August 18th, 2003

Major David Peterson gritted his teeth so tightly he seriously thought that soon he might soon find himself chewing his own shattered dental work.

Satisfied his bodily fluids were substantially drained, he quickly tucked his manhood back inside his camouflage pants and exited from behind the large, ancient pine that had just served as his personal urinal.

Still a good fifty yards from the campsite, he couldn't help but to proceed yelling just as his steel-toed boots kicked aside the broken tree branch in his path.

"Sergeant Chambers, would you please turn that godforsaken racket *down* so that we may enjoy the joyful sounds of nature as they were intended?" He barked in his slightly nasal but nonetheless undeniably authoritative tone.

Entering the wide, sunny clearing, Peterson's ranting halted upon the smell of freshly brewed coffee assaulting his wildly flaring nostrils.

Turning to follow the trail of the intoxicating odor, Peterson was quickly greeted by a stocky young man whose enormously muscled arms were threatening to burst the seams of his rolled-up fatigue shirt. Balancing a steaming tin cup in each stubby hand, the younger man displayed both a broad smile and bright blue eyes filled with admiration for the man standing before him.

"Morning, Sergeant Ezop. My god, who taught you to brew coffee, son?

In my fourteen-year Army career, I never tasted any that could even come close to matching it. Smells like liquid paradise," Peterson practically yelled while reaching cautiously for the offering, the ringing echo of the blaring music causing his right eye to twitch between words.

"My old man took me camping more than once, Major. With him, you either did a job correctly or found yourself on your back nursing one helluva shiner," Jeffrey Ezop beamed, winking playfully before taking a brief sip from his own sweltering cup.

Peterson glared angrily to his right, where the entrance flaps leading into the tent of one Sergeant Isiah Chambers stood open, flapping freely with each passing breeze.

Just as he began to take a step forward, the muscles of his granite-like jaws already in position to bellow, the music abruptly ceased, as if it's power source had been severed by a bolt of lightning conjured from the Major's squinting orbs.

Peterson halted his forward movement and sighed in relief, shaking his head in disgust as he gave Ezop a quick glance. Smiling weakly, Ezop shrugged and turned towards his own tent, which was set up a few dozen yards to the north of the camp. Major David Peterson had spent many an hour digesting security techniques in his youth while serving his country. In this, the first official training mission for the Dark Eagle Militia, he wasn't about to dismiss all he had been taught, despite the contempt he now held for those who had provided him with such valuable knowledge.

The camp was spread out in a ‘V’ formation, each tent at least thirty yards apart, thus eliminating the possibility of each member being taken out by a single strategically aimed missile. Peterson had participated in countless such drills that displayed the cost of laziness as a commanding officer. He wasn’t about to concede to the Gods of Nonchalant Casualness on the horizon of complete national anarchy. Nodding as he scanned the camp set-up in one single twisting motion of his slim, stubble covered neck, Peterson caught movement to his right and was forced to bite his lower lip to prevent groaning aloud.

Private Sandra Kemp, her greasy, frazzled hair hanging over her acne ridden forehead like the edges of a deep shag carpet, entered the clearing from a southern tree line and loped over to him in a bent, slumping gait.

“Zop must have the java brewin’. I could smell it from a half mile away,” she spat indifferently, never meeting the older man’s gaze.

Peterson cleared his throat after a quick swallow of the pitch-black liquid, which seemed to grow instantly bitter in the mere presence of an individual he found utterly disgusting.

“You ditch that bottle of Jim Beam I saw in your gear last night?” he replied sternly, his eyes slowly scanning the loose hanging, badly wrinkled uniform hanging from her slightly tubby frame.

“Yeah, I ditched it alright. Ditched it right down my throat… S*ir,*” she announced without a hint of humor.

Strolling by Peterson, who dwarfed her by a

full foot in height, Kemp paused just long enough to belch without benefit of covering her slug-like lips before doing so.

The scent of rotgut whiskey washed over Peterson for a single flash before fading, but long enough to cause his gorge to rise.

Kemp waddled on towards Ezop's tent, where the hot plate was operating. His watch reading seven-thirty-two AM, Peterson grimaced like a man with a severe case of intestinal gas. His wife's best friend, a squirrelly little woman named Margaret, had insisted the militia was the best and very possibly *last* chance for her troubled daughter to straighten up and fly right. Sandra Kemp was only twenty-three, but had already chalked up a rather unimpressive arrest record that included everything from petty theft to breaking and entering, not to mention an alcohol and drug dependency that had landed her in numerous treatment centers. The military services, to include even the coast guard, had turned her down flat.

Peterson had little sympathy for such pathetic creatures, and had been more than a tad hesitant to allow the girl to join their ranks, but as was the case more often than not over the twenty-six-year span of his marriage, winning such an argument was never really an option. Besides, reality was such that they needed every warm body that was willing. Peterson realized, as he figured Kemp herself did, that her true future lay in the correctional field, on the inside staring *out*.

The Major's train of thought instantly changed tracks as Kemp's slouched body disappeared from site and into Jeff Ezop's tent.

The old man that had rented them the acres had mentioned a state prison site a few miles to the east. Peterson quickly decided that if time permitted within their daily regimen, he might pay a little visit to that particular venue. If all he had heard about that particular unit was true, he figured it might do young Private Kemp some good to witness such a scenario up close. She had spent time in Juvenile boot camps, true, but had never been exposed to anything resembling a 'scared straight' program.

Just as he began to do an about face and head back to his own tent to retrieve his 'daily tasks' clipboard, Peterson heard leaves being crunched at his rear.

"Gooood mornin', sir," Isiah Chambers announced in mock cheeriness, the gold from his front two teeth gleaming like tiny mirrors reflecting the mid-day sun.

Sergeant Chambers was a tall, lanky individual whose mouth never closed, a 'glass half full' type whom Peterson had never warmed up to despite all efforts to feel otherwise.

"Ezop's got the coffee ready, Sarge. Might even have some eggs cooking if you feel like indulging," Peterson replied, his own shot of caffeine tasting instantly better in conjunction with Private Kemp's departure.

Sergeant Chambers stretched his long arms into the air, then yawned as he surveyed their surroundings.

"Not a Java man myself, Major. Quit pouring that crap into my system a decade back, about the time I left the service. I'm strictly an OJ man these days."

Major Peterson started to reply between sips when he noticed the last two of their present group emerge from a thicket a few dozen feet to the left of the camp's center.

Nodding at the slowly approaching pair, he heard Chambers grunt sarcastically.

"Shiiit, here's comes trouble, boss. Way too early for Wilma Chamber's oldest son to be rapping with old 'Bulk and Sulk' there. Think I'll go check Zop's breakfast buffet after all."

Major Peterson smiled behind the cover of his cup, then watched as Sergeant Chambers strode quickly up the hill, the taller man's steps long and purposeful.

Private Lomax Bodine, barely twenty years of age and looking all fifteen of it in the baggy, two-sizes too large uniform he was sporting, along with a mustache that was nothing more than a dozen sprigs of peach fuzz, halted to Peterson's right.

Corporal Ron McIntosh took up position to the Major's left, his own uniform so skin-tight it seemed to have literally been painted on his bulky frame. McIntosh was ten years Bodine's senior, although in the area of maturity it was a dead heat as to which was actually the elder of the two.

"Fine day, Sir. Looks like we couldn't have picked a better one for our first training mission," the Private said, the remnants of fresh sleep still present in his youthful eyes.

Major Peterson studied the younger man for only a moment before turning his attention to his ever-present shadow, the always-surly Corporal McIntosh, who stared ahead as if entranced by the smell being emitted across the clearing from

Sergeant Ezop's tent.

"That it is, Private. You two up to the little paint ball extravaganza planned for this morning?"

His muscled, no-neck appearance giving him the appearance of a competitive body builder, Corporal McIntosh seemed to discard the question entirely, his nostrils flaring wildly above the bushy growth of hair on his upper lip. Major Peterson noticed immediately how blatantly out of regulation the man's mustache was, and made a mental note to take corrective measures once chow had been served. The Major had long been a stickler for regulations, but had always steadfastly refused to take corrective actions on subordinates while nursing an empty stomach.

"Two teams, winners watch the others prepare meals and police up the area for the duration of our stay, correct sir?" Private Bodine blurted enthusiastically, obviously ignoring his partners disinterest.

"Sums it up pretty well, Private Bodine. Classroom battle strategies have to eventually be tested in the proper setting, and what could possibly be more isolated or better designed than this abandoned stretch of forest?" Major Peterson replied, his gaze never leaving McIntosh, who had yet to acknowledge his superior officer's presence in even the subtlest manner.

Bodine didn't reply, just displayed a 'Gee Whiz, Golly Gee' expression that couldn't help but remind Peterson of Wally Cleaver.

"Why don't you boys go grab yourself a bite and tell everyone to meet at my tent afterwards, let's say..." Peterson checked his wristwatch with a quick glance '...oh-eight-fifteen hours."

Corporal McIntosh elbowed Private Lomax playfully in the ribs, then turned and gave the Major a brief wink.

"Appreciate that, Sir. Let's hope that Scrub Ezop whipped up something worth chewin', or I'm liable to throw his worthless hide on the nearest grill and stick an apple in his pie hole."

Major Peterson couldn't help but shake his head in a mix of bemuse and amusement as the two men trudged away, Bodine following a half step behind McIntosh like a younger sibling in the shadow of his older, wiser big brother.

"The odd couple indeed," he whispered to himself before swallowing the last of his coffee. He had never been a morning eater, always content to chow down on a hearty lunch later in the day. He did, however, understand how vital that first meal of the day was to the troops in his care. Camaraderie was built within units in short bursts, to include shared meals. Still, as he made his way towards his own tent, by far the largest, thereby roomiest of the units, Major Peterson couldn't help but linger on the strange, unorthodox relationship between Bodine and McIntosh.

Lomax Bodine was a pencil-thin bookworm, one hundred forty pounds soaking wet, with an IQ as high as his level of experience that involved anything other than an open textbook. Bodine had joined the militia four short months ago, informing Peterson, as well as the head honcho himself, Colonel Barry Tomlinson, that his enlistment was strictly for 'internal maturity' reasons. Unlike the others, Lomax bore no grudge against his government. He simply wanted the military experience embedded into his soul without having to invest at least two years of his life to do so. Lomax Bodine was going to be a journalist; having already set his sights on the University of Southern Mississippi once the militia tour was complete. In turn for the militia's time and training, he swore to uphold their beliefs throughout his lifetime, and even promised to dedicate his first paying job as a journalist to their cause.

Initially, Peterson advised Colonel Tomlinson, who was leaning in the same direction, to reject the young man, but a single fact brought out in their second interview that altered both men's perception.

Lomax Bodine's father was Harry C. Bodine, the honorable fourth-term congressman from the militia's home state of Mississippi. The possibilities for political leverage in future dealings with the State government swimming in their collective heads like Piranha around a floating corpse, the two men welcomed the young man into the ranks with handshakes and smiles that were nothing if not pathetically insincere.

Corporal Ron McIntosh was a different species of animal altogether, the term 'animal' closer to fact than fiction to all who had been unfortunate enough to cross paths with the man during one of his self-proclaimed 'Crimson Rages'. McIntosh was a streetwise brawler from East Nashville, a section of music city growing infamous for its LA and Chicago gang infiltration's within the past few years.

He had pegged his many documented drunken brawls over the years as 'Crimson Rages', claiming that during such scenarios he would literally lose control of his emotions when enraged and 'seek the blood of others'. His arrest record, which he waved around like a Congressional Medal of Honor, actually to the point of keeping a scrapbook of each incident, included charges of Aggravated Assault, Simple Assault, and Criminal Mischief.

By comparison, Lomax Bodine had never so much as littered the street.

Ron McIntosh had been thrice married and subsequently divorced, claimed to have sired offspring in four states that he refused to pay a single dime in support of, and had been discharged less than honorably from both the Army and Marine Reserves within a three-year period in the late nineties. He was two hundred twenty-five pounds of raw meat and illegal muscle builders, all piled on a five-foot ten-inch frame that was immaculately chiseled and as rigid as a stone wall. Unlike Lomax, he knew how to use and/or maintenance the weapons in his arsenal, including a twelve-inch bladed serrated knife that hung from his belt like a mid-evil warrior's broadsword.

Major Peterson had long since dismissed the gay issue between the two, having heard Corporal McIntosh make the point that 'the only good fag is a decomposing one' countless times. Peterson could only deduce that the old saying that 'opposites attract' wasn't limited to relationships in the sexual category, nor to just male and female in general. It was not unlike observing a mongoose buddy up to a rattler on some warped alternate world.

Entering his tent, Major Peterson retrieved the small box of ammo from a side pocket of his well-traveled duffel bag. Sitting on his neatly made cot with a low groan, he could hear the loud, raucous voices of the troops from across the compound. Smiling devilishly, Major Peterson began to load his revolver with the specially designed bullets.

"You kids play with the paint balls while this adult teaches a separate, more *vital* lesson. A lesson that is essential for your growth as soldiers," he whispered in a low, edgy tone coated in a confidence known only to those who have witnessed the true pain only battlefield combatants can ever speak of with unbridled honesty.

Pain in both the physical and mental sense that comes with the experience of shocking, embarrassing defeat.

Soon, the green, unruly, undisciplined troops serving under the good Major's wing would know such pain first-hand, and either learn and accept, or flee and wilt away from the experience.

***

By three PM that same afternoon, Peterson observed as Sergeant Ezop, the unit's only trained medic, performed an impromptu battlefield triage in the center of the compound, where extra cots had been lain out like stretchers earlier in the afternoon.

Private Lomax Bodine stared into the cloudless sky above, obviously fighting back tears as Ezop taped an additional layer of gauze on the quarter sized welt displayed just below his left collarbone.

A few feet away, Private Sandra Kemp cursed under her breath, glaring at Peterson with a primal hatred that was almost a physical presence. The right pants leg of her baggy fatigue pants was rolled up to just below her kneecap, the wrap that engulfed her upper calf unable to completely disguise the swollen knot protruding from the shin.

Down the line from her lay Isiah Chambers, shaking his head in open amusement upon observing Private Kemp's frozen grimace, his grotesquely swollen left wrist resting comfortably atop his midsection.

Sergeant Ezop stood stiffly, patting Private Bodine's uninjured right shoulder ever so gently.

"Just a welt, Private. Those anti-inflammatory capsules will eliminate most of the swelling within twenty-four hours."

Turning to Private Kemp, Sergeant Ezop halted forward progress upon viewing her pained, enraged expression. Major Peterson stepped up; ignoring the furious sneer directed his way.

"I have to admit, Sergeant, I am more than a tad bit disappointed at my aim. Inactivity breeds rust, I deduce. What is the overall status of our people in the aftermath of my sadly off-kilter firings?"

Private Kemp lurched forward from the cot, cutting off any possible response from the comically shocked Medic. Peering up to the man who so comically dwarfed her, white spittle flew from her lips upon the first furious syllable being spat.

"You crazy son of a *bitch!* Was huntin' your own troops down and shooting them in the back all part of your trainin' regimen? I… hell, *we* all ought to *sue* your loony ass for aggravated assault! Not sure you'd enjoy the folks you'd meet in the lock-up, *Sir.* I do believe you'd be the one taking orders instead of giving 'em. My fuckin' leg is on fire, you piece of sh.-.."

His face a study in cool, steely indifference, Major Peterson's right hand swept forward so swiftly that Kemp's final obscenity came forth as nothing more than a garbled croak, the Majors' curled fingers covering almost the entire width of her pudgy neck.

"Private; *that is* sufficient. Please exhibit self-restraint in speaking to your commanding officer in the near future or I will not hesitate to fracture certain bones contained within your worthless, shiftless hide. Do we understand each other, Private?" He barked harshly as the girl attempted in vain to slap his unwavering grip from her throat.

The others observed in shocked silence, only Corporal McIntosh managing to take a single step forward before freezing in his tracks with his mouth agape.

Private Bodine temporarily ceased his whining and tensed, his eyes wide and unblinking.

Even Sergeant Chamber's ever-present smile, normally on display regardless of the seriousness of any situation, faded into a spastic, shaking scowl.

"I will release your throat now, Private. You, in turn, will respond by showing me the respect I have *earned* through decades of helping to mode pathetic individuals such as yourself into something other than the equivalent of a warm dog turd."

Private Kemp's face was growing dangerously purple, her eyes bloodshot to the point of glowing crimson. The only sound escaping her badly chapped lips was a tiny click from the deepest recesses of her severely compressed throat.

"Uh, sir, don't you think you ought to ease up

on..." Sergeant Ezop began, his mouth closing rapidly upon catching Peterson's searing gaze.

"If I need your advice, Sergeant, I'll be sure to inquire," he replied sternly, releasing the young woman's throat at the exact time the last word was uttered.

Private Kemp landed with a muffled thud, tendrils of dust flying upwards from where her ample rear end had made contact with the dry earth.

Major Peterson immediately bent down; resembling a ravenous predator looming over its doomed prey, his grin vicious, maniacal.

"What say you, Private? Still have a problem with certain aspects of the Dark Eagle combat training program, or may I chalk up your miserable, infant like tantrum to the heat of the moment?"

Private Kemp grasped her reddened throat, refusing to meet the man's eyes, instead concentrating them on the dusty tips of Isiah Chamber's combat boots just a foot or so to her right.

"M-my fault, s-sir. W-won't...happen again, sir," she barely whispered, thick tears springing from her eyes.

Major Peterson paused before rising, sighing deeply as he took a full stride back.

"I thought so. Completely understandable, Private. Being taken for a fool in a combat situation does have a tendency to bring out the buried demons beneath. I'm certain your fellow troops here feel the same about their own fates, they were just…less vocal of their inner frustration, and wisely so."

Corporal McIntosh, his arms hideously pumped

and fists clinched at his sides, groaned aloud, then visibly slumped, his eyes trained at his own slowly shuffling feet.

"Something to add, McIntosh? A bit of wisdom from the ranks of a former combat vet?" Major Peterson queried calmly, his head cocked quizzically to one side.

"Nothing to add, Sir, but an explanation of just exactly why we were bombarded with rubber bullets while *supposedly* involved in a strategic paint ball scenario would be damn nice to hear," Corporal McIntosh said politely enough but with a definite undercurrent of sarcasm. Rubbing his bandaged right elbow, he finally met his commander's glare and locked grimly onto it, refusing to yield to the older man's intimidation ploy.

Crossing one foot over the other, the Major's pose relaxed measurably as he pulled a filter-less cigarette from his right breast pocket.

"Simply to catch you off your guard, Corporal. In a real-world situation, there is no comfort zone. You cannot sit back and reassure yourself that even if you are struck by enemy fire, the only casualty will be a fatigue shirt coated in yellow or blue paint. I did more than simply take aim and fire upon each individual. I first studied their posture and evaluated the readiness of each. A certain level of mental readiness must be achieved in a true fire-fight, people."

Cocking his right arm across his chest, Major Peterson took a long drag and proceeded to blow a perfectly circular smoke ring in the direction of Private Kemp, who was only then crawling to her shaky feet with assistance from Sergeant Ezop.

“The point of picking us off one by one is exactly *what,* Major? How are we supposed to defend what we can’t see? What level of readiness are we talkin’ about here, telepathy?” Corporal McIntosh replied through a half-snarl.

Major Peterson jeered, eyeballing the smoke trailing from his left hand. “Allow me to check my personal notes, Corporal, on why being taken by surprise can and *must* be avoided if an assault is imminent. Target number one was eliminated at oh-eight-forty-two hours, a mere twenty-six minutes into the exercise. Private Bodine stood at the base of a large, rotted pine, his paint gun propped at his ankles as he calmly relieved himself into a nearby scrub. I *could* have shot the tip of his manhood into the nearest pile of pine needles if I had so desired, that’s how wide open the target.”

His narrow shoulders visibly drooping, Private Bodine whimpered aloud, then lay back silently.

“Sergeant Isiah Chambers, the second member of team Lima, was a bit better hidden, although the rock formation he choose for cover was far too confining, thereby basically backing himself into a trap easily accessible from the south end. From my vantage point in the tree line I had staked out, I had my choice of body parts to fire upon.”

Holding his damaged arm into the air as if displaying evidence of his own carelessness, Sergeant Chambers nodded solemnly.

“No excuses here, Sir. They don’t bother to write ‘he didn’t see it coming’ on the body bag they zip ya in.”

Mashing his smoke into the gravel with a single twist of his shiny left boot, Major Peterson continued after giving Chambers a quick wink.

"Corporal McIntosh, on the other hand, was hunkered down between two gnarled scrubs, all elbows and knees digging a trail into the tall weeds. It wasn't until he stepped out of his self-made foxhole to investigate the source of a noise in the nearby thicket that he fell between my sites. I had tossed a few strategically thrown stones into said bushes, and the good Corporal allowed his curiosity to get the better of him, as it were. I have to say, however, that amongst all the casualties present, he alone displayed a true warrior's mettle after being hit, rolling first to his feet and then diving back behind his cover with weapon drawn and gripped in his uninjured hand. Of course, I would expect such from an experienced, former army infantryman under my charge."

Huffing audibly, Corporal McIntosh started to reply but was never given the chance as Major Peterson whirled towards Private Kemp, who cringed back instinctively.

"Then there is the Private here, whom I could have strolled up while whistling 'Dixie' at the top my lungs and conked over the head with a rock if I had so desired. Private Kemp was fast asleep, you see, snoring so loudly that I observed small animals escaping the barrage for more peaceful pastures. The shot I bounced off of her shin was fired from less than fifteen feet away, gentleman, possibly less. In a different scenario involving a different enemy, placing it through one of her closed eyelids would have been painfully simple."

Rubbing gently just above her bruised appendage, Private Kemp's expression was a mixture of embarrassment and carefully subdued wrath. She wiped dust-coated tears from the corners of her eyes, her upper body no longer racked with the earlier tremors. Sandra Kemp had clicked into self-preservation mode, a substantial number of the blockages that separated emotional stability and the outer edges of insanity shoved permanently to the side as brain matter never meant to meet collided head on, birthing a strange yet enticing euphoria.

Entering the makeshift circle that the cots had been positioned into to create, Major Peterson stood stoically, as if posing for a sculpture possibly captioned 'Military Bearing 101'.

"Folks, let me sum up so that we may put this admittedly cruel but inherently necessary training session to an end. My reasons for instituting such actions were to bring home a simple but essential point: that being you never, *ever* let your guard down in a hostile situation. Sniper fire can come from any direction, at any time. The enemy each of you sought in those woods was familiar, a bit predicable. You were sent out as teams, but made the fatal mistake of separating into individual targets. Believe me, the Afghans, Iranians, Cubans, North Koreans and various other armies are maliciously efficient in the art of placing snipers within a combat zone. How many Marines and Army infantrymen were taken out in such a manner during the Mid-Eastern conflict just a scant year ago? War never changes in one aspect, regardless of the century it is fought in; the element of surprise is the *most* crucial of any conflict. From Pearl Harbor to Bull Run to the World Trade Center bombings, it is a much-proven fact of history. I picked you off one by one with an ease that at first amused, then depressed me.

I had hoped you would learn a valuable lesson in both personal stealth and the importance of teamwork, all for the puny price of a few harmless welts. I haven't many positive things to say about the Army that discharged and disowned me six years ago, but they did teach me the vital importance of overall readiness within a combat scenario.

In another place and time, more than likely right here on American soil and damned sooner than you might think or hope, the price will more than likely be your very lives."

He paused as if awaiting applause then sucked in a deep breath and lowered his head, revealing a wide bald spot at the center of his closely shaved scalp.

"I understand your anger at what you probably deem the cowardice of my assault, but it is a lesson worth enduring, folks. Trust me on at least that much. I will, however, do my best to even the playing field, so to speak. I realize that I don't have to, but I've always preached that a commander must not limit himself to belting out orders to assign tasks he himself would rather ignore."

Major Peterson retrieved the revolver from his utility belt in a single, extraordinarily graceful wave of his left hand, causing all but Corporal McIntosh and Sergeant Chambers to lean back as if struck by a sudden violent gust of wind.

Shoving the revolver's barrel snugly against the inside of his right shoulder, just above the tip of the arm pit, Major Peterson grinned like a man holding the winning poker deck at a million-dollar tournament.

Sergeant Jeffrey Ezop, immediately realizing the Major's intentions, smiled broadly. At that moment, he felt a father-figure kinship with a man he at times equally admired and feared.

Private Kemp found a different reason to smile just as the Major pulled the trigger, a look of unconcealed peace covering his otherwise haggard visage.

Late that night, the moonlight's rays cutting a spear-like laser through the open flap of his tent, Peterson peered in comical befuddlement at the fingers of his right hand. Although there was no pain associated with the bluish tent underneath the nails, a moist, pus-like infection seemed to be developing at the corners of each. All thoughts of the self-inflicted welt underneath his right shoulder were swept away by fresher, more mysterious pains.

His right ankle ached from the narrow pit he had accidentally stepped into while tracking Kemp, whom he now labeled 'Rip Van Kemp' in honor of her combat slumbering techniques.

Rubbing at the soreness there, he recalled briefly looking down into the hole, which was barely wider than a prairie dog's den, but seemed almost hypnotically, tar-like in its blackness, as well as astonishingly deep, as though it might spread infinitely wider the further it's eerily smooth walls became.

As the throngs of sleep eventually began to take hold a half-hour later, Major Peterson noticed a faint tingling at the base of his scalp.

His fitful sleep was full of dreams that

included, but were not limited to, battlefield scenes of violent decapitations and gut-wrenching dismemberment.

He was shaken awake only when one of the severed heads lying face up in the crimson-coated gravel resembled his own.

CHAPTER THREE
Correctional Measures

Briarston Correctional Facility
Red Bridge, Mississippi
June 12th, 1957

Gripping the glossily coated black billy club like Mickey Mantle standing in the batter's box at Yankee Stadium, Jeffrey Dickenson felt his entire body begin to tingle as if from a mild electric shock. He despised the feeling, although over time it was one he had become nauseatingly accustomed to. His steel-toed boots, the tips of which glistened like reflecting mirrors, echoed off the stone floors like twin cannons as his pace steadily increased.

The cell doors down D block stood open on either side, the dark confines of each foreboding in their eerie desolation. The cons were in the yard, as they would stay for the next hour or so until the mid-day chow horn sounded.

Premature worry lines creasing his otherwise youthful appearance, Jeff's half-jog quickly and dramatically decreased once he neared the East end of the cellblock.

The muffled but still quite distinct sounds of a scuffle were emanating from the next to last cell on the left.

Jeff knew who belonged to that particular cell. The same inmate he had observed being escorted into the block fifteen minutes earlier by Pete Hanley. The same inmate that had instigated a brawl in the exercise area and was on his way to the hole for a still to be determined length of time. The inmate's name was Barkley. Moses Barkley. A small-framed, nervous Nellie type, middle-aged man doing eight to ten for business fraud of some kind. A man who; at least until a few weeks ago, had been the poster-boy for model inmates everywhere. A man, like so many other inmates Jeff had witnessed of late, who had dropped an oar in the water and then fallen off the dead end into a deep pool of lunacy, seemingly without reason.

He had seen Barkley's eyes while working the laundry room the previous day. The man's mind had sprung a major leak, and the state of Mississippi penal system provided no relief whatsoever in plugging such holes.

As if literally walking on eggshells, Dickenson tip-toed forward until he was only a few feet from the open cell door. His cautiousness wasn't fueled by simple fear of his own personal safety, although that was an additional factor. But it was more the almost hypnotic sounds filling his ears from the nearby eight by ten space that prevented him from rushing forward like he realized he probably should.

Just the thought of the skeleton-thin Barkley overpowering Hanley was enough to immediately set his spastic thoughts at ease.

Pete was a muscular bear of a man who had transferred in from a unit near Jackson a few months back. A man of few words but many varied techniques to control the cons under his supervision (most of which involved strategically placed fists), Pete Hanley was the one guard Jeff had shared shift time with who practically oozed cool, calculating menace.

When Officer Pete Hanley walked the block, a true sense of security existed in a place pathetically void of such the majority of the time.

Jeff leaned against the cool stone wall at the outer edge of the cell, and was able to finally recognize the two sets of sounds reverberating from inside the tiny, shadowed space.

One was a series of short, huffing breaths; sounding as if they were being blown from between tightly pursed lips.

The second was the low, almost whispered shrieks of pain that were being released in bursts that seemed strangely synchronized.

It wasn't until he leapt through the narrow cell opening and his eyes had a full three seconds to adjust that he was able to distinguish which voice belonged to whom.

In the five days that remained in the life of Jeffery Ray Dickenson, the horrific scene would be rewound and then replayed without pause.

Pete Hanley, his green uniform pants pulled to his ankles in a jumbled wad, hung like a rather bulky slab of beef from the rear corner of the cell's top bunk. His belt had been made into a makeshift noose, tied to the far bed railing and wound so tightly around his thick neck that even in the dim light, Jeff could see the larger man's tongue sticking from his mouth like a mutated earthworm.

Moses Barkley turned from Hanley's mostly motionless frame and sneered at Jeff like a cornered animal looking down the sights of a twenty-gauge. His bony frame was completely unclothed, his pasty flesh smeared in blood, the coppery aroma of which was now hideously apparent to Jeff's suddenly overtaxed senses.

Just before Barkley lunged forward in his direction, Jeff had noticed the gaping wounds around Pete Hanley's throat and upper chest. He also noticed (an additional vision that would be filed away for further use in the nightmares that dominated his remaining days) that the majority of Hanley's nose was missing. The original version, a large, rather vein-encased bulbous sort, had replaced by a stump of bloody cartilage that looked to have been chewed upon like a pork chop bone lying outside a doghouse.

Managing to snap from his doze just in time to block the smaller man's assault with the club, Jeff nonetheless screamed out like a frightened child upon impact.

As he attempted to sling the growling, groaning form loose from where it had latched onto his weapon like a slug onto exposed flesh, Jeff found himself involved in a macabre dance in the center of a room barely wide enough to accommodate such frantic activity.

With every ounce of strength his adrenaline-laced system could muster, he repeatedly tossed the thin-framed man from one set of steel bars to another, the clanging racket of which was roughly the equivalent to small-arms fire in such otherwise quiet surroundings.

Thirty seconds later, his breath now escaping in harsh gasps, Jeff was mortally terrified to discover Moses Barkley still attached to his weapon, a repulsive look of mockery in the red pits that were his eyes.

Moist garbling noises slipped through the

man's thin, chalky lips, and it was at that moment that Jeff first noticed the horrid condition of the man's skin.

Pink colored sores coated the man's forehead, neck and chest. They were uniformly quarter-sized, and were visually pulsating like major arteries on the verge of a violent eruption.

The short, spider-like hands that grasped the center portion of Jeff's club gleamed a purplish hue, glowing candle-like in the surrounding gloom.

Executing a maneuver taught during the initial days of guard training, Jeff yanked forward with both arms while simultaneously kicking forward with his right boot.

He felt the padded heel dig into Barkley's slim midsection, which seemed strangely gooey and moist on contact.

Flailing back with his pencil-trim arms windmilling madly, Barkley nailed the edge of the top bunk with the back of his skull, then slid underneath atop the lower one like a man settling in for a long-awaited nap. For a few suspended moments, Pete Hanley's slumped form swung back and forth like a mammoth side of meat suspended from a slaughterhouse hook.

Cautiously keeping his distance from the badly trembling but apparently incapacitated form of Moses Barkley, Jeff backed slowly from the cell and then halted, wiping the salty tasting liquid that poured from his pores like a free-flowing stream.

From the center of the walkway, he could still make out the bottom of Pete Hanley's legs and boots, which were crossed over one another haphazardly, like a man preparing to pray at an unseen altar. Despite the choking heat of the cell and his own sweat-soaked person, he felt a series of cool chills envelop his back and arms.

There was no doubt that Hanley was deceased, 'dead as a bag full'a hammer's' Jeff chillingly recalled his father saying at every available opportunity. Still, such lunacy had to be reported as soon as possible, although the temptation to delay medical attention for a currently down and possibly out maniac inmate wasn't easily dismissed.

With a frustrated groan, Jeff sucked in a fresh lung full of air and started back up the cellblock with a slightly wobbly gait.

His ears were filled with the moist, sucking noises just as his stride had begun to expand. Whirling around to his left, he barely avoided tripping forward as his knees clapped roughly together.

Gripping his club straight up in front of his face in a defensive posture, he was initially shocked but invariably relieved by the emptiness that filled his vision. No sounds other than his own inconsistent breathing were apparent. The row was as empty as a moment before, although the soothing, uniquely serene quality of such a picture was strangely missing.

Rising from the semi-crouching combat stance he had instinctively fallen into, Jeff smiled grimly, dropping the weapon back to his side. He had the distinct notion that his oft-times overworked imagination was having itself a field day within the confines of his faintly throbbing skull.

After giving the empty cells on either side of him a quick scan, he turned back towards the cell block entrance and felt the lightest of breezes caress his stubble covered right cheek.

Jeff's nostrils flared wildly, the smell of rotted meat causing his expression to grow instantly sour with disgust.

"What the..." he managed before the movement directly above the bill of his '*BRIARSTON UNIT*' cap caught his attention.

The raucous, mirthful laugh that followed was all his shell-shocked being could think to process upon viewing the nightmarish imagery hanging directly over his suddenly rigid torso.

It was a high-pitched howling that one would normally associate with joyous glee, but within the now-permanently scarred mind of one Jeffery Dickenson, State Employee, faithful husband and father of two grade school daughters, it now held a different meaning altogether.

It served as the mad banshee cry of a hopelessly snapped mind.

Moses Barkley hung from the rock ceiling with his arms and legs dangling, as if suspended from either invisible binding or concealed hooks embedded into his upper back.

The sucking sounds were now ominously shrill, and seemed to be originated from the portion of his body that was connected to the stone, as if suction cups were being used to literally plaster him into position.

A millisecond before Barkley was either freed; or released himself and toppled downward onto Jeff's head and shoulders, the guard caught a glimpse of the squelchy line of moisture and goo that trailed from the upper portion of the convicts cell, across the ceiling, and then to the body itself. It resembled a recently placed slug-line, only a hundred times wider, and more murky than shimmering.

"Aww, shit..." Jeff whispered even as his arms arose and head fell in an instinctive blocking posture.

The impact knocked the air from his lungs in a stifled grunt, his knees driven into the lower part of his abdomen like heavy posts.

The Billy club flew away uselessly, sliding down the hall as if on a layer of recently formed ice.

Jeff swiveled hard to the left in an attempt to toss the gruesomely gelatinous form from his upper back, his mouth stretched wide in an attempt to suck in a fresh supply of oxygen.

The body remained perched, shockingly attached, even as Jeff executed a failed judo flip that resulted in nothing more than his own neck being twisted a full forty-five degrees.

A somehow soft but remarkably stout set of fingers dug into Jeff's mouth, hooking around his top set of teeth, while another gripped the short hair at his forehead. He first smelled and then tasted putrid, rotting meat.

Shoving back with all the energy that remained in his trembling thighs, Jeff attempted to push Barkley towards the far cell wall.

Halfway through the attempt, the weight unexpectedly fell from his shoulders as if never there. Jeff impacted with the wall a split-second later, helpless to halt his own momentum. Bright flashes of sparking light filled his eyes as his shoulders and then the back of his skull landed with an appallingly loud thud.

Someone, or *thing*, was leaning over his prone form when he awoke.

The skin of the face seem to be physically pulsating, small shards of skin hanging free like white ash. Blinking madly but unable to muster the strength to even reach up and rub his bleared, droopy eyes, Jeff heard something similar to a wet belch being released seemingly inches from his nostrils, the stench of decomposition overwhelming. His lids pried themselves open at half-mask just in time to recognize the gaping, gore-drenched maw spreading before him like an open wound stretched apart by a surgeon's tool.

The brownish, thick liquid that spewed forth engulfed Jeff's forehead, face, neck and chest like a wave of warm sewage.

Gagging uncontrollably, he managed to roll over onto his left side, reaching for his own throat. The slimy, scaled appendages found there were just beginning to tighten, like a ravenous anaconda around an intended meal.

As the thing's tentacle-like attachments began to convulse, growing instantly rigid, Jeff became aware of a new distraction.

As the sounds of heavy boots hitting stone from the block entrance grew closer, the pressure around his neck steadily increasing until he seriously thought his head would soon explode, Jeff's final coherent thought flashed forward in a film reel of astonishing clarity. It was not of his beloved wife or daughters, or even of his recently deceased parents.

Jeff Dickenson pondered how it was scientifically possible that a human could suddenly transform into an Octopus.

Such varied solutions as 'radiation' and 'state funded experiments' swam forth, but the recent interruption of shouting voices, some screaming like small girls at the sight of a live rat underneath their feet, eventually broke his brittle train of thought.

Any further queries on the scientific aspects on such a topic would be delayed, as the Gods of Merciful Unconsciousness acquired the controls of his tattered mind.

***

The Briarston Unit burned to the ground on June 17th, 1957, scorched cement walls and soot covered metal bars the only viable proof it had ever stood upright.

Thirty-nine of the eight-six cons being housed were unable to escape, many trapped in their cells behind doors locked into place by the searing flames that swept through the blocks in long-reaching, wide waves of yellow.

The lengthy (two years plus) state investigation that ensued concluded that the fire had begun inside the infirmary, the chemicals encased there providing all the firepower the flames would need to quickly turn the hundred- thousand square foot compound into a pile of simmering rubble and sizzling rod iron.

Neither investigators nor anyone else would ever uncover was the true origin of the blaze.

No survivors would be forthcoming from that section of the compound, only blackened, parched bone and teeth fragments scattered amongst the ruins.

The secret of exactly how and why the first spark of disaster had been ignited would forever remain with the unfortunate few who had witnessed it first-hand.

Barbara Whiten, a veteran nurse of twenty-six years, her skull creased by a solid steel IV stand just as the initial flames began to sweep through the narrow hallway leading to the patient's open bay ward.

Doctor Warren B. Peters, only two short years out of medical school, both his eyeballs punctured by separate syringes, buried to the hilt until the tips of the needles entered the lower portion of his brain.

Bart Carston, a trustee con with only a year remaining on an eight-year sentence for armed robbery, his throat cut from ear to ear by the shiny blade of a surgeon's scalpel just as his tennis shoes and lower pants legs were being engulfed in flames.

Jeffery Dickenson had shaken awake from his coma-state at around eleven PM that evening, his pus-filled eyes itching as if covered with a battalion of scurrying ants.

He felt a sickening moistness as he rubbed them, initially believing the source of wetness spilling from the eyes themselves. Through the bleared, hazy waves he strained to peer through, Jeff soon discovered the warm, sour scented liquid to be leaking from the fingers of each hand, both at the yellowish tips and the grotesquely swollen knuckles. His temples throbbed so loudly he was certain the rest of the ward could hear the persistent pounding.

He could make out the bed to his immediate

right, a crumpled body hidden beneath the frazzled covers. To his left was an empty bed, but beyond that sat a row of occupied ones, all sitting so peaceful and still that Jeff pondered the possibility that it wasn't the med ward, but the unit morgue he presently occupied.

Pushing himself up by the metal railing on each side of the badly sunken mattress, it took Jeff just under a minute to prop himself upright on the far edge of the bed. He attempted to wipe the seeping pus from his hands, then relented once it became painfully obvious that such an act was moot. The wounds were replenishing themselves with each effort to dismiss the present build-up, and Jeff wondered how his body could process such inordinate amounts of infectious fluid without the source eventually running dry in the literal sense.

Rising to his feet, which felt as if they were being simultaneously punctured by ice pick blades through the heels, Jeff first winced and then moaned aloud. The unrelenting thirst that gripped his mouth, throat, and upper chest was one he had never experienced before, driving him forward in a desperate search for immediate relief.

He felt the gown that had been draped haphazardly across his back and shoulders fall free as he made his way steadily down the left side of the ward, wobbling from the center to the edges of each row of beds like a wino trekking down a dimly lit alley.

As Jeff's naked form passed the final bed, the old man occupying it's space lying on his back with his toothless mouth crookedly agape, he spotted the water fountain sitting straight ahead against a far hallway exit.

Slurping hungrily, like a man who had crossed an open desert and stumbled across a lake of clear, ice-cold water, Jeff's speed increased until he came dangerously close to toppling headfirst into the far wall.

He drank from the steady stream of lukewarm H2O until he felt his gut was going to literally pop open. In finally leaning up from the cooler, gasping for fresh air, Jeff spotted the partially opened door, the fluorescent light seeping through the small crack like that of a lighthouse beacon atop a desolate cliff top.

Jeff felt strangely drawn to the room, the outside door of which was labeled '*Extensive Care Unit #1*'. He entered with his right hand over his suddenly oversensitive eyes, as if walking onto the surface of the sun.

As he neared the single bed the relatively tiny room contained, he studied the various IV's and monitors attached to the body it housed. An electronic control panel of some kind released a rhythmic beeping noise every ten seconds or so, the numbers it displayed totally meaningless and alien to anyone other than the med staff. Multi-colored IV tubes ran from the patient's arms, neck and chest like spaghetti strands hanging from the edges of some unseen dinner plate. It wasn't until he actually leaned over the bed's tall side railing and bent down until his vein-infested face was mere inches from the prone bodies tightly wrapped head that Jeff was able to positively identify it's owner.

Even with the majority of his face hidden underneath several layers of mesh wrap with only the forehead and eyes totally exposed (holes had been strategically placed through the mesh for his nostrils, only the right one free of plastic tubes), Moses Barkley was easily recognizable by the man he had attempted to murder five days earlier.

In normal circumstances, Jeff Dickenson might have been inclined to extract a measure of revenge against the man who had come within a cat's whisker of ending his life.

Moses Barkley, had in fact, infected him with some yet unknown, apparently untreatable virus that seemed to be melting his body from the inside out.

Yet, this was far from normal circumstances, and the inner workings of the former Correctional Officer's mind were no longer inclined to such reckless acts against one of his own kind.

Pulling the IV's free from Barkley's arm like so much loose confetti string, Jeff gently placed his greenish colored hand atop the comatose man's forehead, then positioned the other on the man's bandaged chin. He applied only token pressure until Barkley's wrapping was pulled free and his horribly chapped lips pried apart with a low smacking noise.

Resembling a man attempting to resuscitate a drowning victim, Dickenson placed his mouth over Barkley's and paused. His stomach lurched once and then again, the contents heaved forward in the second spasm filling Barkley's jaws and throat with multi-colored bile that pushed the already decomposing skin of his face and neck to the breaking point until the majority was forced downward.

Moses Barkley arose less than two minutes later, his expression bland and his demeanor trance-like. He greeted Jeff Dickenson with a strained, gruesome smile, the remainder of his upper plate of teeth falling free and scattering onto the tiled floor like spilt aspirin.

The two men departed the unit undetected, the lone doctor and single nurse on duty conveniently absent from the front station, and wobbled their way clumsily towards the unit laundry building. This only after systematically strangling the guard on duty at the infirmary entrance, then tossing his lifeless body in a nearby closet. They performed the task with no emotion whatsoever, their stares as blank as the overall expression of indifference that accompanied it.

Within the shadowy confines of the abandoned structure, long since shut down for the evening but rarely locked up, the two stood face to face, their foul-smelling breath causing a thick swarm of flies to congregate near they're bloated, barely parted lips.

They had taken up position at the rear of the building, within a narrow hallway between two locked supply rooms. Almost in unison, they bowed onto their knees as if to pray. Both then subsequently kneeled down, placing their bare hands onto the stony floor and stooping until their fever-racked foreheads made contact also.

From a distance, it would have resembled some mysterious tribal ritual, as if the men were worshipping at the base of a great temple, instead of the dusty, dank floor of a prison laundry.

Beneath the pulsating, gang-green ridden feet of beings that had once answered to the names Moses Barkley and Jeffrey Dickenson; below numerous layers of stone and a foot thick reinforced steel plate, lay a hole in the earth's surface wide enough to drive a bus through. Drawn unconsciously to the spot like vultures to a decaying corpse, the two soon lay horizontally on the cold floor's surface, wriggling around and on top of one another as if under a mad hypnotist's spell. Each arose moments later, leaving a substantial amount of their skin behind, along with spattering stains made up of blood and pus. With renewed levels of raw energy pulsing through their rancid veins, both returned to the infirmary just as the staff had become aware of their missing status.

The doctor and his nurse, along with the unfortunate trustee named Carston, were never allowed to report such transgressions, however, the trio becoming the first of many to perish that evening. Carston, in fact, had been ordered by the good doctor to 'detain' the two men while he contacted the nearest guard station.

Such heroics were never to be, however, as the former guard and convict, respectively, had reveled in the short amount of time it had taken to cruelly dispatch the late shift medical staff that had been unfortunate enough to pull duty on that fateful night at the Briarston Unit.

***

It wasn't until the spring of 1959 that heavy equipment was allowed to move onto the site and begin clearing the site.

As the foundation of what had been the unit laundry room was being bulldozed into a mountainous pile of jagged rubble, a twenty by twenty five-foot sheet of stainless, reinforced steel was exposed. A state engineer, scratching his balding scalp in utter confusion, eventually ordered it removed upon inspection.

Hours later, the plate was set firmly back in place, it's reason for being obvious to all who had stared into the gloomy, impossibly deep pit. The engineer figured that the builders had, more than likely, attempted to fill in the massively wide gap, and found the task both improbable and impossible.

As they proceeded to spread a thick layer of padded dirt and clay atop the metal plated surface, the workers had commented aloud of the putrid stench in the immediate area. "The reek of dead animals" one 'dozer operator had blurted, forcefully pinching his nostrils shut with gloved fingers.

Construction on the newly funded Red Bridge Correctional Housing Unit would not commence until three decades later, when construction crews would verbally note the lack of plant and animal life near the old site.

Many would also comment on the thick, putrid scent of decay present in the air.

CHAPTER FOUR
Undetected Decadence

August 20th, 2003

Interstate 20, eight miles west of Corinth, Mississippi

The man smirked, pushing what his sister liked to call his 'Birth Control' glasses to the highest point the bridge of his prominent nose would allow.

"Jeez Louise, Kara. How exactly is Daredevil gonna manage to take out Wolverine? Using his seein' eye cane? The man is *blind*, woman! Ol' Wolvie would slice his 'radar sensitive' ass into crimson sausage links," he spat sarcastically, just as a newer model Ford Explorer sailed by them in the passing lane, the early eighties Mustang they occupied farting thick black smoke in response.

Brushing the frizzy hair from her forehead and eyes, only to have it blown back into place by the gusts of air blowing through the open car windows, Kara McGuire replied through a pained sneer.

"Why is it that no matter *who* I bring up, your only answer is that 'Wolvie will turn 'em into bologna slices', or 'he'll mangle 'em'. How about giving me a detailed synopsis of exactly how this one scrawny mutant with razor claws can kick the universes' collective rear ends without breaking a sweat."

A small Toyota truck blared its horn as it whizzed quickly past, an action casually ignored by the Mustang's present navigator. William "Wilbo" McGuire had his squinty eyes, which were actually magnified in size by the thick, presently fingerprint smeared, lens of his black-framed glasses, glued onto his twin sister.

"The man is tough as nails and twice as mean, Sister Olive. If I had a C- note, I'd slap it down without hesitation that old Wolvie could hand Superman his balls wrapped in silver foil if they ever scraped."

Kara grinned as her brother finally returned his attention to the narrow two lane they now occupied, a green sign reading 'Corinth-10 miles' visible from a tall growth of weeds. The braces that adorned both her upper and lower set of teeth glimmering in the midday Mississippi sun.

"If I didn't know any better, Wilbo my brother, I'd think you have a serious crush on a comic book character. Besides, don't mix DC with Marvel. You know the rules."

Taking a brief sip from the can of Mountain Dew stashed away at his crotch, Wilbo sighed, rolling his eyes comically.

"You sayin' I got homosexual tendencies, my dear sibling? I beg to disagree. It's the Scarlet Witch that heats my meat, so to speak. Although I will admit that Captain America does have a nice caboose, depending on whose drawing him at the time."

Kara howled, slapping her brothers sinewy arm, which was undersized for a man his height, a little over six feet, but nonetheless layered in tightly wound muscle, as was his entire frame.

"How much longer to the triangle, anyhow? I'm starting to develop butt- cheek scarring from the springs sticking out of this seat," she grumbled playfully. Kara was her brother's senior by exactly two minutes, twenty-six seconds, having just turned twenty-six, but looked a decade younger when they were stood side by side.

She had also inherited the trademark McGuire frame, lanky and bone thin. Both wore their father's nose, narrow and a shade lengthy. They carried a trait of their presently missing mother, as well. The McGuire twins, known during their school days in Paris, Texas as "Freak and Geek", were as stubborn as a summer day in the southeast was long. Kara's female peers had begun calling her "Olive Oil" sometime around the 4th grade, due to her gangly look and high-pitched voice. Little had changed since puberty in her case, including the pancake flat landscape of her chest, although she hoped the braces would at least correct the unevenly set teeth displayed since her early teens.

"Another two hours, at least. It's two-lane from here 'til there. Grab me another Dew outta the cooler, will ya, Sis?" he answered while stifling a yawn. The Red, White and Blue striped T-shirt he sported (the phrase '*Eye for an Eye*' barely readable above a faded photo of former Mid-Eastern Terrorist Bin Laden) stained in various colors from the collar on down.

"We did cover all of our bases on this, didn't we?" She asked a bit cautiously after handing him the only slightly chilled beverage.

Wilbo didn't meet her timid gaze, instead keeping his dark blue eyes trained on the bumper of a Semi a few dozen feet ahead.

"You read the stats, Kara. This place is a freakin' *black hole*. Swallows people up like

Marlon Brando with a bag of M&M's. *Coincidences* don't come in sevens, eights or tens. Numbers don't lie, am I right?" He asked grimly through tightly set jaws.

She nodded, sipping the Diet Pepsi she had retrieved for herself.

Leaning back to study the serene, pasture filled countryside as they sped past the truck and into a clear, flat stretch of highway, Kara exhaled quietly.

Twenty-six years old and out playing 'X-Files'. Sometimes she didn't know whether to laugh or cry.

Paternal twins who shared many of the same interests, to include a comic book collection (mostly superhero comics of the seventies) with an estimated worth in the high four figures, the McGuire's were happily content misfits in a world neither deemed worthy of their concern.

Both toiled in the everyday workforce, Wilbo as an armed security guard for a chain of local Paris banks, and Kara as a policy specialist for a large insurance company. Both had dated occasionally, but never experienced a relationship resembling anything remotely 'serious' in nature. Amongst co-workers, the rumor of an incestuous relationship between the two had been whispered about, along with the popular 'they're not really brother and sister, anyhow', in an attempt to explain the seemingly unbreakable bond that existed. The twins scoffed at any and all such ramblings. The basis for their co-existence as siblings who resided together without neither shame nor self-consciousness was simple: save money by sharing bills, at least until the time a possible mate came along for either of them.

Wilbo kept his eyes glued to the asphalt, his pointy chin only an inch or so from resting atop his admittedly narrow but still finely toned upper chest. While his regular diet rarely called for anything more filling than a tuna sandwich or Campbell's soup eaten directly from the can, the set of four weighty dumbbells that rolled freely inside the Mustang's rusted trunk never yearned for attention. William McGuire was what old timers referred to as naturally 'cock-strong', and felt it was his personal responsibility to remain such.

With his Icabob Crane looks and whiny, nasal tone, he had been forced to defend himself more times than he cared to recall. The McGuire twins had seemingly been born with a 'kick me' sign permanently attached between their shoulder blades, and realized that within their lifetimes, respect would always be something earned as opposed to freely given.

Departing the cramped, two-bedroom apartment in Paris they had shared for the past three plus years, the mission ahead was a simple one; uncover the truth behind their parents disappearance, while simultaneously blowing the lid off of a twenty-square mile area they had deemed 'The Red Bridge Triangle'.

In early March of that same year, the twins had received a call from their father, Martin, a retired civil servant, and mom, a lifelong housewife. They were in the midst of what their father called 'The McGuire World Tour,' a six-month road trip in the recently purchased RV that Martin had purchased upon retirement.

Things had been going swimmingly, according

to both. They were snapping pictures at every spot along the way even rumored to be a local landmark, sticking mainly to back roads and two-lane highways in order to experience what their mother called 'Genuine America'.

The call had originated from just outside a tiny Mississippi burg named 'Red Bridge'. Martin and Rose McGuire had been on their way to Biloxi for a three to four-day engagement with the 'one-armed bandits' located inside various casinos.

The twins had received a second phone call from Red Bridge three days later, this one not from their vacationing folks, but the local Sheriff's Department.

The RV had been found lying within a deep, grassy ravine on the outskirts of town, a few miles east of the 'Oak Mountain Campsite'. Martin and Rose McGuire were mysteriously absent from the badly dented yet still serviceable vehicle, which had been pulled from the steep ditch by a city-owned crane and taken to the Sheriff Department's impound lot for safekeeping.

Even upon their initial visit to Red Bridge, a small township tucked neatly away between thick, hilly forests and flat, carefully cultivated farmland, a few days after the call, the twins had felt an unexplainable foreboding, a sensation of pure dread.

The Sheriff's department, with a total staff consisting of a single dispatcher, two deputies and the top dog himself, had no answers as to the whereabouts of the senior McGuire's, and even seemed a bit apathetic to the twins predicament. At least, it had seemed that way to Wilbo as one of the deputies, a skinny young man who looked as though he was still a year or so away from shaving, gave them a tour of the wrecked RV. As they filled out the required Missing Persons Reports, the Sheriff mumbled such gems as 'we'll do our best' and 'call you when we hear something' in a casual, bland tone that might as well have been saying 'don't give a shit long as my paycheck arrives each week'.

The town itself wasn't exactly Rockwell material. Most of the three to four blocks that made up 'main street' were made up of stone buildings that looked to have been constructed in the early 1900's, and at least a quarter of them wore padlocks on the front doors and faded signs of businesses gone bust.

There was the usual outlet shops that featured clothing long out of style with Madison Avenue; grocery and hardware stores which featured half-empty parking lots, and a farm implement store that displayed tractors, lawn mowers, and garden tillers coated in dust and cobwebs. Two separate, ancient looking gas stations were positioned at each end of town, presumably to catch travelers who might be passing through in either direction.

After staying overnight in the only hotel available, a fifteen unit spread named 'Sandman's Stopover' which made Motel 6 resemble Embassy Suites, the twins left early the next AM. Feeling confused and hollow within the mystery they were leaving behind, the twins remained mute for most of the eleven hour drive back to Paris, neither able to verbally express the vibe each felt. The vibe that their parents hadn't been kidnapped *or* taken hostage. The vibe which whispered that no phone call asking for a ransom was impending.

The twins later discussed the vibe in detail, both equally shaken and enthralled at its similar definition within each of them.

William and Kara McGuire knew their parents we no longer alive.

They also knew that Martin and Rose McGuire's bodies were still within or just outside the borders of Red Bridge, Mississippi.

Now all they had to do was find out where and why.

Further contact with local and federal authorities was quickly considered and then discarded. The twins had witnessed first-hand the indifference of the locals, and figured the FBI had bigger fish to fry than taking up precious agency man-hours searching for two missing senior citizens. There was also another reason they wanted to handle the search themselves, with minimal to no outside interference. Both William and Kara McGuire became acutely aware of one concrete fact while within the city limits of Red Bridge, Mississippi: something was terribly *amiss* other than just the disappearance of their parents.

They began to slowly investigate and record an impromptu portfolio of strange; unexplained events that had taken place near or around the area over the past century. Utilizing nothing more available public records (obtained through snail mail) and the world-wide web, a macabre pattern began to form, taking shape as clearly as a child's jig-saw puzzle within the expert gaze of an experienced architect.

Within the county of Davenport, state of Mississippi, city of and around Red Bridge, folks had dropped off the map in groves, more than a truckload of milk cartons could possibly account for. A few weeks before their scheduled return to the region of their parent's last known occupancy, the McGuire twins dubbed the area 'The Triangle' without the slightest hint at humor.

With the trunk of his rusty Ford 'Tang supplied with an ample supply of canned and dry goods, matching sleeping bags and two-man pup tent, Wilbo found his sister an enthusiastic ally in the bizarre mystery they were both determined to solve, no matter what the cost.

He hadn't, however, bothered to inform Kara of the loaded thirty-eight revolver and twenty-gauge shotgun, plus enough additional ammunition to start a private war, tucked beneath the bald spare tire within the car's trunk.

Just past what looked like a handmade road sign that read '*Red Bridge- Filled With Old Friends You Just Ain't Met Yet - 8 miles this here way'*, Wilbo made the slight left onto an alien, pothole ravaged stretch of two lane. The twins sighed simultaneously, evicting wry grins from each.

"Not long now, Olive. You're not getting cold feet, are ya?" He queried with a playful wink.

Kara sat up as straight as the badly sagging car seat would allow.

"Wilbo my brother, right now I believe even Wolverine himself would cower before my unmatched resolve."

His wide smile revealing a set of upper teeth both jagged and unevenly spaced, Wilbo nodded before reaching out and punching his sister lightly on the shoulder.

"Okay Iron Man versus Power Man."

Kara hesitated, placing her chin into her right hand thoughtfully.

"Definitely Iron Man. Two punches; IM nailing PM, and PM going through the nearest wall."

"Sis…' Wilbo sighed, '...you're finally startin' to get it.."

Fifteen minutes later, they pulled into the parking lot of the 'Sandman's Stopover', and were eventually greeted at the check-in counter by a short, silver- haired man that reminded both of the senile old codger played by Tim Conway on the old Carol Burnett Show.

The motel parking lot had been empty save for a rusted Monte Carlo that was parked by the office entrance.

"Looks like tourist season has passed, Sis," Wilbo had quipped while removing their sparse luggage from the back seat.

"Real hotspot, alright. Bet the roaches put on a real dandy floorshow," she replied while scanning the mostly deserted main street to their left.

After situating themselves within the sour-smelling confines of the cramped room, the contents of which would serve solely as a supply depot for the next few days, the twins walked to a nearby eatery named 'Harry's Burgers 'n Fixings' for a quick bite.

The few locals within the establishment, mostly older folks either nearing or past retirement age, paid the twins only passing attention as they placed their orders.

Wilbo was scarfing down cheeseburger number three and Kara Tuna melt number two when the peaceful mood was suddenly shattered like a boulder thrown through a plate glass window.

The doors flew open as if blown apart by a level-five funnel cloud, and two men staggered clumsily inside, the larger of the pair almost toppling headfirst into an older couple just preparing to depart.

"Goddammit, Buck, I know what I saw. It was one of them National Guard Patrols, man. Those nosy sombitches are creepin' around the prison site for a reason, I tell ya. Might have some cons on the loose up there," The smaller man blurted, his speech badly slurred. The camouflaged hunter's hat he sported was dangerously close to sliding off of his wobbling, badly tilted cranium.

The larger man scoffed sarcastically, his gait a bit steadier, but still obviously under the influence.

"J.C, if I had sucked down thirty Bud Ice's like yourself, I'm sure I would've seen George W. Bush humpin' a grizzly. Pipe down and let's grab some grub."

The men practically fell into the nearest booth, the scent of recently consumed alcoholic beverages filling the air around them.

Wilbo and Kara quickly looked away, deciding the view through the nearby glass windows onto the barely occupied main drag infinitely more attractive, not to mention safer. The twins could easily define trouble upon viewing it. The other dozen or so inhabitants of the relatively small establishment turned and stared at the two men as if viewing a newly acquired Zoo exhibit.

"Harry! Get your flabby butt cheeks out here pronto, will ya? Ya got two starvin' hunters to feed!" The larger man yelled through cupped hands, so loudly even his drunken partner covered his ears.

"Jesus Crow, Buck, could you yell any louder? I think I shattered a drum," he replied, staring at an open menu as if viewing some strange hieroglyphic writing tablet.

Both men were younger than they appeared, Wilbo guessed. The scruffy, thick beards and long hair each displayed adding false years to their twenty- something visages. They were also vulgar, crude, and more than likely the definition of sadistic redneck if offended in even the most innocent way. He had met and dealt with their kind practically all his life, drawn to such individuals like a magnet to steel. He shot Kara a quick glance, rolling his eyes worriedly, then proceeded to finish off the last of his burger in a single, comically oversized bite.

"Let's get rolling, Sis. The Duke boys over there are gonna spot us pretty soon, and no doubt will want introductions. We can't afford to be cooling our heels in the town lock-up a half hour after arrival," he whispered between chews, the two men continuing to ignorantly bellow away in the background.

Kara didn't respond verbally, just nodded in agreement before taking a final sip of iced water.

Wilbo tucked a twenty beneath the edge of the large glass saltshaker as they rose as one to depart.

Kara's chair squeaked slightly as she had pushed it back, and she grimaced and shot her brother a worrisome look. The two men had immediately grown quiet, and the twins became instantly aware of the intrusive stares now following their every movement.

Just as Kara turned to join her brother, who had

already turned in the direction of the exit, the bellowing voice at her back caused her to cringe involuntarily.

"How goes it there, missy? Ain't seen you or your buddy there in these parts before, have we?" It barked with a sarcastic insincerity that was ludicrously obvious.

Taking a single step forward, Wilbo calmly gestured for his sister to step forward just as he caught a glimpse of the larger of the two men stand up in the background.

"You two deaf or just dumb? I'm speakin' to you. We don't cotton to snotty outsiders around here," the man continued, the façade of friendliness replaced by slurred rage.

Kara wheeled around, her smile wide and toothy. She hoped her lips weren't trembling.

"Just passing through your fine township, sir. We, that is, my…"

She turned slightly just as Wilbo stepped up and hugged her tightly to his side, his own grin equally as manufactured as her own.

"Her better half, she means," he blurted cheerily, a large hunk of bread clearly displayed between his two front teeth.

"On our way to the gambling Mecca of the south, Biloxi. Got our income tax check a few days ago, and can't wait to piss it away by pullin' levers on every one-armed bandit that crosses our path."

The larger man, earlier identified by his drunken pal as 'Buck', began to wobble forward, the scowl covering his unshaken face a mask of disgust. Wilbo felt the muscles in his arms and chest tighten like coiled bands. He felt his sister tense up as she sucked in a quick breath and held it.

"Mister, I don't give a rat's ass if you're own yer way to meet the Pope at a Roman orgy. I just want to be shown simple courtesy, that's all. When I speak to someone, I expect a reply. Better teach your woman some manners, you hear?" Buck exclaimed, standing a mere two feet away from the conjoined couple by the time the slightly garbled message was completed.

"Damn straight. You tell 'em, Buck. Look like a couple'a road rats to me, anyhow," his partner chimed in matter-of-factly, still perched crookedly atop his chair, but at an awkward angle that made it seem as though he were leaning forward on his tiptoes.

His smile never wavering, Wilbo nodded amiably and turned to Kara, whose own calm demeanor was beginning to fade. He felt her body begin to shake, and realized he had but a few moments left before things were apt to get outrageously out of hand.

"I humbly apologize, my man. Names Bill, Bill James. This here is my ever-patient spouse of seven years, Claudine. Nice to greet and meet ya. Hate to rush off, but we gotta..." he began, forcibly twisting Kara's body to turn her towards the front door.

"You ain't going nowhere 'til you pay *our* check, mister. I believe it's the least you can do after insultin' us so. Whaddaya think, JC? Sound fair to you?" Buck asked, clumsily leaning back on one leg in order to visualize his inebriated buddy, who was slapping the tabletop in hysterics.

"Damn tootin', Buck-O. That's the least the two snotty asswipes can do." The intensity and speed of his heartbeat picking up speed like a runaway freight down a vertical slope, Wilbo somehow managed to retain the outward appearance of the three C's: calm, cool, and collected, despite the instinctual urge to rush forward in joyous abandon. Years of experience in dealing with ridicule in its cruelest form did provide advantages at such times.

"Well, we'd really like to, fellas, but we're kinda on a limited budget, you know?" He replied with a shrug as Kara released a thankfully muffled groan just inches away.

Buck lurched ahead, barely avoiding tripping headfirst into the suddenly braced twins.

"Do you see 'gives a shit' splashed across the bill of my cap, four eyes? Either you and ol' tin-foil teeth divvy up the cash for our spread, or both of you won't leave this here establishment without a noticeable limp."

Sighing deeply as he peered up at the taller man who undoubtedly outweighed him by at least fifty pounds, Wilbo's self-restraint peeled away like a snake's shed skin. As he gently pushed his sister to one side, he couldn't help but embrace the feeling. The fighting pose he struck was a side-stance; his legs spread wide apart, arms to the side with fists tightly clinched.

"Tell ya what, Goober, the wife and I are gonna turn and walk outta here now. If you and your shit-faced cohort there are feeling extra froggy, you can hop on over and try to stop us," he spat from between yellowish tinted teeth, winking at the larger man as if to ring some unseen fighting bell only he could hear. "...but I wouldn't advise it."

The smaller man practically fell from his seat, wobbling to his feet before regaining his balance. He came close to tackling his larger partner as they stood a few feet to the right of Wilbo.

"God damn faggot lookin' street bum. Buck and me are gonna plow your lousy ass into the tile, then borrow a meat cleaver from the kitchen and chop off that greasy, hippie hair'a yours," he barked furiously, his fists held out from his chest in a classic boxer's pose.

"Son, you just opened a can of whoop ass that you ain't prepared to put the lid back on..." Buck smirked, preparing to lunge.

"Buck! JC! Cut the bullshit!" A gruff, impossibly gravelly voice boomed out, causing all involved, including the scattered patrons of the establishment, to wince in shocked surprise.

The man charged from behind the long counter like a wild boar. His ample gut shook from underneath the gravy-stained white T-shirt he sported, his bald- head glistening with fresh sweat. He carried a thick-headed baseball bat in both hands like an ancient talisman.

"You two want me to call up Woody at the plant and tell 'im two of his dedicated but sick-for-the-day employees just strolled into my eatery smellin' like the inside of a JD bottle and pickin' fights instead of workin' the assembly line? Is that what ya want?" He screeched, his eyes squinting until it looked as though he were peering through narrow window slants.

"Let these people get on with their business, boys, or I won't hesitate to do a Mark McGwire on your drunk-ass noggins, you hear?"

Giggling nervously, Buck held up his right hand palms out in mock surrender. His grin was twitchy, his knees visually wobbling.

"White flag, Harry, white flag. Jesus, we were just funnin' anyhow."

"Yeah, Harry, don't blow a gasket. Yer libel to seize up right here and now, and I'll be damned if I'm gonna do CRP on your fat ass," JC added a bit hesitantly.

"That's CPR, you brain dead moron. Now, sit down and I'll have Marge take your order. You piss *her* off and she won't be so understanding as these good folks," Harry said, shooting Wilbo and Kara a quick nod.

Returning the gesture, Wilbo stepped forward and clapped Buck playfully on the right shoulder, causing the man to jerk back involuntarily, his eyes laughably wide.

"Appreciate the effort, sir, but like ol' Buck here was saying, no harm, no foul. My si...uh, wife and I will just be on our way. Good grub, by the way. Sure hit the spot, right hon?" He asked while squeezing Buck's shoulder until the man flinched.

Kara beamed, the reflection from her braces firing rays of light in every possible direction.

"Best we've had in days, sweetie-pie. We'll make a point to stop again on our way back."

His blood-red eyes now parked only inches from the larger man's bearded chin, Wilbo's expression never faltered, although the smile now seemed more predatory in nature than amiable.

He spoke in a low, whispered tone targeted for Buck's ears only.

"Fuck with us again, Billy Joe Bob Buck, and

there won't be enough *left* of your drunken hide for the vulture's to pick clean."

Buck's lips trembled, despite the stern look he attempted to display.

JC had stepped up, his mouth forming words that were never forthcoming. He had absorbed the lightning quick glance the small yet somehow startlingly menacing man had shot his way just as Buck's shoulder had been released. Frozen in place much like the deer both men reveled in illegally spotlighting and then killing on a regular basis, Buck and JC were in silent agreement that at that particular moment in time, discretion was easily the better part of valor.

"Have a safe trip, son. Take care of the little lady," Harry proclaimed just as the twins stepped from the establishment.

Sucking in the fresh, pollution free air that assaulted their faces once free of blocking walls, Wilbo saluted the man through the glass window.

"Holy *Deliverance*, Batman, we were a gerbil's whisker away from a WWF Slam-down match," he whispered from the right corner of his pursed lips.

"You hear what they were spouting as they walked in, brother of mine?" Kara asked, her shining eyes darting back and forth along the main street as if attempting to pinpoint a potential follower.

Wilbo dug the car keys from his faded jeans and halted at the driver's door.

"Yep. National Guard unit wandering around the woods near the prison site, which is located very near *you know where*."

"We headed in that general direction, I take it?"

Flinging the driver's door open as if pulling the hatch from some ancient, badly rusted space capsule, Wilbo flashed a smile that was much kinder than the one he had revealed to the patrons of Harry's Burger's and Fixing's just moments earlier.

"We can take five at the roach motel, then head that way. Sounds like a clue to me. I'm beginning to feel like we're stuck dead center in an old 'Scooby Doo' episode."

As her head disappeared below the partially dented hood of the Mustang, Kara couldn't help but sneer sarcastically.

"Just don't call me Velma, Shaggy."

***

Buck chewed his steak sandwich in total silence, his cheeks flaring red. A large, wide vein protruded prominently from his left cheek, just below the eye. It was a vein that only reared its head in times of great rage, one that symbolized the complete meltdown of what little rational side that Buck Lomax the Third currently (or for that matter, *had ever*) possessed.

JC Carlyle, or 'Lil' Bastard' to his equally mean-spirited, happily ignorant pals, knew better than even attempt to initiate a conversation when Buck was encased within the tightly wound throngs of such an ill, potentially violent mood swing.

Both men had sobered up in record time since the confrontation with the two strangers.

Sucking down the remains of a still-steaming mug of coffee in three quick gulps, Buck gently wiped a thick collection of breadcrumbs from his beard, then slowly turned his unblinking gaze to his friend.

"The Sandman. That's where they're stayin'. Saw the piece of cow-shit Mustang they was drivin' parked there as we pulled in. No other strangers in town, so it has to be that scrawny shithead and his main squeeze, ol' tin-foil teeth. Gonna pay 'em a visit, JC. Gonna show 'em some *true* southern hospitality."

JC blinked madly while sipping his own Java, strategically hiding his tremor-racked left hand underneath the cloth tabletop. The desire to stroke his quickly hardening manhood was maddening.

"I want the girl, Buck. Let *me* have the girl. I got some pliers in the truck perfect for pullin' that metal off her choppers, one at a fuckin' time."

"Keep your voice down, crap-for-brains," Buck whispered harshly, although the diner was now empty save the kitchen staff, who were currently out of sight behind a set of closed swinging doors.

"We'll stake 'em out, nab 'em, and take to the drop-off site. First I'm gonna find out exactly *why* in the hell they've paid our peaceful little valley a visit. That gambling story was bullshit from the word go."

"Finish up your sandwich, JC. We got work to do."

JC Carlyle flashed a lunatic's leer, what few teeth his head still possessed flashing like yellow slugs from the fluorescent lighting positioned above his pumpkin-shaped dome.

"I was hopin' you'd say that, Buck old buddy."

Watching his obviously deranged cohort chomp and swallow down the remainder of a somewhat undercooked double-cheeseburger like a caged animal with a handful of fresh roadkill, Buck Lomax the Third felt his stomach lurch and spasm in mild disgust. For many varied reasons, some even moderately justified, he truly despised the man sitting crookedly across from him. Always *had.* They had known and hung together since both were in lower grade school, linked by some mysterious, inexplicable bond they both loyally adhered to but never quite understood.

Buck found JC Carlyle an irritating, ignorant, dumb as a stone individual whose only apparent talents were malicious mischief and the strange ability to fart at will, not necessarily set in that order.

He hated the man's constant whining, the nasal tone of which could have driven even the sanest man clawing up the nearest wall.

Of course, being that Buck Lomax the Third pretty much hated or at the very least *begrudged* everyone he had ever come into contact with, the odds of his dislike for one such as JC would be a Vegas gambler's dream.

Born the son of Buck Lomax Jr. in the Year of Our Lord 1972, Buck the Third had been a screaming banshee of an infant, his early years filled with a constant barrage of high fevers and severe stomach ailments. His father had vanished from Red Bridge when he was but less than a year old, never to be heard from again. A man known for his quick temper and even quicker way with a bottle of whiskey, Buck Lomax Jr. had simply walked away from their shack-like abode one fine fall morning and never returned. He left behind his wife of twelve years and a screeching infant, not to mention unpaid debts that would only be squared with the selling of the family truck and the majority of their meager assets.

Buck Jr. wasn't the first Lomax male to perform the 'vanishing husband' act. His father had instituted the tradition some twenty- four years earlier, leaving Junior's mother lying in a battered, bloodied heap in the same bedroom he had later grown up in. Locals deduced that Lomax Sr. had fled to avoid prosecution from the assault of his wife, although relatives on both sides of the family had serious doubts concerning such a simplistic epilogue.

Mira Lomax had passed away on Buck the Third's eighteenth birthday. The town sawbones had taken one look at her grotesquely swollen, bloated form and had scribbled two words on the medical report under the heading 'cause of death': massive coronary. He hadn't deemed it necessary to examine the body, refusing to even lean down and give it a careful once-over.

At the time of her husband's inexplicable disappearance, Mira Lomax had been the consummate happy homemaker (minus the occasional beatings from her continuously ornery better half), satisfied to keep home and board for the two men in her life. She had also been the proud owner of what Buck's father had called 'the sweetest, shapeliest rear end in the county'. Lithe and wiry in build, Mira had done the ultimate about-face once Buck had seemingly fallen off a corner of the earth in year twelve of their marriage. Over the next five years, while living off the involuntary charity of Mississippi's taxpayers, Mira discovered a love of fried foods and sweets that she hadn't known previously existed (or had unconsciously held at bay with pure willpower) until Buck was no longer around to keep such cravings in check.

By the time Buck the Third was preparing to enter Red Bridge Elementary at the tender age of five and a half, Mira had added sixty pounds of loose blubber to her once slim, housework-toned frame. During year one of the Ronald Reagan administration, Mira piled on an additional twenty-five pounds, sucking down store-bought cakes and pastries on a daily basis, and rarely missing a regular meal in between. She had tipped the scales at two-forty by the time Buck the Third had entered high school. The death certificate would list her weight at two-sixty-five just four scant years later. Mira Lomax had literally resembled a bowling ball with a head on the day she breathed her last labored breath. Buck had not wept at his mother's gravesite the day she was placed in god's good earth. He had, in fact, felt nothing short of sweet *relief.*

He had considered his mother an embarrassing annoyance, nothing more. She had frowned at his childhood hobbies, which had including collecting the heads of any stray dog he might run across and immediately terminate with his dad's twelve-gauge, followed by a precise, meticulous dismemberment with the machete and bone knife he kept stashed away in their barn.

She had never understood his fascination with World War II books that displayed the graphic scenes of torture utilized and perfected by SS and POW camp Commandants.

She badgered him on several occasions upon finding the S&M magazines he had purchased from his confidant at the Middle School. Magazines that featured tightly bound, gagged, and sometimes even bloodied females at the mercy of their shadow-faced or mysteriously hooded masters.

Mira hadn't considered such interests normal teen curiosity as much as downright *perversion.*

In turn, the teenaged version of Buck the Third never missed an opportunity to belittle the woman that birthed him. He nicknamed her 'Mack-Ass', thus comparing her ever-expanding caboose region to the wide grill of a semi- truck. Buck would purposely leave half-eaten food stuffed between his bed mattresses for her to clean, wipe fresh boogers onto the walls of his room, and conveniently 'forget' to flush the toilet after a particularly nasty bout with diarrhea.

On the afternoon of his mother's passing, a cool April wind blowing through the surrounding hills like a searing scythe through semi-melted butter, Buck the Third had simply come to the end of his rope. The night before, Mira had discovered Misty's butchered body hanging from the metal hook Buck had wedged it upon. Misty had been Mira's favorite of the three cats that occupied the homestead, a large-boned tabby that his mother had taken a somewhat wicked pleasure in fattening up over the years.

Seen from a distance, one would have thought Misty to be an overweight Bobcat or perhaps even a mutated rat in the H.G. Wells tradition.

Buck had despised that animal, *all* animals in fact, for as long as his fevered brain could recall. He had made a daily habit of tossing rocks (some as big as softballs) at all three of his mother's feline companions since his early grade school years.

Having dropped out of school two years previously (along with who his mother called his 'evil twin', a boy named James Carter Carlyle), and having established himself as one of the major pot growers and distributors in the country, Buck found both ample time and targets for his inexplicable rages. Over that particular winter, he had made Misty the focus of his unrestrained cruelty.

Upon returning home at mid-morning after an all-nighter spent toking weed and sucking down Pony Millers, Buck had been both pleasantly shocked and gleefully surprised to find that mama's favorite pet had run underneath the front wheels of his tank-sized Mercury Cougar.

Of course, being that he *had* spotted the cat strolling casually across the dirt drive and proceeded to shove the gas pedal to the floor with enough pressure to bruise the bottom of his foot, such a 'tragic accident' was inevitable. Peeling the still alive but badly wheezing cat from the clay rut it had been driven into within the driveway, Buck had proceeded into the barn to hang it by it's shattered, mashed paws from a metal chain he had positioned for just such an occasion. He then leisurely gutted it using the sharp-edged bone knife, the steely erection that bulged in his jeans throbbing madly as he literally felt the animal's heartbeat fade to nothingness.

Mother had found her precious baby a few hours later, its mangled head dangling from a single strand of thin, shredded flesh. She had noticed the fresh blood stains on her son's denim shirt as he passed her through the kitchen that morning, and had suspected the worst.

As was the case at least twice a week since he had turned fifteen years old, Mira had first ordered and then begged him to leave her house, the hot, flowing tears that spewed from her eyes born of rage but manufactured by fear and self-pity. She feared her son, true, had since he had grown enough to pose a physical threat to her years before. She pitied herself, both for what she had become since Buck JR's evaporation act from their lives, and also for the beastly offspring she had turned out into an unsuspecting world.

In her hysterical rage, she had tossed a can of mixed vegetables at her smirking, leering son. The can had nailed him flush on the forehead, leaving a perfectly circular outline in its wake.

Hours later and fast asleep on the living room couch, Mira never felt the presence of her brooding, stone-faced son at her back.

The fingers that gently wrapped around the sides of her puffy throat were unshaken, moving with a mechanical preciseness. They bore into the soft, bloated flesh like twin steel bands. Mira's eyes never opened in the few moments it took to end her pathetic life. If she had, and managed to lean back while the strangulation was transpiring, she would have been greeted by a face only vaguely familiar to her. The flesh of the face would have looked moist, sickly. The fingers performing the task were tinted a light shade of blue, while underneath the nails the skin looked to have been recently singed, dark black splotches clearly visible.

Buck the Third had executed the parricide expertly, not a single bruise left behind to arouse suspicion. He waited four hours to phone authorities, allowing the initial stages of rigor to set in.

Late that night, staring into the full moon posed over the thick elm tree line just outside his room, Buck's heart fluttered in sadistic delight. After eighteen years of walking the planet in an uncertain, confusion-laced haze, he had finally realized his true calling.

Weeks later, drawn to the rolling, thickly forested hills on the eastern edge of town, Buck the Third was naturally accompanied by his right-hand man, the equally sadistic JC Carlyle, whose own warped family tree included the rape of his grandmother and numerous suicides. Both were conspicuously silent during the drive and subsequent hike towards the seemingly preordained spot, which drew them like fevered male canines to a bitch in heat.

A half-hour into the trek, they discovered an inner energy source that both realized had been present in their lives since birth; compelling them to certain actions, instigating unnatural urges not entirely of their own making.

The circular edges of the chasm looked peculiarly bare, slick and weed- less, as if daily maintenance were being performed to keep it so.

Almost hypnotically, both sucked in the dank, sour-smelling scent that arose from its shadowy center and spread over the adjacent area like natural gas trapped within a confined space. Their eyes glazed over with jelly-like mucus, Buck and JC fell to their knees at precisely the same moment, happily surrendering to an unseen God neither could visualize but nevertheless accepted as the ultimate savior.

Their bowing, weaving movements were slow yet eerily graceful, just as their grandfathers had been all over four decades earlier. The small clearing at the center of the oak and pine tree infested grade would become their own personal oasis as the months and years passed like the pages of an opened calendar within a wind tunnel. They would come, usually together but sometimes separately, to bask in the stench of consummate evil, to inhale the putrid air like a cocaine addict leaning over a fresh line of white powder. Peeking into its sinister, blackened maw, careful to never actually step near the edges, both would draw raw strength in its presence like a battery hooked to the cables of a powerful charger.

Over the next decade, neither Buck Lomax the Third nor JC Carlyle would accomplish a great deal within the pathetically mundane structures of their personal lives. Both would get jobs at the local canned vegetable plant, easily the largest employer within the city limits. They would continue to harvest and sell marijuana on the side, although on a much smaller scale as time progressed. Both men would never marry or even date seriously, a monthly trek to Jackson or Biloxi and the warehouse district whorehouses located there providing the only sexual outlet either desired.

Each reveled in the verbal belittling and physical ravaging of the usually drug-addicted, decease-ravaged women on display. They could beat, rape, and humiliate until their black hearts desired, then return to Red Bridge wearing broad wide smiles and sporting bloodied knuckles.

Both had other friends and acquaintances, but only of the 'BS' variety, none of which were remotely trusted with the secret of their chosen God. Buck and JC had an unspoken, unwritten pact about the 'Circle of Joy', as Buck had so cheerily nicknamed the clearing and the spectral chasm within its tiny perimeter. *No* outsider would witness its glory and live to tell about it.

Over the many years that followed, many would answer to that particular pact, some involuntarily and by brute force at the hands of its originators. Many others by sheer force of will, a will not of their own making, but from within the mystifying force that lay deep inside its ominous walls.

Walls that seemed to call out, yearning for frequent feedings of the human soul.

CHAPTER FIVE
The Gathering

August 19th, 2003
Oak Mountain Campsite

Jimmy Rollins was just topping the steep, rock-infested hill that sat just west of his campsite when he halted abruptly in his tracks, accidentally dropping the triple-compartment tackle-box from his left hand onto the tip of his imitation leather work boot.

Tilting his head to the left while wincing from the blow to the toes of his left foot, Jimmy stared unblinkingly through the spaces in the tall oaks encircling him. For the next minute in time, he was transfixed by the intermediate sounds his perked ears absorbed.

It sounded like cries, the echoing wails of small children from a faraway distance, the gist of which was obviously being blocked and muffled by the surrounding forest.

Just as quickly as they had begun, all noises ceased, leaving only the occasional breeze blowing through tree limbs and scrubs, as well as the intermittent late afternoon insect choirs to fill the silent void.

What in the wide world of sports was that about? Sounded like very young children crying out. Either that or the Vienna Boys' Choir got their collective testicles ensnared in bear traps.

Could be my overactive imagination working some serious OT as well. After last night's little dream-feast, anything's possible.

After bending to retrieve the bulky tackle-box, and releasing a loud, squeaky fart in the process, Jimmy trudged slowly ahead until the grille of the Jeep came comfortably into view.

It had taken him a full two hours to reach the fishing pond, only to discover it resembled nothing actually qualifying as such. It looked as though someone had taken a shovel and dug a deep, wide hole, then filled it with tap water. Needless today, fresh fish would not fill the main portion of his dinner menu.

"Looks like Campbell's Tomato Soup instead of Catfish delight, old buddy," Jimmy whispered to himself while propping his fishing rod ('best you can buy' the salesman had blurted, 'they'll practically jump onto the pole') against the South end of the tent.

Forty plus minutes later, with the radio blaring an old Joe Walsh tune ('Ordinary Average Guy' Jimmy deduced, and couldn't help but grin at the irony), and while sipping boiling hot soup from a plastic mug, Jimmy caught the initial scent of distant fire smoke. The tiniest of butterflies took flight within the pit of his warmed abdomen, set free by an equally small pang of panic.

Great. Simply wonderful, and Smokey the Bear nowhere to be found. Now what?

***

A few miles to his immediate west, standing at the center of a clearing surrounded on all sides by camouflaged tents, Major David Peterson stuck his flaring nostrils into the air and slowly leaned his head back.

"Let's get a move on, troops. The smoke is originating from the west, possibly only two short miles from this site. According to our map, that's directly atop the prison site. Shouldn't take us more than thirty minutes tops, if we haul ass like we're capable of. Let's move! Sergeant Ezop!"

Jogging from his tent, the infrared binoculars swinging freely from the base of his thick neck, Ezop slowed only as he neared the fading campfire.

"Sir?" He huffed, his body stiffened to robotic extremes.

"Kindly go see what is keeping Private Kemp from joining our little excursion. I worry about no one else here, but she sometimes requires…*extra* motivation."

Sergeant Ezop whirled around to instantly obey, then stopped. Turning back to his stoic commander, his face was a mask of contorting discomfort.

"Sir, you think this is the correct time and place to practice night Brairs? I mean; if there is a fire at the prison, there could be real world trouble."

Shaking his head from side to side, his eyes rolling back, Major Peterson smirked in comical disbelief.

"Sergeant, such a scenario is *precisely* why we must complete the exercise tonight. Walking into the unknown is something a professional soldier must become comfortable with, least he be transformed into a shivering, yellow- bellied coward. I realize it's extremely difficult for the 'Internet' generation to comprehend, but survival of the species lends credence to my ideals. Now, please see where Private Procrastinator is keeping herself, Ezop, and be quick about it. Time and precious daylight are wasting."

Sergeant Ezop sprinted away as if propelled by a strong gust at his back, his leaden combat boots thumping noisily onto the hard dirt trail leading away from the campfire Peterson had already begun to stamp out.

Minutes later, Major Peterson stood at the center of the improvised formation and executed a brief inspection of his charges. Satisfied that each, including the severely scowling Private Kemp, were properly geared, he glanced at his watch and then over at Sergeant Chambers, who stood propped with his elbow atop the barrel tip of his M-16.

"Sergeant, we will treat this as a simple surveillance mission. Take Private Kemp and Corporal McIntosh and circle around from the west. Sergeant Ezop and Private Bodine will accompany me from the east. Synchronize your watches to exactly six-forty-two PM. Keep radio contact to a minimum; no less than five- minute intervals at the outside. Once I evaluate the scenario, we'll go from there. Got it?"

Pulling a badly chewed toothpick from the right corner of his mouth, Sergeant Chambers casually nodded and turned to Corporal McIntosh as he began to gather his gear.

"Don't wanna hear no more bitchin', Mac, you hear? Let's keep this little nature walk as silent as possible, as if the trees were full'a terrorists just waitin' to part our hair with sniper fire." He whirled around and stood over Kemp, who hadn't bothered to budge from her trance-like state.

"You with us, Private Kemp, or are you plannin' on staying behind to do dishes? Let's get the molasses out of our butt-cheeks, what do ya say?"

She didn't bother to respond verbally or even meet his eyes while scooping up the small back-pack and her own rifle, choosing instead to concentrate her steely glare onto the back of Major David Peterson, who was busy instructing the others.

Corporal McIntosh brushed by her just as the trio headed for the southern end of the forest line.

"You'll get your shot at Major Jackass, Sandy, but don't rush it. Bide your time and don't be so damned obvious," he whispered before picking up speed to take point.

"What do you…" she began, then broke into a lumbering jog to catch him. Isiah Chambers shot the Major a quick, loose salute before following close behind.

"Really appreciate you teamin' me with those two goldbricks, sir," he grinned.

Major Peterson returned the gesture, his own salute crisp and professionally executed.

"No problem, Sergeant. A good commander has to be an expert at delegating his authority."

"Write if you get work, Sarge," Private Bodine blurted as Chambers rambled off.

Sergeant Ezop reached over and punched Bodine forcefully on the right shoulder. The skinny Private backed away as if bee stung.

"You think you can handle being separated from your conjoined twin long enough to get in some night training, Private?" He asked, slinging the backpack over his massive shoulders.

Stepping back to rub the point of impact from the surprise blow, Private Bodine shrugged, obviously embarrassed.

"Mac isn't part of my family tree, Sarge. Wouldn't claim him if he were, actually," he smiled, reaching down gingerly for his gear.

Major Peterson stepped forward, his expression completely humorless. "Don't let that man's influence effect your performance, Private. The good Corporal is not exactly what I call 'polished', although I'd definitely want him on my side in the middle of a firefight. Just refrain…' the Major reached over and placed his right hand on the Private's left shoulder and stroked gently '..from joining the ranks of the malcontented. Those positions have thankfully been filled for now."

Moments later, as they headed to the opposite end of the clearing from the earlier trio, Private Bodine found himself dwelling on a topic other than the mission ahead. At first he discarded it as his imagination performing a tap dance on his already hyped senses. He then deduced it was the shadows overtaking the nearby landscape that had provided such a grotesque play on the shapes and colors of the objects within his visionary range.

As they trampled through a waist-high growth of weeds and entered the darkening forest, Private Bodine felt a ponderously moving chill begin to climb his lower spine on its way to its final destination at the base of his slim, clean shaven neck. It hadn't been his mind *or* the shadows, he soon reluctantly conceded. Major Peterson's hands had been tinted purple, the fingertips of which held a yellowish hue. They had also stunk, reeking like decomposing meat not long from sprouting a thick harvest of starving maggots.

Walking a few feet behind Major Peterson and just in front of Sergeant Ezop, Private Bodine noticed the Major's left hand, which swung freely at his side. The fingers were twitching madly, as if propped atop unseen piano keys. Even from a distance of at least four or five feet, Bodine could smell the putrid stench left in their rotted wake.

Private Lomax Bodine felt a sudden tingling in his gut.

Despite the inner humiliation at such a thought, he wanted nothing more at that very moment than to run screaming in the other direction.

***

Five miles to their east, clouds of black smoke billowed harshly from the tailpipe of a Ford Mustang in dire need of both engine maintenance and a new paint job. The vehicle slowed and then departed the black top two-lane for a slim dirt road to the left, a bent metal sign proclaiming '*OAK MOUNTAIN CAMPSITE* - 3 MILES', followed soon by a larger, more prominent one that read 'BRIARSTON CORRECTIONAL FACILITY', next left. *DO NOT PICK UP HITCHHIKERS!'*

His glasses bobbing wildly on the edge of his nose, Wilbo's laugh was less enthusiastic than exhausting.

"Only in Mississippi do they build prison and campsites side-by-side. As dad used to say 'dumb as a box of hammers'. I thought we had the market on imbeciles back home. Can you belie-..."

"Where are we *going* exactly?" Mara broke in, sighing nervously while attempting to bite her nails around the tight braces encasing her teeth.

Wilbo eyed the narrow road and slowed for a series of deep ruts, his lips pursed so firmly it looked as though he were about to begin whistling.

"Hold your water, sis. We're just out here for a look-see. Finding a spot to camp won't be a problem. Might cost us a ten spot for the night. We're just gonna...look around, that's all. Don't get your drawers in a wad. Just concentrate on what Phoenix would do in such a situation. Ol' Jean Grey would never pee her tights over..."

Her hand slammed against the dash with such force it sent an empty coffee cup and various fast food wrappers sailing into Wilbo's lap, causing him to shriek out and jerk the wheel involuntarily to the left. He wheeled quickly back to the center of the road, barely avoiding side-swiping a nearby pine that was bent at the base and looked to be literally reaching into the path with its dry, dead limbs.

"Cut the bull, will you? I'm not Jean Grey, *Dammit*! I'm about as far as being a super-heroine as I can possibly be, William. I'm nothing right now but simply scared shitless. What are we really a*ccomplishing* here? Tell *me* so we'll both know!" She bellowed, her eyes brimming with tears as she stared into a black forest that she felt was surely swallowing them whole.

Finding a small dirt clearing a few hundred feet ahead, Wilbo parked the car and cut the engine, the many sounds of the woods instantly filling their ears as if someone had plugged in a 'Echoes of a Southern Forest' CD.

He reached over and patted her arm somewhat clumsily. Providing comfort had never been his strong point, but he realized the sensitivity factor involved in dealing with his twin sibling and knew he had to find a way to calm her.

"Kara, it's not exactly undercover work for the CIA. I... we both feel we have to at least *try* to find out what happened to them. Don't think I don't know it's like looking for a glass eye in a marble factory, but we owe it to 'em, don't we?"

A low sob escaped her as she turned to him.

"Something's wrong here, William. I can feel it. It hit me like a load of concrete bricks once we drove into Red Bridge. It has something to do with their deaths, yes, but there's something else too. I can't put my finger on it, but it's nothing we want to mess with. I was going to tell you back there when we left the hamburger joint, but I figured you'd just think I'm backing off. It's *not* that. There's serious danger here, brother of mine. Danger even your boy Wolverine might sprint from."

Leaning back, his face masked in frustration, Wilbo began to reply, then reached down to start the engine instead.

"You gotta be a bit more specific here, sis. We've come a long way to be hauling ass in the other direction now."

Kara began to reply, found no suitable words, at least none that weren't laced with either obvious cowardice or sheer panic, and instead fell silent after a low click at the back of her suddenly parched throat.

"Just a few nights, sis, that's all. Maybe we find nothing at all. If not, we treat it as that long-delayed 'trip back to nature' we always talked about, okay?"

His eyes left the road just long enough to shoot her an openly irritating glance.

"Okay?"

Kara nodded, her tone one of frustrated defeat. "Fine."

"Good," he replied with a huff, smiling as he returned his concentration on navigating the absurdly narrow path of dirt top.

"Besides, Wolverine would never run nor pee his tights. Spider-Man might spring a leak every now and then, but never, *ever* my man Logan."

As they topped a particularly steep hill, a rustic, tin-roofed wooden cabin came into view, a painted sign reading 'Red Mountain Rentals' covering the whole of the otherwise brightly red painted bar blocking the roadway just to its right.

"Well, I see a light on at least. Let's go check out the 'commendations," Wilbo whispered mostly to himself, his fingers instantly growing tense and slick on the steering wheel.

The black Ford F-150 pick-up glided to a silent halt just as it topped the same hill two minutes later. It's headlights had been strategically left in the off position for the past mile, only the driver and his passengers familiarity with the road and it's varied bumps and craters allowing for such a risky maneuver.

"They're campin' out? What in blue blazes, Buck? I mean, they got a hotel room at the 'Sand bought and paid for. That's damn strange, don't you think?" The passenger said while stuffing a fresh handful of chewing tobacco into his stubble-coated jaw.

Buck the Third lifted his left leg from the truck seat and farted loudly; then began playfully waiving the air towards his cringing cohort.

"They're up to no good, no doubt. What say we wait a few and then proceed to the office for a little talk with ol' Bart. He'll give us the scoop or lose a lung…his choice entirely."

Both men sat silently for the next few moments, each using their pinky fingers to jab and poke at teeth growing increasingly loose, secretly reveling in the soothing pain such actions created.

***

With a thick-handled, twin beam light gripped in his left hand, Jimmy turned and gave his camp a final, forlorn look. The hood of his jeep, as well as the top portion of his tent disappeared from sight as he whirled back around to negotiate the rocky, uneven hill ahead.

The smell of smoke was growing stronger, more pungent. The decision to check the origin of the burning had been an easy one. He had to find out if relocating his campsite might be necessary, least he awake the next morning to discover the clearing (not to mention his own hairy ass) engulfed in swooping flames and the choking fumes associated with such. Yes, he was depressed and anti-social at the moment. No, he definitely *wasn't* on a suicide mission due to those particular facts. If a bug-out was necessary, so be it. He figured the old man at the cabin would have contacted whatever qualified as a local fire department near Red Bridge if a potential forest fire held even the tiniest of possibilities. The old man lived at the cabin year-round, or so Jimmy had assumed. The smoke was coming from the opposite direction from the campsite's headquarters, however.

Jimmy had thought about contacting the old man himself, but decided instead to strike out on his own, doing his best 'Grizzly Adams' imitation while attempting to solve the mystery without actually having to contact another human being if at all possible.

The forest grounds were dry, no denying that fact. Jimmy recalled the old man saying it had been a 'few weeks' since the last measurable rainfall, so the area was parched dry and undeniably flammable. On the other hand, there hadn't been any 'dry thunder' that Jimmy could recall hearing in the last two days, so what might have triggered the blaze would most likely turn out to be the usual suspect, that being man.

Some jackass hunter lighting up a Camel and tossing either the remainder of his match or the cigarette itself into the nearest pile of dry pine. Sucked down a case or two of beer with his moronic buddies before heading into the forest, no doubt. I'd better be careful not to get a backside full of lead myself. I sure make a large enough target. Get enough alcohol in their veins, and everything that moves becomes potential game to such morons.

Darkness was swallowing the space around him; its appetite insatiable, veracious. Jimmy could hear his own heartbeat in between the echoes of leaves and dry limbs snapping beneath his heavy boots. As he scrunched down to duck a low-lying birch tree limb, he heard the first series of voices in the far distance. Propped against the ancient birch, which leaned to one side as if to better eavesdrop on the nearby valley; Jimmy had brief hopes that it had simply been his imagination. Possibly nothing more elaborate than a wind gust blocked from his flesh by the tree itself creating an echoing band of blurred whispers. A moment later, such hopes sunk along with his suddenly slumped shoulders.

Two distinct voices were clearly audible to his west, just past a line of thick pines and knee-high weeds, perhaps no more than seventy-five to a hundred yards away.

Jimmy couldn't make out actual words, just garbled, muffled mumbling. He briefly considered turning back towards his camp, figuring the voices belonged to either campers (thus the smoke from their campfire) or local fire department folks already on the burn scene.

His bladder aching for release, he unzipped and calmly watched the faint steam rise towards his face from the spray of warm urine.

The stream halted in mid-release just as Jimmy crouched instinctively to his knees.

The piercing, hollow wailing ceased as quickly as it had begun, allowing Jimmy a moment of tranquility to tuck his badly shriveled manhood back into its stall while remaining balanced on the balls of his feet.

What in God's name was that? Sounded like someone got their fingers hung in a trash disposal. Firefighter in trouble, maybe?

The voices were closer now, Jimmy realized, as a portion of their conversation suddenly becoming clearer, more understandable.

Regaining his position at the base of the warped tree, Jimmy turned his flashlight off while sucking in an ample supply of oxygen and then holding it. He perked his right ear in the direction of the voices, his head tilted to the extreme.

“Why…stay? …no real military obligation. Peterson is…asshole, so...why don’t you…quit?” A male voice bellowed.

“Cause If I do…parents will…my ass to the nearest county lock-up. I have…choice but to put up with…miserable jackass… Peterson,” a female replied, her voice overly shrill and the tone obviously irritated.

His nostrils unconsciously flaring, as the smoky stench seemed to grow stronger around him, Jimmy waited until the voices faded slightly to the north, again mostly unintelligible, before breaking his position.

The wide, piercing beam provided by the flashlight again pointing straight ahead, Jimmy followed the trail of voices to where he knew the origin of the mystery fire certainly must lie.

Surprised by his own curiosity, he was careful to maintain a distance just within audible range of the hushed voices, all the while ignoring the ever-present voice at the back of his mind which begged the body below to turn and run wildly in the opposite direction.

***

Approximately sixty yards ahead, Corporal Ron McIntosh blazed an uneasy trail through a patch of wiry thicket, a narrow beam of light bobbing wildly in the lead. Private Sandra Kemp marched in a permanent slouch just a few feet to his rear, angrily pulling her rifle barrel free from a tangle of weeds.

"Ya mean your folks would actually toss you into the stir if you don't maintain your militia status?" McIntosh asked while entering the center of a small clearing.

Kemp huffed, almost tripping into the same clearing.

"Damn straight they would. Dear old dad wants my rear out of the picture anyway, family embarrassment that I am. I got no choice but lick Peterson's sadistic boots for the next year or so, at least until the statute of limitations is up on that little shoplifting charge nipping at my heels."

The Corporal smirked while checking the lit pocket compass attached to his right wrist.

"They don't mind you trekking around with a bunch of government bashing, pessimistic war-mongers like the Dark Eagle clan?"

Between labored pants, Kemp replied with obvious distaste.

"Ron, they don't give a rat's behind if I'm hangin' with Mid-Eastern terrorists as long as I'm out of sight, out of mind."

The Corporal again checked his mini-compass, then retrieved a diminutive walkie-talkie from his utility belt that resembled nothing more than a modified cellular phone.

"D Eagle one, this is D Eagle two, over," he spat, his face a mask of indifference. He nodded after a moment, his expression unchanged.

"Roger, one. We're just a few clicks from the site. Perimeter road leading to the Briarston compound should be only a few hundred feet dead ahead. Should we proceed or wait for your signal?"

The Corporal grimaced as if suffering from a bad case of gas while receiving the reply.

"Affirmative, Major. Sergeant Chambers took point and is currently out of sight, out of mind. D Eagle two out."

Snapping the device back onto his already crowded belt, Corporal McIntosh turned back to Private Kemp and smiled, kneeling to meet her at eye level.

"General Stone-Balls says to hurry up and wait for his go sign. He wants us at full strength as a unit before moving forward near the correctional facilities' outer perimeter. Jesus, guy thinks he's fucking US Grant and Colin Powel morphed into one big dictatorial package. Where the hell is Chambers, anyhow? I'm getting damned tired of coverin' for his lethargic black ass."

Placing her backpack on a layer of dried leaves while positioning herself 'yoga style', Kemp stared sheepishly at the Corporal, just the slightest of smiles taking form at the corners of her mouth.

"You don't exactly seemed thrilled to be here either, Ron. What's the deal? I haven't heard one positive phrase, nor word for that matter, escape that sewer pipe mouth of yours since we left razorback country."

"Elementary, my dear Private," he said, simultaneously yawning while peering into the star-filled sky through the slight circular space provided overhead between oak tree limbs.

“Simple matter of camouflage. As you’ve undoubtedly heard, I’ve had more than a few scrapes with the men in blue through the years, not to mention numerous nasty scenarios originating from a handful of problematic marriages. The Dark Eagle Militia is a perfect cover. You surround yourself with similarly troubled individuals, the spotlight dims on your own fragmented ass. It also keeps my hands and head occupied, despite the BS involved therein, thus avoiding the temptations the outside world offers. Hell, one more fight scene within the confines of any establishment serving alcohol and Betty McIntosh’s only son will be makin’ plates up state for quite a few years. Besides, I find myself calmer within the ranks, maybe because of the freedom of excess violence it promises whenever the world does turn sour for good. You get all that, or do I need to rewind my sewer pipe lips?”

Kemp reared back as if receiving a mild shock.

“Jesus, Ron. Are you on medication for that split-personality kick? For a minute there I thought I was jawin’ with a law school grad. Your militant act is a good one, no doubt. I hate to take a chain saw blade to your rainbow, but being a card-carrying member of an illegally operating, ‘gun-toting without a license’ militia isn’t exactly the preferred way of keeping a low profile from the law.”

Straightening from his crouching position, the Corporal exuded cockiness with a single wink of his right eye.

“Sure gives ya other folks to pin shit on though, don’t it? I was just following orders, after all.

Besides, Sandy, what we're doing wandering around the woods of Mississippi does make a warped kind of sense. The world as we know it is goin' down fast. We're gonna be ahead of the game when the boat finally does submerge for good."

Just as she was mentally preparing a heated counterpoint, Private Kemp halted with parted lips as the buzzing noise reverberated from the Corporal's belt.

He raised a gloved finger into the air as if to cut off any attempt she might still make to speak.

"D Eagle two. Affirmative, Major. Um, sir? We have no idea of Sergeant Chambers present whereabouts, truth be told."

The Corporal doubled over a moment later, attempting with little success to avoid giggling directly into the device.

"Y-yes, sir. We'll do a quick police up for his location before we converge with the other groups. Affirmative, sir. I'll inform the Sergeant he'll be less an ass cheek upon greeting you at said site. Yes, sir. D Eagle Two out."

Howling until warm tears sprouted from both of his partially squinting eyes, the stocky Corporal reached down and playfully patted the grinning Private between the shoulder blades.

"Let's move it, Sandy. Peterson just blew a vessel over Chamber's absence within our ranks. We will, as the Major just ordered by the way, 'Scour' the area for his AWOL butt before moving on down to perimeter road."

Gathering her pack and weapon, Private Sandra Kemp released the first genuine laugh she could recall for days.

"Unreal. Not even at the designated checkpoint and we've already got MIA's. Probably gonna get greeted by armed Correctional Officers who'll lead us and our nut-ball leader right to a series of waiting cells especially chosen for our kind."

Corporal McIntosh overstepped a gathering of thorn bushes and disappeared momentarily into the dark underbrush to their left.

"Just consider the worst-case scenario and set your mind at ease. We'd be lookin' at three square meals and a roof over our heads, my dear. Not a bad deal, all things considered."

***

A half-mile to the west, Wilbo was just hammering the final tent stake into place between the massive trunks of two mountainous elms, when he lifted his head upwards and sniffed loudly, as if suffering from a severe case of congestion.

"You smell smoke, sis?"

Kara stood over him, a steaming metal cup grasped within the curled fingers of both her hands.

"As a matter of fact, I was fixing to ask you the same."

Standing up quickly, his knees popping like the twin barrels of an exploding twelve gauge, Wilbo turned his sights to the grass covered hill just within the range of the oil lamp he had positioned at its overgrown edge.

"Shit on a shingle, getting stronger too. Coming from the direction of that Prison site. Hope we're not wasting our time putting up stakes here just to pull 'em up again while dodging flames. Smells stout, not like a campfire to cook catfish over, neither."

Kara hugged herself and stared at her brother worriedly.

"Up for a little stroll in the woods, sis?" He finally asked with a shrug, reaching for a nearby flashlight.

***

Major David Peterson stepped gingerly onto the dust covered, paved two- lane road, a twelve-foot high, razor wired chain fence visible no more than ten yards past the opposite shoulder. Although not clearly seen, the overwhelming smell of freshly seared metal and wood filled the air like a stifling, musty blanket.

"Something is definitely amiss, Sergeant Ezop. If not for the bright moonlight, we could have walked directly into the compound fence."

Sergeant Ezop temporarily dropped the hand that had been covering his nose and mouth. He was peering intently over the fence at the looming guard tower just a few feet past its base.

"Check out the tower, sir. Black as a pit and not a single sign of life. A sentry would have spotted us before we topped that last hill."

His eyes darting from both ends of the desolate highway to the equally so prison perimeter grounds, Private Bodine's thin lips noticeably trembled.

Peterson removed his black beret and wiped his bare forehead, then turned to scan the dead space of the eerily deserted highway they had just crossed. He then proceeded to reach down and casually reclaim the Com device from his belt loop.

"D Eagle Team Two, converge upon the site immediately. We have a situation that warrants a bit of investigation here."

A moment later, Corporal McIntosh responded with a quick series of clicks and a cheerily spoken 'affirmative, Major'.

"May have evacuated the site before our arrival, Sergeant, don't you agree?" Peterson asked while keeping his sight locked on the discordantly foreboding tower looming in their wake.

"Possible, sir. But I didn't hear siren one or any similar commotion that normally accompanies such activity, correct?"

Peterson cleared his throat and stepped back, finally breaking his self- imposed daze.

"True, but remember how isolated this particular correctional facility is. Sirens to ward off pedestrian traffic are uncalled for.

You would think if a fire was the cause of a bug out, authorities would still be on hand, however."

"The whole place looks deserted, sir. Maybe t-they bugged out days ago and the smoke is coming from a separate location," Private Bodine injected, his words cloaked in nervous energy.

Peterson grunted apathetically.

"We saw an inmate work crew on its way out here just yesterday morning, didn't we, Private Bodine? Those were inmates, not contracted workers."

Departing a broad treeline a few hundred feet to the south of Dark Eagle Team one's present position, Corporal McIntosh effortlessly climbed a steep, gravel-infested grade onto the highway, followed closely thereafter by an obviously out-of-breath Private Sandra Kemp.

The bulky Corporal double-timed towards the Major, who faced him with an expression of pure dismay.

"Where the hell is the Sergeant, Corporal McIntosh?" Peterson barked just as the Corporal grunted to a halt, kicking a fresh pile of gravel and dirt onto his commander's highly polished steel-toed boots.

Private Kemp stumbled forward just as Corporal McIntosh had begun to reply, her flushed face moist with sweat. Her breathing was almost comically labored, her face ghostly white as she huffed and puffed.

Peterson shot her a disgusted look before turning his attention back to the Corporal.

"Hide nor hair, Major, and we covered some serious ground looking for 'im. No radio contact, either."

"How long since your last contact with him, Corporal?" Ezop interrupted, his eyes periodically darting back and forth from the ominous tower to the frighteningly still highway. Without even the slightest of breezes present, it was almost as if they were standing inside a domed greenhouse. Even the noises of the forest seemed strangely muted.

"It's been at least a half-hour, Major. Maybe he fell into a hole, gung-ho jackass that he is," the Corporal answered, his own breath calm and steady, not a single bead of sweat visible on his rugged, sparklingly clean-shaven mug.

Pulling the Com device from his utility belt in one fluid movement, the Major glared at the

Corporal sternly.

"That's quite enough, Corporal. Sergeant Chamber's reckless actions will be addressed, but it's not the place of a lower ranking troop to comment upon a superior's shortcomings."

His lips pursed and pale, Peterson whirled around with the device planted tightly against his face and granite-like chin.

"D Eagle Team Two team leader, come in, over."

Scowling, Corporal McIntosh shook his head slowly from side to side and looked around at Private Kemp, who was still attempting to catch her breath.

"What a goat-rope we are tied into here, Sandy. It is to laugh," he whispered, though loudly enough for Sergeant Ezop to hear. Kemp nodded in silent agreement, her huffing and puffing finally beginning to subside. Sergeant Ezop stepped forward until the tips of his boots were only inches from the Corporals. In the background, Major Peterson's upper body began to shake in barely concealed rage.

"God dammit, Chambers! You are needed at the east perimeter road just outside the Briarston Unit…. sound off, mister!"

While Sergeant Ezop and Corporal McIntosh held an impromptu stare-off just a few feet away, Private Kemp went down to one knee to better view the combatants and also retie the mangled strings of her right boot.

"You might want to think about displaying a semblance of respect for your commanding officer, Corporal, not to mention the NCO's assigned to this unit," Sergeant Ezop whispered callously, baring his teeth like a cornered animal.

His body language nothing less than a portrait of casual cool, the Corporal nonetheless refused to back down from the taller, equally hulking Sergeant, his own gaze never faltering.

"Hard to respect incompetence in any form, Sarge." "Meaning what, precisely?'

"Meaning I think our presence on posted Government property, *armed* presence, I might add, isn't exactly comforting. Some serious shit has gone down here, might *still* be as we speak. Don't you agree?"

"More than likely, so?"

"So you want the blame on whatever has transpired placed directly on your Non-Commissioned ass, Sergeant Ezop? I do believe Isiah answered no to that particular question and decided to take the high road."

Sergeant Ezop finally blinked after a lengthy pause, again turning to give the abandoned tower a once over.

"Somebody might need help in there, mister, you ever think of that?" He asked in a tone usually reserved for adults while scolding small children. The Sergeant had never felt particularly fond of Corporal Ron McIntosh, a man he deemed an irritating whiner who was about as trustworthy as your standard public official. Corporal McIntosh was the malcontent every unit seemed burdened with, but Sergeant Ezop understood his dislike for the man had deeper, more subtle roots. Both men made sculpting their bodies a daily ritual, despite the years of sacrifice and countless lost years sweating and straining inside a weight room to first build and then maintain such a look. He considered Ron McIntosh nothing more than a red neck barroom brawler, and the type of individual you didn't dare turn your back on during a firefight. He had pushed hard for McIntosh's dismissal after an incident during training maneuvers in Jonesboro a year earlier, to no avail. The Colonel had decided that such 'admittedly reckless but viscously competitive' men had a place within the militia. Sergeant Ezop had the distinct feeling that the Corporal knew of his disapproval of the man's status within the ranks, and never failed to capitalize on pushing the Sergeant's buttons whenever the occasion arose.

"You think we're qualified to assist if there are? There are probably quite a few former city and state workers serving time in there, Ace, imprisoned by the government we are known to despise. We get caught in there and the higher authorities might just decide our ultimate goal might have been assisting in a well-mapped out prison break or some such happy crap."

Private Bodine stepped up at a snail's pace, apparently concerned about the consequences of interrupting the conversation. A full ten yards away now, the Major was practically hissing into the palm-sized Com device.

"E-either of you guys notice anything about the Major?" Private Bodine injected, rearing back as the last word escaped his chapped lips as if expecting to be backhanded. Sergeant Ezop turned to him with a look of disdain.

"Other than the fact that he's pissed enough to

chew steel and crap nails?" he blurted a bit louder than he meant to, then turning to ensure the Major hadn't heard.

The Corporal and Private Kemp both stepped closer to Bodine, who now huddled in between the three other bodies as if seeking warmth.

"H-his skin…the skin on his hands and face."

Private Kemp carefully studied the Major's turned back as she spoke. "What about it?"

Bodine's voice cracked like a teen in the throngs of puberty. Even in the murky darkness of their surroundings, the light of a half-moon the only element of illumination, all could easily read the stark fear in both the young man's voice and in the spastic movements of his darting eyes.

"I... uh, n-noticed it when we left...camp. His skin is...yellow in places and brown in others, mostly on the backs of his hands. I think h-he has a fever of some kind. There's also a strange odor around him, and I'm not just talking regular every day, stress-related BO either."

Sergeant Ezop coughed coarsely into his cupped right hand, then laughed mockingly.

"Son, I think we all could use a bubble bath about now. I haven't noticed any-..."

Corporal McIntosh cut him off abruptly, holding his left-hand palms up, then wordlessly pointed a single finger in the direction of their fearless leader. All three slowly turned in unison to observe the man they had so blindly followed into the midst of a beguiling mystery each would have much rather avoided.

The Major paced back and forth on the same path of gravel, digging a noticeable (even though shrouded in shadows) groove within a five by three-foot radius. He seemed to be trying to literally shove the Com device into the flesh of his left cheek as he shrieked, his free arm windmilling wildly as if warding off a swarm of insects only he could visualize.

"Sergeant Chambers, I will have your ebony ass hung from the highest oak limb if you're not standing before me within the next one-hundred twenty seconds, you understand, soldier? Sergeant Chambers? Useless piece of SHIT!"

Rearing back like a quarterback attempting a last second Hail Mary pass towards some unseen end zone, Peterson proceeded to lob the device over the prison perimeter fence with a loud, raspy groan escaping his lips with the follow through.

"All right, dammit, let's form up here, people. We've got a job to do, despite a certain worthless NCO's absence," he then relayed with a sudden calmness that caused even the blonde, peach-fuzz like hair atop Corporal Ron McIntosh's thickly muscled arms to rise and stand at instant attention.

"Uh sir, exactly what job are you referring to?" Sergeant Ezop asked somewhat timidly.

Major Peterson motioned towards the fenced-in compound, the thick shadows of the night unable to completely mask the look of complete befuddlement being displayed beneath his tucked down beret.

"Wha-? What job, Sergeant? There are possibly injured parties inside this compound. Despite our differences with the establishment and what they currently stand for, we are still human beings, aren't we? It is our obligation to investigate the situation and assist if possible."

Corporal McIntosh stepped forward, his hands held palms up in a pleading gesture.

"But Major, won't our presence inside the compound, regardless of the reason, be misconstrued as trespassing on Government property? Our collective butt-cheeks could end up hanging from a skyscraper high sling if..."

Dropping his backpack to the ground nonchalantly, the Major leaped forward until his protruding chest bumped lightly into the Corporal's own. McIntosh refused to flinch as the taller man bore down until their noses were just inches apart. An even mix of building fog and drifting smoke surrounding both men, levitating near their heads as if actually emitted from their rigid torsos.

"Corporal McIntosh, if you want to remain a part of his unit, unpack your night-vision goggles and follow my lead into the compound. If not, stroll back into the forest and be prepared for a militia court martial when we return to base camp. I really don't think you want to choose the latter, son. Your sorted past is just waiting for such an opportunity to leap up and *bite you* on the ass, am I correct?"

Without a moment's hesitation, the Corporal quickly stepped back, his right hand a blur as he executed a graceful, entirely flawless salute.

Obviously taken back by the gesture, it took the Major a full five seconds to return the gesture, his eyes peering into his subordinates for even the slightest trace of sarcasm.

"Yes, sir. I'm with you. Sorry 'bout that, Major. As you undoubtedly know already, I have a bad habit of covering my own hide above all else. No more questioning your decisions, Sir."

Private Bodine walked up and slapped the Corporal playfully between the shoulder blades, the young man's forced smile failing to conceal the uneasiness gripping his being.

"Loosen up, Mac. Maybe we were meant to be here. We might even get to play hero."

Sergeant Ezop joined the Major near the perimeter fence, both men peering through the thin metal links through squinting eyes. They kept their voices low, exchanging worried, haggard looks. Moments earlier, the Sergeant had observed the Major pull a set of black wool gloves from his small duffel and pull them gingerly over slightly gnarled fingers.

Leaning down to dig into his own backpack, careful to ensure the Major was out of listening rage, Corporal McIntosh grunted sourly.

"Fuck that crazy bastard, man. I made a choice, that's all. I decided to back away and play solider for hire instead of renovating the old coot's teeth with a quick right to the jaw. Peterson knows all the shit he has on me back at Dark Eagle HQ is one helluva ace in the hole when it comes to keeping me on a short leash. Colonel "Iron Balls" has a file as thick as my dick with my name attached. If I walked now, they'd have me tossed into some local lock-up in the blink of an eye, pinnin' crimes on me that I had nothing to do with."

His eyes growing wider and his state of mind ever more paranoid, Private Bodine's next words came out choked, exasperated. "You really think they...would *do* that?"

Placing the wide elastic band of the slim

goggles around his bulky neck, Ron McIntosh beamed.

"In a heartbeat, partner. Where do you think most of their recruits come from? Broken homes? Malcontents ready for radical change in lifestyle? Try people hiding from something in either their past or their immediate futures. That man over there will plant a combat knife between your shoulder blades without hesitation if he believes such an occurrence is 'vital' to the mission. Take my advice and watch your back, Lomax, and watch it close."

Adjusting his own set of goggles around his painfully thin neck, Private Bodine stood shakily, barely avoiding stumbling into Private Kemp, who had been donning her gear a few feet to his rear. His words were choked, as if he were straining to hold back impending tears.

"The Major's sick, I tell you. I saw his hands. I…*smelled* them."

Her jaw muscles set as tight as pressed steel bands; Private Kemp elbowed him lightly in the side.

"No doubt he's sick, Lomax. Mad as a hatter on barbiturates, but he also holds all the cards. He speaks, we follow, and there isn't a damn thing we can do about it."

She shot Corporal McIntosh a quick glance while strolling away towards their stalwart CO.

"Ain't it a pure bitch?"

Five minutes later, the majority of their gear (including all automatic weapons) stashed into a nearby gully, five individuals donned in camouflage uniforms and steel-toed combat boots marched in single file at double-time speed, their destination, the main sally-port entry to the Briarston compound, less than a quarter mile away.

***

Jimmy had observed the group from a rocky hill a good two hundred yards to their south. He had watched them congregate initially from a thin tree line almost directly across from the guard tower, but then backed away in fear of being spotted. He couldn't make out their garbled words, but had studied the taller man, the one Jimmy now deduced was the leader, rant and rave openly at a smaller, stocky individual who had eventually responded with a stiff, rather humorous-looking salute.

The group had grouped together and hidden their small duffels in a nearby ditch, then quickly proceeded around the west perimeter of the chain-link fence.

It had taken less than two minutes for them to fade into the vast darkness that enveloped the entire compound.

Jimmy paused, clicked his flashlight back on, careful to point it into the ground below, and pondered his next move.

Must have been a fire at the prison site, maybe that's why the electricity is out. But then, why is it so quiet? I can hear my stomach rumbling. Must have already evacuated. Funny, I didn't hear any commotion normally associated with emergencies. Not even the first siren. What are those guard people doing sneaking around like Navy Seals raiding a terrorist camp? Couldn't get close enough to see their insignia. Must be Special Forces of some kind, though.

A distant cousin of Jimmy's was a Paratrooper in the Air Force, or had been the last he had heard of him, which had been at least five or six years back. Jimmy had briefly considered joining the service himself. It had been during the early Reagan years, even going as far as calling a local Army recruiter, an action he would later regret as the Sergeant's initial less-than-hard sell of how to 'be all that you can be' soon resembled nothing less than all out harassment. He found himself dodging a never-ending series of phone calls and mailed flyers from the man, who was obviously in the middle of a quota drought.

Staring down at his ample midsection, and still badly out of breath despite the inactivity of the past ten minutes or so, Jimmy couldn't help but giggle at the thought of playing soldier. A thirty-minute hike through the woods had worn his chubby frame to a frazzle. Leaning against a waist-high boulder that was the perfectly sculpted image of a woman's breast, he sighed heavily.

What the hell am I doing here? Am I this bored with solitude already? Playing forest ranger detective just because I get a scent of smoke in the air? Jesus, the wife would be rolling over, howling until her sides ached. I'll let the professionals handle the crisis, I believe. Besides, there's not a single flame in sight, so my humble abode seems safe for now.

Shoving himself forward with his free hand, Jimmy hadn't taken a single step before catching the sudden movement to his left.

A few hundred feet to his east, the two figures

emerged from the forest, slowing cautiously to ensure the perimeter road ahead was indeed deserted.

Ducking back behind the rock, the protruding stone nipple of which almost jabbed him just below the right eye, Jimmy felt a tingling at his gut that, for once, had nothing to do with inner hunger.

***

"Why is it so dark, William? Is the site closed down?" Kara asked, crouched down as if avoiding live ammo fire.

Pushing his thick-framed glasses from the tip of his sweat-soaked nose to the equally slippery bridge, Wilbo shrugged while keeping his eyes trained on both the highway ahead and the perimeter fence that formed it's background.

"Dunno, sis, but if not for the moonlight, we'd be stumbling around like two blind mice in a room full of set traps. I wish I felt safe about turning on the flashlight, but I don't wanna give away our position. By the way, you smell something other than fire smoke or is it just me?"

Joining her brother at the center of the paved road, her multi-colored tennis shoes straddling the badly faded yellow line, Kara placed her right hand onto his lower back and quickly pulled it away as if bee stung.

"What exactly is that stuffed inside the back of your jeans? You didn't..." she began, then halted abruptly as an altogether new, toxic odor assaulted her already heightened senses.

"God, smells like an open sewer," she

proclaimed before covering her mouth and nose with one curled hand.

"I was gonna say a toilet that hadn't seen a flush in a month of Sundays, but your analogy will do just fine," Wilbo replied before trudging slowly forward and straight for the compound fence.

"You didn't answer my question, William. Tell me you didn't bring something from that insane arsenal you have stashed in the basement back home. Something that could get us either arrested, shot at, or possibly both. Tell me I'm *wrong*, William."

Motioning for her to follow his lead, Wilbo avoided his sister's gaze, which he knew at that moment would most likely resemble two fire-red pits. He secretly cursed himself for bringing the thirty-eight along, especially with his sister's less than casual attitude on the subject of firearms, but had considered it a necessary measure as they had departed their makeshift camp.

"Kara, we need some protection out here. We can take care of ourselves in most situations, I realize, but right now we're smack dab in the center of the unknown. I ain't planning on plugging anybody 'less I have to, okay?"

Huffing loudly, his sister started to rebuff his comments, but discontinued such action as a wave of mild nausea rushed through her midsection.

"Let's just see where the soldier boys are going. We don't have to introduce ourselves to 'em. There's gotta be a valid reason for them to be sneaking around the site, looking more like a swat team than plain old army grunts, weekend warriors at that. Maybe we'll find out something useful, maybe not. Never know unless we follow up, am I right? Damn, it stinks out here."

He turned to his sister, who jogged a few feet behind him, now with both hands cupped around her nostrils and lower jaw.

"Maybe they've created some kind of shit-bomb for future wars and are experimenting on the convicts," he blurted in a miserably failed attempt at humor.

Kara waived him ahead without response, the disgust easily read between the fingers that covered the majority of her face.

In the gloomy, cloudless sky above, a few scattered sparks of blackened ash blew freely towards the dry, brittle grounds of the surrounding woods.

***

Buck sat posed with his knees buried into a pile of moist, sticky oak leaves, studying the form lying before him like a Medical student hovering over a rotted, reeking cadaver.

JC stood on the opposite side of the body, vigorously scratching his head with both hands. Buck kept his flashlight's thin, tight beam aimed directly at the center of the man's blood-spattered face, as if waiting for the man's eyes to flutter and eventually open from the effects of the light.

"Right through the noggin, Buck. Dead center, too, like someone drew a circle there and then shot through it," JC muttered while holding his hands high to block the moonlight. The backs of both, most noticeably around the scarred knuckles, shone with a sickly moistness. He brought the left to his nostrils and sniffed, then turned and spat in disgust.

"Yep, this boy was done up right, no doubt. Could have been our boy four- eyes and that spidery lookin' sister of his, but more than likely one of his own troopers plugged old Sergeant Happy here. Jesus, that smile of his is giving me the Willies, and I didn't even know that was possible at this point," Buck said, the light now concentrated on the eerily frozen grin, the lips parted in an expression of inner satisfaction. A perfectly horizontal line of semi-dried blood had blazed a trail from bullet wound at the forehead, dribbled down the length of the nose, and finally settled between the lips and onto one of two shiny gold teeth on display.

"Must'a died a happy man, Buck. Sure didn't do any suffering."

Shuffling his boots from side to side like an apprehensive child, JC began fidgeting with his own light, patting it against his side nervously.

"We gonna…take the body to the site, Buck? One's as good as another, right? I mean, just cause we didn't..."

Buck arose wearily, quickly twirling the light forward until it landed on JC's face, the skin of which now resembled partially settled putty.

"Don't get so damn antsy. We know where the body is if we need it. Right now we got two live ones to track. Let's move on before we lose their trail. I wanna catch 'em completely off guard…see their eyes just before we..."

"I still say we should'a just stayed at their camp and waited on 'em, Buck. Hellfire, why do we have to play pioneer and spend half the night climbin' mountains and the other half pullin' briars out of our ball sacs?" JC whined as a small fleck of skin from his left ear lobe dislodged and sailed into the night atop a cool breeze.

Buck stepped over the body in a single leap, accidentally kicking the man's face and causing the head to whip around violently, spitting a trail of saliva and caked blood.

Grabbing JC by the crook of his right elbow, Buck planted the tip of the flashlight between the other man's breastbone and instituted a series of short but forceful jabs.

"Because, asshole, I *say* we do. I ain't waiting around some tent, ducking behind a tree like some yellow coward. What the hell kind of fun is that? You're getting lazy in your old age, JC old buddy. The thrill of the hunt was always what jacked my meat, and it use'ta do the same for you. You remember the ones we ran off the road and then released into the woods? We always gave 'em a chance. Just seemed the sporting thing to do. I get the feelin' our pops would'a done the same."

Backing away to escape the blunt assault of the flashlight being jammed into his already sore and lightly throbbing chest cavity, JC snarled in anger.

"Tonight is.... *different* though, Buck. I don't think I've ever felt this bad, this...weak. Something is happening to us, don't you feel it, man?"

Leaning his head back and sucking in the night air like a nocturnal creature escaping it's underground dwelling for the first time in months, Buck Lomax the Third howled through blackened teeth.

"Yeah, I feel it alright, old buddy. I feel

stronger tonight than I've ever felt, son! The change has *never* been this damn sudden…this urgent, this…stout. I'm walking around like I'm on a mix of Ultra-Viagra and black beauties!"

Reaching over with both arms, he hugged JC close, vehemently squeezing the cringing man until he heard a low, muffled shriek, then slowly releasing the pressure until it was no more than a gentle hug.

"Damn, boy! This just might be the night we finally meet the man, and you're as weak as a friggin' kitten. I must be feedin' off you or something, cause I ain't never been this strong. Nothing beats this surge, JC my man. Booze, dope, pussy, *nothing*! Nothing compares to this."

Peering down at the sprawled body to his left, Buck stepped away from JC in a sudden lurch, leaving the other man to trip back into a large shrub.

Buck planted his size ten left boot onto the dead man's chest, then raised both his curled fists into the air and whispered harshly in a voice that was less than human, it's vicious tone nothing short of predatory.

"This is our night, JC…this is *his* night. The true shit is gonna roll downhill like a rocky mountain avalanche, and whoever is unfortunate enough to stand in its path is gonna discover a level of pain humans were never intended to know."

Moments later, Buck the Third dragged the body by its boot heels and tossed it headfirst into a nearby ditch as easily as a man might a large sack of potatoes.

"Let's hit the trail, buddy boy," Buck then blurted to JC through lips literally coated in foamy white spittle.

"I get the feeling that gaining entrance to the prison site ain't gonna be the least bit tough."

JC paused before wearily jogging after his partner, who had already made tracks into a nearby thicket.

"Briarston? What the hell are we gonna do there, Buck?"

As he jogged forward, JC Carlyle spat another goo-lubricated tooth from between his pus-coated lips. In reality, he already knew the answer to that particular question. It was one he had been provided at birth, but managed to stubbornly deny for multiple decades until just moments earlier. Deep within his fast-rotting gut, JC felt both a strange exhilaration and a nerve-wracking dread.

Sometime later, a black-winged crow landed gently atop the crushed, bloodied chest of the discarded corpse. The bird nipped at the man's exposed neck only once before fluttering wildly as it attempted a panic-stricken take-off. Its ascent was woefully short of clearing a nearby pine whose spidery limbs had long ago been stripped of life and seemed to exist solely for such a moment. The bird sailed directly into the tree's slightly cracked but still solid base, breaking its neck instantly. It landed mere feet from the body it had so enthusiastically nibbled at just seconds before, it's talons stretched out as if to reach the dead man's similarly splayed fingers in a grasp of solitary passing.

Within minutes, the birds' previously shiny, darkened coat of feathers were transformed to a murky white tone, the texture of which reeked from the decomposition taking control beneath its skin.

CHAPTER SIX
Changing of The Guard

The state of Mississippi began the arduous task of rebuilding the Briarston Unit on February 13th, 1986; almost a full thirty years after the mystery blaze had demolished the old site. With crime rates at an all-time high nationwide, state and county correctional units were being constructed at a record pace in a somewhat feeble attempt to keep pace.

The state had never given up it's deed to the land the old site had stood upon, and logically deemed it more efficient to utilize such an established area instead of scouting out a fresh one.

The old unit had been conscientiously simple in both its basic construction and set up. It had consisted of four buildings, each one connected to the last by glass-encased breezeways.

Briarston Unit 1987 was nothing less than a state-of-the-art penal colony, complete with all the bells and whistles then available from a state fund driven by overburdened taxpayers residing in the poorest state within the Union.

Within its fenced perimeter (double linked with razor wire making up the top two feet) lay seventy thousand square feet of cold stone and hard wood structures, all spaced a mere dozen feet from one another and connected by glass dome walkways. Thirty-foot high stone towers with bulletproof, sliding glass windows were erected at each corner of the squared compound. The roofs of these sentry-points were bricked and pointed like the tips of arrows, giving them the look of ancient castle towers from centuries past.

The compound itself had only one entry/exit point, that being the sally port on its western side. Persons and vehicles alike were greeted and inspected within the cramped square, enclosed within a pair of electronically controlled double doors that were never to be opened simultaneously. A rectangular shaped two-man guard shack lay within this space, while an additional sentry post, this one not much larger than a phone booth, stood just outside the second entry fence.

Upon gaining entry, one would find themselves at the entrance to the unit administration building, where all incoming inmates were initially taken for in- processing. This was easily the largest of the unit's structures, twenty thousand square feet of offices, conference and supply rooms, and closet space reserved for the mountains of paperwork generated on a daily basis. All but the correctional officers and chow hall workers assigned to the unit slaved from the two-story admin building, which was easily labeled as the nerve center from which all tasks, great or small, normally originated.

The single-story structure at its rear was the compound dining facility, from which three square (but not always entirely edible) meals were served twenty- four seven, three hundred sixty-five days per year. The unit housed a steady inmate population of one hundred-ten to one-hundred twenty-five at any given time, all but a handful of which took their daily bread within the hall's dingy green colored walls. Only those assigned to the Administrative Segregation Unit, the building to the dining hall's immediate south, were fed elsewhere.

The inmates housed in the relatively small cellblock known amongst the inmates as the ‘Mole Pits’ had been separated from the general population for many reasons. Some had continuously broken unit rules or simply couldn’t get along with their fellow inmates; others were labeled snitches and kept in Admin Seg for their own protection. They received three squares and one hour outside their cell each day, a monitored sequence within a break lounge that consisted of exactly one chair and one TV.

The ‘Mole Pits’ normally housed no more than ten to twelve inmates at a time, but had a total cell occupancy of fifteen.

Within the same structure as the tiny Segregation was the compound gymnasium, which held a basketball court, two handball courts, a weight room Joe Weider would have envied, and adjoining sauna room. No expense had been spared to produce a bigger, badder, increasingly bulked up breed of inmates, a much-debated subject in and around all state penal units nationwide as the century came to a close.

Covering a space one hundred yards long and fifty wide, the exercise yard centered the compound, thus providing ample space between the inmate cellblocks and the other structures.

As was the case in correctional facilities worldwide, the fenced in yard was the hub of all activity, illegal and otherwise, within the inmate population. Deals went down. Bodies were auctioned off like cattle. Souls were sold for the briefest of human frills. The cellblocks themselves were contained in a single three-story, red brick building that made up the entire Eastern end of the compound. Block A was floor one, Block B the second tier, and Block C the top story. Simplicity in itself, just as it had been mapped out to be by those in the know. Daily inmate counts were made every hour on the hour, including a final tallying done at midnight by the oncoming night shift officers.

Cell doors were also electronically controlled, a total lock-down of the facility within a single buttons reach.

The New Briarston Unit had been a model of modern technology, held in regard by those within the state as the singular example of how a unit could and should be run at the outset of the twenty-first century.

The first several years went as smoothly as initially advertised, with a minimum of bugs that were quickly and efficiently stamped out and otherwise corrected. The warden, a stone-faced bear of a man named Wharton, had ruled with an iron hand and shown little patience for complacency from either his staff or the housed guests of the state that were his to reign over.

It wasn't until the final months of his tenure that things began to dramatically change for the worst. Things that eventually drove Wharton to a retirement he fervidly insisted had been 'long planned' and had 'nothing to do' with the inner turmoil that had floated over the compound like a monstrous storm cloud waiting to explode.

On Thanksgiving Day of 1989, the first of several horrendous, unexpected events transpired. Events that would serve not only as a foreboding catalyst for things to come, but also to haunt the grounds of Briarston in an almost mythological way, and only then in muffled whispers, like ancient ghost stories told around a crackling campfire.

A small, bookish man named Jackson Dennis, known to CO's and fellow inmates as a quiet, reserved individual serving five years for check fraud and related convictions, had been sitting alone in the B Block TV lounge after the inmates annual turkey day meal.

Peter Baldwin, a bull of a man at six-three and two-hundred twenty pounds of solid muscle, had subsequently entered the room in a huff, his usually flat midsection a bit swollen from the massive meal just consumed. Baldwin had instantly decided that the World War II documentary Dennis had been viewing was, spoken in Baldwin's Southern Cajun twang, 'borin' shit nobody gives a rat crap about' and proceeded to switch the TV station to a cable sports station.

According to Larry Coring, a trustee inmate who entered the room just a few moments later, Dennis had asked Baldwin several times to change the station back, requests that the larger man refused to even acknowledge.

Coring, later treated with sedatives to allow his frazzled nerves to settle somewhat, reported to state investigators that Dennis had slowly, ever so calmly risen from his chair, placing the paperback he had been thumbing through onto a nearby coffee table. He then had stepped towards Baldwin, who had been lying lazily across the full length of the couch that centered the room, his face slack and eyes concentrated on the TV screen fronting both men.

Coring said what transpired next was so surreal it was as if he were watching it as a spectator of some bizarre Home Theater presentation, the involved parties movements blurred in 'Matrix' type motions.

Dennis, according to Coring, pulled a yellow number two pencil from behind his left ear and rammed into the lower left side of Baldwin's exposed neck, just below the ear lobe, then leisurely backed away as if to survey his handy work. The pencil had been buried almost to the eraser, and Baldwin had rolled off the couch onto the floor, grasping at his punctured neck as if trying to reach a particularly bothersome itch.

Coring said that the pencil finally pulled free with a tiny sucking sound, a gush of crimson shooting from the small, perfectly circular wound in a fine line, the initial gush of which splashed against a far wall, a full fifteen feet from its former host.

As Baldwin struggled to his knees, all the while clamping his right palm to his wound and lapping his left over that, Coring reported that Dennis stood prone, his chin propped upon his right fist, like a man studying a rare species on display at a local zoo.

Coring then stated that Dennis waited until Baldwin regained his rather shaky footing, then stepped forward and planted the fingers of his left hand squarely into the other man's eye sockets.

The remainder of Larry Coring's statement was spotty at best, being that he was later found unconscious just outside of the lounge room door and couldn't recall at exactly what point the shut off button inside his brain had been pressed. He did recall images of Dennis wrestling Baldwin to the ground and 'tugging' at the man's face, the smaller man's fingers submerged deep into the ravaged sockets until only the bloodied knuckles of his fore and middle finger were visible. Coring said it resembled a man with his hand stuck in a bowling ball, and recalled being amazed at the ease in which the frail, sickly looking Dennis could manhandle a bulky brute such as Baldwin without 'breaking a sweat'.

Upon discovery of the body pulp that remained of Peter Baldwin a half-hour later, the unit 'force cell' team was quickly dispatched into the cellblock. Once a quick investigation had ensued, they found Jackson Dennis sitting quietly inside his eight by ten abode, his entire body literally drenched in bodily fluids, not all of which belonged to the deceased man he had so efficiently dispatched of earlier. The cell team's lead CO later reported that Dennis had been 'licking the fluids' from his fingers like a man relishing warm barbecue sauce from a stack of recently devoured ribs. Still another guard stated that Dennis had been sporting an erection through his red-stained prison issue pants at the time, and that the skin of the man's face was a light shade of yellow. Both men's written report on their handling of Dennis (he was taken to the infirmary in wrist and ankle shackles, then monitored by a select team of CO's during treatment) was similar in nature, although they did differ in all but one precise statement. A statement that was scribbled in separate styles but almost word for word in content.

Jackson Dennis had reeked upon capture, and not solely the stout coppery scent associated with large amounts of blood. It was described as both 'sickly' and 'infection-like' in both reports. Dennis was placed in one of two 'quarantine cells' at the far end of the infirmary. Meanwhile, Warden Pierce Wharton and a hand-picked homicide investigator from Tupelo went through the contents of the man's empty cell, looking for a possible clue to explain why a man, known as a model inmate, could go off the deep end so rapidly and without a single warning. Normally in such a rare case, the answer could be found from either the use of narcotic drugs or an inmate grudge. Unfortunately, neither instance fit the individual involved.

Jackson Dennis was one who other inmates had sworn wouldn't even drink coffee, a man who had never asked the compound medical staff for even a single aspirin tablet within the previous two years of his stay. He kept to himself, spending most of his duty-free time in the site library or reading inside his cell.

It wasn't until the Warden began surveying the man's chosen reading material that a strange tingling surfaced at the base of his mostly bald scalp.

A line of thick, hard bound novels with titles like '*Ancient Myths – Legends of Buried Evil*' and '*Lucifer's Minions - The Ones Who Once Ruled*', all found to be specially ordered by Dennis within the past year, were carefully placed between more commercial reading. Dennis had been known to be a lover of the occult, at least within the books he browsed, but no one had ever considered the man anything other than a bit strange and genuinely harmless.

Wharton was later informed that the TV program that had essentially cost Peter Baldwin his life, the one that Jackson Dennis had taken great offense to being cut away from, had indeed been a documentary covering certain aspects of World War II. The title of this specific program had been 'Inhuman Practices: Torturous Methods of the Third Reich."

Eleven months later, a medical panel from John Hopkins University had concluded that Jackson Dennis' homicidal rage had indeed been caused by 'delusions of fantasy role playing', and insisted the man had been obsessed by all things ancient and evil, a true prophet in the study of mankind's eventual Armageddon.

In short order, the man who had fatally stabbed and gouged out the eyes of Peter Baldwin had been nutticr than a three-pound fruitcake.

In the weeks following the incident, Dennis was treated for everything from anemia to AIDS, his condition steadily worsening despite the constant bombardment of various antibiotics. Although his mysterious ailment wasn't considered contagious, he was nonetheless kept in the same sealed off room for its duration. A specialist was flown in from Dallas during the third week of treatment, and drove away literally scratching his head in disillusionment once a specific diagnosis was deemed impossible to settle upon.

Dennis' putrid smelling, infection-ridden form was discovered on the morning of his twenty-seventh day of treatment. A CO had been strolling from the admin building towards the cellblock structure at just before 5 AM when he spotted the splayed-out body at the center point of the exercise yard. Dennis' pale, skeletal form was completely nude, his skin casting an eerie glow in the light of daybreak. Torn IV's hung from both his bony elbows like severed rope. It looked as though he had been digging at the space beneath his body by wriggling his rail-thin arms and legs into the grass and dirt below, the outline left behind resembling the markings of a snow angel.

The CO took his station that night with an unsteady hand and nerves frazzled to the snapping point. He told co-workers that Dennis had displayed a wide, gruesome, almost completely toothless grin that had covered his yellow- tinted face as if painted on. It seemed to him, as well as the medical personnel who would later retrieve the body, that Dennis had been literally trying to 'dig and bury' himself into the yard's midsection.

The CO would dream of such an expression for months to come, its distorted features ever-present within the hazy realms of his most terrifying, reality- based nightmares.

That particular CO's name had been Jerrod Dickenson, whose father had once served in such a capacity while walking the same grounds. Jeffery Dickenson had died tragically in the blaze, which destroyed the original site, his infant son barely a year old at the time. A veteran of three other correctional units within the state, Jerrod had requested a transfer to the Briarston site immediately upon its completion. The night he stumbled across the body had been his ninth shift as a member of the Briarston CO staff.

Within his first year on station, he would witness scenarios that made the strangeness of Jackson Dennis' passing seem utterly pleasurable by comparison.

More deaths would follow, a total of thirteen in as many years, the majority of which caused by an illness that the state medical board could never quite pinpoint, although such varied culprits as diabetes, pancreatic cancer and advanced HIV were listed as 'likely' suspects.

Rumors were tossed about freely among both staff and the inmate population. Rumors that covered every possible cause from 'bad drinking water' to 'asbestos' poisoning, from an overabundance of rats in the surrounding area to the site itself being built atop an ancient 'Navajo burial ground'.

Questions as to why the landscape encircling the site seemed consistently more barren and less fruitful than in the nearby forest had always lingered throughout the seasons, as had the constant complaints of a strange, toxic odor lingering within the compound on certain occasions. Inmates called such days 'SS Days' as in 'shit-sniffing' days around the compound.

Despite the abundance of highly imaginative, over-exaggerated guesses, *no one* could logically explain why so many of the victims who had passed so inexplicably had turned so brutally violent in the weeks before succumbing.

The site medical staff had reported the same tendencies in each case, that being the victim's seemingly unquenchable appetite to bludgeon, rape, and otherwise feloniously assault whoever happened to be unfortunate enough to stand in their path as the illness progressed.

Additionally, each victim save one had been

found in the same manner as Jackson Dennis, sprawled face down with their gnarled hands digging into the grounds of the exercise yard, their faces frozen in an odd mix of unrivaled pleasure and excruciating pain.

The lone exception to this macabre pattern had occurred in late nineteen ninety-eight, on the very day Warden Owen Gates was quietly celebrating his first anniversary on the job.

A rookie CO named Albert Weems, only weeks removed from CO school, had begun to show symptoms similar to earlier cases of the illness; the yellowish tint of the skin and darkening of the same underneath his fingernails. His family physician, a man who had served as Red Bridge's main sawbones for over three decades, had taken one look at him and instantly suggested (in an uncharacteristically shaky tone) that he report to the Briarston staff pronto.

Weems began to exhibit severe mood swings in the days following, and was soon placed in the same quarantine room that had been the final resting place for so many others treated for a similarly bizarre condition.

There were episodes of savage assaults on the staff, including an almost fatal stabbing of a nurse with a discarded syringe (according to the file report, the nurse had suffered over forty separate puncture wounds) and the attempted choking of one of the staff physicians.

Like his predecessor, Warden Gates had a specialist flown in (this time from a large Baptist Hospital in Nashville), as well as a team from the CDC in Atlanta to ensure the illness was indeed non-contagious.

Gates, a thirty-five-year veteran of the correctional trade, and a man of few words and even less patience, had been briefed concerning the compounds past casualties and the shroud of mystery surrounding them. On the day he observed both the CDC team and the viral specialist depart Briarston, all of whom had no more answers than when they had arrived, he spent the majority of the afternoon tucked away inside his dimly lit office, chewing aspirin and antacid by the handful.

Albert Weems expired exactly three weeks to the day of his admission into the infirmary. The room door had been electronically sealed in recent years, and not just to prevent unauthorized *access*. Warden Wharton had implemented the locks mainly to avoid any further 'night maneuvers' by dying patients in search of a particular patch of grass within the exercise yard. No such stroll had been taken by Albert Weems on this particular occasion, but it wasn't as if the man hadn't given it the old college try.

His body weight down a full hundred pounds from the robust one-ninety of mere weeks earlier, he had been placed on a respirator and given less than a week to live by staff doctors on the eve of his passing. Surgeons had removed a marble sized tumor from his lung, as well as an unidentifiable growth from his right kidney a few days before, but still had no definite answer to the family as to what had caused such fatal abnormalities within his system.

A staff resident was the first to enter the room that morning, sipping a hot cup of coffee while balancing a large clipboard underneath the other arm.

Upon viewing the horrific carnage once the door was fully ajar, the young doctor practically tossed the steaming liquid onto his own neck and chest, leaping back into the hallway as if gut punched. Five minutes later, a weary and haggard-faced Warden Gates, along with his top-ranking CO and a team of medical personnel stood at the threshold of pure, primal madness.

Albert Weems, all ninety pounds of nothing more than gangly bones and sickly, pus moistened flesh, had somehow managed to not only rise from his deathbed, but totally *dismantle* it, along with every other free-moving object within the fifteen by twenty room.

One of the doctors present would later state in a medical journal that it looked as if 'a funnel cloud consisting of shredded skin and jagged bone' had torn through the room, using Weems' decimated torso as its personal battering ram.

Thick folds of pulped skin had been pasted to the inside of the door, glued to the surface by a purplish ooze that dripped downward like trails of spilled paint. Despite his obviously critical condition, and despite the fact that Albert R. Weems had not yet regained consciousness since his surgery over forty-eight hours earlier; the skeletal waste he had evolved into had somehow awakened with a vengeance during the night.

Awakened, arose, and had wanted *out.*

All that remained of his threadbare arms was shattered bone, both broken at the forearm and practically skinless.

He lay on his side at the base of the door, giving the onlookers just enough room to push the door open without inflicting further damage on his shell- like figure. Albert Weems' face peered upward, the skin of his face ripped in thin, horizontal sections, like someone had taken a cheese grater to it. His almost lip- less mouth was parted impossibly wide, what few teeth that hadn't previously fallen out laying atop his bony chin like aspirin tablets that had missed their target and subsequently stuck there.

His dark, pit-like eyes were opened only partially, but enough to reveal an inner anguish only the near dead could ever begin to either comprehend or properly define.

Blood and other bodily fluids were spattered about the surrounding walls, the collapsed bed mattress, and even the misplaced and dented medical equipment, most of which had been completely overturned.

Warden Gates found no explanation as to how a comatose man with practically no remaining working muscles on his emaciated frame could initiate such a self-mutilating atrocity, but as to the reason *why he had* was no mystery, at least not to anyone privy to the past history of Briarston.

Albert Weems had received a call. He had been drawn to a small patch of ground at the center of the exercise yard, but unlike his long-dead and buried predecessors, had found a blockade in his path too difficult to pass. A blockade that had prevented his passage to that spot that yearned for his wasted carcass to occupy. A blockade that had driven him to a final, maniacal, frenzied act of suicide. Albert

Weems had been unable to answer the call, and had in turn lashed out in a fevered assault upon his own rotting, decaying soul.

Later that night, rinsing his mouth with lukewarm Milk of Magnesia, Warden Gates sunk into the comforting confines of the high leatherback chair that had accompanied him on four similar posts since he had traded in his CO uniform for a suit and tie.

Owen Gates wasn't a man to worry easily. He had been legendary for his no-nonsense, by-the-book attitude in dealing with inmates while a guard, an approach he had personally deemed 'don't bend *or* break'. Even as times and procedures shifted to a more 'politically correct' atmosphere, Gates had remained stoic in his stance that the majority of the men housed under his care were not 'victims' of their upbringing' as was the popular media and public opinion. He viewed them as thugs who were simply incapable with normal society; men and women, who, in most cases, were not victims of abuse or 'unfortunate circumstances', but uncivilized dregs who had no one to blame but themselves for their incarceration.

He tolerated the states' softer, gentler methods in dishing out additional corrective measures only because he had no choice in the matter. In his day walking the blocks, consistently troublesome inmates eventually found themselves within the unit infirmary short a few teeth or owning a few cracked ribs. Funny what a club to the temple or a swift series of kicks to the testicles could do for one's attitude. He secretly yearned for the same procedural freedom in what he called 'the era of touchy-feely', but to keep a job that kept him in a three hundred-thousand-dollar home and driving a new vehicle every few years, he could certainly learn to be 'flexible'. His two girls would be headed to Starkville within a year to become freshmen at Mississippi State, and tuition for two didn't come cheap.

After concocting a mix of Magnesia and Evan Williams Rye into a tall glass, Gates sipped cautiously and instantly grimaced.

"Nectar of the Gods, not," he had whispered, holding his left hand under the nearby lamb light and failing miserably to control the nearly overwhelming panic causing it to shake and tremor.

The nails were a faint purple color, and the fingers on both hands tingling madly, as if in the initial stages of contracting a severe case of poison oak.

Raiding a nearby metal file cabinet, Warden Gates removed a fresh bottle, this time a pint of JW Dant, and quickly broke the label and poured himself a tall glass.

As his chest and midsection warmed from the effects of the first few swallows, the Warden discovered a new emotion begin to overlap the earlier fear. His entire being was sweeping within the folds of euphoric waves, electric surges that he could only compare with sexual orgasm. Casually pushing the bottle to the far end of his paper and file-folder cluttered desk, Warden Gates wholeheartedly welcomed the intrusion, and instantly felt all earlier pain melt away as his subconscious was being properly introduced to a presence he never could have dreamed existed.

A presence he would soon come to realize was the true Warden of the Briarston Correctional Facility. As time progressed, Warden Gates found the process of handing over said reigns a maddening mix that was simultaneously pain-filled but also strangely pleasurable. The everyday pressures fell from his slowly mutating shoulders like cement bricks from an overturned semi.

He hadn't felt as free since his early teen years, and the warm rinsing of relief associated with such a complete surrender created the pleasure equation of the process.

The inner rage nestled beneath his cool, calm exterior bubbled and festered like volcanic liquid in the months ahead, and managing to control such maniacal anger without spinning into meltdown mode brought the pain. Pain that kept him from any form of sleep for several days at a time, while turning his bowel movements into pudding-like masses of crimson and yellow covered pus. He would sometimes masturbate five, six times a day, usually ending in immensely painful ejaculations, all in an attempt to subside constant, uncomfortable to the point of irritating erections.

Owen Gates had been instructed to bide his time, an order that had come not in the form of a memo or typed transcription, but from a home office only he could hear or adhere to. The order had been clear and concise, despite the lack of actual verbal communication.

The exact spot of the command center should have been apparent from the beginning, once he dwelled upon it without the blinders of his own kind blocking his inner vision, the extra site that had been added since the transformation.

Each day after confirming his suspicion, Warden Gates made it a habit of walking through the exercise yard just to pass over its exquisite entryway. Although buried beneath dirt, clay and rock, and capped by thick metal, it might as well have been paper-thin and transparent for the effect it produced.

The engorged, pulsating rage that beat at his temples would be released in all its unhinged glory in due time, but only when the proper command was given. He did find subtle ways to feed its insatiable appetite as time passed: altering inmate's files in order to hinder their chances for parole. Constantly altering regulations in and around the blocks to keep inmates in a continuous state of confusion. The occasional (usually unwarranted) chewing out of a subordinate just for the sheer kick of it.

Owen Gates waited, albeit sometimes impatiently, driven to fits of jabbering rage whenever alone, for the hammer to fall.

He didn't even want to contemplate the consequences of disobeying such an order. He had seen men suffer both mental and physical anguish in horrific extremes during his time in the Correctional field, having inflicted his fair share of it personally.

The Warden understood one single, indisputable fact very clearly and without question: such pain would pale a hundred-fold compared to what was lingering on the horizon for so many unsuspecting of his own kind.

Whenever he thought of this, more frequently as the calendar pages sailed past as if caught in the path of an industrial strength fan, Warden Owen Gates would smile like the raving lunatic he had truly become.

He had traveled to Red Bridge to instill his own brand of penal discipline, to leave his mark as a man unbiased when dealing out punishment to those deserving, and unabashedly fair to those truly seeking redemption and rehabilitation for past mistakes.

What he had become after a decade-plus since the Jackson Dennis affair, was a *sentinel.* A well-dressed, equally well-respected gatekeeper for the one true King of Red Bridge, Mississippi.

A King seeking an infinitely larger kingdom. A King he was slowly being prepped to hold to task. Warden Owen Gates would no longer exist on the day of reckoning, only a hollowed-out shell of what had been human. The species taking his place would face a challenge many lesser beings would deem an impossible endeavor. The Ancient One had to be stopped, and a lone Sentinel stood erect and defiant as it's menacing shadow gradually rose from the depths.

Defeat would not be an option, least the wraith of the one true master be felt.

The Sentinel patiently waited while the Warden slowly faded from view.

CHAPTER SEVEN
A Melting of the Minds

Private Sandra Kemp considered herself worldly in many, varied ways, despite her relatively young age. She had taken a sip from her first beer at age nine (an Uncle on her mom's side), toked on her first joint at eleven (an Uncle on her father's side), and had her first sexual encounter at age twelve (same Uncle, Mom's side).

She had joined her first gang at age thirteen (initiation to which included sleeping with five male and three female members on the same night and assisting in a car theft) and spent a large majority of her teen years awaiting trial for one criminal count or another.

Sandra Kemp could count the times she had been literally scared shitless on one hand within all those trying times.

As the makeshift formation cut a final sharp corner and the main entrance and sally port to Briarston Correctional Facility came dimly into view, she could have lifted a shaky finger in acknowledgement of such an incident presently taking place.

Something was truly amiss, that much would have been obvious to anyone in possession of even the weakest instincts. The entire compound was draped in darkness, the infrequent tendril of floating smoke cutting through the air as if in rapid retreat, accompanied by a nose-curdling stench that had initially caused her to gag and spit repeatedly before growing somewhat accustomed to its putrid company.

She was pretty certain that Major Peterson was more than just your everyday run-of-the-mill asshole anymore, but something distinctly worse, and infinitely more dangerous. He had gone off the deep end since their arrival in the woods. He was wandering the two-lane highway towards Loonyville. She could see it in his bizarrely glowing and bloodshot eyes. Private Bodine had been right, also. The man stunk like he had been dipped in raw sewage. All that said, and they continued to follow. Like suicide bombers in line to dive into the nearest destroyer, following the lead plane into the fire. An illegally formed militia trespassing on posted, fenced-in government property. Private Kemp shook her head in quiet disbelief. She didn't know whether to laugh or scream, although she could have effortlessly managed both simultaneously.

Bringing up the rear, her gear suddenly seeming twice as heavy. She considered her options, the gist of which was sadly limited.

Fight or flee, stay or go, adapt or retreat. If she ran, Major David Peterson would see her locked up within days, no ifs, ands or buts. If she stayed, she had a gut feeling some seriously nasty shit was lurking just around the corner.

As they grew ever closer to the sally port, its main gates open and resembling the outstretched maw of some prehistoric creature at feeding time, Private Kemp carefully scrutinized those around her, seeking an air of comfort and finding such a condition sorely lacking.

Major Peterson and Sergeant Ezop had point about fifteen yards ahead. She could hear the Major babbling, and saw Ezop nod in agreement every three seconds or so. Private Kemp had the belief that Sergeant Ezop would not only take a bullet for his leader, but also might dive onto a grenade crotch-first if the situation arose. If trouble arose, she hoped Ezop was as good a soldier as he was a blatant kiss ass.

Private Bodine followed, the kid's head darting around as if attached to a slinky, occasionally attempting to wipe the disgusting odor from his nostrils with a vigorous wipe. He reminded her of those 'GI journalists' you saw in war movies, the ones who hid inside bunkers or behind other soldiers, gripping a pen and pad instead of a rifle.

Private Kemp could easily envision Private Bodine curled inside a body bag with a neat little hole embedded between the pimples on his forehead.

Corporal McIntosh hopped along just a few feet ahead of her, his loose posture and slack movement like that of a man taking a peaceful midnight stroll through the park.

She had been introduced to Mac at a recruiter party back in Little Rock almost a year previous, and had spent countless hours in his loutish, pessimistic presence since. She had gotten drunk with him, high with him, even slept with him on at least a dozen occasions. That said; Private Sandra Kemp would have been hard pressed for answers if asked to describe the man. She was turned on as much by his 'everyone can smooch my hairy white butt cheeks' attitude as by his muscular frame, which seemed carved directly from granite, exquisitely toned and seemingly always on display by its proud, though at times dreadfully vain owner. It wasn't love, nothing remotely similar. That specific word, at least in Sandra Kemp's vocal, oft-heard opinion, belonged in back-shelf romance novels and movies from the early twentieth century, but certainly had no place in real life. Distrust, resentment, and hate were a different breed altogether. Those terms were at least based in reality.

Her eyes temporarily glued on the skin-tight buttock region of Corporal McIntosh's person, Private Kemp wondered what type of warrior he would be if the need actually arose. She deduced without hesitation that if she had a choice of whom to duck behind if the shit cut loose in a big way, good old Mac would serve such a purpose just fine and dandy. She did, however, secretly wish Sergeant Chambers were nearby. While she had little respect for his choice in music or the way he seemed to revel in demeaning females at every available opportunity, she knew he could take care of himself in a combat situation.

She had witnessed Isiah Chambers take out three loud-mouth bigots in a Baton Rouge bar just a few months past, his arms and fists spinning like twin lawn mower blades, his feet work lightning quick and gracefully efficient, despite the half case of Michelob he had ingested throughout the evening. Big mouth thug that he was, she wished like hell that he was marching beside her as they neared the gates of the compound.

Just as they got to within twenty or thirty feet from the opened gates of the sally port, Major Peterson raised his gloved right hand in a 'halt' gesture.

All froze instantly in their tracks, the gravel and dust of the only partially paved roadway beneath their boots kicking up in cloud-like bursts. A paved parking lot to their left held few vehicles, certainly not a nightshift's worth.

The Major strode purposely forward, then halted in front of the inwardly shoved double-door fence, his gaze never leaving the eight to ten-foot space between the two.

Turning to Sergeant Ezop, his haggard face, most of which was drowned in shadow, was literally locked in a pained frown. To Kemp, the Major looked like someone who hadn't been able to complete a bowel movement in several calendar years.

She watched him move back to where Ezop stood stationary and whisper into the Sergeant's left ear.

Seconds later, Ezop had the others huddle together in a tight circle while the Major remained near the entrance, adjusting the night goggles around his neck.

"Listen up, folks. We're treating this as a potential rescue mission exercise. We get in; do a quick sweep of the compound, not to include offices in the main building, just the outside grounds. If the opportunity arises, we assist any potential victims. We'll split up in teams once we pass the outside of that initial building, which is more than likely the main administrative hub."

Feeling a bit like a desperate fifth grader raising her hand for permission to go pee, Private Kemp nonetheless could not refrain from interrupting. Her voice cracked with nervousness, and she could almost feel Corporal McIntosh smirk a few feet to her right.

"Sergeant E, does the Major realize the gravity of this bullshit stroll onto very restricted government property? Has the Major considered this rotten smell might actually be a chemical spill of some kind? We could be standing here sucking it in while our insides slowly turn to oatmeal, you know. I can't speak for no one else, but..."

Ezop cut her off with one raised hand, the fingers of which shook noticeably.

"Private, calm the hell down. There will be no *consequences* to speak of, all right? The place is obviously deserted, probably has been for weeks. The crew we spotted yesterday was probably for post clean-up of some kind. The smell is probably an old sewer line that's been penetrated for cleaning or repair, nothing more. The Major simply feels this is a good chance for night patrol training with the goggles. We're not even armed, remember?"

"Yeah, but Jesus H..." She began before turning slightly as Private Bodine's left hand landed onto her right shoulder with a low thud.

"Don't worry, Sandra, we'll be in and out of there in ten minutes tops, right Sarge?" He whispered, his mild tone a bit eerie within the surrounding air of almost dead silence.

"Damn tooting, Private. Nothing more than a FOD walk on an old prison ground, that's all. Treat it seriously though, folks. One day we may be tasked for similar duty within a terrorist camp inside our very own borders," Ezop replied with a tight smile aimed at Private Kemp, who in turn sighed so loudly it caused the Major to turn towards their circle with a somewhat irritated expression.

"Let's move, Sergeant. There might be people inside needing medical assistance. We're all up to date on CPR procedure, I take it. This damn smoke is getting thicker by the second, and that rancid smell increasing as we grow closer," the Major barked, every other word seeming a bit slurred.

"On our way, sir," Ezop replied, flashing Private Kemp a final, trustful look. "In and out, walk on the beach, right?" He asked while adjusting his own goggles, this time speaking to no one in particular.

"Sarge?" Corporal McIntosh asked, his own eyewear already in place. "What is it, Mac?"

"Just where in the hell is Chambers? You hear from him at all?" As he walked away, Sergeant Ezop shrugged uneasily.

"No idea, Mac. Major couldn't reach 'im. Knowing Isiah, he's off banging a moose somewhere."

The Corporal replied without a trace of humor, that of course being his trademark, as he arose from his crouch.

"Either that or the bastard found an open bar somewhere."

Private Bodine began to assist the other Private to her feet, his goggles swinging crookedly over his narrow chest, and was brushed back with a light elbow to the ribs for his efforts. He backed away, comically startled.

"Don't bother, kiddo. I'm *hunky-dory*. Better watch your own ass in there. I get the distinct feeling we're walking right into a hornets nest that just caught a stout whiff of pesticide," Private Kemp snapped with a dark scowl.

"Damn, pardon me for breathing, lady," Private Bodine spat harshly once conveniently out of range of his intended target.

Seconds later, five members of the Dark Eagle Militia stepped cautiously through the opening, all save one within their small group holding their collective breath as if stepping nude into a frozen lake.

The sole member void of such inner dramatics led the way with a single sentence replaying in his mind as if glued onto a jammed conveyer belt. His badly swollen lips stuck to the morbidly rotted stubs his teeth were fast becoming like slugs to a stone wall.

Lambs to the slaughter, lambs to the slaughter, lambs to the slaughter.

***

Jimmy watched the shadowed forms vanish past the range of his limited sight as he leaned behind the wide, hollowed out trunk of a long dead birch tree. Still panting despite little movement in the previous five minutes, he promised himself for the hundredth time since the forest jaunt had begun that he would shed fifty pounds or more within the next calendar year.

The last regular exercise regimen he could recall being a part of was when Jake had been in his early teens, when they'd spend a few hours in the afternoon tossing around the old pigskin. Jimmy had been at least sixty pounds lighter in those days, and Jake had yet to spend a single minute in juvenile court, a structure to which his son would sarcastically quip was his ‘home away from home’ in later years.

Scanning the surrounding woods, which was both abnormally still and quiet for such a late hour, Jimmy wished he had thought to bring a fresh canteen of water along. The rancid scent that had earlier threatened to literally bring him to his knees in full barf-mode had either subsided or he had finally begun to grow immune to its souring effect.

He was still unable to pinpoint exactly why he had felt compelled to follow the voices this far into uncharted territory, eventually chalking it up to rabid curiosity, a bothersome condition that had created nothing but trouble for him as a teen and young adult.

The aged two-lane road a few dozen feet ahead of his position seemed to exist solely as a perimeter for the darkened compound on the opposite side. He instantly recalled the old man, ‘Harry’ or ‘Henry’ he believed had been his name, mentioning the Briarston Facility more than once the day he rented the camp space. What he couldn’t remember for the life of him was the old man saying anything about the prison being closed down or otherwise deserted.

With his eyes long-adjusted to the darkness, Jimmy could easily make out the chain fences outline and the numerous signs proclaiming it’s off-limits status to anyone other than correctional employees.

Despite the thick smoke massing in the adjacent sky, his earlier concern of a rapidly spreading forest fire had been abated being that there wasn’t a single flame or glowing horizon in sight.

Several times before reaching the facilities perimeter road, Jimmy had considered turning back to camp, but instead hiked enthusiastically ahead as if under some sinister magician's hypnotic spell.

After observing the small group of soldiers (*guardsman perhaps*?) first halt and then proceed through what he deduced was the opening to the compound, Jimmy had heard a different voice bark an unmistakably clear command from within the deepest pit of his subconscious. The voice was Patty's, utilizing a tone he only heard when she was at the torn end of a very frazzled rope when dealing with his incisive 'need to know' in matters she deemed trivial.

The sentence was short and agonizingly clear in its meaning.

Jimbo, please retract that nosy probe of yours before someone cuts it off.

His beloved Patricia had only called him 'Jimbo' in times of great annoyance, usually when his intrusive nature threatened to send her shimming up the nearest wall, manicured fingernails first.

The two other figures, a male and female both void of uniforms and obviously shadowing the soldiers cautiously, had ducked behind a wooden storage building a few hundred yards to the east and had yet to emerge.

Parking his bulky frame on the thick torso of a fallen pine, Jimmy inhaled the cool night air and peered into the smoke and star-filled sky above.

Take five, my man, before that overtaxed ticker of yours implodes from all the unplanned activity. This is as good a place as any to lay back and enjoy nature, what little of it is still actually alive around here anyhow. Maybe that damn smell has something to do with it. Never seen so many dead trees, gnarled weeds and dried grass in one area. Seems to worsen the closer you get to the prison site. Let's just sit back and see what transpires. It's not like you've got anything better to do.

After releasing one final strained huff, Jimmy felt his second wind begin to emerge as his pulse rate slowly decreased. For the next few moments, the only sound that reverberated within the small circle he occupied was the muffled growling originating from deep within his abdomen.

"Just like playing spy when I was a kid," he smiled, although the tingling sensation at the back of his scalp refused to be entirely diverted. He knew exactly why he was staying put. Something major was going down on this night, and he was somehow destined to either participate in or at the very least, witness the proceedings.

***

Approximately two-hundred yards to the east of where Jimmy sat, Wilbo peeked from behind the far corner of the small shed to ensure the uniforms had indeed moved ahead far enough for he and Kara to remain hidden from their site. "Well?" She whispered impatiently, her slim back shoved forcefully against the hard wooden planks of the rear wall like someone avoiding sniper fire.

Wilbo turned to her, surveyed her stiff pose and quickly covered his mouth, concealing the broad smile held there. Small beads of sweat had formed on his forehead, dribbling down the bridge of his nose and causing his glasses to slide ever downward.

"Jeez, sis, don't have a bowel movement, they've broken formation and moved straight into the heart of hades itself," he replied drolly, resetting his glasses and turning back to view the now deserted paved enclosure fronting the main gates.

"Tell me *one more time* why we're doing this," she asked, relaxing a bit and allowing her folded arms to fall to her sides.

"Y'know, you don't make much of a Scully to my Mulder, sis."

Kara smirked, simultaneously shaking her head and rolling her eyes. "That may be due to the fact that you make one pathetic Mulder, Bro." Each stood quietly for a full minute, the lack of both movement and sound from the adjacent forest raising the level of uneasiness already present.

"Sis, you recall that old issue where Captain America, during his 'Nomad' stage, had that knock down drag out with the Sub-Mariner? I think they were near the Lincoln Memorial at the time."

Covering his nose as a fresh breeze of foul air shot by, Kara nodded without speaking.

"Ol' Cap, Nomad I mean, got his head handed to 'im as I recall, am I right?"

"Yeah, I believe, but he didn't have a shield as Nomad, and old fish-boy was one stout amphibian," she pointed out, her stature suddenly like that of a campaigning politician addressing a gathering of would-be voters.

"Well, I gotta tell ya, sis. I get the feeling the solider boys there are playing the part of Nomad, *without* the shield."

"What do you mean, William?"

The expression he displayed was stoically grim, and for the first time that night, utterly humorless. Kara felt a sudden shudder and rubbed her arms through her cotton shirt.

"There's a Sub-Mariner lurking somewhere in that compound, sis. The *bad guy* Sub-Mariner from the old days, and a very pissed off version at that."

As if sprung from a catapult, Kara practically leaped forward until her upper body was mere inches from that of her taller sibling, who cringed back from the sudden, unexpected movement.

"Then what the hell are we doing here exactly, you stupid…*asshole?* If you feel that strongly that were stepping into some kind of ambush, and you obviously *have* since we got to this steaming turd of a town, then why aren't we back at camp roasting marshmallows instead of standing in the open like circled targets on a *shooting range*?"

Gripping her trembling shoulders firmly, Wilbo locked his eyes into hers until she broke the stare by peering down at her own feet. The twins shared only two very distinct and similar characteristics, one physical and in attitude. Their eyes, from the dark brown color to the almond shape, were jarringly analogous, and had belonged also to their missing mother. The basset hound/mule-like stubbornness each displayed was a trait plucked from their father's genes, and was normally unyielding despite the ultimate outcome of the argument involved.

"Kara, don't ask me how, but I know without a shadow of doubt that those GI's creepin' around this old prison has some sort of tie-in with mom and dad's disappearance," he released her suddenly limp form and punched his own chest with a clinched right fist.

"I know it in here. Deep down there's a nervous tingling I can't explain, and it isn't just fear causin' it."

His sister looked back up with a building moistness at the corners of eyes that could have easily been his own. Her look was beyond grave; it was nothing short of an expression drenched in total, devastating defeat.

"We're not leaving…this place alive, are we William?" She whimpered.

He placed his left hand upon her slumped shoulder, but this time with a tender gentleness previously absent. William had rarely had to play the role of 'manly brother' with his twin sister, who he knew to be the toughest, both mentally and physically, person he had ever known. He hardly relished the act, but saw it as a necessary action if they were to ever know what had become of their folks. He realized Kara was retreating into herself at lightning speed, and had to be snapped back just as quickly before the process passed the point of no return, where she would become nothing but a hindrance in the trying task facing them.

"Sis, do you really think I'd allow that to happen? We're here investigating a matter the authorities have chosen to ignore, remember? A matter that *only* you and I give a shit about, or ever will, it seems. I ain't gonna lie to you, there's a menace present here, and we may have to face it down before the night's done, but I need to know you're strong enough to accept that before we begin to follow-through."

He hesitated, giving her a full ten seconds to respond. Kara instead looked back to the outline of her shoes in the dusty ground below, her pursed lips seemingly welded together.

She had just begun to nod from side to side in a spastic 'no, no, no' gesture when the open palm connected with the left side of her face with a loud pop. Kara's head whipped hard to the right, then bounded back into its previous straight ahead position like a child's old weeble-wobble toy. No longer draped in fear, her expression swiftly shifted to one of shocked outrage.

"Chicken shit female. I should'a known you'd be about as useful as a white man on a basketball court out here. What's happened to you? I used to consider you the toughest broad I'd ever met. Scarlet Witch my ass…you're more like the *Yellow* Witch..." William blurted in utter disgust, his hands clinched in tightly wound fists at his sides. He found it an almost impossible task to refrain from laughing wildly. He could only hope the strategy paid off as predicted. If it backfired instead, he would be dealing with a total basket case for the remainder of the night.

"You son of a...! *ARRRGGGH!"* She screamed, charging forward with her head bowed like a makeshift battering ram.

As he tried to turn to one side to avoid his sister's wild rush, Wilbo's left foot slipped atop the slick dust pile it had been braced upon. As her rock-hard skull landed with a muted thud onto his breastbone, William performed an impromptu dancing jig, cackling wildly as the convulsing moon-dance sent him flying onto his back with his sister attached to his upper torso as if glued there.

"K-Kara, it's…I…it's okay...you don't have...to..." he babbled maniacally as she wriggled atop his temporarily pinned frame, just before the perfectly placed punch to his solar plexus emptied the remaining contents of his lungs.

"Miserable rat bastard! Nose picking, ass-digging shit-heel!" She continued to rant, pelting downward with a series of meticulously aimed punches and jabs, most of which were blocked away with frantic haste by her battered brother, who was choking from lack of oxygen.

Shoving upward with what little energy remained, his mouth wide open and lips sucking wind like a discarded fish lying on a creek-bank, Wilbo managed to toss his sister aside and roll away in a cloud of dust and tossed weed fragments.

"G-get...a-away...can't...c-can't b-breathe..." he mouthed, although the actual words were hardly audible.

Just as he managed to regain his footing, the left heel of her Reebok nailed him on the right side of his ribcage, just below the nipple. Slumped with both hands on his injured side, he was unable to visualize his sister's perfectly executed three-sixty maneuver, nor the clothesline backhand that accompanied it.

The side of her left fist landed with a loud smack behind his right ear, sending him crumpling to the ground with a hand dedicated to each separate wound.

Before he could inhale a single breath, she leapt

atop his back and wrapped both her slim arms around his throat in a makeshift 'sleeper' hold, steadily increasing the pressure while attempting to balance her weight.

Wilbo stumbled to his feet, kicking thick waves of dust, dirt and dead weeds into the air, a good majority of which landed in his open mouth and eyes.

After finally being able to brace himself without leaning too far in one direction, his sister growling while propped atop his back and head like a conjoined twin gone mad, Wilbo began to whirl and twist in an attempt to sling her off.

From a distance, they looked like two figure skaters attempting a show- stopping finale, the female athlete balanced atop the male as he executed a series of tightly wound spins.

Sometime between the third and fourth completed circle, she lost her grip and they both sailed airborne in opposite directions as if an invisible rubber band had unexpectedly snapped.

Kara flipped head over heels and landed on her back with a harsh gasp, her arms splayed out to her sides limply while her legs slowly curled up towards her chest.

Wilbo fell back onto his right side, the ribs there already throbbing like a rotted tooth from the earlier kick.

A moment later he stood over her, the palms of his hands balanced on his kneecaps. His breath was still labored, his left nostril bleeding slightly and his neck burning from the throttling it had endured. Despite the fact that his entire upper torso felt as if it had been beaten like a rug during an annual spring cleaning, he couldn't help but smile through the pain while looking down at his slowly reviving sister. He realized with not a small amount of relief that the fall she had taken had curbed, at least temporarily, the fight in her. The rage had subsided, or at least been re-directed elsewhere.

"Damn, Sis. I *meant* to touch a nerve, but not short-circuit 'em *all* at the same time. You okay?"

Leaning forward on her hands and knees, Kara spat dust and then coughed, all the while eyeballing her brother distastefully.

"You...*wanted* me to blow a fuse? You know how much I hate losing control and... using foul language like that," she mumbled, holding her lower back and grimacing while pushing herself up.

"Bad language? My internal organs feel like they've been pureed and my neck plucked from a vise, and your concerned about uttering the word 'shit' out loud?" He replied with an expression of pure bemusement.

Finally able to stand, Kara couldn't contain a giggle while staring at the unholy mess that was her twin brother.

His frazzled hair stood up in the front like some fifties pompadour, his face coated in dust like an actor from the silent film era. His shirt was pulled out from his jeans and hung freely from one side like a battered flag. Miraculously, his birth-control glasses had stayed glued to his nose throughout the tussle.

"Well, brother of mine, you did ask for it."

Nodding in obvious discomfort, Wilbo soothingly massaged his neck.

"True enough, but it had to be done, sis. I was

gonna lose you if I didn't light a quick fire beneath your rear end."

Like an embarrassed child, Kara watched her shoes make wide rows in the dust below.

"Wow. I can't remember the last time I went that ballistic, at least with you as the target. I blacked out there for a few."

Wilbo stepped forward and held out his right hand as if greeting her for the first time.

"I do. We were in the seventh grade and you caught me swiping the fiftieth issue of Spider-man from your wall closet. My right eye has never been the same, truth be told," he grinned.

Kara shook her brother's hand forcefully, then gave him a quick hug before backing away and wiping the fresh moisture from her eyes.

"I did nail you that time, didn't I?" She laughed, her voice cracking slightly. "Damn tootin'. I guess that self-defense class you took a few years back is still paying dividends, huh?"

As they strolled back to the rear of the shack, both were surprised at how much distance their little scrap had covered.

"I... guess. Those Taebo tapes hadn't hurt either. William?" "Yeah?"

They fell against the shack as one, both sighing in unison like marathon runners a few minutes past the finish line.

"I can't promise you I won't fold up in there, regardless of what we do or don't find."

Staring into his sister's wide, wet eyes, Wilbo felt an inner twinge that held two meanings. One was undeniably pity. A pity for the lives he and his sister had been forced to endure from those with little or no tolerance for anyone who didn't fall into a specific, 'cookie-cutter' category of looks or personality. A pity for those things he and his sister would never experience, regardless of the night's outcome.

They had existed with their own personal storm clouds flowing overhead and trailing them since birth. There was no understanding such a condition; it was simply what a small percentage of society were dealt at inception. You either accepted it and bravely trudged forward or perished underneath its suffocating, intrusive presence.

Kara and himself had always fallen into the former category, battling their way through the seemingly endless pitfalls with forced grins and constantly shrugging shoulders.

Wilbo knew this was the night one or both of them would surrender the stigma once and for all. They hadn't just been brought here to solve the mystery of their missing elders, but to test their own mental fortitude against a force that normally fed upon such as themselves like a ravenous grizzly upon it's wounded, crippled prey. A presence that reveled in toying with, torturing, and invariably *consuming* the very souls of the isolated, downtrodden masses that were its main source of energy and the very life-force that sustained it.

Winking playfully, William shot Kara a smile that beamed of sincerity, and for once, felt entirely just so.

"You'll be just fine, Tigress. Keep those claws of yours honed and at the ready, just in case we need 'em. I also brought ya this. I believe you know how to use it."

The taser gun fit snugly into her right jean pocket. It was the same weapon she had been forced to use on a would-be parking lot assailant months earlier, and one that her brother knew she felt the most comfortable handling. He had considered bringing another handgun along, possibly the Glock nine millimeter, but knew Kara's feelings about revolvers in general, and decided on the taser instead. Kara pocketed the tiny weapon without argument or hesitation.

Peering past the shed and into the waiting gloom that would soon envelop them both, Wilbo took a deep whiff of the rank wind as it breezed by.

"I guess no one heard our little WWF match, or we'd sure as hell have company by now. You ready to motivate, sis?" He asked while turning to gauge her expression, which was beginning to harden a bit as seconds passed.

"I'm right behind you, old sharer of wombs. Thanks for the wake-up call. No doubt I desperately needed it," she replied stoically.

As they cleared the shack and stepped forward, their pace increasing as the main entrance danced dimly into view under the sparse moonlight provided, Wilbo reached back until his sisters hand was tucked securely into his own. He felt the rigid stiffness of the thirty-eight digging into the pit of his back, but oddly felt no sense of security associated with it.

"Where's the Avengers when ya need 'em, huh?" He quipped.

Kara whispered back, struggling to keep in step with her taller, lankier brother.

"Right about now, I'd settle for Mighty

Mouse."

***

Jimmy had watched in morbid fascination as the two combatants had rolled about the grass and dirt behind the old shed, the larger and presumably male of the two taking a defensive measure against the smaller, possibly female, aggressor.

He felt as if he were watching some sort of pay per view event, only live and staged for his own personal viewing discomfort. By the time the two figures had made peace and then tracked off into the same direction as the soldiers had before them, Jimmy's breathing had at least normalized somewhat.

This is growing weirder by the minute, Jim old buddy. Those two didn't seem to be wearing uniforms, as far as I could tell anyway. Maybe they were escaped inmates or...yeah, sure. Escaped inmates breaking back into the prison. Jeez, Louise, pull your head from your...

A distinct popping sound, a brittle branch being stepped on and shattered, not only instantly broke Jimmy's train of thought, but sent him flailing backwards, slipping off of the tree and landing butt-first into a pile of wind-blown leaves.

"Who's there?" He croaked weakly, now ducking behind the thick log and peering over its slick edges. Jimmy realized with some degree of terror that the noise's originator could have been standing less than two feet away from him, and he'd never know it until *they* decided to be properly introduced.

The laughter that ensued was a*nything* but soothing, its tone equally satirical and sarcastic in nature. It was also strangely garbled, as if the originator spoke through a jaw full of marbles.

Jimmy started to call out just as he spotted movement to his right. His mouth opened to inquire just as the bright sparks of light filled his senses. He felt no pain as his body rolled over on its side, just a hapless feeling of being levitated just above the ground as if connected to wiring from the dangling tree limbs hanging overhead.

Jimmy heard giggling, faint and unreal, as if it were being broadcast from a TV or radio transmission miles away. He was able to visualize the shape of a man's head leaning upside down over his own, the facial features of the mysterious visitor blurred and unclear. The head was nothing more than a large black dot, while the breath that emerged from the cackling skull to slap Jimmy's forehead was easily identifiable, nauseatingly so. It was the same rank, sewage- like air that seemed to encircle the prison compound like a sweeping mist.

Jimmy managed to gag, or at least attempt such a reflex just before the dark, comforting blanket of unconsciousness was lay atop his prone form, the throbbing wound at the base of his skull finally revealing itself through the slowly fading numbness.

"Who is this fat jackass, Buck?" JC queried, keeping his distance from Jimmy's still form, the flashlight beam he aimed scanning it repeatedly from feet to head.

Buck was bent over the body like a doped-up mortician prepping a corpse for drainage. JC noticed his partner actually sniffing the man's face, particles of yellowish skin falling away like flecks of dandruff from Buck's cheeks and forehead.

"Dunno, JC old fart, but he sure as heck picked the wrong night for star gazin', am I right or am I right?" Buck finally replied, rising to his feet and sizing up the body like a starving man peering down at a fully cooked turkey posed atop a silver platter.

JC pulled a bottom tooth free and casually tossed into some nearby weeds before again speaking.

"You think he's from the prison? Not wearin' a uniform or inmate duds." "Not sure…don't care. Whoever he be, he be comin' with us, JC old bud, old confidant. Large one, ain't he? Man ain't missed a meal in many, many moons, I'd venture to say. The master is gonna like him for sure. Nice and plump, and probably damn juicy to boot."

Feeling a sudden stomach cramp, JC turned and projectile vomited for at least the fourth time that night. Afterwards, wiping the reddish drool from his bearded chin, he secretly wondered if a man could actually barf up his own innards and still manage to remain upright and functioning.

He could have sworn he saw something resembling a hunk of liver sail onto the trunk of a nearby elm. It had hung onto the bark for a split-second, like a slimy black slug, before slowly descending onto the dirt below.

"Buck, I'm gonna hurl up a lung if this shit keep up…what's goin' on, man? You gotta tell me. I ain't never seen it like this..." he practically pleaded through pus-coated lips.

His head again thrown back like a howling wolf, Buck's shrieking howls echoed through the dead air like a klaxon inside a narrow tunnel.

When he finally spoke, the tone revealed had been altered somehow, deeper but at the same time bizarrely flat and mechanical.

JC shuttered despite himself.

"Surrender to it, man, don't *fight* it. You're refusing to accept the change, that's what it boils down to. Part of you wants to hang on to the shell. Natural response, I guess. But you gotta let it go, JC. It's nothin' less than ecstasy, I tell ya. It's like havin' a thousand orgasms at once, and the feelin' *don't fade*! Let it go, old buddy, just flow with the glow!"

Like a man afire, Buck ripped his cotton shirt apart with a savage series of jerks, sending buttons flying loose like shrapnel from an exploding grenade.

The skin of his chest and abdomen shone like the bulb of a child's fluorescent nightlight. Previously coated in rich black hair from his lower neck to just below his navel, it was slick and moist, as if recently shaved and moisturized. Even from a dozen feet away, the pungent aroma of decomposing flesh overwhelmed all other scents, including the rancid smell already enveloping the area around the Briarston compound.

JC, void of most of his teeth and reeking like death himself, his entire body a half-ripe boil of infectious bodily fluids, couldn't help but cringe back from the spectacle.

"Hellfire, Buck. Y-your skin is g-glowing like a sparkler on the 4th of July!" He croaked, backing away in disgust.

Buck flexed his chest and bare arms like a

bodybuilder executing a rehearsed routine. His sinewy arms, flabby chest and midsection contorted and shook wildly, pieces of soggy skin falling free in long, thin strands.

"Burnin' up, dude! Feel like I've been swimming in lit charcoal! Damn, this hurts like hell *and* feels like the best damn sex I've ever had at the same time! Ya gotta love it!" He bellowed while dancing about like a street break-dancer from two decades earlier.

"B-Buck? What are we gonna do with fat boy here? Leave 'im be like the spook GI or what?" JC asked somewhat timidly, viewing his friend and co-conspirator for the past two decades plus with a queasy uneasiness.

"Nope, negative, no way. Old chubby cheeks here is gonna walk right onto the site with us, JC old salt. I could chunk his lard coated behind on my back, but I do believe we need to save our energy for more…*pressing* issues to come."

Buck's multi-layered gut, meticulously constructed over decades of heavy beer drinking and a diet consisting mostly of carbohydrates and starch, sagged over his belt line like layers of thick flour dough as he bent down and placed the palms of his hands on either side of Jimmy's scalp.

"Let me see if I can revive old sleeping ugly," he whispered in demonic glee.

"Parties about to begin, JC my brother. Just thinkin' about meetin' the MC of this little skin-dig has my Willie swollen like a New Year's Day parade float," he added, just before he began to apply subtle pressure to the fallen man's skull.

***

Once they had passed through the deserted sally port and through to the compound grounds themselves, Private Kemp felt the tingling begin in the lower section of her gut.

The sally port's paved surface had been riddled in what seemed like hundreds of sets of shoe tracks. Shoes tracks that had been embedded in a dark, sticky substance that all realized instantly *was not* red paint. The coppery smell that should have accompanied such ample bloodshed was strangely absent, but that was easily explained due to the overpowering fragrance already present within the site.

"Couldn't smell a rotted stiff if ya stepped on it," Corporal McIntosh had commented as they tiptoed their way through the second double-door entrance/exit doors that led into the compound.

Private Bodine had mentioned, in a tone better suited for a parched man begging for a glass of water, if the Major might reconsider leaving the firearms behind and have the unit retrieve them instead.

Sergeant Ezop, although hesitant to do so, had begun to pass on the query when Major Peterson, stepping forward at a snail's pace but still a good twenty-five yards from Lomax's position, answered in a voice that sent cold chills through everyone present.

"Move forward and await further instructions. Someone in there needs aid, not shot at," he had barked gravely, the words sounding as if they had been spoken from a closed coffin already half-covered with freshly tossed soil.

"How did he hear...?" Private Bodine had cried to no one in particular. Corporal McIntosh snickered, a reaction Private Kemp found utterly astonishing. She felt as if she were being led directly into the gaping gates of Hell itself, unarmed at that, although the urge to turn and haul her carcass in the opposite direction wasn't the least bit enticing. She knew the others felt the same way, but were also inexplicably drawn forward, reluctant to refuse the madman's order to proceed. It was like they were being controlled like pawn pieces, unable, and in some ways *unwilling* to escape the playing board they walked upon.

"As Isiah might say if he had been so kind to accompany us, this shit is getting downright *whack,*" the Corporal had quipped after Private Bodine's half- spoken plea, his own words laced with a barely masked anxiety that Kemp suddenly realized was dangerous close to being revealed. Revealed in all its glory despite the false bravado at its core. If Ron McIntosh was on the verge of cracking, Private Kemp secretly wondered how long it would take before she began to scream aloud.

The admin building loomed roughly fifty yards ahead, everything but the metal sign proclaiming '*Briarston Correctional Facility In-processing/Visitor Center*' cloaked in shadows and the occasional trail of smoke. Taking in the perfectly squared building with its flat red brick construction and lack of windows (at least on floor one), Private Kemp couldn't help but be reminded of all the horror films she had viewed that were set in institutions for the criminally insane. The lack of trees, scrubs, or any other type vegetation around the building increased the overall mystique of impending dread, and Private Kemp could see everyone in front of her visibly tense as they neared. All that is, save one, who led the blind charge with nothing less than a cheery skip in his walk.

Major Peterson halted at the front steps of the entrance, his gloved hands on his hips, stoically waiting for the rest of the unit to catch up.

One by one they formed a horizontal formation just to his left, all staring ahead at the stone building ahead as if it were a recently discovered Aztec pyramid.

"Sir, are we...going to investigate inside or just stick to the outside grounds as discussed?" Sergeant Ezop asked a bit fearfully, his arms posed stiffly at his sides as if preparing to snap to attention.

The Major was eyeballing the heavy oak double door entrance further up the paved walkway, his arms now crossed over his chest. Private Kemp noticed the Sergeant keeping a fair distance from his fearless leader, and it wasn't the least bit difficult to figure out why. Even with the thick stench of fresh sewage all around them, the rank odor emanating from their commander was impossible to escape. He smelled like walking diarrhea and recently vomited buttermilk.

Turning around slowly, his movements a bit robotic, Major Peterson reached up and tugged the front of his beret downward, leaving it a bit lopsided as it covered the majority of his forehead.

"Sergeant, you and I will do a quick policing of the admin building, first floor only. Corporal McIntosh, Private Bodine and Private Kemp will do the same around the perimeter of his structure only. We will meet at the back exit in...' he paused to check the camouflage banded sports-watch on his right wrist, 'exactly ten minutes. Corporal, you *got* that?"

Corporal McIntosh, his head cocked to one side, had been staring at Peterson with the curiosity one might associate with a biologist scrutinizing a new strain of virus. He straightened his pose just before responding, seemingly shocked to have been addressed at all.

"Uh, got it, Major. Ten minutes at the rear door. Sir?"

Major Peterson answered while turning his attention back to the front entrance, his words still mysteriously garbled, as if he were chewing on a mouthful of red hots.

"What is it, McIntosh?" He asked wearily.

"I don't know about the others, Sir, but I couldn't see my own prick hangin' out here. Can we go ahead and don the vision goggles?"

When Peterson didn't provide an instantaneous reply, Private Kemp took advantage of the opportunity to inject some (what she thought at least) was some much needed humor.

"In your case, you might try using a magnifying glass, Clyde."

When the only snicker to follow was her own, Private Kemp paused before huffing in embarrassed frustration.

"But seriously folks," she added, a new wave of fear punching her solar- plexus like an anvil.

"By all means, utilize the equipment. Great opportunity to get in that much-needed training.

Plus I don't want anyone coming out of here with broken bones from sauntering around blindly. Radio if you run across anything you deem out of the ordinary, Corporal."

"No problem there, Sir. If a mouse farts in my vicinity, you'll know about it ASAP."

The Major grunted, motioning a 'dismissed' gesture with his right arm. "Sergeant, let us investigate the mystery ahead," he muttered in the same low, guttural tone as earlier, stepping forward only after donning his own goggles.

The doors swung open freely, creaking a bit as they were shoved inward by the gloved palms of Major David Peterson, whose entire body shuddered upon entry, racked by a series of orgasmic-like pleasure that threatened to induce a temporary black-out. Sergeant Ezop did not witness his commander's upper body jerk spasmodically or his legs grow rubbery just as he stepped into the pitch-black foyer. The Sergeant had instead been entranced by the outside surface of the left door itself, which was coated in countless thin streams of semi- dried liquid. Liquid that shone bright crimson within the circled lenses of his night vision goggles. Sergeant Ezop now understood what the Major had been staring at from the entrance steps, although how the man had visualized the coppery smelling substance from that distance was a mystery he had little time to dwell upon.

"Sir, did you see the d..." he croaked, holding the door at the top to avoid the paste-like gobs drying just inches from his face.

"I saw it, Sergeant. Possibly there are survivors of whatever massacre has transpired here. Let's search them out post haste," the Major barked, already standing inside the narrow foyer. An electronic checkpoint, like those commonly seen in airports, was positioned just a few feet inside. Peterson shot it a wry glance and walked through towards the center of the room, which seemed so wide as to take up the majority of the floor itself.

The Sergeant allowed the door to shut behind him, and made his way past the security point like a man walking in a minefield. He could see the Major a dozen feet ahead, heading towards a crooked maze of office partisans and filing cabinets.

"Sir? Don't you think we should, um, arm ourselves in case we engage the hostiles responsible for...?"

"There are no hostiles here, Sergeant, at least not anymore. Whoever is responsible has obviously made tracks. More than likely it seems we've stumbled across a rather messy prison break. Let's keep the chatter to a minimum from here on out. I want to be able to hear any injured parties who might not have to strength to raise their voices."

The Sergeant, stepping past a series of office cubicles manned with identical PC's, matching desks, sliding chairs, and small metal filing cabinets, started to disagree and stopped short. He peered up and caught a glimpse of a hanging sign which read 'Visitors Center- check in to the RIGHT - Outside Law Enforcement Officials to the LEFT', and came dangerously close to tripping over what looked to be a woman's leather purse lying between two cubicles.

The purse contents were spilling from an open pouch, although he was unable to identify anything specific through the goggles.

When he looked back up, the Major was nowhere in sight. Proceeding forward at a double time pace, Sergeant Ezop winced at the shooting pains at his bladder. He cursed himself for the jolts of cowardice bubbling to the surface of his usually rock-solid psyche. Half-sprinting towards the only hallway the entire floor provided, he reached down with his right hand and felt for the familiar bulge strapped to the outside of his left thigh. The camouflage casing made it almost invisible to the naked eye when it was tucked next to the similarly designed uniform pants. Ezop secretly thought of it as his 'Ten Inches of Instant Courage', a serrated stainless-steel blade with a marble handle, the letters 'D.E.-NCO' (Dark Eagle Non-Commissioned Officer) engraved within. Satisfied he wasn't sailing into the unknown completely unarmed, he jogged down the slim hall with his arms tucked in like a tailback preparing to streak through a break in the defensive line.

The hall circled around to the left, a line of offices coming into view on each side. Ezop was able to read a few of the attached door plates as he sailed by, such titles as 'Parole Staff Supervisor' and 'Chaplain Mizer' scanned over and just as quickly forgotten.

As he neared a set of metal doors with a clearly marked 'EXIT' sign hanging above, Ezop thought of turning back and retracing his steps, pondering how he had managed to lose the Major.

"Where in blue blazes?" He whispered, removing his beret and scratching his sweat-moistened scalp.

Instead of reversing his direction, he carefully shoved the metal doors ahead a few inches and peaked through the opening like a peeping tom through an open window.

The 'Exit' actually led into a spacious conference room, complete with two lengthy oak tables with at least a dozen padded chairs on the outside, an audio/video set-up and instructors table at the center, and a speaker's podium fronting a wide, pull-down white movie screen at the far end. A trio of large candles burned atop a desk at the room's south end, allowing the Sergeant to hastily remove his night goggles.

After executing a perfectly choreographed double take, Sergeant Ezop spotted the posed, motionless figure standing just to the left side of the podium.

The Major stood at parade rest, his hands cupped at his back, as if waiting to be introduced as the guest speaker of the evening.

"Sergeant, I do believe I'm beginning to comprehend our roles in this little drama," he said without turning. Sergeant Ezop felt a new series of chills shoot up and down his spine like an endless roller coaster ride fueled by his own fear.

"Sir…the sign outside lists this as an exit. I thought you had already cleared the building..." he began while stepping into the room in a semi-crouch, as if an attack were eminent.

"Actually, I deduced the same just a few moments ago, Sergeant. There actually is an exit door at the rear of the room, but I'm not at all sure why this conference room was left unannounced."

The Major remained motionless as Ezop made

his way forward down the center of the oak tables, the Sergeant's head whipping back and forth in an effort to at least marginally scan the immediate vicinity. It was pure instinct to do so, the nature of the beast. 'Born and bred a grunt' Ezop would tell others whenever asked about his stoic outward appearance and rigid, cut-to-the-chase attitude.

"You found something significant, sir?" He asked while taking the first series of steps upward onto the roomy stage area.

The Major finally shifted as his second in command neared his position, twisting his upper torso to the left just enough to remain concealed.

"I indeed have, my son. The most significant thing one can discover in this lifetime, I personally believe..." the Major replied, swinging around in a lurch, his arms held out in a classic shooters pose, his gloved left hand resting just beneath the right.

"…that being the moment in time we accept our true lord and savior into our hearts and allow him to cleanse our rotting souls."

Almost toppling backward from the edge of the podium, Sergeant Ezop regained his balance only after flapping his arms wildly, like a man literally attempting to take flight. The barrel of the Glock .357 being pointed at his chest was easily recognizable as one the Major had used at a Little Rock firing range both men had frequented in the past.

"Uh...Major? What the hell, over? You...uh...feeling all right?" He managed, never taking his eyes off the weapon being held so stiffly in his direction and at such a horrifically short distance.

The Major's stance relaxed a bit as he casually backed up a step.

"Sarge, I have to say, in all honesty, I've *never* felt better in all my years. Hard to explain, but it's kind of like experiencing a never-ending climax coupled with the finest alcohol buzz ever known. Can't say it's doing much for my physical appearance, however. Then again, I've never considered myself the 'pretty boy' type."

The Glock's gleaming eye still staring him down from less than two feet away, Sergeant Ezop's sputtering mind could only manage two reasonably logical explanations for the mad scenario being played out. Number one: the whole compound had been laced with some sort of mind-altering chemical weapon, and the Major had been the first to succumb to its initial symptoms. Number two: Major David Peterson was executing perhaps the most warped practical joke ever conceived, and would soon drop the revolver to his side and burst out in hysterical laughter.

The Sergeant silently prayed for explanation number two while, in case the nod was eventually given to number one, slowly dropped his right hand towards the blade tucked against his thigh.

"Leave the steak knife be, Sergeant. Courage is one thing, but stupidity is quite another," the Major barked, his voice nothing more than a gravelly croak. The Sergeant instantly straightened and placed his hands on his sides in frustration.

"Sir? Is there something I should know about this particular mission? Some sort of elaborate gag on my behalf?"

The Major didn't respond other than a brief

side-to-side nodding of his shadow-engulfed head, the positioning of the weapon unwavering.

"I get the feeling some serious greenbacks are being passed around, and that I was conveniently left out of the loop, is that it?"

The Major scoffed while tugging at the goggles hanging from his neck with his free hand.

"Money, Jeffrey? I must say; I'm beyond disappointment in the light of such an accusation. I will admit, however, that until a few hours ago, it would not have been *beneath* me to entertain such unscrupulous acts of greed or personal gluttony. Things have changed dramatically within such a frighteningly short time period, however. Attitudes have been adjusted and souls have been *guided* onto the correct path, Jeffrey. I stand here a new man, washed in the clear waters and bursting at the seams to share my happiness."

The words of his commanding officer were only partially heard, as Sergeant Jeffrey Ezop, a life-long Southern Baptist and hard-line believer in both heaven and hell, carefully studied what he figured must be a clear sign from the latter of those locales.

Major Peterson's eyes spewed forth a yellowish glare that had previously been hidden by the goggles, twin beams of light that not only enveloped the entirety of the older man's sockets, but allowed his shocked subordinate a crystal-clear view of the melting, dripping horror his face had become.

"I simply want to invite you to look into the light as well, Sergeant Ezop," the Major gurgled through lips that drooped downward as if weighed down by some unseen force, and which seemed to be literally peeling away like a fat, wriggling worms from moistened dirt.

The Major's forehead was riddled with what looked like fish scales, his exposed neck layered in moist, shedding flesh like that from a recent burn victim.

Sergeant Ezop raised his arms and revealed his palms in a defensive gesture, as if to block out the grisly vision.

"Sir…I... uh, you need medical assistance. M-maybe we can find the infirmary..." he babbled, unable to refrain from staring into the other man's hypnotic glare despite great effort.

Without warning, the Major rushed forward, jamming the revolver's barrel against the center of Sergeant's Ezop's chest with a muffled thud. The muscular NCO felt his bladder twinge, begging for immediate release.

"Keep quiet a moment, Jeffrey. Give me a chance to explain my small but pivotal role in this large-scale production. I feel it essential to do so."

"Sir, y-you're ill. I mean, really, really ill. Y-your face and neck..."

With his free hand, the Major waived him off, his smile hideously warped but somehow sympathetic.

"I found the opening during our 'search and destroy' mission, just before spotting and taking out Sergeant Chambers and the two privates with the rubber ammo. Almost fell in the cursed thing, actually. Damn near snapped my left ankle before managing to regain my balance enough to at least land on my butt cheeks in some tall weeds instead of taking a header into a bottomless sinkhole."

The barrel of the revolver pushed through the Sergeant's uniform shirt and the black T-shirt underneath until it pressed firmly against the center of his breastbone. Sergeant Ezop sucked in quick breaths and tried to hold them as long as possible to avoid the arid stench sweeping through the room in sickeningly heated waves.

"I recall rolling to my feet, hoping the excess commotion from my fall wouldn't alert my quarry, when the first breeze of that heavenly odor blew my way. Truth be told, Jeffrey, I considered it quite sour and unpleasant at the time, but after a time it kinda grows on you. Honestly, grows *in* you might be more accurate.

Regardless, by the time I arose from peaking inside the opening's seemingly infinite interior, my perspective was already altering in subtle yet dramatic ways."

"S-Sir? I'm fairly sure you've been exposed to a chemical agent of some kind, possibly buried within this 'hole' you mentioned. Maybe something the Briarston folks were experimenting with.

P-please, let me seek help for you. Any or all of us might be next," the Sergeant practically pleaded as he managed to focus his attention squarely upon the Major's suddenly heaving chest.

"Sergeant, there is no 'might' factor here. You and the rest of the Dark Eagle militia present here tonight will most definitely be…*next,* as you called it. I brought you and the others here to revel in the wondrous, unspeakable joys of his majestic company.

This is a night like no other, Sergeant Ezop."

Feeling as if his entire being was one massive

nerve ending, Sergeant Ezop purposely tensed the muscles in his arms, legs and chest to fight off the tremors building within. The last thing he wanted was to visibly display the stark fear that was gradually sweeping over his being like a paralyzing dose of snake venom.

"All the past conflicts, arguments, frustrations that this life rings upon us mean absolutely zilch now. I know you don't comprehend the big picture yet, but fear not; it will come to you in a single blazing moment of realization. First, however, measures must be taken to ensure compliance. Nothing personal here, Sergeant, you understand. I've always trusted and depended on you, something I cannot say about the others within the unit. I thought I could trust Chambers, but he reverted to his hard-headed, argumentative, 'what's in it for me,' self, and left me no choice but take decisive action."

Swallowing hard, Sergeant Ezop felt the pressure at his bladder intensify to the point of bursting from within.

"What did y-you do with Isiah, Sir?"

The Major's gruesome sneer faded, the few teeth that remained in his rapidly deteriorating mouth cloaked by slug-like lips that curled together like purple maggots upon a chunk of rancid meat.

"Sergeant Chambers will be retrieved from the wooded area I left him lying in, but unfortunately, he will remain soulless in death, a useable yet tragically discarded blimp on the screen within the grand scheme of things. I met...others in those woods. A kinship was instantly formed between us. Your enlightenment will not be long in coming,

Jeffrey. Fear not, all of this will make perfect sense very, very soon."

Bowing his head slightly as if in mourning, The Major titled the revolver's barrel to the tip of the Sergeant's pug nose.

"Our savior can find a use for Chamber's damned soul, as he has many others who passed before absorption, but he truly prefers a living, breathing sacrifice. One he can absorb and gain immediate power from for the mission ahead. I only wish my own pathetic contribution to his cause could be of a higher significance."

Just as a tiny droplet of sweat fell from his left nostril onto the tip of the Glock's shiny barrel, Sergeant Ezop's last remaining fuse within the realm of sanity's control box simmered, crackled, popped and finally burned away in a single blink of his bloodshot eyes.

He first leaned back and then lunged forward like a man attempting a head butt. Veins the size of cable cords stood out on his neck and forehead. His hands were clinched clubs, the fingers balled up inside the palms like nesting rattlers.

"Who the *FUCK* is this savior you keep jabbering about, you raving fucking *LUNATIC?"*

The Major never flinched, just raised a single finger to his bacteria-ridden mouth in a mock 'shushing' gesture.

"Now, now, Sergeant, let's not have any of that. Like I said, you'll understand soon enough. Like I also said, it's nothing personal."

The Sergeant's gaze was still locked on the Major's twitchy, jiggling lips, the bottom of which fell loose with a small sucking sound and landed to the right of his commander's left boot. Peering down at the purplish, larva-like object in total dismay, Jeffery Ezop was prepping for a combination howl/scream just as the lengthy, circular object made forceful contact just above his left ear.

By the time the sparks cleared from underneath his closed eyelids and vision was restored, he seemed to be levitating above the scene formed on the conference table below.

The Sergeant was lying flat on his back as the Major stood stiffly at one end of the relatively narrow table, while an additional uniformed (although not of the militia) man bent down over his motionless body from the other side.

His line of vision began to rotate from table to ceiling level, as if he were being allowed separate camera angles with each fluttering of his spastic eyelids.

From table level he could read the nametag hanging above the right shirt pocket of the mystery man, illuminated in part by the same scarlet-shaded eyes afflicting his commander.

The tag read 'J. Dickenson'. As the man knelt beside him, the bill of the faded blue cap he wore also came clearly into view, the words inscribed there adding a baffling new chapter to the building mystery. It had read 'MDCJ', thus explaining the dark colored uniform the man sported as being that of a correctional officer.

Just before his ground view once again switched to the 'eye in the sky' monitor, Sergeant Ezop caught a whiff of the man leaning over his torso. He held the same toxic stench as the commander, but astonishingly intensified.

Floating a few feet from his own outstretched form, the Sergeant seemed to be witnessing a ritualistic act performed solely for his own viewing displeasure. His floating self was unable to object to what was taking place, for if such had been possible, a banshee like scream would have echoed off the quiet walls of the conference room as a Klaxon of dire warning to his militia comrades presently roaming the prison grounds.

"Careful not to sever any major plumbing, Jerrod. The last thing we need is a gushing wound at this point. Enough damn blood spilt on these grounds tonight as it is. I wish I could have simply shot him in the feet and hands, but the retorts from the Glock would have set off a most extreme reaction from my troops, I'm afraid."

The younger man leaned up, the mutilated, ravaged features of his face like that of a wax dummy in the aftermath of a blazing fire.

His mouth was all gums, void of lips and teeth, and his nose nothing more than two marble-sized punctures.

"No problem, Major Peterson. After the fiasco with the other guards, I've learned my lesson. The inner rage should be suppressed until the master himself releases the reigns. How's this?" He said huskily, revealing yellow gums that dripped gelled gobs of pus onto the table below as he backed away from the table like an abstract artist awaiting critique.

Major Peterson, his right hand massaging his scalp and pulling away chunks of his short-cropped hair and layers of flesh in the process, leaned down over the body and gave it a quick but thorough once over.

The floating spirit of Sergeant Jeffrey Ezop recoiled, realizing his physical self would spend the rest of his days, however limited that might turn out to be, without the ten cleanly severed fingers that lay atop the table like an uncooked entree prepared by a mad, cannibalistic butcher.

The disembodied spirit drifted downward into its disfigured shell just as the Major leaned back up and seemed to grin directly into its progressively descending, panic-stricken eyes.

"Perfectly executed, my good man. What are those called, bone shears? Look more like the tree limb variety."

The guard held the scissor-like instrument eye-level to the Major, the curve blades still dripping red.

"Got 'em in the infirmary, along with some other goodies that might come in handy. Ready to cauterize the wounds, Major?"

Retrieving the small handheld torch from a nearby white tray, Major Peterson thumbed a switch and the room was instantaneously filled with a thin streak of blue flame. The younger man held up the left hand of the downed man from the elbow and nodded amiably.

"I do believe this will curtail any worries about young Mister Ezop putting up a fight during transportation to the site, don't you agree, Officer Dickenson?" the Major beamed, reaching over to scorch the ends of the bloody nubs, the scent of burned flesh overcoming all others present.

“Right as *rain,* Major. And besides, we both know the savior is a peaceful soul at heart,” Jerrod Dickenson replied, happily inhaling the rising tendrils of smoke like a man leaning over a batch of freshly cut roses.

“It is a bit puzzling why we… weren’t instructed simply to drug them with the readily available tranquilizers, but I… have to confess, it wouldn’t have been near the fun,” Peterson replied between coughs as the scent of cooked meat filled the conference room.

***

Private Sandra Kemp dug her gloved left hand deep into the crotch of her loose camouflage pants. The irritating, burning itch between her butt cheeks was only getting worse. Hours earlier, long before the moonlight excursion into the dark, desolate grounds of the Briarston Correctional Facility, she had enjoyed a long, satisfying bowel movement at the base of a rather ragged looking spruce tree. It was her first such occurrence in over forty-eight hours, her system finally adapting to both the outdoor locale and the lack of deep, peaceful slumber associated with such. The campouts were the closest she would ever come to actually experiencing jetlag, the combination of night air, nature’s midnight chorus of sounds, and assorted biting and stinging bugs normally the culprit in temporarily snapping the springs of her inner clock.

As luck (or lack thereof) would have it, Private Bodine had decided to take a nature-stroll in her general vicinity just as the task of self-cleaning had begun, forcing her to halt the procedure before completion. Thus the searing itch and pinching, probing fingers, which followed suit.

Corporal McIntosh led them down the narrow, paved walkway that led past the admin building's eastside, the only such trail within the fenced compound that allowed bypassing the structure altogether.

Private Kemp noticed that the Corporal walked with his knees slightly bent, his arms held chest high in a blocking stance, and his head pointing straight ahead. In complete contrast, Private Bodine trailed behind like a lost pup in a sea of fog, his arms hanging loosely and his gait as wobbly as a drunken sailor on a three-day shore leave.

Private Kemp, her scalp tingling underneath her beret as if swarming with ravenous fleas, figured Private Bodine was simply in a state of fear-induced shock at their mere presence inside the compound. She would have bet a month of militia pay (not exactly an outlandish wager due to her rank) that an inspection of his underwear would reveal a Hershey squirt trail as long and winding as the concrete path they now trudged along.

The side of the admin building they visualized while passing was entirely windowless, nothing but the outline of its jagged brick walls perceptible through the night goggles each donned.

Shivering involuntarily as her left shoulder brushed its unexpectedly cool surface, Private Kemp quickly sidestepped to the right to expand the distance between herself and the wall. For some unknown reason, she felt safer near the perimeter fencing on her right than the looming structure on the opposite side. She couldn't help but feel a negative vibe being emitted from somewhere inside, like they were strolling past a stony, mass gravesite.

Looking forward as they neared the rear of the building, she noticed Private Bodine staring down at his boots, his frail arms waving back and forth lazily, like a bored child kicking a stone along a deserted pathway.

"Lomax, are you still with us?" Corporal McIntosh's voice broke in harshly. Private Kemp saw the Corporal had removed his goggles and was walking backward, staring at Private Bodine in total befuddlement.

The Private didn't respond, instead choosing to continue be-bopping forward with a low hum escaping his pursed lips.

"Earth to Private Lomax Bodine, come in, *Dumb*-ax..." the Corporal spouted, reaching forward with one hand and lightly punching the smaller man's right shoulder, instantly stopping him in his tracks.

"W-what? Did you say...*what?"* The Private mumbled, his mouth and hands trembling with equal verve, the tightly donned goggles giving him the look of an ancient miner.

Private Kemp slumped to a dragging halt a few feet to the rear, pulled her own goggles free and then began digging at her rear end with both hands.

"Are we having fun, sunshine? You wanna pay a little more attention to your surroundings, Lomax? This ain't exactly the *playground* at the Y were roaming through, y'know," the Corporal said sternly, taking a quick look over his shoulder at the fenced in exercise yard a few hundred feet in the distance.

Smirking, Private Kemp turned briefly to check their flank and immediately released a low gasp. She pulled her goggles back over her head and hurriedly re-scanned the same area. There were two distinct shapes moving cautiously through the second set of sally port fences a full hundred yards back. Ducking down on pure instinct, despite the openness of their location, Private Kemp threw her right arm back and waived spastically, attempting to catch the Corporal's attention without having to speak.

"What the hell is it, Kemp? You got hemorrhoids or what? This ain't the time nor place to squat and pee," the Corporal, after re-fitting his Night Vision headgear, finally responded, looking past the deflated looking Private who stood between them. His body instantly stiffened as the shadowy forms came into view.

"Looks like company. Let's double-time it over to the rear of the admin building and wait for the Major," the Corporal whispered before reaching over and grasping Private Bodine by the shirt collar and jerking him brusquely forward.

"Pull your head *out*, Lomax. We may actually need you later, and a walking veggie ain't very useful. Let's go."

Private Bodine's face was only inches away, and Corporal McIntosh could smell the sourness of the younger man's breath. He could only compare it to undercooked pork gone to seed.

"Isn't going to matter, Ron old buddy. We're all dead meat, pal. Don't you feel it?" Private Bodine replied in an apathetic tone that fired a bolt-like shiver up the visibly perplexed Corporal's spine.

Private Kemp dashed by, heading for the glass-domed breezeway a few dozen feet to their left.

"Face it, Mac, young Master Lomax has misplaced his testicles," she quipped while walking briskly by, adjusting her goggles for at least the tenth time since entering the grounds.

"He's right though, something stinks here, and it ain't just the air."

The Corporal kept the slowly moving shapes in his sites even as he pulled Private Bodine ahead, eventually forced to physically haul the smaller man towards the breezeway, which connected the admin building to a smaller, single story structure. He could read the body language of the two mysterious new arrivals to the darkened compound, their movements rigid and supremely cautious.

"They're blind as bats, not even a flashlight between 'em," he mumbled, finally forced to break visual contact as he rounded the squared edge of the admin building.

The dark tinted, circular dome breezeway was fronted by a mini-guard shack, consisting of a one-room wooden structure that was just roomy enough to house a single individual. The glass door entrance to the breezeway swung open effortlessly as Private Kemp entered first, followed by the conjoined bodies of her comrades, one huffing angrily as he practically wrestled the other inside.

"What a friggin' goat rope. I had a feeling some crazy shit was going down," the Corporal spat as he shoved Private Bodine against a far glass wall a bit harder than he had actually intended.

Bodine let out a small, pathetic whimper as he crumpled to the floor, his night vision goggles hanging crookedly to the left on his narrow face, the skin of which was pasty white.

"What are we gonna do with Mr. Potato head over there for the rest of this little shin-dig?" Private Kemp asked, removing her goggles with one hand and digging into her ample rear end with the other.

Scanning the dome, which was meticulously clean, as though it had been recently scrubbed with glass cleaner, Corporal McIntosh shrugged his massive shoulders, his upper body visually pumped from the sudden physical exertion.

"That's the Major's decision. I just work here, remember?"

He shot Private Bodine a disgusted look.

"Hell, I'll probably end up giving him a piggy-back ride the rest of the way. Damn, I wish Isiah was here."

Private Kemp nodded in agreement, leaning down in a crouch against the dome entranceway.

"I'm with you there. He was one annoying SOB sometimes, but he could take care of himself."

The Corporal kneeled beside her, pulling his goggles free until they hung from his thick neck.

"Darker than a mule's asshole in here. Sandy, you have the same vibes as old jelly knees over there? You think we're up to our collar-brass in deep shit?"

Pausing to suck in a lung full of fresh, albeit slightly rank, oxygen, Private Kemp stared blankly ahead into the darkness of the night.

"Affirmative, Ron. I haven't felt dread like this since the first night I spent at a juvie work camp."

"Right you are, girlfriend. We should have all given ourselves an M-16 enema before stepping onto these grounds. At least the suffering would've been less extensive. Swallowing a bullet is a *peaceful* passing compared to what's in store for us this night," Private Bodine whined, his eyes unblinking and staring trance-like at his peers.

"Son, your constant cheeriness is gonna turn my stomach, that is, if the air were breathing doesn't beat you to it, I..." Private Kemp said with a tight smile, just as the remaining words hung in her throat like stale crackers as the admin exit door swung open with a loud creak.

Corporal McIntosh and Private Kemp leaped up in unison, their hands posed as if they held invisible revolvers.

"Shiiiit!..." Private Kemp babbled wildly, causing the Corporal to laugh hysterically in the aftermath.

As the Major strolled stiffly towards them, Private Bodine began to whine like a cat whose tail was caught in a metal grinder.

Moving a quickness that belied her bulky frame, Private Kemp reached over and slapped him viciously across the right cheek. The whine became a low whimper as Private Bodine curled his knees to his chest and buried his head between them.

Seemingly disinterested in the origin of such behavior between the privates, the Major halted his forward progress a full ten feet from Corporal McIntosh, still locked in a fighter's pose with his hands high and his knees slightly bent.

"Corporal, come with me. We've got injured parties inside," he barked, the voice gravelly and the words badly slurred. The Major's head was tilted to one side, as if he were favoring an injury to either his neck or back.

"Who is it, Major? What happen..." the Corporal began before being cut off in mid-sentence.

"No big surprise. They had a prison break a few hours back. Come on, we've got to transport these people to the infirmary a few buildings down. Leave the Privates here for now. We've got enough people stumbling around in the dark as it is."

The Major turned his back on them and motioned awkwardly with his left arm in a 'proceed' gesture before walking back towards the admin building entranceway.

Corporal McIntosh shot Private Kemp a worried glance and slowly moved forward. The re-donned goggles prevented him from actually seeing her expression, but he could feel the fear her being emitted like a physical presence. "We'll be right back, Sandy. Take care of old Cauliflower ears over there."

The heavy metal door leading into the admin building slammed hard behind the Major, drowning out the two words that Private Kemp had cried just before the Corporal pulled the door open and stepped inside and out of her sight.

Her voice had crackled with desperation as a feeling of almost unbearable panic swept through the enclosure like a gust of blazing hot air through an industrial fan.

If he had heard them, the Corporal had not responded, leaving her standing dead center inside the breezeway with nothing more than a whimpering, sniveling basket case for company. The Major's sudden appearance had infested the air with the smell of rotted eggs, and had subsequently begun to dissipate almost immediately upon his departure.

The words still echoed in her fevered mind as she bent down and began to dig into the side of her right boot.

"Don't go," she had pleaded, somehow knowing that the Major had been lying. The man had led them into the compound with an agenda, possibly one he himself had been unaware of when their journey from camp had begun. After pulling her goggles free to rest upon her greasy forehead, Private Kemp held the small penlight in one hand and the zap gun in the other, the weapon only inches from her eyes. Satisfied that she indeed would have at least a thousand volts of self-protection close at hand, she re-donned her goggles and reached down, gently massaging the short, moist hair on Private Bodine's bowed head. She had seriously considered making tracks back to the front gate once the Major and Corporal McIntosh had departed, but quickly rejected such a reckless and potentially fatal scheme. They had no idea who the two figures were floating about the compound, and a zap gun wasn't much defense if you were targeted from long range. She might have tried it if her M-16 weren't buried in a ditch outside the gates, but even then the thought of trekking out into the great wide open that led to the sally port wasn't the least bit appealing.

The thought of leaving the semi-comatose Private Lomax Bodine hanging in the wind also factored in the equation; although she would have had to admit under oath she wasn't *incapable* of doing just that.

The main factor keeping her glued to the walkway's tiled flooring was one she had little trouble accepting.

Sandra Kemp had always been the curious type, a troublesome trait that had assisted in keeping her locked away for most of her teenaged years. She had been curious about alcohol and felt the need to indulge. She had been curious about sex and felt the need to indulge. She had been curious about all and any mind-altering drug offered to her, and felt the need to indulge.

Standing within the deafening quiet of a glass domed breezeway at the center of an apparently deserted state correctional facility, she felt the familiar burning sensation begin to overcome the tingling pangs of fear gnawing at her gut. As much as she would have liked to deny it, the gist of her soul welcomed, gleefully *relished,* the feeling.

"Don't fret, Lomax. I'll get us outta here with our skins still intact. You just follow my lead and don't trip us up once all the hell breaks loose."

As if proving he was still somewhat aware of his surroundings, Private Lomax released a short series of mucus-filled snorts.

"Make no mistake about it, little buddy, hell is definitely gonna break loose *real* soon."

***

The prone form lying across the relatively narrow conference table was donned in prison guard gray, the bulky, burning candle sitting between his slightly spread legs like a surgeon's probe. The light shine was limited in scope, filling the room with floating shadows that were greatly exaggerated in both depth and width. The Major had held the door open upon entry, allowing Corporal McIntosh to step inside first.

As he neared the body, its head turned away towards the podium at the rear of the room, the Corporal was unable to visualize the form that crouched directly beneath the table, tucked neatly between two pushed-in chairs.

"Is he...alive, Major? I don't see any blood," he began, kneeling down with his hands floating mere inches from the man's pasty white face, as if about to initiate some type of voodoo healing ritual.

"Look closer at his face, Corporal. Take a *good look*," the Major replied almost cheerily, his croaking voice laced with sarcasm.

Within the span of mere moments, three things transpired in almost perfect harmony of one another. First, Corporal McIntosh gently grasped the man's chin and pulled his face into view. Secondly, Corporal McIntosh gasped aloud once his mind had verified a positive ID on the chalky-white face below. Third and lastly, Corporal McIntosh cursed loudly upon feeling the steely grip curl around his ankles just before pulling him onto the cool tile floor.

"Ezop? Son of a BI-..." he yelped, his upper back smacking the floor as his arms pin-wheeled wildly.

The form pulled itself forward onto the Corporal's squirming body like a cat shimmying up a tree, the overpowering scent of spoiled meat filling the air.

"Major, g-get if off me, w-will ya?" The Corporal moaned, crossing his thick forearms in front of his face in a blocking stance as the piston-like fingers dug into his sides for leverage.

"Afraid I can't do that, Corporal. I told Jerrod there that you were one stout SOB, and he saw that as a clear-cut challenge to his newly formed manhood."

Whirling his head around as far as his pinned down body would allow, Corporal McIntosh spoke through bared, tightly gritted teeth.

"What's the h-hell's g-goin' on, Major? I ain't in the m-mood for anymore BS war games," he spat just before a set of hands that held the look and texture of half-melted candle wax wrapped around each side of his throat.

"No more games necessary, Big Mac. Our savior had simply seen enough and made the decision to grace us with his presence in order to accomplish some long overdue house cleaning," he heard the Major declare as the pressure gradually increased on his windpipe.

Clutching the wrists of his attacker, Corporal McIntosh got the first clear look at the thing's face that sat atop his heaving chest.

"J-Jesus C-crow..."

Jerrod Dickenson had always been considered a handsome man, one whose gentle demeanor and smooth-talking ways had sent many a female heart a flutter in his younger days at Red Bridge High School. In fact, the nickname his peers had tagged him with, 'Stud-ly Do-right', had been mainly for his eerie resemblance to the sixties cartoon icon of similar name. The blond, curly hair and dimpled, square chin, along with the wide shouldered, muscular build.

Those same peers would be hard pressed to recognize the warped, bloated features of the face that hovered over Corporal McIntosh with a hideous, lip-less grimace frozen into place.

Ron McIntosh had been known to bench press four-hundred pounds and squat close to five on prime lifting days in his home gym, and was proud to display his nineteen-inch biceps, or 'Anaconda Erections' as his latest girlfriend liked to call them, to anyone willing to stare.

Struggle as he might, gushers of adrenaline pumping through his veins as his anxiety level arose, he found the task of loosening his attackers grip on his neck appallingly difficult, only managing to budge them less than an inch before they regained their original grip.

"Now don't kill the boy, Jerrod. As with Jeff over there, the master needs, actually demands might be a better word, breathing specimens. I hesitate to disobey such a request. Call me a worry-wart, but I would like to be around to experience the rapture," the Major said, placing a hand on the CO's shoulder and stroking it gently.

The thing that had been Jerrod Dickenson peered upward with his left eye, the right frozen in its lid-less socket. Coughing in between gasps, Corporal McIntosh thought crazily about a chameleon he had once captured as a teen, it's roving eyes set atop scaly stalks.

"Digit removal, I presume?" The thing cackled though raw, bloodied gums that seemed to glow orange in the dimly lit space.

It wore Ezop's militia uniform, although the moistness leaking from its putrid pores had already darkened the shade of the fabric considerably.

The Major looming directly over his face, the Corporal could make out a similar series of grisly changes in his former commander's once less-than-peachy complexion. Ron McIntosh could only deduce that Major Peterson had stepped in front of an operating flame-thrower.

"You got it, ace. Despite our seemingly effortless capture, Big Mac here could be a hindrance just as Ezop might have been. The other two are hardly worth a thought. I will personally take care of both, with *relish.*"

A moment later, the two-hundred-plus pound Corporal was slung roughly across the opposite conference table as the unconscious Sergeant Ezop, the back of his skull thudding loudly against the shiny oak finish.

"Do the honors, Major, and make it snappy. This boy's getting stronger by the second," the Dickenson-thing muttered, its slug-like tongue hanging from its mouth like a thick, overcooked sausage.

The Major stepped up and casually reached for the Corporal's left hand, the arm of which was being forcibly positioned before him as he brought forth the gleaming instrument with its cutting blades already separated like the razor-sharp teeth of a growling predator.

"My pleasure, Jerrod. Just a few quick snips and the good Corporal here will lose *his* grip, so to speak."

With a sudden, sharp crunch, Corporal McIntosh's right arm ripped free and connected solidly just below the Major's left collarbone, sending him sprawling backwards in a comical break dance, the weapon slung free and sailed end over end into a far wall.

Quickly planting his right foot into the Dickenson-Thing's midsection, McIntosh shoved forward while simultaneously whipping his free arm across his body in a wicked backhand motion. Both movements had the desired effect, the push shoving the former CO free while the backhand landed solidly on the right side of Dickenson's neck, sending him flying into the center of the conference room floor like a high-diver onto a grouping of jagged cliffs. The Corporal rolled to his left and over the high back chair in his path, then leaped to his feet while ripping a metal leg free from the same. It wasn't until he was in full fighting stance that he first felt and then observed the strangely familiar object dangling from his right forearm.

A single bone protruded from the torn stub, the color so white it seemed bleached in comparison to the purplish skin and reddish/black muscle that held it in place.

McIntosh began to sling his arm about frantically, like a panicked child attempting to rid his body of a stinging insect. The shattered, mysteriously bloodless forearm of Jerrod Dickenson finally shook free, clearing almost the full length of the conference room before landing with a nauseating plop against the movie screen hanging just beyond the wooden podium.

It slid to the floor like a swatted fly from a glass

window, leaving nothing more than a few green and yellow spatter marks in its wake.

"I ain't *believin*' this shit...on my long-suffering mama's headstone, I ain't buying a second of it," the Corporal quipped in a tone more suited for a perplexed sitcom actor.

The Major, who had been lying flat on his back just a split-second earlier, seemed to literally glide across the room towards him, leaping the three foot plus high table with shocking ease.

Flinging the chair leg forward like a power hitter at a hanging curveball, Corporal McIntosh shrieked like a cornered animal.

Metal met flesh and bone with a muffled clanging noise, the Major's head snapping back violently, then forward again with equal velocity.

Corporal Ron McIntosh's minds-eye captured a single snapshot of his former commanders visage just before his inner light was shut off from behind. It was a minds-eye photograph he wished by everything holy hadn't been processed at all.

The Major's right eye had been ripped from its socket, leaving only a hollow pit that trickled a pinkish ooze onto his badly crushed jawline, which had been shoved horribly inward from the blow.

The smile Major David Peterson flashed was void all but the swollen gums that smelled of dead fish basking in the midday sun atop a sandy dune. Corporal McIntosh fell like a sack of tossed potatoes just after the baton raked across the top of his scalp. He landed in a loose heap directly between the wide-legged stance of former CO turned walking nightmare Jerrod Dickenson.

The room swirled into focus a section at a time,

the size and proximity of each object surrounding him first ridiculously exaggerated but eventually normalizing as the cobwebs cloaking his senses began to gradually float away.

He was tied to a chair, bound at his wrists, chest and ankles by thick wire that was cutting into his exposed skin with even the slightest shift.

The Major stood directly in front of him, leaning down with his badly mangled jaw balanced on his right fist in a hideous parody of 'The Thinker'.

"You waking up, cupcake? Damn, he's stout, Jerrod. It's only been a few minutes since you thumped him. I honestly believe the baton got the worst end of that scrap. Must have been one of the good Corporal's legendary 'Crimson Rages."

The thing that had once been Correctional Officer Second Grade Jerrod Dickenson shambled into view to the Major's left, his right arm conspicuously missing below the elbow.

"Tough cookie, no doubt. You sure the binds are necessary now that's he's been rendered pretty much useless?"

Their voices sounded more slurred than before, truly alien in nature. Corporal McIntosh shook his head from side to side in a pathetic effort to wipe away the effect. His binds instantly dug in, and he winced and ceased movement. He felt a distant stinging in both hands, but easily dismissed it as his chin fell forward.

"I won't underestimate him again, Jerrod. You watch both of them closely while I dispatch of their much weaker comrades. I won't be long."

The Major stood stiffly, his knees popping like

twin canons. He had hardly turned to depart the conference room when the voice instantly cut short all movement.

"Hey, a-asshole, hold up…one d-damn minute," Corporal McIntosh mumbled barely coherently, his chin resting atop his chest but his eyes peering upward.

"I g-gotta know… why? A-actually, *what* a-and why?"

The Dickenson/Thing chuckled, although it sounded less human than mechanical.

"Might as well enlighten the grunt, Major. I figure he has the right to know."

Major Peterson reached down and filled his gloved hands with the dazed Corporal's short, blood matted hair and pulled upward, staring into his former subordinates partially opened eyes with his remaining working orb.

"Damned if he doesn't at that, Jerrod. All right, Corporal Mac, you just get comfy and let me fill in some of the blanks for you."

Leaning against the edge of the opposite conference table, Sergeant Ezop's motionless frame just inches from his propped hips, Major Peterson sighed heavily, the emission of air sounding like someone sucking ice chips through a straw.

Corporal McIntosh was without either the will or strength to attempt a visual search for Dickenson, who had temporarily disappeared from his line of sight.

"While tracking during our early morning maneuvers, I stepped into a flat clearing and came dangerously close to diving headfirst into a perfectly circular opening in the earth that looked to have been drawn and carved out there. Nothing grew around the hole, which was probably three feet wide at the outset, and the spruce and elm trees nearby looked dry and brittle, as if burned without a flame ever actually touching them. I even noticed several separate piles of what looked to be animal bones near the loop. My curious side got the best of me, I have to admit, something I rarely fall victim to when logic dictates otherwise."

A soft moaning sound interrupted the Major's monologue, albeit briefly. It took Corporal McIntosh a few heartbeats to realize he was the originator of the cries. The Major's mouth, his jawline horribly distorted, commenced to ramble, ignoring the grunts and groans after the initial series. The Corporal's fingers began to throb like ten separate toothaches, but he was again unable to manufacture a suitable amount of energy to check the source of the pain.

"The odor was like no other I have ever experienced, unlike any natural or manmade scent this old Officer had ever had the displeasure of inhaling. I was leaning over on my hands and knees, staring into the abyss, when Officer Dickenson appeared seemingly out of nowhere and proceeded to open my eyes to a *new* existence, one that actually had a meaningful purpose. A short scuffle ensued, one that I had little prayer of winning despite my wealth of experience and combat savvy. Officer Dickenson was about to toss me headfirst into the opening when I received an unexpected stay of execution, isn't that correct, Jerrod?"

His temples throbbing like twin Jackhammers attempting to crack a marble surface, Corporal

McIntosh heard the former CO's response from what seemed like a great, open distance, as if the man were replying from the center of a vast field and bellowing his reply from in-between cupped hands.

"Yes-sir-re, Bob. The message I received was loud and clear, and simply stated 'not *this* one. He, as well as the people in his charge, can be vital in the birthing to come'. Simple as that, like a lightning bolt to the senses, it was."

The Major interjected, his left hand now massaging Jeff Ezop's head playfully, as if he were nonchalantly petting the family dog.

"I had already begun to change, Corporal, fast on my way to shedding this useless shell that, even now, still hangs on stubbornly to its pathetic existence. Jerrod had not just run upon me by accident a full mile and a half from the Briarston unit. He had driven his Jeep Cherokee up one hill and down another to reach that neat little hole punched so perfectly into Mother Earth.

It had long been a sacrificial drop-off point, and he had stashed a fellow guard, crude unbeliever this man had been, inside his vehicle and had come to offer the man's shell as the initial stage-setter for the glorious events to come.

Jerrod, as well as the master, received two for the price of one, it seemed, and I was right where I was ordained to be. We tossed the body inside like so much loose garbage, which in reality isn't an altogether incorrect definition, and then proceeded to sit near the well and jaw like the oldest of friends. My first course of action, after a magical, I guess I'll call it a *conference* call, to our savior, was to ensure the Dark Eagle Militia make an appearance at the Briarston compound this evening. My second was to immediately eliminate the most potentially dangerous deterrent to the mission, that being Isiah Chambers. Fear not, Corporal Mac, he never saw nor felt the bullet that ended his life. I still feel it's a shame that such a healthy specimen was relegated to 'dead soul feeding' status, but it couldn't be helped, I'm afraid."

The pain in his hands and forearms becoming unbearable, Corporal McIntosh used what little strength he could muster to squeal at the top of his lungs until his voice was ragged and coarse, his entire body shaking as if undergoing radical shock treatments.

"WHAT THE FUCK IS YOUR POINT, PETERSON? SPIT OUT THE FUCKING EPILOGUE OR DO ME A FAVOR AND SHUT THE HELL UP!"

His one remaining eye shining like a gold musket ball within the gleaming light of the candle's high flame, Major Peterson stood in the center of the room, directly between the fallen, bound bodies of two former comrades.

"Now, now, Corporal, let's not push insubordination. We still have a chain of command here, although the highest-ranking official is yet to make an appearance. I personally have no 'point', except to serve. Within the hour, we will *all* serve. It was a simple matter for Jerrod and his only alley within the compound to prepare the grounds in a proper manner. CO Marvin Settle had felt the power of the savior years earlier, and actually served as an unofficial tutor for Jerrod when his preliminary urges kicked in. The plan had been mapped out in record time once Settle received the 'Go' command from a higher source a few weeks ago. As you well know, Corporal, nothing runs smoother than a well-prepared, finely tuned machine that truly believes its ultimate goal can and *must* be reached."

His lips pursed and teeth grinding from the onslaught of a new series of painful spasms, the Corporal closed his eyes and feverishly attempted to wish it all away. He never saw Dickenson scoot next to Major Peterson, both looming over his quivering body like vultures over fresh roadkill.

"This is taking far too long, Major. Let him *see* for himself. We have other matters to tend to within the next half hour or so."

Major Peterson reached down, placing his left palm onto the Corporal's sweat-soaked forehead.

"Easy enough, Jerrod. I rather enjoy displaying my newfound telepathic skills. We can go ahead and transport the bodies while the visions bombard his mind like detonated Claymores. Hopefully he can handle them without pissing himself, unlike poor Sergeant Ezop."

Closing his eye while bowing his gruesomely twisted neck, the Major began to sway gently from side to side, his sunken jaws tensing as if he were fighting off a powerful sneeze.

"Let the show begin..." former CO Jerrod Dickenson quipped in a voice straight from the deepest, dankest pits of a world filled with fires that never ceased burning and souls that were repeatedly fed upon without mercy.

***

“Let’s go little buddy. Your mom’s waiting to pick you up by the swing sets at the edge of the playground,” Private Kemp whispered kindly, her mouth just inches from the left ear of Private Lomax Bodine, who took a full thirty seconds to respond with the most fleeting of nods.

Her eyes darting back and forth between the Admin building door and her slowly rising comrade, Sandra Kemp bit her lower lip nervously.

The commotion she had clearly heard a moment before wasn’t the type one would normally associate with a rescue operation. Just as she had suspected from the time they had first stepped onto the compound grounds, something was undeniably amiss.

“Bad vibes, Lomax old pal. Vibes that make me wanna make Malted Milk in my drawers, you know?”

As she reached around Private Bodine’s slim waistline and pulled him next to her, she felt a sudden aching for the presence of either Isiah Chambers or Ron McIntosh, either of whom carried with them an aura of confidence and cockiness unmatched within the unit.

Turning in the opposite direction from the door she had so somberly watched Corporal McIntosh stroll through less than ten minutes earlier, Private Kemp was relieved to feel Bodine pick up his pace on his own just before they reached the door leading into the adjoining, unmarked building.

“We’ll find a choice spot to stake out, partner. Like I said, everything is gonna be groovy, all right?” She asked timidly, reaching for the knob and praying that it would turn freely beneath her sweaty palm.

Seconds later, Private Kemp's petite penlight cutting a fine horizontal beam a few feet into the murky distance, they shambled inside as if escaping monsoon winds. The night goggles had grown burdensome and weren't nearly as effective within enclosed areas. The distant scent of recently prepared food filled her flaring nostrils almost instantly, a welcome relief from the rancid smells that had permeated their senses for the majority of the evening.

Private Kemp's left hand gripped a metal railing, and she pulled them both along the trail it followed cautiously, keeping the pen-light's beam directly in front of her scuffed boot tips. Private Bodine suddenly lurched heavily to the left, almost tipping both of them over in a flailing heap. Almost dropping the pen-light while struggling to right their postures, Private Kemp felt her inner rage meter soar to red line heights. She fought off the urge to simply dump the entranced Private and concentrate on her own survival, instead patting his side gently and again utilizing the 'motherly love' tone that he seemed to respond to at least moderately.

"Easy, little buddy. I smell eats. Let's you and I go see what's on the menu, what do ya say?"

"E-eats," he murmured in passive response.

Pushing through a set of swinging double-doors, Private Kemp couldn't help but roll her eyes and sigh.

"Jesus, Mac. I told you not to follow that bastard inside," she said, not realizing she had spoken aloud.

Just as they rounded a long, metal table littered with dishes and tableware (Private Kemp stopping only long enough to pocket a small steak-knife), the pen- light's beam fell upon the walk-in freezer's wide-open doors, the air surrounding them turning instantly twenty degrees cooler.

A step further revealed the freezer's inner contents through the Privates' thickly frosted breath.

The piercing scream that followed was only slighter louder than the maniacal laughter that would soon drown it out.

***

Ducking inside the cramped guard shack, Jimmy could feel the tip of Buck's knife puncture the flesh atop his ribcage through his wool shirt.

"Quiet, fat boy, or I'll gut your worthless carcass here and now," Buck spat just millimeters from his left ear. Jimmy fought off the urge to gag from not only the warm moistness now felt there, but also the nauseatingly sour breath that had accompanied it.

JC Carlyle's back facing him; Jimmy could see the huge circles of wetness literally dripping through the man's shirt.

"Could be the Sheriff or some of his boys, Buck," JC warbled, his words muffled as if spoken underwater.

"Shut your pie-hole, JC. He just cut the engine."

They had spotted the headlights nearing the main gate of the compound just as it had rounded the far West corner a full two hundred yards away, obviously traveling in from the main highway.

Kerry Cructhfield cursed under his breath as he threw the rusty Accord's driver door open and practically leaped from its coffee and powdered donut stained font seat.

"Late again, Crutch. The Captain said just last week that one more butt- drag on my part might be fatal. I'm gonna end up baggin' groceries at the Winn- Dixie again for sure," he muttered, not bothering to ensure he had locked his ride upon jogging haphazardly away while simultaneously adjusting his uniform's shirt collar.

It wasn't until he got to within a dozen feet of the main sally port that the tall, painfully thin young man halted dead in his tracks, as if he had ran face-first into an invisible force field.

"Wha-?...Who turned out the lights? Now that I think about it, perimeter road was a bit on the dim side. Where's the...?"

He gave the open gates and deserted sally port within a final grave look and winced. He then peered back at his waiting vehicle sitting among the sparse gathering of POV's that normally made up the night shift, a gathering of no more than fifteen or twenty cars and trucks tucked together in an almost perfect square within the spacious parking lot.

"Gang's all here, it seems. But, the gates…"

Officer Crutchfield wiped the fresh, clear snot from his nostrils with his left sleeve, his eyes darting spastically from the gates to his car several times, his knees locked securely into place as if permanently bent.

"Maybe they're testing me. Y-yeah, that's it.

See if Crutch has the testicular fortitude to find his way to the weapons room in total darkness. Well, never let it be said that this boy ever backed down from a challenge."

Giving the rusty Honda one last forlorn look through the blackness of the night, he turned on a single heel and strolled towards the waiting gates with a cockiness born of pure youthful ignorance.

On his third step into the sally port, his right boot slid forward as if it had come into contact with a freshly discarded banana peel. Falling back, he landed with a grunt on the thin padding of his narrow rear end, his hands planted onto the soft stickiness of the pavement on either side.

"FUBAR caught on film. Good show, Crutch. I'm sure they'll save this film for posterity."

Raising his right hand to his face as he arose somewhat crookedly, he was unable to identify by color but instantly recognized the faint yet still odorous smell of the jelled substance stuck there.

"Blood? Smells like blo..."

Officer Kerry Crutchfield, not yet two months on the job and as green as a freshly bottled pickle in regard to handling real-world situations within a maximum security correctional site, whirled around clumsily just as the figure fell upon him, both of his arms shooting towards his face in a cross-blocking stance.

The slender, somewhat bent blade of the pocketknife effortlessly bore through the cotton shirtsleeve and sank into the soft flesh of his thin forearm with a soft, puncturing noise. As he fell back, this time both of his size eleven boot heels sliding helplessly over the same semi-congealed substance whose origin was no longer a mystery, Crutchfield stared at the blade's ridged handle protruding from his wounded appendage like a turkey thermometer.

Rolling to the left, his lips forming a scream that he was somehow unable to haul to the surface, the young guard first smelled and then visualized the half- naked form standing over him.

"Howdy, pard. Talk about the wrong place at the wrong time. Son, you just *bought* the farm."

Moving on pure survival instinct that would have made even his jaded superiors proud, Crutchfield rolled away to his right while pulling the blade free with one lighting fast tug.

His roll ended as his upper back made contact with the western side of the sally port's inner fencing. He lurched to his feet, the pocketknife's moistened blade slashing first forward and then evenly from side to side. From a distance he resembled a man frantically waving away a swarm of bothersome insects with an invisible flyswatter.

"Step away, man! Keep your d-distance or I-I'll..." Buck Lomax the Third held the lens end of the flashlight just inches from his chin before initiating the 'on' switch.

"You'll do what, sweet-cheeks? Crap your diaper? Pee your state issued jeans? It's a short list, but I'd bet even money on 'em both transpirin' within the next thirty seconds or so."

Crutchfield's mouth opened wide to cry out just as the mangled monstrosity disguised as a man leaped forward in a frenzied blur, wrapped it's mangled fingers around his neck and began to systemically squeeze the life from him. Fingers that held almost no flesh to speak of, but that were astonishingly strong in performing the deed, held airborne by arms bloated to twice their original size and riddled with yellow-tinted boils the size of golf balls.

The sound of bones crunching from immense pressure ensued, followed by a final, exasperated escape of oxygen from lungs already void of life.

Moments later, Buck tossed the lifeless corpse to the other side of the sally port, grinning revoltingly as it landed head over heels and came to rest in a yoga-style 'mantis' position.

It slumped like a life-sized puppet with severed strings.

JC then joined him at the center of the port, his right arm propped atop Jimmy's left shoulder, giving them the look of drinking buddies prepping to paint the town.

"Why'd you waste 'im, Buck? Should've brought him along for sacrificin', ya think?" JC warbled indifferently.

"We've got all the ripe bodies we need, JC old sap. The master probably would have spit up this pimple faced runt, anyhow."

Jimmy leaned over suddenly and retched; heaving several more times even after his tank was entirely emptied of all substantial contents.

Buck looked at him disdainfully, scratching his head and pulling away what little had remained of his hair.

"What the hell's his problem? Was the kid a *relative* or somethin'?"

Leaning on one knee, Jimmy gave Buck a disbelieving look while wiping his hands across his still-trembling lips.

"Y-you killed him for...n-no reason. Why in God's name?"

JC reached down and gripped Jimmy's jeans at the belt line and hauled him to his feet roughly, gleefully giggling as he awaited his partner's forthcoming response.

"Why, you said it yourself, buddy-boy. It wasn't for no reason, but precisely for God's sake, though probably not the God *you're* referrin' to," Buck replied curtly, his words so badly slurred that Jimmy had to replay them in his mind several times before the translation was complete.

"Let's get inside, JC old comrade, old salt. I have the distinct notion that we're holdin' up the shin-dig of the Century."

Pulling Jimmy by the nape of his thick neck, JC nodded and followed his slumped shouldered, badly limping partner past the guard shack and into the main compound.

"No more talk from you, blubber-gut, or I'll turn your lights out for the duration. Don't make no n to the master whether you're conscious or not, understand?"

Jimmy jerked his head away and turned on his captor, stepping beneath his grip and throwing a hard right jab, followed by a vicious left uppercut.

The first only grazed the tip of JC's chin, but the second caught him full- force in the solar plexus as he had unexpectedly staggered forward.

For a moment Jimmy felt strangely adrift, as if suspended in time and unable to determine his exact whereabouts or the sudden events that had led to such an unreal state of mental flux.

He was staring at two pairs of feet, his own muddied shoes and those that stood just on the outside of each, the brownish toes protruding from the tips more akin to fat slugs than human digits.

In a desperate attempt to pull back from the reeking form that was clawing at his hair and upper body, Jimmy realized with a mixture of shock and comical bemusement that his left arm was hopelessly stuck at the wrist. Huffing madly, he found it impossible to budge regardless of how hard he jerked and tugged to retrieve it.

Turning his head away from the man's putrid scent, which was dangerously close to inviting a new wave of gags from his already lurching midsection, Jimmy heard what at first he deduced to be harsh coughs originating from two separate locations.

It wasn't until his own labored breathing slowed somewhat, once he had given up pulling his hand and arm free from the apparently unbreakable bonds ensnaring them, that he realized the coughs were something else altogether. His captors, one of whom was now doubling over just a few feet to his rear, were in the midst of separate but similarly dementia-fueled laughing fits.

They were weaving and moaning like two teenaged boys sharing a stale joke only pot-induced joy could transform into one of outlandish hilarity.

Buck Lomax the Third's repugnantly distorted head popped up from over Jimmy's entrapped, quickly cramping left shoulder like some grotesque Jack-in- the-Box, winking playfully with his one remaining eye.

"Hey, Dimple-butt, you mind removing your

arm from my best pal's midsection? You diggin' for gold in there or what?" He croaked, the word midsection had been pronounced 'mif-sex-son' through the gaping red hole that had once been a human mouth.

Regardless of the monumental effort put forth to avoid acquiring such information, Jimmy eventually peered ahead at the source of their warped, deranged humor, and discovered in the aftermath of such a sight that merely closing one's eyes did little to evaporate the memory permanently stored away for all time. Stored away to be drudged up on those nights when sleep was elusive due to a loose shutter banging against a distant pane or a neighbor's howling canine parked beneath a nearby window ledge. Stored away to emerge within tranquil, peaceful dreams suddenly transformed without warning into stark, unrelenting nightmares filled with graven images that induced night sweats and gnashing of teeth.

Buck had moved behind JC and had positioned his head on the other man's right shoulder, giving the two the appearance of some mythical two-headed beast whose arsenal of weapons included unbearable body odor and the ability to meld into one another's putty-like bodies.

Just before the blood rushed from his head in a single flushing wave and the plug was pulled on his inner-electrical system, Jimmy got the full gist of the trap that had so effectively gripped and held his fist and arm at bay. It wasn't some ancient marital art hold or steely arm-lock straight from the annals of the World Wrestling Federation. Just as his eyelids clapped shut, allowing his brittle mind to drift into the merciful realm of a motionless, colorless dreamscape, Jimmy would have given up a year of his life for either of those particular explanations in lieu of the true source of both his capture and subsequent unconsciousness.

His arm had sunk into and become submerged just underneath JC Carlyle's rib cage, puncturing the abdomen like an iron spear through partially congealed Jell-O.

Immersed to just past the midway point of his forearm, Jimmy's arm had then found itself within a vice-like grip at the wrist, one which he could only associate with an old Disney cartoon he had seen as a kid. He was playing the role of Briar Rabbit, and JC Carlyle's bulging; mutated gut was the Tar-Baby of 'Song of The South' fame. The soggy, lightly tinted flesh that encircled his forearm was smooth and tearless, as if the wound had been measured and cut out to fit his arm exclusively. With each tug or jerk Jimmy attempted, the grip on his wrist became firmer and was accompanied by soft, stomach-churning sucking noises around the perimeter of the wound, as if his arm were literally being fed upon.

"Find something you like in there, sunshine?" JC had quipped, sending his evil twin mutation into a new series of unbound hysterics.

Jimmy had felt something touch the palm of his enslaved hand just before the lights went out. He could have sworn it had been the gentle licking of a rough-edged *tongue*, like that displayed by a yawning feline. Jimmy's main fuse blew just as the object dragged across the top of his opened hand towards the crook of his elbow.

Never had sweet slumber, even a session as

abrupt and without warning, been so utterly welcomed.

"Damn, JC. Don't that *smart*?" Buck had snorted while observing in morbid fascination as JC pulled Jimmy's arm free with a low 'plopping' sound, like a champagne cork being released.

Jimmy's arm looked to have been dipped in beef gravy from the elbow down, but no wounds of any kind were apparent to the skin itself. The gaping hole created by his fist and arm closed almost immediately following the extraction, retracting to its former shape and texture like rubber sealant being poured into a narrow tube canister.

Buck clapped enthusiastically, as if he had just witnessed a particularly snazzy parlor trick.

"Honestly, Buck, it feels kinda ticklish. Like old tubby there was tryin' to reach an itch I couldn't quite get to on my own. Somethin' is…moving around in my gut. I can...*feel* it in there…swimming around."

"Holy hoppin' catfish! JC old friend, you are becoming somethin' new and different altogether! I'm almost jealous, pal. You ready for the final curtain to be raised on this night of nights?" Buck asked with child-like glee, wrapping a right arm that was beginning to bear a striking resemblance to a squid's tentacle around his friend's narrow waist.

"Gotta admit, Buck, I was lost there for a while. Scared enough to leave a trail of Hershey nuggets since we left the main road and trekked towards the compound," JC replied with an expression that, if still remotely human, might have been defined as overly dramatic or even sappy.

"I may be comin' apart at the seams, but I've

never felt so damn robust in all my years. I do believe I could down a handful of Valium and still 'boot scoot boogie' til the cows come home."

Buck reached down and took Jimmy's left ankle, then proceeded to nonchalantly drag him towards the prison compound with alarming ease.

"Glad you've finally come around to our side, JC, and don't fret, the biggest cow of 'em all is knockin' on the door as we speak."

They shuffled crookedly through the inner gate, their spindly legs and skinless feet liquefying atop the smooth pavement of the main walkway, leaving four distinct slug trails in their wake. With each wobbling step, the remainder of their clothing peeled away like discarded snakeskin.

Both knew their ultimate destination without exchanging a single garbled word, drawn to its essence like ravenous birds of prey to torn, bleeding meat.

***

"Come on, sis, it'll only take a few minutes to scan the place now that its relatively safe to use the flashlight. Once we've shaken a few doorknobs, we'll be outta here faster than a politician's secession speech," William whispered while pausing on the bottom step of the staircase leading upstairs, his flashlight's beam balanced between himself and where his twin stood with her arms crossed tightly across her narrow chest.

"We're not going to find anyone. At least…no one *alive* anyway," she replied while rubbing her arms vigorously as if struck in a sudden, cool breeze.

Since they had baby-stepped inside the first floor of the administrative building some five minutes before, Kara had felt her feelings of intense dread and foreboding dramatically increase. It was as if she and her twin brother had stumbled into a massive fog filled with all things bad, and it was just a matter of time before unholy terrors would step forward for formal introductions.

She considered herself a relatively brave type, not prone to nervous jitters or uncontrollable anxiety when faced with overly stressful situations. Her brother was, and had always been, the closest thing to fearless a human being could possibly be, especially in the matter of their missing parents. A primal obsession had formed in the previous months since their mysterious vanishing act near Red Bridge. An obsession that she realized long ago would lead to something bigger than either could possibly fathom, and possibly result in an outcome both exhilaratingly upbeat and tragically fatal for one or both of them.

"Let's go, sis. Elevator ain't an option. I know in my bones that somewhere in this building lies a key to the overall mystery."

She stared at him gravely just before walking forward toward the waiting stairs.

"The key you're talking about smells a lot like death personified, brother of mine, don't you agree?"

He waited until she took up position a mere step behind his own before proceeding up the winding path.

"Just stay close behind me and keep those baby

blues peeled, youthful sibling. I do believe whatever fatal harm has been done on these here premises is long since history. No foul in being cautious, however," he said while removing the revolver from his belt and holding it in line with the flashlight's scouring beam.

Once within the confines of floor number two, they passed countless office doors either completely closed or only half open on either side of the hall, Wilbo's light carving a path directly down the tunnel-like confines.

They eventually dead-ended, facing a wall of reflective black glass and a stainless-steel door with the markings 'COMMAND CENTER – Have Badges Properly Displayed' in comically large print engraved at its mid-point. Wilbo thought crazily that the word 'ACME' should have been included in there somewhere. The door was knob-less, a calculator-type keypad mounted in its place.

"Former nerve center of Briarston Correctional Facility, I presume?" Wilbo quipped while stuffing the revolver back into the front of his jeans and then placing his left palm on the exterior of the door, as if checking it for some sort of vibration from the other side. They both gasped audibly when the door opened with a low click from the slight pressure he had applied.

"Command Post doesn't *lock* when the power's out? Man, now that's 21st century security at its finest," Wilbo worded through a throat parched from lack of available spit.

Kara's voice cracked as she gripped his shoulder with badly shaking fingers.

"Let's get back outside, William. I don't need

or want to know what's behind that door."

"I'll only be a minute, Kara. Stay put, okay?" He replied, already with one foot planted inside the enclosure.

His twin rolled her eyes and blew out a nervous sigh.

"My *ass*. I'm right behind you, old reckless one. If you hear a sudden thud, it'll just be me fainting."

Despite the apprehension filling his gut like an over-inflated balloon, Wilbo managed a quick guffaw.

"Spoken like a true super-heroine. Possibly 'Chicken-Girl' or maybe the 'Yellow Streak.' You ready, sis?"

"Lead the way, Captain Steel-balls."

Upon entry they were greeted by a lengthy wooden console equipped with various sized PC's, multi-lined phone pads and what initially looked to be a giant flat-screen TV. Upon closer inspection it appeared to actually be an electronic status board of some kind. Wilbo flashed the light across the labeled strips attached to the board's upper portion and read the words 'Block A, Block B, and Block C' stenciled there.

"This must be where they tally the counts and make sure that all the state- fed cattle are present and accounted for. The central nerve center of all that is the 21st century slammer in modern society," he mumbled quietly, as if to avoid drowning out any other unanticipated sound that might be forthcoming within the general vicinity.

"Do you…s-smell something? I mean, something other than that aromatic pig-crap scent from earlier?" Kara replied somewhat hesitantly. She had removed her hand from her brother's person and was now walking stiffly with both arms held up and out from her sides, the taser squeezed tightly into her left fist. If viewed, one would have thought she was walking a circus tight rope.

"Now that you mention it, yeah. Kind of like raw beef that's on its way to turning a mean shade of green."

Turning towards the single door at the relatively small room's rear, Wilbo allowed the light to remain glued to the words attached there on an oversized doorplate.

Warden Gates – D.N.D.O.I.Y.A (DO NOT DISTURB OR IT'S YOUR ASS!)

"Must be a cordial, even tempered sort of a fella," Wilbo smirked, the light trailing down to the slight crack between the edge of the door and it's closing point.

"I think we should heed those words and make tracks, William." This time, there was no hint of underlying humor in her tone.

"Come now, Kara, we're through the hard part already. You think I like stumbling around like a blind mole? I still think there's something in this room were supposed to.... *need* to see."

His sister coughed, then nodded in defeat.

"Be my guest, blind mole-man. I-I'll man the fort out here, if you don't mind."

The barrel of the thirty-eight situated just to the right of the flashlights carving beam, Wilbo used the tip of his elbow to push the door open just enough to allow his narrow frame to slip through.

"Back before you can say 'Ghost Rider,' he

murmured.

"Great choice, that," his sister replied, frowning at the ever-increasingly pungent odor filing the dead air around them.

The warden's office seemed even larger than the control room that fronted it, but Wilbo figured that was simply due to the fact that it held considerably less furniture and equipment. He flashed the light across the oak desk (complete with a Dell computer set-up substantially more up to date than the PC's in the command center) and top edge of the leather recliner chair behind it, then quickly to the cloth couch that faced it from the opposite side of the room.

A three-tiered metal filing cabinet sat in the far West corner, while the far eastern side was occupied by a large-leafed plant that was dangerously close to brushing the low tiled ceiling.

Wilbo had just started to turn back towards the control center when the office door tapped against his left shoulder. As he reached to push it aside, the form that had been slumped against it shifted to the right and slammed it shut with a loud crack, trapping him inside.

Wilbo shrieked, leaping back a few steps and pointing the revolver at the suddenly unmoving, statue-like shape, the wildly bobbing light beam not locking fully onto the target until two to three heartbeats later.

"Hold it right there, amigo. I don't wanna have to….h-holy s-shit..."

"Howdy, son. You really ought to have *heeded* the warning on my door, especially on this here night," the voice croaked, sounding as if the speaker was gargling on something significantly thicker than water.

The light quivered and quaked from side to side and then up and down on the inhuman monstrosity it so spastically revealed to Wilbo's rapidly blinking eyes.

"I'll be done here in just a sec, pal. Then we can have us a nice, long chat," the thing spat in a garbled, wavy tone that reminded Wilbo of a badly interrupted radio frequency.

The man, or what had once been such, stood before him practically skinless, peeling away his own flesh in chunky, moist gobs that fell to the freshly waxed flooring below like stringy strands of discarded biscuit dough.

"W-what's going on...here?" Wilbo began, attempting with great difficulty to kept the light centered on the stranger's pulpy red face and shredded, hairless skull that was strangely void of ears.

The thing's penis and testicles detached and fell away into the larva-like pile a moment later, prompting a muffled giggle from their former owner, who peered down at them with casual aplomb.

Wilbo trained the light on the building mass, feeling his own scalp begin to tingle as if sprinkled with itching powder.

"Guess any further additions to the family are out of the question, huh?" the thing cackled, now bent and briskly rubbing the flesh from its legs and ankles. "William? What…who is it? *William!*" Kara screamed from just outside the door, the sound of which forced the flashlight from Wilbo's hand as if it had suddenly become red-hot in his fingers.

It clanked to the floor at his feet, rolling to a stop with the light shining directly into the mushy pile of gore the thing continued to dislodge as easily as one might peel dead skin from a nasty sunburn.

"Stay there, Kara! I-*don't open the door!"* Wilbo bellowed while reaching to retrieve the light, the revolver in his other hand shaking like it was being pointed by a person in the latter stages of Parkinson's diseases. He was, without nary a doubt, more scared than he had ever been. He could hear his own heartbeat at his temples, thumping like the most thunderous drum solo imaginable.

Kneeling, he pointed the light at the space the thing had occupied just seconds earlier, only to instead be greeted by an empty void.

Rising in a single, fluid movement, he whipped both the revolver and light around towards the door.

Both objects landed just inches from the back of a blood-spattered scalp that looked to have been peeled by a straight razor.

"H-hold it, mister, or I-I'll..." Wilbo began just as the figure pulled the door open and backed slowly to the left, like a hotel doorman politely performing his duties.

"You plan on plugging me with that peashooter? Go on with your *bad* self, then. Won't matter, I'm afraid. At this point, I'm way beyond being effected by such mundane efforts."

The light fell across Kara's terrified visage as she stood at the entrance; her thin but well-toned arms held in a classic boxer's pose, the taser gun gripped in the lead fist.

"William? Who are you talking to?" She

groaned, her shoulders relaxing just a bit.

"Get the hell out, Kara! There's somebody, *s-something* in here with us...he's got some kinda virus that m-melting him like a snow-cone in the Alabama sun..." Wilbo ranted, instinctively taking a step forward in his twin's direction. Just before the impossibly strong arm landed across his upper chest, sending him flailing backwards into the oak desk at waist level, he heard the thing laugh in a mocking, sarcastic tone that was no longer remotely human.

The force of the blow sent him careening over the desk headfirst, his head banging hard against the computer modem and monitor stationed there. Wilbo landed with the modem crushed beneath his shoulder blades and the monitor shattered under his battered thighs. He could feel tiny shards of broken glass embedded into his butt-cheeks and lower back as he attempted to roll away from the carnage. The room was a black pit without the light's intrusive beam.

His sister's shrill screams ensued just as he had stumbled to his feet and stood waving his arms about like a blinded boxer in search of a deathly quiet opponent.

Wilbo jogged wildly forward just as the room unexpectedly lit up like a planetary Supernova.

"The name is Gates, *Warden* Gates. Welcome to my nightmare, children," the guttural voice spat just beyond the source of the pupil-expanding light show.

Once his vision cleared, Wilbo instantly wished for the blind state to mercifully return.

CHAPTER EIGHT
The Lesser of Two Distinct Evils

The unbearable pain that had been building to extreme heights finally beginning to subside, Corporal Ron McIntosh strolled along the twisted, turning roads of a starkly real, crystal clear street of dreams he quickly realized was not entirely of his own making. In fact, as the images began to alter and mutate with rapid-fire speed and intensity, the fact that it was a totally foreign dreamscape he had been cast inside was readily apparent. He was merely playing the role of powerless, unwilling spectator. The scenes, some as brief as the blink of an eye and still others minutes in duration (although this was purely a guesstimation at best), played out like a haphazardly produced home video filmed within the confines of the most fevered of schizophrenic minds.

Scene one consisted of Officer Jerrod Dickenson arriving at the compound's sally port, cheerily 'giving some skin' to the somewhat overweight black correctional officer who had allowed him access inside. The clouds overhead were puffy and foreboding, an occasional flash of distant lightning present on the far horizon beyond the facilities southernmost tree line. The two figures stood inside the sally port, the speed of their movement increasing suddenly, like a VCR stuck in fast-forward mode, their lips trembling blurs as they spoke, their hand gestures spastic and frenzied.

The scene then altered drastically, first halting altogether, as if in pause mode on the same inner cassette recorder within the Corporal's brain, then released into a more deliberate, slow motion pace.

A third uniformed guard had joined Dickenson and the black officer within the port. He was an older man with a stocky build, strands of straight, gray hair poking out from beneath his 'MDCY (Mississippi Department of Correctional Justice)' baseball hat, displaying a gut usually associated with a heavy beer consumer.

The older guard's name tag was shown to the Corporal in a single, full- screen flash, as if a camera had been briefly shoved forward for an extreme close up just above his uniform's left shirt pocket.

It had read, "Settle."

Movement returned to a more normal speed just as the two white guards descended upon the black one like predators from the same pack bickering over a slab of raw meat. The tape sped up as the two men continually beat the larger one repeatedly with their clubs, only pausing to add a swift, ferocious kick or wildly thrown punch for good measure. A joyous lunacy filled each man's eyes as the massacre ensued, like small children relishing the torture of a small, helpless animal or insect.

As if carefully edited, the scene rapidly altered to show Dickenson and Settle loading the man's battered body into the back of a half-ton truck that had been pulled into the sally port since the attack.

Another quick cut revealed two additional guards, each with labored breath and darting eyes, joining them inside the port. Both were subsequently treated in the same manner as the black guard from earlier, caught completely flat-footed by the sudden blows that rained down upon them, rattled off of their head, face and midsection. Tossed into the truck like so much excess baggage, their weapons confiscated beforehand, it was apparent that they had been duped into thinking their fellow officers needed assistance of some kind, and were instead mercilessly ambushed for their efforts.

The inner camera then revealed Dickenson and Settle carefully huddled together near the rear of the truck, their somewhat subdued yet undeniably intense conversation littered with vivid hand gestures and robotic, stone-like expressions. It would have been obvious, even to the most casual of witnesses, that the details of a plan long since mapped out was being discussed and dissected one final time.

They left the sally port of Briarston Correctional Facility unmanned as the next scene flashed into view, leaving the truck they had so casually stashed three dead bodies inside of parked between the two locked gates.

The next scene transported Corporal McIntosh inside a narrow corridor, his movements fluid and smooth, as if he were floating atop the shoulder of a camera man whose feet levitated above the carpeted floor below.

The door ahead read "Authorized Personnel Only", and McIntosh witnessed the fingers, the nails of which were tinted a light shade of purple, reach over and punch in a series of numbers onto a mounted keypad.

Spastic, turbulent images of savage violence ensued like snippets from a thousand snuff films whose most vile acts had been carefully edited together in a 'best of' volume, sparring Corporal McIntosh few of the gruesome details of each.

Throats were slashed, fine lines of crimson liquid sprayed into thin air as serrated steel blade met tender flesh. Faces and skulls were pounded ad nauseam; some long after the spark of life had departed the battered shells of the victim. Corporal McIntosh spotted a singular similarity, a lone MO that tied all the brutal homicides neatly together in an unmistakable theme.

All had worn the same bland, grayish uniform that distinguished them as correctional officers for the state of Mississippi.

The Corporal was unable to establish an accurate count of just how many men his mind's eye watched butchered and bludgeoned due to the overwhelming montage of imagery as a whole, but quickly deduced the final tally to be no less than ten, possibly even twenty.

The next scene showcased the bodies being casually and systematically stacked into a dark, cramped room like freshly cut cordwood.

Corporal McIntosh sensed a cold presence within the mysterious confines of the squared space that would house the recently slaughtered. Even within the cloudy barriers of the hazy dreamscape, he could have sworn he felt goose bumps envelop his prone form from head to toe.

Proceeding further into the recent past, he next bore hapless witness to a cruel, sadistic killing that was showcased in excruciatingly vivid show motion detail before being rewound and shown again at normal speed. The victim had exited a back office in a lurching jog, a revolver held shakily in his left hand, his round, sweat coated face a mask of pure, primal fear. His rounded shoulders had displayed the bars of an officer, although his shocked, terrified expression was comparable to that of a terrified child peeking from underneath a bed frame to avoid the ghosts and goblins their mind had created on a dark, stormy night.

The Captain's lips were moving, more than likely inquiring as to the source of the commotion to the two subordinates that stood so smugly before him.

The doomed man's eyes widened with awareness just as Officer Settle leaped forward and sunk the previously stained knife blade deep into his upper abdomen.

Managing to squeeze the trigger of his revolver while jerking back from the impact of the stabbing, the Captain's aim had been wild but miraculously accurate.

The thirty-eight slug grooved a neat, bloodless hole just above Settle's left eyebrow, fiercely snapping the man's head back and then forward again, his cap sailing away in a high, circular arc.

A single trickle of pinkish ooze dribbled down the man's nose and into his mouth from the dime-sized wound, to which he licked away with a devilish grin as he motioned for Dickenson to join him at the spot where the Captain lay spread eagle. Settle pulled his knife free from the man's midsection and gleefully licked the dripping edge of the blade while shooting his partner a sly wink.

As the two proceeded to take turns using the officer's own revolver to pelt his body with calculatedly aimed shots that were meant to maim more than kill, the Corporal couldn't help but marvel at Officer Settle's continued involvement in the malicious scenario. The forehead wound no longer seeped bodily fluid of any type, much less the porous amount one would have expected from such blunt trauma.

The two unloaded the weapon into the Captain's exposed limbs, leaving his legs, knees and arms ravaged and torn from the multiple gaps blown into each. They had laughed like teenaged boys lighting farts beside a campfire as the damage was inflicted, ending the mad ritual with a concluding shot to the side of the man's lolling head.

Both threw a mock salute to the corpse before dragging the body down a distant hall to be unceremoniously added to the growing pile of human remains collected earlier that evening.

Cut to a wide clearing, the afternoon sun fading into the distance as just a trace of fog drifted onto the edges of the dream's increasingly ragged perimeter.

The half-ton truck from the sally port was parked near the base of an ancient, dead-limbed oak as the two guards were turned in the opposite direction, their heads bowed as if each were deep in prayer. The Corporal's view of the surreal portrait transferred from rear ground level to front overhead in a blink, leaving the source of the two men's concentration plainly in sight.

The crater was so unnaturally round it looked to have been painted into the dusty, flat surface, like one of those 'instant ACME holes' Willy Coyote had always attempted to snag the Roadrunner within old Warner Brothers cartoon shorts. The smothering darkness below the lip of the hole was so complete that not even the faintest of outlines could be seen. The abyss was *nothingness* personified, a bottomless black pit of mystery with a heart of pure menace pounding at its rotted core.

Officer's Dickenson and Settle moved as if entranced, their facial expressions bland, almost catatonic, as they went about the task of removing the three deceased guards from the back of the truck. Each body was tossed into the crater with special care, pushed into the tube-like opening with a gentle reverence that had been sorely lacking as they had been so ruthlessly eradicated.

The bodies fell into the pit as if swallowed by a ravenous cavity that had as much sucked them in as simply welcomed their intrusion.

After the last, the large black guard, had been sacrificed to the gaping maw, Corporal McIntosh could have sworn that Dickenson and Settle bowed slightly in the same direction, as if confirming that some malevolent quota had been met.

The closing act in the plethora of lunacy-filled visions to fill Corporal McIntosh's inner eye-lens was one laced with equal amounts of calm tranquility and impending chaos.

Officer Settle sat inside a room that appeared to be a command center of some type, his chubby, chalk-white fingers tapping furiously at a small keypad linked to a large-screened computer monitor. The screen displayed what seemed to be cellblock layouts, the words '*institute LOCKDOWN mode*' flashing in red while an asterisk-coded password was being typed in waiting spaces below.

Officer Dickenson tapped the older guard on the right shoulder, as the last entry was complete, the pudding-like substance the skin of their faces had become gleaming in the overhead fluorescent lighting. As if on cue from the younger man's touch, Officer Settle arose from the tall-backed chair he had been slumped into and stepped towards a large metal transformer in a far corner of the room.

After keying and then removing the large Master lock held there, Officer Settle then reached up and placed his thumb and forefinger on a switch labelled 'main power grid'. The sneer on his bloated, sickeningly moist face widened to physically impossible proportions just as he pushed downward.

All went instantly black, only the desperate, haunted voices of men trapped in eight by ten cells and engulfed in unrelenting darkness conveying the blunt message. A message meant solely for Corporal McIntosh's drifting mind through the otherworldly channel opened to him by his former supervisor.

The guards were dead and the inmates trapped like coalminers in a collapsed mine.

As the Corporal fell back into an unconscious daze that was no longer being controlled by outside influences, a single query still besieged his tattered mind.

A simple question but still one with ample ability to gnaw and grind at one's subconscious, even in times of great physical pain (his hands again) and confusion.

What was the *purpose* of it all? What unholy

mess had he and the rest of the Dark Eagle militia stepped into? And what role did Peterson play in the deadly drama that would more than likely cause many more their lives before all was said and done?

The Corporal's next vision was of a solid white sheet of nothingness that bulged in the center like an ice age beast shoving itself through a frozen, ivory force-field that was just moments from certain collapse.

Something huge was on its way. Something huge and not the *least* bit pleasant.

***

"Bodine? Damn it, where are you?" Private Kemp moaned, the pen-lite's pathetically narrow beam sailing about the room like a mini-laser show on concert night.

Upon viewing (performing a perfectly executed double take in the process) the neatly stacked bodies with their freezer-burned skin and crystallized wounds, she had instantly flung Bodine aside and hit the floor as if avoiding incoming mortar shells.

"Come out w-wherever you are, Limp dick. I ain't hanging here with the dead-end kids until you decided to crawl from whatever hole you ducked into," she blurted, careful to avoid placing the light anywhere in the general direction of the open freezer.

Despite her best efforts to sound unfazed in the face of the gruesome visions now permanently welded into her subconscious, Private Kemp found it impossible to keep either of her hands even remotely steady in the aftermath. She had hardly taken the time for an accurate count, but figured there were at least seven to ten bodies stashed inside the closet-sized freezer, the portions visible from each looked to have been beaten, shot, stabbed, or a mixture of all of the above. A veritable buffet of fatal injuries stacked atop one another like a freak show exhibit in a Madman's sideshow, the few faces that had flashed into view horribly distorted, their frosted lips curled, their jaws frozen in mid-clinch. She saw a dangling eyeball hanging from a mashed socket like a cat's toy on a string. Fingers were bent and gnarled, as if grasping for something to pull them free from the grisly fate they had been dealt.

"Guards. The inmates wasted 'em all. I guess the Major was right. Prison break for sure," Private Kemp whispered while kneeling down onto her hunches. The light landed on a pair of partially scuffed but still-shiny boot tips, parked behind a three-tiered metal tray dispenser a few feet to her left.

"Bodine? That you back there, kid?" She asked a bit shakier than intended.

The shrill whimper that followed gave her the obvious answer, and she moved quickly to his side, pulling him up roughly by the armpits.

"Sorry 'bout the push, Lomax. Lost my bearings there for a sec. Meat lockers full of dead correctional officers always seem to bring out the chicken shit in me, sorry to say."

His entire body shivered beneath her touch as she attempted to push/pull him towards the kitchen entrance. Despite the chill present from the open freezer, Private Kemp could feel the immense body heat radiating from his slumped form.

"We're as d-dead as they are, S-Sandy," he managed between lips so chapped they seemed to be coated in partially dry Elmer's Glue.

Keeping just enough distance between them to avoid tangling their legs together, Private Kemp aimed the light over his left shoulder and pushed lightly at the pit of his back.

"Damn, Lomax. I thought *I* was a pessimist. Let's just keep moving and hope for the best, okay? I get the feeling that the damage has been done here. I doubt whoever did this is around to give a rat's round ass about a group of roving militia troops."

As they passed through the swinging doors and back into the somewhat comforting open space of the mess hall, Private Bodine suddenly gripped the metal railing with both hands, instantly halting his forward progress. Private Kemp's chest bumped into his bony back a moment later, and she barely avoided tossing the penlight forward, grunting in frustration.

"Move it, Lomax. This ain't the time for meditation. We need to haul ass for the main gate, pronto. Do *not* pass go; do *not* collect your AWOL balls. Move it, son, I'm fast losing my patie..."

He whirled to face her, his hands leaving the railing and instead grasping her upper shoulders with an intensity and strength she would have never thought possible considering his earlier semi-comatose state. Her light balanced on the center of his pasty, snowflake white complexion, his top row of teeth magnified somehow in the odd angle of the beam. At that precise moment, Private Kemp's only thought was that her cohort resembled a man who had taken a peek inside death's open chamber and discovered the doorman to be himself.

"Sandy...the gates are l-locked. Locked up, t-tight. He's on his way. The one we w-were brought here to greet. Th-this has all been p-pre-ordained, don't you see? The M-Major knew what was transpiring. He brought us here to be...s- sacrificed. N-not like those guards. Nothing t-that simple or m-mundane. Something *special* is p-planned for us."

No longer able to maintain the façade of bravery and indifference to their plight, Private Kemp discovered she was dangerously close to actually peeing her fatigues. It was something about the other Private's voice, the ancient doom contained within its stark tone that made her realize that he might not be so damned crazy after all. Whatever lunatic babbling he was spouting, it might well be equal amounts fact and fiction.

"W-what...who are you talking about, Lomax? Who are we supposed to greet?"

Private Bodine's throat clicked as if the inner workings were in dire need of lubrication. His eyes bulged like fleshy manhole covers being expanded from within by some unseen pressure valve on the threshold of release.

"I f-felt it before we ever left c-camp tonight. The M-Major wasn't h- himself. He was sick, afflicted with some sort of virus, I think. He k-knew what was happening at the compound. Somehow, he *knew*..."

"Why are we here, Lomax? For what and why the hell us anyhow? It ain't like we really matter in the great scheme of things. It's to each his own now, every fuckin' man for himself, I say. I told

Mac not to follow that bastard Peterson. I told 'im...I said..."

Private Bodine raised his right hand palms up, as if shushing a small child. "Doesn't matter, Sandy. We do matter, or we would not be here. S-simple as that. The damned never realize they've been chosen until the moment the reaper arrives and taps them on the shoulder. We are the damned on this night. But at least we can take a matter of solace in the fact that we're not alone. No we are hardly the beginning. A tiny appetizer placed on a dinner table as long and wide as infinity itself."

Slapping his remaining hand from her shoulder, Private Kemp brushed past him in a controlled jog, the outline of the mess hall exit just a few feet ahead. "If you're trying to scare me, Bodine, let the record show you've succeeded with flying colors. Now, let's see what we can do about securing some real weapons...*after* we check the main gate, that is. I don't know 'bout you, but Beatrice Kemp's only granddaughter ain't about to lay down and die without a scrap. She was a fighter, old Granny was, nothing at all like my folks. I only hope some of her genes found a cubbyhole inside me somewhere. So, you coming with me or staying here to pray?"

She stopped with her hand atop the exit's door handle, turning back to shine the light on his face one last time.

His expression was less slack, a bit more animated than before, as he looked to the dark ceiling above for an answer. Ten seconds ticked by before it was forthcoming.

"I... I'll...I'm with you, Sandy, although I know deep down it's a fruitless effort, however valiant it may be."

Private Kemp smiled crookedly, her tone instantly reverting back to its former sarcastic self.

"I told ya, Chief, don't be so damn optimistic. Besides, at least you'll have the pleasure of expiring in the company of a beautiful, exotic warrior princess like myself."

They strolled back into the covered breezeway like cat burglars balanced on the edge of a hotel terrace.

"Man, could I use a drink," Private Kemp exclaimed as they tiptoed back onto the grassy compound. Behind her, Private Lomax Bodine sucked in the putrid night air, realizing without meditation that it would most likely be some of the last he would ever inhale.

***

It had long despised the restraints of time that had been its constant advisor. Countless centuries spent in a perpetual state of suspended animation, with only the drudgery of never-ending time as a companion had taken its toll. A torturous toll that could only be reversed through restitution. Restitution paid in full on not only the pathetic hordes of soon to be soulless minions residing above, but on the judge and jury that had bred such a vastly different being than the one that had been originally tried, convicted and sentenced.

Sentenced in a time not measured in simple numbers but in dusty, dank strolls unraveled in bright fiery pits by beings supposedly of its own elk. Beings that might have once been his equal in terms of malevolence and sheer wickedness, but now paled pathetically in comparison. Decades spent lying in forced wait for the freedom that was at last forthcoming had created an impenetrable layer of determined resolve that went beyond the simple borders of extracting revenge.

As it squirmed and wriggled its lower extremities, all of which moved more fluidly since the last absorption of human carrion, it felt a jolting surge within its massive chest cavity that both terrified and exhilarated its festering soul. The pulsating power spilled into its cord-like veins as if fueled by a planet-sized generator. It felt the orgasmic spasms reach into its skull and massage the brain beneath with a million separate digits.

The surface world and its insignificant masses had provided the key to escape once a means of commanding and controlling their thoughts had been mastered. An infinite amount of time had been spent feeding upon small, soulless creatures that provided little satisfaction. Bouts of insurmountable rage that made it feel as if it would literally split into separate entities had instead provided the power to tunnel to the surface in varied directions from the imprisonment space. From there, the calling had begun. A silent wailing heard only by those select few with the inherited talent to receive the transmissions. A select few who would heed the instructions of what they understood to be their only true master.

Failure had come often in those early attempts, coming as no surprise when dealing with a species it considered insignificant and weak from the outset.

The breeding of his spores through human hosts

had provided only scant success, and it quickly dropped such feeble attempts in lieu of direct feeding methods. Despite the overall failed attempt, the initial breeding methods had paid off rather handsomely within the past two decades, however, as two surface dwellers possessing the seed had provided it with consistently hearty souls to feed upon, each one adding a muscle to its building constitution.

The being felt a strange kinship to the trio, despite their obvious shortcomings within the rank and file, a feeling not unlike fatherly pride.

They had listened and obeyed willingly, although the slacked pace of the project tended to burden the timeline of overall completion, driving the being to unnecessary dramatics that might have easily given warning to those who would surely attempt to prevent his escape. It wasn't as if the being feared such measures from his captors, actually welcoming the forthcoming struggle with joyful glee, but the element of surprise could never be overemphasized in such cases. It had, in fact, felt a vague presence recently. A presence that it perceived as a viable threat, thus patience was required to build its strength to unknown heights in preparation for the glorious conflict to come. It knew the threat waited above surface, but was more than likely a core-dweller acting as a sentinel of sorts. It realized that nothing spawned at the surface could possibly bode such a threat to one such as it, so it was the lone explanation for such a premonition.

The last of the mortal flesh consumed, it fought the overwhelming urge to dig forth and begin the task at hand despite being not yet complete in either physical stature or suitable mental prowess.

A final feeding would be necessary before extraction. Commands had been transmitted and thusly received to set such activities into motion.

The being forced itself to settle back into the marble stone that had been its only home for eons. What would have been the equivalent to a human smile was parked on a maw as wide as a Mack trucks grille, the spear-like teeth contained within dripping with a thick, jelled liquid equal parts human and animal blood.

Time would soon no longer be viewed as an enemy in a world void of a soul to call its own.

***

"Can you feel it, JC? Man, I smoked some extra-fine Colombian grown wacky-backy a few years back that had me seein' goats wearing tuxedos and pigs with human hands. That wasn't diddly-shit compared to the singular space- trippin', ass-glidin' ride I'm in the middle of right here this minute, old buddy old rag," Buck Lomax the Third, or at least what remained of his former self, exclaimed joyfully. His ragged voice was inhumanly deep and inexplicably shrill at the same time. As they made their way painstakingly down the concrete walkway that led towards the exercise yard in the near distance, JC Carlyle struggled to keep pace with his cohort, sagging a full step behind on legs that were nothing more than shredded bone and seeping, infectious bodily fluid. Each held one of Jimmy's ankles, his footwear long since pulled off and discarded since entering the Briarston compound. With JC's pained efforts to keep up with Buck failing miserably, Jimmy's lower body seemed to be dancing a drunken jig, his right leg spread wide from the left at an angle that would have caused extreme discomfort in a more aware state.

"Slow...d-down, Buck. I'm 'bout to lose a lung in the literal sense."

His hairless, badly distorted scalp bent back as he studied the star-filled sky above, Buck fell back a step without responding to JC's whine.

Sucking in a deep, expanding breath of the rank, rather chilly night air, he spat free what few teeth had remained inside his hollowed mouth and coughed harshly.

"See it up there, JC old salt? See that spot just to the right of the second fenced-in basketball court? It's shining like a lighthouse beacon at the dead of night, ain't it son? Grandest damn sight these rotten old orbs have ever settled on, I can tell ya that."

JC, happy just to be on an even cadence with his oldest friend, tried to respond with a manner of enthusiasm but managed only a dismal squeak. JC's well of energy was shrinking fast, pulled from his very being by Buck's own insatiable appetite for the same. JC found he didn't really mind too much. What were friends for, anyhow?

"Only a hundred yards or so, and we'll be stomping around in our own version of the Garden of Eden, huh, pal'a mine? Y'know though, JC old canker sore, I get the feelin' we're gonna have some company other than old jiggle-buns here."

Jimmy's left eye began to twinge as the initial

stage of consciousness re-emerged. The back of his skull bounced and rocked along the concrete, long since scraped raw from the base of the neck to the top edge of his scalp.

"Wh-Wha...what…?" he stammered incoherently, his fingers reaching weakly for something, *anything,* to clutch in order to halt all forward movement.

Buck the Third peered back at him through the red, pulpy pits of his eye sockets and guffawed. The sound was like razor blades being whisked across a glass surface.

"Looks like sleepin' ugly is comin' to, JC old fart. His timing couldn't be worse, at least from *his* point of view, I mean."

JC spat and stuttered for a moment before working up a semi-coherent reply, his naked face and chest coated in what from a distance would have looked like partially dried oatmeal.

"Ya think we ought to cold-cock him again 'fore the arrival, Buck?"

Now only a few dozen feet from their ultimate destination, a sharp right turn moving them onto the exquisitely manicured grass of the exercise yard, Buck nodded while adjusting his grip on Jimmy's exposed ankle, ripping the dirt- stained sock free in the process.

"Let 'im be. I won't mind hearin' him scream like a spooked girl-scout once the feeding begins."

The patch of dirt they stood before seconds later looked to have been measured off and cut out like a patch of expertly removed shag carpet from a living room floor.

The clearing was amazingly circular in shape,

with a diameter that covered roughly the space of a larger than normal street manhole cover.

"Ah, our lord and master's main portal, I presume," Buck the third announced as both men dropped Jimmy's bare feet to the ground in harmonic unison.

JC fell immediately to his naked knees at the south edge of the circle, his face turned to the sky in silent prayer, before bowing as if at the base of a recently dug up artifact.

Buck joined him there, although remaining upright, as both performed a brief self-inventory of their gruesomely distorted faculties. A fierce breeze swept by, dislodging JC's left ear and sending it sailing into the misty night.

"Geez, ain't we a grisly twosome? Looks like somebody used a 'tator peeler on our asses," Buck barked while studying the dry white bone protruding from the tips of each of his ten fingers.

"Just happy to finally be at ground zero, Buck. It won't be long now, will it? Tell me it won't…I'm s-so damned tired."

Buck tapped his friend gently on the right shoulder, leaving a permanent indention matted into the gelatinous flesh.

"Mere minutes 'til all is revealed, JC old bud. Moments until the true rapture."

They turned as one to face the huddled shadows trudging their way from between the admin and mess hall buildings.

"Ah, looks like the rest of *Our Gang* has arrived, Spanky," Buck warbled on an alien wavelength only he and JC could possibly comprehend.

The man at the head of the line was tall and wide-shouldered, the dark fatigues he donned sagging a bit at the waistline, a circle of sickly wetness hugging him there like a burst inner-tube that had leaked half its air content. The man's face sagged on the left side like a victim of life-long paralysis, his eyelids hanging down like an aged basset hound, leaving only the narrowest of slits to peer through.

A smaller man dressed in equally moist CO gear brought up the rear, pushing a pair of metal gurneys roughly across the grass. Each gurney held a body, only one of which displayed even the slightest of movement.

"Here for the unveiling, I take it?" Buck managed through a mouth that seemed to be slowly sewing itself closed.

The larger man stepped to the north edge of the circle and peered down intensely.

"Affirmative, my brothers. We come baring fruit for the feast. From what I gather, these last few morsels will provide all the boost needed for final extraction."

Buck the Third wobbled over to the man's side, studying him carefully. "And your name, soldier boy?"

"It's…not that it really matters now was Major David Peterson, Commander, Dark Eagle Militia. My comrade behind the entrees is former Correctional Officer for the great state of Mississippi, Jerod Dickenson. And you two might be?"

JC arose, his brittle knees firing off like twin cannons.

"Buck Lomax and JC Carlyle, just a couple'a townies out for a peaceful moonlight stroll within the confines of our local state pen," he croaked with renewed vigor even as a thick line of goo flew from his nostrils as if fired from twin water pistols.

"Damn. I thought the change was turning me into a walking pile of pureed plasma. You two are melting like ice cubes in a hothouse," Peterson said with a wink of his remaining functional eyelid.

"Who's the meat?" Dickenson asked, nodding towards Jimmy's prone form, the legs of which were now twitching more visibly.

"Some wanderin' camper who picked the wrong location and night to be pullin' his pud in these here woods," Buck replied calmly, his consistently hyper state finally beginning to subside somewhat.

JC limped over to the first gurney and peered downward at the unmoving form strapped there.

"C-comrade of yours?" He asked Peterson wryly.

"Unbeliever. Strange how some of us receive the calling and others do not. Sergeant Ezop was a good troop. Could have been a problem if not for the bit of...selective surgery Jerrod and I decided to perform. Same with Corporal Mac here. Big, strong, stubborn SOB, he is. Their bleeding stopped after we took a torch to them. Hope the master doesn't mind the missing digits. For as I understood, he wanted them alive. Didn't specify what condition."

Buck joined JC in hovering over the body. Sergeant Ezop's face was frozen in a pained scowl; his breath whistling through his partially pinched nostrils.

“You cut off their fingers?” Buck asked with child-like curiosity, studying the singed nubs pinned at the man’s sides.

“You must understand. Ezop and McIntosh are trained combat veterans whose talents include transforming even the most mundane object into a potentially dangerous weapon. I…was given a… hazy order to ensure they be disabled after capture. Disabled but not fatally.”

Peterson stared at the circular clearing with his chin balanced on his left fist, his feet spread apart in parade rest position.

“At least, I believe that’s the command I received. Perhaps...it was just...a *suggestion* from the master, not an actual order. Possibly he decided a little fun was in order for our efforts, after all, how much damage could mere mortals inflict on such a grand being?”

He turned to grin at Buck the Third, a single tooth hanging crookedly from the center of his spongy, mutated maw.

“Regardless, I have to admit it was a real kick, wouldn’t you agree, Jerrod?”

Dickenson stood directly over Jimmy, his black boots straddling the fallen man’s head and shoulders.

“Damn tootin’, Major. It kind of scares me how much I enjoyed the entire process. Kind of…liberating.”

“Anymore in here with us besides the inmates?” Buck asked a bit wearily. His upper body had begun to rock back and forth, like a drunken wino on the verge of collapse.

“Two of my troops are still roaming about, but

they're pretty much helpless. I thought about going after them, but didn't even deem them fit as suitable sacrifice material. They can join the general population in the initial sweep."

Turning his flared nostrils towards the sky like a blood hound on the scent of nearby quarry, Buck the Third sniffed several times before holding up a single gnarled finger.

"We know of at least two more. A brother and sister act we were hot on the trail of before we ran into tub-a'guts here. One or both of 'em may be strapped, though the damage they might cause would be minimal at best. Couple'a real fruit-loops."

Dickenson leaned down and gave Jimmy a quick, viscous slap across his right cheek, which flared instantly red from the contact.

"Get up, fat man. I know you're faking the sleeping bit. Open 'em up and be first witness to the greatest unveiling of all."

"By all means, yes," Peterson rang in happily, bowing like a stage actor receiving a standing ovation.

"How many get the opportunity to view an all-powerful force, a true God, just before it begins the glorious task of absorbing and transforming everything around it?"

Jimmy suddenly lurched to the right, initiating four full rolls before rising to his shaky bare feet, his hands raised over his face in a defensive pose.

"Who are a-all you crazy son of a b-bitches?" He managed, instantly taken back by his captors blasé attitude in wake of his sudden awakening.

"Mister, do yourself a favor and relax. You

ain't goin' nowhere anyway. Number one, the gates are locked and the keys been tossed. Number two, the resurrection is a cat's whisker away. Number three, from the looks of ya, you couldn't fight off a head cold," JC quipped with his arms, stripped raw and void of almost all skin, crossed across his equally skinny, concave chest.

Slapping the left side of his head just above the ear, as if attempting to eradicate fluid build-up after a lengthy swim, Jimmy caught only minute portions of the garbled vocalization. He thought he had heard 'relax', 'gates locked', and something similar to 'head case', but was uncertain about any specific meaning.

"L-listen, you're all very s-sick. Look at y-your faces, y-your skin, for God's sake. You need a doctor, don't you see that?" Jimmy pleaded, all the while scanning the perimeter of the exercise yard for a possible escape route. Despite only the dim moonlight available and the fact that his vision was still a bit blurred from the blow on the head he had endured, Jimmy could visualize the freakish, distorted forms better than he would have ever wished to under more normal circumstances.

It was like standing before a group of scientific lab experiments gone awry, the subjects of which had been cruelly, horribly disfigured both in a physical and mental sense.

"W-was it a chemical spill or something l-like that? W-where are the prison inmates?" He asked, unsure of exactly why he bothered considering the incomprehensible answers likely forthcoming.

The wobbling, slowly scurrying pile of disintegrating muscle, tendon and bone that mere hours earlier had answered to the title of Major David Peterson took center stage, the grating, grinding voice surprisingly clear in reply to Jimmy's two-part query.

JC Carlyle and Jerrod Dickenson had joined the Major at the far edge of the circle, the two metal gurneys parked with care on its eastern and west sides. Jimmy thought crazily that the trio resembled a barbershop quartet from the deepest regions of hell.

"We are lost no longer...the tunnel is opening...the all-consuming darkness will show us the way...his way. We die to serve and please him..." Peterson chanted in a robotic trance, evoking a fresh batch of chill bumps to envelop Jimmy's entire person.

The ground at their feet began to rumble and crack, the surface of the clearing splitting like a rotted elm beneath a lumberjack's axe blade.

Jimmy saw the three figures fall instantly to their collective knees as if solemn prayer.

He turned to bolt just as the ground exploded.

***

"Looks like somebody finally found the light switch," the thing croaked, its slim, peeled body revealed in all its grisly glory from underneath the fluorescent lights illuminating the office.

"Bought damn time. Do either of you realize just how difficult it is to shed your skin in total darkness?"

Wilbo leaped in front of his sister, who stood at the office doors threshold, one foot planted firmly inside while the other remained posed to sprint in the opposite direction.

"J-Jesus, man…what the...y-your..." Wilbo sputtered like a man with a mouthful of ball bearings.

Kara's lips trembled futilely, the hand grasping the taser a blur of jerky spasms.

"I know I must look a site, kind of like a walking, half-defrosted TV Dinner. If I'd known company was coming, I could have put on my Sunday best. As it is, you two will just have to accept me as I am. I have only one quick question to pose. Just who in the name of Elvis Presley's undertaker are you two bozos?"

Steadying the revolver that had come dangerously close to literally shaking from his quivering hand moments before, Wilbo set the front site directly between the thing's eyes, which were ivory white and pupil-less.

"Keep your d-distance man. We don't want to contract whatever you're carrying. We j-just…uh..."

The thing moved forward in a blur, so quickly that Wilbo never saw it take an actual step, as if it had levitated ahead without benefit of moving either legs or feet.

The barrel of the thirty-eight stuck against, and submerged into, the soggy flesh of its ruined forehead. The smile it revealed was overflowing with both sardonic wit and barely withheld rage.

"Let me repeat…who in the hell are you people, and what are you doing in the Warden's office smack dab in the middle of a major league *FUBAR*?"

Despite the paralyzing fear gripping every fiber

of her soul, Kara glared at the monstrosity standing before them with her head slightly cocked in comic confusion.

"Fu...b-bar? What's that s-stand for...a prison break of some kind? Did the in-inmates use chemical weapons or some..."

Wilbo's right hand shot up to her face palm up, instantly quieting her.

"I'll explain later, sis. No time for definitions…" he whispered to her in an apologetic but stern parental tone, before turning his attention back to the reeking figure whose skull had readily swallowed a full inch of the revolver's barrel.

"I'm William and this is my sister K-Kara. I... we came to Red Bridge to search for our m-missing parents. We followed the smoke to the compound, and I had a …feeling that the mystery going on here might be connected to their whereabouts…"

The thing that had so casually discarded the flesh of Warden Owen Gates and presently stood posed as a living testament to the walking dead groaned in obvious annoyance, the revolver's barrel site now hidden beneath the soft tissue that seemed to be slowly engulfing it.

"Yeah, yeah, blah blah, yadda yadda. Couple of amateur detectives, I deduce. Well, to be honest, the proceedings on this particular night more than likely *do* hold the key to your kin's missing status. Be forewarned, dear children, that it's a key that opens a doorway you may later wish had remained double- bolted."

The thing's hands twitched at its sides, the whole of its form seeping body fluids from every visible wound, providing a shiny, grotesque coating not unlike clammy wax build-up on a shiny metallic surface. Wilbo noticed with morbid fascination that the thing's upper body near the chest and upper abdomen seemed to be stretching and expanding without benefit of any accompanying movement on its part, as if being altered and reconstructed from *within* by an invisible team of plastic surgeons.

"A-re you d-d-dying?" Kara chimed in, her tiny, terrified voice barely audible.

The thing eyed her around the blockade her brother's hand and the adjoining revolver provided.

Wilbo perceived the look as nothing short of maniacally lustful. His finger grew instantly tighter on the thirty-eight's trigger mechanism.

"In a manner of speaking, yes, my dear. On an altogether different plane, however, the word I would use is 'restructured'. This day has been on the near horizon for what's seemed like an eternity for me. The fate I've inherited is the ultimate in double-edged swords, you see. Impossible to dismiss and improbable to even try, despite the strained efforts to keep it at bay with such words as 'lunacy' and 'raving drivel'. Over the years I tried to convince myself that my mind was drifting into delusional regions only logically explained by symptoms of mental illness. Countless unexplained, *unexplainable* to be fair, incidents over the years on these very prison grounds finally convinced me otherwise. I was placed here on a mission, and the rehabilitation of incarcerated individuals was only a very small, insignificant part of the plan, as it turned out."

His entire arm aching from the continual pressure applied in holding the revolver forcefully in place, Wilbo wanted desperately to switch hands. His entire right arm had grown numb and tingled excessively.

"W-what mission? What's going on in this freaking looney-bin? We s-saw what we thought were National Guard troops bolt onto the grounds in front of us." Its eyes still glued onto Kara, who had yet to twitch a muscle other than her shuddering lips, the Warden/Thing replied in a bored, openly irritated tone. "Probably just part of his plans, no doubt. He's a leech, no more. To be liberated, he's forced to depend on those beings he despises only a fraction less than his captors, ones that he only exists to eventually destroy and subsequently damn. Impatience will be his ultimate undoing. Impatience and underestimating his enemies, to be exact."

"Who a-are you talking about? Mister, you a-ain't right in the hea..." Wilbo began, his voice cracking wildly, like a man on the verge of a hysterical laughing jag. The sentence was never completed as the tiled floor beneath his feet began to noticeably vibrate. It felt as if a room full of jackhammers had been simultaneously plugged in and rammed into the tile directly between his legs.

"What the…earthquake?" He mumbled, struggling to keep the weapon in place while executing an impromptu break dance to avoid tripping forward.

The thing howled, throwing its head back like a baying wolf. "Not quite, kid. More like Showtime at the O.K. Corral."

"W-William? Don't you think we really need to leave now," Kara asked timidly while shuffling backwards unconsciously.

The shaking halted a moment later, leaving Wilbo in a stance more appropriate for a surfer riding a wave's building crest.

"Stand your ground, sis. This sick asshole knows something about our folks, and he's gonna let me in on it in the next ten seconds or so or somebody's gonna be able to use his head for a planter."

The Warden/Thing grinned devilishly.

"Fire away, Kid, by all means. Another hole or two in this dilapidated shell won't affect the inevitable."

Wilbo could actually feel the surging vibration, like a mild electric shock, beneath the man's skin. Muffled cracking noises were accompanied by moist, sucking sounds as the muscle and tendon shifted, loosening like severed guitar strings before eventually tightening again.

"Damn it, *what* are you?" Wilbo screamed just as the floor and surrounding walls seemed to slide violently to the left, sending him sprawling in the same direction in a makeshift combat roll.

As a new series of aftershocks ensued, the overhead lights began to flicker frenziedly.

"Time to settle an old score, kids. Come on with Poppa now. You don't wanna dare miss this...," the voice croaked amid the sickening echoes of snapping tendon and cracked bones.

Wilbo was in the midst of a desperate search for his dropped thirty-eight when he felt something soft and wet wrap around his left ankle just above the edge of his high-top tennis shoes. He whipped his head around, almost losing his glasses in the swiftness of the motion, and caught only spastic flashes of the object whose grip grew ever tighter as the seconds passed. Wilbo's eyes grew wide as the tentacle-like appendage; complete with human fingers that were abnormally thick and nail-less began to tug at his calf, pulling him towards the center of the room.

Swinging his arms madly in an attempt to clamp hold of the nearest object, Wilbo heard someone screaming in the background of the small confines of the room, which seemed to literally be coming apart at the seams. It wasn't until he was violently jerked to his feet and swung around the room like a clock pendulum that Wilbo realized the piercing screams weren't originating from his twin sister, as he had so hastily presumed, but from himself.

The room went jet black just as the tremors abruptly halted.

"Time for introductions at last..." the voice bellowed as it bolted forward with a speed that belied it's new, thicker size, ripping free large sections of wall plaster and ceiling tile in the process.

***

"Bingo. I'm feeling more secure already," Private Kemp beamed, staring through the wire mesh fence into the weapons armory, a metal gun rack littered with twenty and thirty gauge shotguns lighting up the pupils of her eyes like lit bulbs on a freshly cut Christmas pine.

"Waste of time, Sandra. Guns won't hel..." Private Bodine began before being cut off as the bony elbow of his comrade thumped off his ribcage.

"Stow it, Private Killjoy. I don't care what's waiting for us out there. I'll feel a damn might safer with a little firepower leading the way. Remember what they say..." She quipped, pushing past his prone form and through the already pushed open solid-steel door that led into the armory. "...guns don't kill people...*people* kill people."

After a few moments, Private Bodine joined her inside; his shoulders slumped in total, desolate defeat.

Private Kemp had already chosen her weapon of choice as he strolled next to her between two wall racks hanging directly across from one another. Slinging the thirty-gauge over her shoulder, she spoke without looking at him.

"Sure glad somebody saw fit to turn the juice back on. Maybe the Calvary has already arrived. Never hurts to be prepared though, am I right or am I right?" The ground began to tremble just as she had stepped behind a large counter marked 'AMMO – Sign it Out or Be Reprimanded – ***IT'S YOUR CHOICE!'***

The shakes quickly intensified ten-fold, the wall and floor gun racks rattling ferociously in unison.

"What the fu..." she blurted, almost falling backwards and taking the contents of a metal fire drawer full of bullets and packed cartridges with her.

"It's beginning," Private Bodine announced calmly while hanging onto a nearby partition.

Even as the quaking subsided to a low rumble, both hung to their respective positions until only a slight throbbing could be felt through the soles of their boots.

"Bomb just detonated somewhere in the compound. Nothing else it could've been. Far as I know, Mississippi ain't exactly prone to quakes," Private Kemp remarked solemnly, her hands gripping the top edge of the heavy metal cabinet for support.

Private Bodine hugged the partition, his eyes glazed and unblinking. "Wasn't an explosive, Sandy. Wish it had been. Afraid we won't get off that easily."

Breaking her stance, Private Kemp strode towards him with her fists balled at her sides, a contorted scowl covering her red-cheeked face.

"You buggin' out on me again, Bodine? I swear I'll leave your schizoid carcass right here if you don't start making some sense. We've got t-..."

A series of echoing thunderclaps swallowed the remainder of Private Kemp's rant, the suddenness of their onslaught sending her ducking into an impromptu combat crotch.

"What's that, happy boy? Low flying ducks fartin' into the breeze?" She sneered once the echoes had died down.

Private Bodine didn't respond as he backstepped towards a lower gun rack and scooped up the first available rifle. Halting in front of the ammo cabinets, he finally turned and met her eyes, a small, sad smile stretched across his badly chapped lips.

"What the hell…like you said, it can't *hurt*, right?"

Private Kemp giggled girlishly despite the stark

fear gripping her gut in a vice.

"C'mon, Rambo. Lock and load that baby and let's go check out the opposition, if there is any."

Each stood quietly, loading shells into their respective weapons. The rumbling cracks and booms sounded off intermediately, each of which was invariably followed by a low-centered vibration that was little more than a mini- aftershock.

"Ready, fellow Private?" Kemp asked firmly, taking the lead towards the exit.

Private Lomax Bodine nodded agreeably; the twenty-gauge hugged tightly against his narrow chest like a talisman to ward off evil spirits.

"I'm with you, Sandy. Like the man said, *whoever* he was 'cause I'm beyond recalling names at this precise moment, let's be *careful* out there."

Before disappearing through the wide double doors, she shot him a curious glare.

"Ron McIntosh actually hung out with you, man? Un-freaking- believeable."

Following closely behind, he observed Private Kemp grip the exit door and push it slightly ajar.

"At least I didn't bump uglies with 'im," he exclaimed proudly.

Private Kemp turned swiftly, her initial anger quickly fading after viewing her comrade's wry expression.

"You don't know how relieved I am to hear that, Lomax. There were rumors to the opposite, you know. C'mon, let's go check out what all the commotion is about."

They exited the building's rear exit mere seconds before the concrete walls caved in like stucco beneath a wrecking ball.

***

"Holy sweet Lord! What the...?" Jimmy screamed just before being flung airborne by the level-five wind gust that had exploded from the circular clearing like an invisible funnel cloud, tossing rock and chunks of earth the size of semi-trucks sailing into the foggy night like paper confetti.

He landed flat on his back after what seemed like a shockingly lengthy flight, what little oxygen his lungs had previously held knocked free in a single huff.

Dirt, clay and small shards of gravel rained down onto his face and into his mouth and eyes before he had a chance to roll over. Wiping his eyes furiously while resembling a beached fish attempting to suck in a fresh supply of air, Jimmy could feel the heat of the compound's perimeter and interior lights touching his exposed, dust coated skin.

The deadly gust had evaporated almost immediately after its initial release, leaving the air thick and reeking with the same rancid aroma as earlier. The overpowering stench of rotted meat seemed increasingly stout, and it wasn't until Jimmy was able to clear his eyesight somewhat and prop himself onto his battered, unsteady knees that he understood why.

Various sized mounds of what resembled burnt meat and charred bone littered a wide area of the exercise yard, billowy waves of smoke visible from each. Jimmy's only rational thought was that the earth had literary tossed its cookies from the circular clearing he had so briefly glimpsed before sprinting away.

Taking in a few extra breaths before attempting to rise, he saw his captors again congregating near the clearing. The two metal gurneys sat overturned a few hundred feet from where he had last seen them, and the man who had been introduced earlier as Major Peterson was slowly dragging the bodies they had held towards the open earth.

Even from a fair distance and peering through roving clouds of smoke and fog, Jimmy could see the darkened outline of the crater they stood before, tendrils of black smoke spewing forth from its gaping center.

Jimmy wanted nothing more at that moment than to turn tail and haul in the opposite direction. Two distinct factors prevented it from transpiring, and bravery had little to do with either. His lower body quivered weakly from the constant beatings he had endured in the last half-hour and was unable to respond to such a demanding request. Also, and most beguiling of all from a logical standpoint, a part of him had to know both *why* and *what. Why* the obviously diseased and deranged people who dragged him onto the compound had done so, and precisely *what* they had brought him to see inside the smoking crevice that they stood before like some unveiled artifact.

For at least the third time that evening, Jimmy could hear his deceased wife's voice barking within the confines of his muddled subconscious, telling him that this time his curiosity might very well be his undoing. Also for the third time that evening,

Jimmy dismissed the tiny voice with a shrug.

The compound lights had indeed powered back up, the yard and surrounding buildings appearing from the black night as if they had been transported into the area at the exact time the earth had shot forth its fetid innards amidst funnel cloud winds.

Struggling to his feet, his palms restfully atop his kneecaps, Jimmy watched the one who had called himself Buck join Peterson at the far edge of the opening, both holding their blood-soaked hands into the air in joint salute, their hands waving back and forth in spiritual harmony.

Jimmy took a few steps back and stood erect, ensuring he had sustained no major injuries upon impact with the relatively padded grass he'd been so roughly tossed onto.

The former correctional officer whom Peterson had identified as Dickerson or Dickenson joined the first two men, stepping clumsily onto and then over the two downed bodies that had been dragged and discarded a few feet to the hole's south side.

Jimmy heard the three begin to chant, although nothing they said would have been remotely comprehensible even at closer range. To him it sounded like a trio of lost animals baying at the sky in an attempt to contact the pack they were misplaced from.

Jimmy turned to the left and gave the front gate a quick once-over; its outer edge just observable beyond the left corner of the first brick building within the compound. Even through the drifting smoke, he could see the gate was closed and more than likely locked tight.

Sudden movement caught the corner of his

right eye, and he whirled around a step, barely avoiding tripping over his shoeless feet as a wave of dizziness swept over his vision.

What strongly resembled one side of a human rib cage, burnt to a turn and still smoldering, lay just inches from his sock-covered right foot.

As his vision cleared and his gait stabilized, Jimmy caught himself rubbing his eyes once again, only this time it wasn't due to dust or dirt build-up, but simply astonishment and shocked disbelief at what was being revealed. His legs, which had been slowly building strength for the gallop ahead, immediately fell back into 'instant noodle' mode.

"Oh…shit. Wake up, Jimbo. Nightmare City, my man, nothing more. Has to be, Nightmare City. Wake…*up*…please..." he muttered, cupping his hands over his eyes in order to tunnel his vision and block out all other possible distractions.

The form's shape was only vaguely human, and roughly the size of a F150 pick-up with an extended cab. What Jimmy first thought were thick robes or vines hung from its scaled sides, and dangling from their ends and being dragged haphazardly across the yard were two medium sized human beings, both of whom were struggling desperately for release.

The thing had a head; a bulb-shaped skull riding on a body three times too large for the spindly neck which held it aloft, and at least four separate appendages besides the tentacle-things that could have either been legs, arms *or* none of the above. It was making a rambling B-line towards the clearing, tearing deep twin grooves into the grass along its path.

Jimmy strolled hastily to the left, although he

was totally unaware of such instinctive motion until the banshee-like wailing began, splitting the thick air like a blaring siren.

He turned back towards the crater just in time to see something crawl from its depths that made the earlier monstrosity look downright cuddly by comparison.

"Oh y-yeah, the old alarm clock needs to s-sound off, Jimbo. Needs to s- sound off right...about…now…," Jimmy blurted, followed by a series of delirium- fueled guffaws normally reserved for those under heavy medication.

From the hundred yard-plus distance from which he observed, Jimmy could only compare the scene with that of a round, plump watermelon emerging from the end of a water hose.

The top portion poured out of the crater and instantly thickened once it found the room sufficient to do so, the base of what Jimmy deduced to be its neck at least fifteen, possibly twenty, feet in width.

Major Peterson and his worshipping trio backed away to avoid contact, their arms still swaying back and forth in a macabre version of an arena 'wave'. Jimmy could barely make out the chants they continued to spout, and realized that even if he could, a literal understanding of what was being said would have been utterly impossible.

They were resuscitations from an alternate world; a language spoken in tongue that more than likely would pose a baffling mystery to even the most astute professors and biblical scholars.

Jimmy found himself actually moving closer to the site, although completely oblivious to such a fact. His eyes darted from one unearthly scene to the next like a line judge at a tennis match.

To his right, the thing with a human head, squid tentacles and a lower body that seemed to levitate barreled ahead without even the slightest hesitation, the prisoners within its grasp bringing up the rear at least ten feet behind. He recognized them as a young man and woman, both of whom punched and kicked furiously as they were being hauled along like crustacean in a fisherman's net.

Jimmy could hear their muted screams as they gouged and jabbed at the thick, cord like tentacles that held each at the lower legs and ankles.

To his left, what looked crazily like a hundred legged, yellow-colored worm littered with black splotches and roughly the size of a Mac truck emerged to what essentially qualified as a standing ovation. An ovation from a small group of men that might have once been human, but now were nothing more than mutated sculptures that hardly qualified as such.

Jimmy closed his eyes to the surreal play being staged before him just long enough to reach down with his right fist and shove his knuckles forcefully against his testicles. Falling to his knees, he waited for the familiar throbbing in his lower abdomen that normally followed such contact.

A few moments later he opened his eyes to the stark realization that what he was witnessing wasn't simply a hellish dreamscape manufactured within the confines of his darkest subconscious, but instead a horrific reality to be dealt with and not simply dismissed once an alarm clock sounded off.

His stomach ached and his balls pulsed in pain. No dream could so accurately imitate such discomfort.

While still positioned perfectly for prayer, Jimmy looked ever so briefly into the black, hazy sky and did just that.

He whispered the word ‘amen’ in a raspy whisper, then leaped to his feet and darted towards the compounds main gate, all the while keeping his sites on the utter madness transpiring to his immediate right.

***

“H-hang on, sis…Kara? C-can you hear me?” Wilbo yelled just before the back of his head bounced forcefully off the edge of a sizeable rock, filling his eyes with flaring bolts of light and causing him to bite deep into his tongue. The coiled appendage that pinned his ankles, shins and thighs tightly together was ice cold to the touch, instantly numbing any portion of skin that it came into contact with. He had tried several times to reach the small serrated blade taped to the inside of his right ankle, but found the task of budging the Warden/Thing’s coil virtually impossible, like tugging on a massive, slime coated tree trunk.

Glancing over, he could see the blur that was his sister, her labored cries barely audible as they were being towed along as if tied to the back of a speeding vehicle’s back bumper.

The back of his neck was raw from being first pulled across pavement and gravel, followed by blades of grass transformed into thousands of potential razor blades due to their excessive traveling speed.

Despite the obvious desperation of the situation, Wilbo felt an eerie calmness begin to sweep over his tattered psyche as seconds ticked by. His rational side simply deduced that if the Warden/Thing meant to kill Kara or himself, it would have already happened inside the office. What exactly the creature *did* have planned was a subject he refused to address until forced to do so.

"Let…us...go, *damn* you!" Kara blared between teeth gritted so tightly she thought she may have already cracked or displaced her braces.

She was fairly sure her right arm was broken at the forearm, more than likely snapped as she had been rammed hard against a stone wall while exiting the admin building. She had it tucked beneath her left armpit to prevent further damage while half-heartedly slapping at the crushing bonds at her thighs with her remaining good hand.

Kara had never been a bible-thumper, hadn't actually attended a church in over three years, but had always had the belief that a higher being did indeed exist within the vast cosmos. Her mother had instilled such in her and William during their childhood, or at least made the effort. As her brother and herself were being heaved along the prison yard with ridiculous ease by an abomination straight from a sweat-soaked nightmare, she felt no embarrassment whatsoever in praying for such a being to aid their seemingly hapless cause.

***

"Ain't it beautiful, JC? Beats anything I've seen before, I can tell ya, even the first piece of ass I ever mounted! Not even the time I shot that lawyer whose car had broken down on Bull Creek road a few years back! Nothin' on this planet compares, man!" Buck the Third announced, his lower jaw no longer able to meet the top half due to the constantly shifting bones beneath the clammy, near transparent skin of his misshapen head.

JC didn't respond, just kept swaying his bony, elongated fingers towards the massive shape that continued to painstakingly free itself from mother earth like an overgrown bug from a cocoon.

"I guess it didn't need the extra sacrifices after all. After so many countless centuries, I guess patience is a hard virtue to come by," Major Peterson said while standing just inches to JC's left, the crooked, toothless orifice serving as his mouth drooling a thick, brown substance that bore a striking resemblance to chocolate pudding.

"No problem-O, General. I'm sure he's gonna get his fill 'fore the night's done. A few billion's worth, more than likely. Ain't this the shit? Tell me, ain't it though?" Buck replied with demented delight, digging a finger deep into his sagging right nostril before pulling free a wad of torn meat that held the distinct color and texture of brain tissue. Buck the Third flicked it away casually and returned his undivided attention to the being he accepted without question as his true lord and savior, the one he had been unknowingly waiting to appear since birth.

"What a ride this is gonna be! A trip like no other, men. We're goin' on a journey that few can claim...*I'm* finally goin' home!"

The trunk of the thing's body was as thick as an

ancient sequoia, the surface of which was riddled with cord-like veins the size of a man's arm. What seemed like hundreds of various sized limbs protruded from its pulsating frame, the majority of which wriggled and squirmed like half-submerged larva from the enormous torso.

It took another thirty seconds before the back end emerged from the crater with a resounding plop; the tails tip narrowing to spear-like dimensions.

"Behold the one true messiah, boys. Ain't it spec-fuckin'-tacular?" Buck announced, taking a tentative step forward towards the mammoth specimen.

Major Peterson wobbled forward, his one good eye wide and boggling within its rotting socket, his arms spread wide in a hugging pose.

JC Carlyle quietly stood his ground a few yards behind, the steady twitching of his head and neck the only apparent movement he remained capable of. The smile painted across his snail colored lips revealing the complete, unabashed awe he was feeling in the presence of what he too deduced to be nothing less than a God.

The thing swiveled to the right, a dome shaped attachment swinging around like a wrecking ball to focus on the men that stood a few dozen feet beneath it. A single orb the size of a dinner plate concentrated on them momentarily before the entire structure that served as its body shifted over in the same direction.

Behind it, the crater no longer smoked, the sides of the entryway as smooth as molded clay, as if an implausible, immeasurable heat had molded them into place.

The being scooted ahead a few feet, the ground beneath it crushed down as if fallen upon by a demolished skyscraper.

Major Peterson did not hesitate nor slow his momentum, strolling ahead with his arms spread wide and shrill, pained whimpers escaping his ruined throat. “Let me be the first! I offer myself wholeheartedly, old great one...” he screamed, nearing the base of the thing’s smooth midsection, which was strangely translucent and dripped of moisture.

The being studied him curiously from above for less than a full second, then the bloated, engorged head arose in a swift jerking motion, the orb suddenly aware of the frantic movement from the eastern side of the exercise yard.

“I apologize, my savior, for not recognizing your obvious influences in my life up until now. My purpose was never clear until these last few hours...” Peterson bellowed as if he were delivering a dramatic mountaintop sermon to an audience of star-struck worshippers.

Officer Dickenson and Buck the Third cringed back as the flesh just below the being’s neck split open as if carved by an invisible axe blade, opening a vertical gash at least two feet long and a foot wide.

Major Peterson stepped back until all three stood shoulder-to-shoulder, ‘oohing’ and ‘ahhing’ as if standing in some vast arena, witnessing a historic sports feat. JC garbled loudly and began to clap enthusiastically, losing a forefinger and pinkie in the process as they spun wildly into the air.

He alone got a clear, unobstructed look at the object that ejected from the being's open wound, and the clapping halted as abruptly as a bird sailing into a brick wall.

For all practical purposes, JC could only compare it to a catcher's mitt, not unlike the kind he had worn while mastering the position at Red Bridge High some twenty odd years before. The arm or stalk it clung to was narrow and octagon shaped, with jagged edges that resembled cartoonish versions of drawn lightning bolts.

The colossal mitt, which seemed to possess bulky (yet pointed at the tips) fingers encircling the concave palm, shot straight out with a fluidity that belied its bulk, leaving its intended targets little time to respond whatsoever, much less dive or duck out of its path.

Major Peterson arm's made it not quite halfway to his face, while Jerrod Dickenson and Buck Lomax stood stoic, expressions of comic shock frozen on their horribly distorted mugs.

JC figured he must have blinked, although he didn't recall doing so at that precise moment, or even possessing the ability *to do* so without benefit of eyelids.

The next scene he clearly viewed was that of the beings' wound closing up, zipping up might have been the more correct term, from top to bottom, leaving no proof the skin had ever parted at all. It then rocked and surged back until its body was perfectly horizontal, moving as gracefully as an eel in calm creek water, leaving JC to study upon what it had left behind.

Falling to his knees as if shoved from behind,

JC peered ahead at the three sets of collapsed legs and bare feet, all of which looked to have been sliced cleanly across the lower thigh, and felt his earlier giddiness sail away like a feather caught in a typhoon.

Buck's hairless calves and bunion-infested toes were easiest to identify, lying dead center between the other two pair. Not a single drop of blood spilled from the severed limbs, each wound perfectly horizontal and the color of burnt ash.

Broken from his daze just as the thundering commotion from behind his kneeled frame became apparent, JC started to turn around just as the being to his north lurched forward.

"Holy…sweet...*JESUS*!!!" JC shrieked, twisted his severely weakened, fever-racked body to the left as the thing's gigantic bulk rolled over him.

Once it had completely cleared the patch of grass he had occupied only a split-second before, the only evidence that JC Carlyle had ever existed was a mashed outline of his contorted body that dug a two-foot trench into the hard clay below.

On the south side of the crater, Corporal Ron McIntosh's propped himself onto his elbows and slowly opened his weary eyes. His vision was slightly blurred, no doubt from the pain medication so haphazardly administered by his former commander and his mad sidekick, but several sessions of rapid blinking to refocus his pupils began to gradually lift the fog.

He turned his neck to the left and allowed his numb frame to eventually follow, using simple leverage to pull off the arduous task. His mind's initial reaction to what he visualized transpiring at the center of the exercise yard was one of droll disbelief, chalking up the insanity filling his sight to a drug-induced hallucination. What else could explain a worm the size of a Peterbilt semi rumbling across grounds? Or the octopus with a human head and legs (nearer the size of a large garbage dumpster) steamrolling in from the opposite direction?

Twisting around further for better positioning, Corporal McIntosh decided to give himself an additional minute before even attempting to rise. As he reached for the edge of the crater in order to get a better handhold to pull himself along by, he noticed two unconnected but similarly disturbing facts: the first was the marble smooth walls of the tunnel itself, virtually impossible to grasp, like black ice build-up on asphalt. The second fact was easily the worst of the two. The good Corporal no longer possessed fingers to grasp *with*. Rolling onto his back and raising his digit free hands into the misty air, the sense of loss he felt was almost instantly sheered away by primal rage. The screams, which ensured were not born out of self-pity, but a warrior's howls. A badly wounded but still undeniably dangerous warrior with a single, piercing thought that dismissed all others.

Retribution.

***

The Warden/Thing glided across the gravel and grass like an out of control locomotive down a steep grade, that is, until he grew ever closer to his intended target. He had observed it dispatch of the four on-lookers like so many mashed insects, no surprise there, but the sheer size and bulk of its slug-shaped frame left him questioning a proper angle and strategy of attack.

He could feel the gnat-like kicks and punches from his two unwilling allies bringing up the rear, although he had serious doubts as to their use upon viewing the opposition. Still, there was something about the siblings, a mysterious aura surrounding each, that convinced him to not only keep them alive, but also close at hand for the tussle ahead.

As the distance between them swiftly narrowed, forty yards and closing, the Warden/Thing felt himself pass through a wall of pure unreleased energy, one he knew full well had nothing to do with his own transformations.

His enemy was not only larger in size and scope than he could have ever envisioned, but astonishingly superior in terms of mental preparedness for the battle to come. Centuries of incarceration spent frozen at the planet's darkest core, awaiting liberation that might never emerge could send even the most even-tempered soul spiraling into unrivaled madness.

This specific being had been created to destroy and evoke thoughts of malice into lesser beings. Festering in its own fury for thousands of earth years had spewed forth an incarnation void of the patience necessary for a slow, premeditated takeover. It simply existed to annihilate with extreme prejudice, discarding the time-consuming mind control games that had been necessary for its escape.

The Warden/Thing had little doubt of the talent and skill it held within its grasp to perform the monumental task at hand. Its bulk had already widened dramatically since absorption of the four ill-fated worshippers just minutes before.

The two were a scant twenty yards apart when the skies above them opened up, unloading a torrential mix of rain, sleet, and hail, the chunks of the latter roughly the size of a regulation baseball. The Warden/Thing peered upward for just an instant, just long enough to observe that the downfall seemed to be originating from a single cloud, a low hanging mist shaded in a black color so extreme it resembled a puffy hole carved into the sky.

A shard of ice shaped like a tiny spear punctured Wilbo's left shoulder as he was shielding his eyes and face from the bombardment with his crossed arms. He pulled the pencil-sized shrapnel free with a wince and instantly felt the warm blood trail down his biceps. The temperature seemed to have dropped thirty degrees in a matter of mere moments, coinciding with the sudden cloudburst, his huffing breath clearly visible.

Wilbo prayed that his sister was able to visualize the same strange phenomenon a dozen feet to his left. He could no longer hear her frenzied grunting or enraged squeals, and the tentacle that held him had twisted his body around at a side angle, making it impossible to view her on the opposite side.

Kara hung limply in the thing's grip, her head thrown back until the top of her scalp was dangerously close to making contact with the matted grass whooshing by, her legs and arms (especially the broken one) swinging along like severed puppet strings.

She dreamed, as was often the case when faced with situations deemed overly stressful, of personal transformation, both physical and metaphysical. Her alter ego was a mix of two decidedly different heroines; the Scarlet Witch with her tenaciousness built on years of personal strife and family tragedies (as a teen, Kara had actually cried upon reading the issue in which Quicksilver had passed away), and the X-Men's Storm. The power of flight, especially when supplied to the women of comics, had always enchanted Kara, giving her the sense whatever shortcomings the heroines displayed, it assisted in equaling a playing field overflowing with testosterone-laced, macho-spewing male heroes and villains.

Storm's ability to control weather conditions also fascinated, as Kara had toyed with the idea of studying meteorology during her middle grade years. The day the first X-Men film was finally released, Kara was among the first in line with cash in hand.

She hoped someday that Hollywood would see fit, in its anxiousness to bring seemingly every costumed hero ever created to celluloid, that the Avengers to include the Scarlet Witch would soon follow suit.

Her rain-soaked eyelids fluttering wildly as the rain/sleet pelted downward, Kara glided above an open wilderness in a sun-drenched dreamscape, elm and oak treetops stretching out to her just inches below.

Cruising over a wide clearing between sloping

mountain ranges, Kara noticed a series of perfectly circular holes within its perimeter, all of which were lined up and spaced as if placed there by a giant-sized three-hole punch.

As she descended upon them, her red-booted feet landing with the force of a feather upon the mostly dirt surface, Kara noticed a stench filling the air, one which instantly reminded her of decomposing animal flesh.

Nearing the first of the three evenly spaced craters, she was suddenly blown back by a gust of wind stout enough to temporarily hoist her skyward. Brushing dust and dirt from beneath her crimson mask's eyeholes, her vision cleared just as the figures began to crawl forth from the holes like hordes of roaches from a cramped opening within a rotted orifice.

Piled atop one another, the bodies poured from the craters as if being shoved forward by a surging geyser.

As the mass of naked arms, legs and torsos rolled and squirmed free of one another, it wasn't what Kara was seeing that chilled the marrow of her bones like a stiff winter breeze, but what she didn't see.

They stumbled gradually towards her, some upright and some crawling, pulling themselves along the hard dirt surface by their fingers and arms. None were whole, some missing hands and others void of entire arms. Still more hopped along on a single leg, while the most unfortunate of all shambled along with their arms out in front as if sleepwalking, their missing heads leaving them hapless to navigate a proper path to Kara's position.

The ones handicapped with missing limps looked to have been badly burned, their faces charred and their scalps hairless and coated in freshly formed blisters.

Fighting the urge to simply leap into the air and fly away from the grotesque wave of mutilated humanity that seemed to have been awakened exclusively for her viewing horror, Kara stood her ground and struck a pose familiar to the readers of a certain adventure comic. Her arms pointed straight out with hands that were spread wide apart with slightly curled fingers, the task of conjuring a circular force field around her body second nature in such a situation. "It's up to you now, Sweet pea," a voice suddenly croaked from behind her, breaking her concentration just as the invisible wall was beginning to form.

Kara whirled around and her breath caught in her throat. Only two people had ever called her that, stopping only when she hit her late teens.

"Mama? D-daddy?" She lipped, although hardly any volume accompanied the words.

Her mother and father stood before her, both completely nude and each missing several body parts, her mom's baldness and her father's lip-less sneer making them resemble a grotesque, partially erased portrait. Neither had teeth, just purple gums that seemed far too large for the mouth's housing them.

"It's up to you and William, dear," her mom said calmly, her eyes brimming with tears which ran down a face that looked to have been recently blow torched. "You can't help us now, darlin', but

the rest of the world is up shit creek without an oar. Only you and Will can stop the rampage," her father added, his pale breasts sagging like overstuffed burlap bags.

While facing them, Kara felt the hands massage her upper shoulders, her calves and ankles from behind. Several pair dug deep into her hair just above her mask and tugged ever so gently, as if trying to divert her attention away from her apparently long- deceased parents.

"Listen to the Warden, Dear, and follow his lead..." Mother said in a corrective, scolding tone.

"But be cautious of his words, for he is merely the lesser of two evils..." father chimed in as he reached down to scratch genitalia that were buried in gray pubic hair that looked as thick and long as spring kudzu in an Alabama forest.

What seemed like a hundred separate sets of hands clamped down on every inch of Kara's body, fingers as numerous as a hundred millipedes digging into and then through the fabric of her costume to the warm flesh beneath.

"M-mom? W-what about you? Dad? I want to h-help y-you. What happened? Are you d-dea...gone?" She asked timidly, dreading an answer she unfortunately already knew the answer to.

Her mother's head bowed, as did her father's a moment later.

"M-mom? I h-have to know. William and...we have to know, don't you understand that? We have to have some type of c-closure...," Kara pleaded as the hands began to pull her downward, her spandex covered knees precariously close to buckling.

When her parent's heads finally arose, their hangdog, downtrodden expressions had vanished, replaced by twin smiles that were both impossibly wide and filled with pure malice. Sharp-pointed teeth as long as twenty-penny nails hung from gums coated in crimson.

Their eyes were empty pits with tiny yellow flames shooting from the sockets like that from butane lighters. Her parents had long, pointed ears and noses that narrowed to a fine point.

"...get along now, Sweet Pea. Your true master awaits. He's gonna enjoy sucking down your brothers bones, oh yes. I believe he has...other plans for you. Special plans, oh yes indeed-y, oh my..."

Mother spouted hatefully, her hands clapping together in enthusiastic glee. "Right you are," the other demon masquerading as her father bellowed, the tips of his nail-teeth clicking together excessively.

"...my darling girl has to be saved for last...savored like the rare dish that she is, and served only to the one true master of the new world, or underworld, if you will."

Pinned into place as if her body had been dipped in fast drying cement, Kara was unable to force a single muscle free from the army of steely fingers holding her so effortlessly at bay. Her fantasy powers were no longer an ingredient within the darkening dreamscape, her costume vanquished into thin air. She peered downward at her own naked body, the skin of her tiny breasts and abdomen pasty white.

When her head again arose, it was just as her parents leapt at her with teeth bared from mouths astonishingly wide, the froth of hunger leaking from each corner in bubbly waves.

Kara awoke to find herself rolling roughly atop the grassy earth until her momentum carried her into the chain-link fence perimeter of the yard's westernmost basketball court. Sticking the fingers of her unbroken arm through the mesh fencing, it took her a full two minutes to find the energy to pull herself into a sitting position.

She winced painfully as she attempted to turn around, shooting pains from both her lower back and the left side of her neck bringing her perilously close to blacking out. Her shattered arm felt numb and detached, as if most of the assigned vital nerve endings had been unplugged or similarly disconnected. Two deep breaths and a quick inventory of her body parts later, she finally managed to instigate a turn and spot her twin brother lying a few hundred feet towards the center of the exercise yard. Wilbo was sprawled onto his back, his arms and legs wide part. After a quick hitch of her breath and a few skipped heartbeats, she finally saw him move. His right arm rose to cover his field of vision. For all practical purposes, Wilbo looked like a man taking a long overdue nap.

Still on her knees, her cotton shirt ripped at the waist where she had been so tightly subdued, Kara began to crawl towards him, ever so mindful of the surreal, inexplicable, utterly illogical scene playing out a few hundred feet to her immediate left.

His head simultaneously ringing and throbbing at equal pitch, Wilbo decided a few more seconds of a motionless siesta were in order before attempting even the slightest of movements.

He wasn't sure why the thing had released them (he had watched his sister roll away from the other side just before he landed face first in a pile of what felt and smelled like charred bones), and didn't really care to investigate. He rolled to the right and caught a glimpse of his sister crawling over. She was holding her right arm tightly against her body while crawling forward using her left.

She shot him a quick nod and continued forward, allowing her eyes to dart to the left every few seconds.

Wilbo felt a stinging at his upper right thigh and quickly found the source of pain that overshadowed all others. A shard of bone, the upper portion chalky white and the lower scorched and blackened, protruded from the meatiest portion of his outer thigh just below the hip. With one smooth jerk, Wilbo pulled the ballpoint pen-sized bone free and tossed it aside, ignoring the thick flow of blood that instantly followed and instead focusing his full concentration on the bizarre confrontation ensuing to his right.

The Warden/Thing had discarded the twins just early enough to place them out of immediate harm's way. He wasn't totally sure of why he had decided against using them as a possible decoy against his formidable opponent, but somehow had simply understood that it was vital to the battle's overall outcome to do just that.

As the giant spawn drew to within ten yards of his position, its rotund form had begun to discharge several dozen pieces of itself into each direction of the yard, like makeshift eggs being hatched in a ritualistic birthing. Shoved from the being's skin like burst pimples, they were approximately the size of an adult Saint Bernard and held the shape and color of a ripe pumpkin stood upright onto one end, their outer skin literally engulfed in quarter sized suction cups. Picking up speed once outside their hosts' bulky frame, the mutant offspring seemed to glide over the grounds without benefit of actually making contact with the grassy surface, leaving no visible tracks in their wake.

By the time the Warden/Thing was within striking distance of his cumbersome opponent, what resembled an army of yellowish sponge-balls were scattered about the yard, each seemingly making an independent B-Line towards a target they alone were aware of.

From where he now sat upright on bleeding kneecaps, Wilbo couldn't help but believe he and his sister were living pawns in a Pac-Man computer game come to life.

The Warden/Thing sprung forth and head-butted the being directly below its neck stalk, then attached his two upper tentacles around it while searching for a similar hold on the massive trunk with the lower set.

"Ride 'em, cowboy! Yeeeeee-haaaaaaaaaa!," He shrieked as the stalk slung his two-ton frame about like a paper string trapped in a wind tunnel.

The Warden/Thing's chest cavity stretched and finally split apart like rotted pine beneath a chain saw's carving blade, a tube-shaped arm spilling forth like a striking cobra towards the beings colossal midsection. At the tip of the slick appendage was a set of pinchers that were equal parts lobster and backhoe blade. Lodged between the pinchers like a Scorpion's stinger was a single pointed spear that was the perfect imitation of an Olympic javelin.

Just as the tube/spear descended upon the being's flesh, it shifted its bulk to the left with surprising quickness, as if it had understood it's attacker's strategy. The pinchers tore through the outer layer of skin and then slid harmlessly off to the side, shreds of flesh hanging free in slimly clumps.

The Warden/Thing retracted the tube just as he was being slung airborne by the slashing stalk.

He landed a dozen feet away, his body weight digging a three-foot gorge with his head, arms and upper back doing the damage.

The being stood its ground, its single orb eyeing him curiously as a drawn out, unearthly groan escaping the thin horizontal line representing its mouth.

Once again balanced on the thick, square shaped poles that served as his legs, the Warden/Thing smiled sarcastically and nodded towards the shiny, unblinking orb.

"You're faster than I was told to expect, Clyde. I would've had you cold turkey if you hadn't boogied out of range, you do *know* that, don't you?"

The thing's body grew eerily still, the orb-eye abruptly glazed over with a white substance that seemed to be coating its frame like fresh sweat.

"Buddy boy, you're either damned scared or damned pissed off, and I don't have to guess which."

The hundreds of tiny legs that jutted forth from the being's skin like porcupine quills began to wriggle and quiver frantically, while the frame itself remained motionless.

For the first time since the being's arrival onto the surface, the Warden/Thing was finally able to positively identify them as something other than mutated antenna the being possibly utilized as 'feelers'.

They were human legs and arms, melded into the thing's hide like half- submerged grub-worms, the still intact and somehow alive appendages of the victims it had absorbed in its never-ending quest for freedom. The victims it used to fuel its all-consuming rage.

"You gonna flap your arms and fly away, big boy?" The Warden/Thing cackled, albeit a bit apprehensively.

He never even saw the thing that cut him in half like axed cordwood a split-second later.

The impact had been like that from a bazooka fired at extremely close range, an object at least a dozen feet in height but hardly more than an inch in width, with jagged edges like a circular saw blade constructed of bone and tendon instead of metal. It had exploded from the widest point of the being's upper torso like a heat seeking missile, slicing through the Warden/Thing like a red-hot scythe through moist tar, then circled back and re-entered its masters womb through the same invisible opening it had exited five seconds before.

The Warden/Thing stood upright for an instant, managing a gurgled sigh just before impact, then toppled to the ground like a dismantled puzzle in two jarringly equal sections.

The being sauntered over and bent down, ogled the mangled remains for a few fleeting moments, then slithered away in the general direction of the prison block building, where the majority of its 'sponge' offspring had glided towards earlier. As it blazed a destructive path between and then past the two fenced in basketball courts, carving a trench a dozen feet across and at least four deep, it was accompanied by a low, shrill sound that could have easily been mistaken for a human giggle magnified ten-fold.

In the foreground, the muffled screams of those trapped behind steel bars rang out like a choir made up of the eternally damned.

***

Private Kemp was unsure of just exactly how long she had been holding her breath before the burning, throbbing sensation in her chest begged for relief. She and Private Bodine had been cowering behind the large metal dumpster since departing the armory. The plan had been to double-time it over to the main gate and hopefully discover it unlocked. The ground had rocked and belched before they even got a dozen feet from the armory exit, leaving them frozen in their tracks and hapless to do anything but silently witness the insanity which followed. Private Kemp had murmured something to the effect of 'has to be special effects. Must be making a Sci-Fi movie', knowing even as the words escaped her trembling lips how utterly ridiculous such an explanation sounded, even to herself.

About the same time that Major Peterson and his small band of mutated worshippers were being swatted aside and subsequently inhaled into the thing's slug-like midsection, Private Bodine finally managed to string a few substantial words together other than 'holy shit' or 'what the?' He had straightened as if snapping to full attention and clapped Private Kemp on the right shoulder with the enthusiasm of a convicted pyromaniac witnessing a nasty explosion involving vehicles filled with highly flammable materials.

"That's one honking big tequila worm, Sandy! It wiped 'em away like they were dust balls! Did you see that? Did you see that *wild shit,* Sandy? That was some wild, wacky shit!"

She thought of slapping him out of his hysterics, but reconsidered once she realized how dangerously close to coming completely unhinged she was herself.

Staring at the shotgun balanced at her side, Private Kemp couldn't decide whether to laugh or cry. *Whatever* that thing was, nothing short of a ballistic missile was libel to do anything other than give it a bothersome itch.

"Pea shooters aimed at an elephant's hide," she had whispered just as her fellow Private had pointed past her line of vision, his voice cracking like a teenage boy in the throngs of puberty.

"Like, check out the sea monster! Jesus, and in *this* corner..." he barked in a pathetic imitation of a boxing ring announcer, his voice soaked in fear.

"Shut the hell up, Bodine! Shut up and keep that cone-head of yours down, got it?" She scowled, scrunching down instinctively until she was almost performing a full squat.

She had intended to add a resounding 'jackass' or 'dumb shit' but found the words hung at the center of her parched throat like mashed portions of a saltine cracker once her eyes locked on the creature streaking across the yard from the opposite side of their position.

"W-what...what is? Okay, s-somebody has definitely spiked my canteen water," she finally mumbled, her entire body growing instantly chilled, and not just from the suddenly dropping temperatures. Through the inexplicable cloudburst of tennis ball sized hailstones and sweeping walls of cold rain, she glared wide- eyed at the newest abomination to join the already otherworldly fray. She could barely make out the human forms being hauled roughshod on each side, wrapped inside what looked like squid tentacles, only three times thicker.

"Un-freaking-real. I only have one quick question…w-where the hell is Godzilla when you really need him?" Private Bodine ranted, his own shotgun now lying worthlessly at his booted feet.

"Quiet, you crazy son of a..." She began, the rest of the sentence trailing hopelessly away as the exercise yard before them was suddenly filling up with what she could only identify as football shaped eggs. A virtual army of them spread about the field, most heading directly for the compounds southernmost building.

"What the…what's all over them? S-suction cups?" Private Kemp asked mostly to herself while shaking her head in comic disbelief.

"Look like brillo pads. The giant tequila worm

burped them out like rabbit pellets. Unreal…what's next, flying toaster ovens with basset hound heads?" Private Bodine replied humorlessly with surprising calmness, a fact not lost on his fellow grunt, who shot him a brief but worried glance. They crouched down, peeking around opposite ends of the dumpster just as two of the yellow-tinted forms darted by like weather balloons supplied with rocket boosters.

Private Kemp hugged the edges of the stone pad the dumpster sat upon, her shotgun falling from her grasp and landing against the side of the metal container with a resounding thump.

The next sound she heard was that of Private Bodine's strangely soothing voice whispering just a few inches from behind her left ear.

"They're gone, Sandy. Whizzed on by like they needed to find a restroom reeeeal bad. I saw 'em cut to the right just as they neared the armory. Turned like beams from a flashlight. I think they just...missed us."

Pushing herself into a makeshift mantis position, Private Kemp blew a strand of matted black hair from between her lips and sighed.

"Maybe they're blind, w-whatever they are. Or maybe they had a different target in mind. Could even be h-harmless."

Private Bodine laughed a bit sarcastically. His face was painfully gaunt, his eyes bulging and his jaws set tight.

"Harmless? I wouldn't wager the old homestead on that. Did you get a good look at Mama? Anything that walking intestine spat out cannot be anything short of seriously harmful to your health."

Private Kemp replied with a disinterested grunt as she scanned the exercise yard from her knees, her left eye barely clearing the squared edge of the dumpster.

"I don't see a-anymore of 'em. Let's haul ass to the gate, Lomax. I get the feeling we ain't nothing more than fish bait to whatever those things are, otherwise they would've stopped to at least say hi," she whispered while observing the larger of the two entities dispatch of the smaller by manner of what resembled a wall-sized buzz-saw.

"We either find a way out of here or end up a smear on that mean mother's boot heel."

Private Bodine gripped her right shoulder, causing her to flinch involuntarily.

"They're aliens, Sandy. They...have to be, right? I mean, I realize a prison compound in rural Mississippi is a strange landing site, but what do they know about our geography, you know?" He asked timidly.

Private Kemp brushed his hand away gently, rising to her feet like a woman forty years her senior and racked with crippling arthritis.

"The Jolly Green worm over there crawled from the ground, man, remember? If it was hatched from a spaceship, then home is buried somewhere near Briarston, more than likely about five stories deep. Anyhow, X-File or *not*, it don't seem overly friendly. Let's make tracks before it decides we belong under the heading midnight snack."

"Looks like someone else has the same general idea," Private Bodine said, observing the two dark forms sprint across the field towards the gate, the first approximately twenty to thirty yards ahead of the other, who was limping noticeably.

"Damn, the pudgy one is making some serious tracks," she replied, shoving Private Bodine to the side with a well-placed shoulder.

"The other guy is closer to crawling than running, though. You think one of those floating pumpkins got hold of him?" Private Bodine asked, gripping the side of the dumpster like a man scaling the edge of a skyscraper.

"Could be, not our problem. You ready to pick 'em up and put 'em down, Private Bodine?"

He sighed heavily before slowly circling to the front of the container. The worm creature had vanished from their line of site, the wide row its bulk had carved into the ground trailing towards the same building as its mutated offspring. "Coast looks c-clear. As the King once sang...it's now or never," he croaked pathetically.

"You would paraphrase a corpse," Private Kemp said just as she jogged forward into the clearing, the shotgun held snugly across her chest.

Racing across evenly coifed sections of grass, which were periodically sprinkled with what seemed to be pieces of charred bone, Private Bodine found keeping pace with his smaller female counterpart more difficult than it should have been. After covering less than fifty yards, his breath was badly labored and his legs were already beginning to feel like twin retreads on the verge of a double-barreled blowout.

"S-Sandy, what if…what if the gates are locked electronically? I m-mean, the power's back up now. M-maybe they m-meant to lock us in, you know?"

"We'll blow that particular bridge when we reach it. Just shut the hell up and run, Lomax," she replied curtly, maintaining a steady speed while keeping her eyes frozen on the two forms growing gradually closer. They were close enough to recognize as males, the second of which donned the colors of the Dark Eagle Militia, the uniform shirt partially torn away.

A dozen steps later, Private Kemp had a name to go with the limp the man so obviously displayed.

"Get the lead outta your ass-cheeks, Lomax! That's Ezop up ahead!"

***

As his bare feet slapped against the paved walkway leading away from the exercise yard, Jimmy squinted in the direction of the main gate. He was unable to get a clear visual of the gates due to the eastern edges of the admin building, which jutted out just enough to block his view.

Whirling around for final assurance that the larger of the two creatures had indeed wobbled away in the opposite direction, Jimmy spotted not one but three uniformed personnel headed his way.

"Fantastic. Friend or foe, I wonder," he mumbled, jogging backwards and almost tripping as he again shifted his substantial weight forward in a shambling lurch.

He hadn't gotten ten more steps when he heard the pleading voice split the night air. A voice that was equal parts desperate and terrified.

"Hey man! Hey! H-help me, w-will you? Slow…slow down, man!"

After initially attempting to increase his pace, Jimmy hesitated and then stopped, bending over with his hands atop his knees. He turned just as the limping man wearing torn and ripped camouflage made it to the edge of the concrete walkway.

As he sucked in several lengthy breaths of misty, lightly fogged air, Jimmy looked past the gimpy soldier to the two similarly dressed individuals huffing along about midway across the yard.

The lead one was definitely female, the fluidity of her movements belying her chunky frame. She held the rifle to her chest like a combat savvy veteran, while the thin, gangly male at her heels slumped along clumsily, his own weapon being dragged haphazardly by the stock, the barrel dragging the ground behind him.

"G-give me a h-hand, will you, man? My…my hands are bleeding r-really bad…I'm think I'm gonna p-p-pass out again…," the soldier gasped as Jimmy finally began to move towards him.

"Stay right there. Try not to move for a few. If I have to, I'll carry you on my b-...." Jimmy yelled, a bit louder than he had originally intended. He was within a few dozen feet of the man, who had laid back onto the stone pathway with his bloodied hands resting on his heaving abdomen, when the frantic waving of the two other uniformed sprinters caught his eye.

The female was yelling something, her shotgun held over her head as if she were treading rising creek waters. The male had dropped his weapon and was waving madly with both hands, his head turned sharply to their right.

Jimmy halted instantly, his naked feet stuck to the concrete as if super- glued. The egg-shaped object was headed straight for their position, sliding along the top of the ground with cheetah-like speed, not a single blade of grass left dented in its path.

"Run…get the hell *outta there*!" Private Kemp finally managed in a low croak, white spittle flying from her lips in a fine mist.

Jimmy almost laughed at the absurdity of her suggestion, as the closest safe haven, that being the covered breezeway between the compounds first two buildings, was a good fifty yards to his right.

Simply stated, there was no place to run nor hide.

"Damn. I left civilization for *this*?" He babbled while bracing his body as best he could despite the stark fear freezing all blood flow within his veins.

The form's trajectory altered for just an instant, as if it had briefly picked up the female soldier and her cohort on its radar screen and might target them instead, before shifting back into its original course. The sudden alteration hadn't been lost on the soldiers, who had almost instantaneously dived to the ground with their hands covering their faces and heads.

As it neared to within a few dozen yards of where Jimmy stood completely motionless sans his trembling lips and matching hands, it seemed to actually increase speed, like an attacking lioness closing in on a young, winded Wildebeest.

Cringing haplessly, Jimmy peeked from between his own splayed fingers at what he had already consented to be the instigator of his own violent, sure to be extremely painful demise, and realized with a sense of guilty relief that a different target had been chosen.

As the object grew closer to the battered man lying no more than twenty feet to his north, Jimmy got his first clear look, however fleeting, at its yellow shaded hide and the hundreds, if not thousands, of tiny suction cups that covered every square inch of its oval shape.

Suction cups that pulsated and throbbed. Suction cups that Jimmy wouldn't have been shocked to discover contained separate sets of jagged, razor edged teeth akin to that of a piranha fish.

He watched helplessly as the thing bore down on the man just as his head had risen from the pavement, eyes springing open and stretched to the size of dinner plates. It was like witnessing a potential car wreck from a far distance and being utterly helpless to warn the unknowing participants.

Jimmy started to yell out, but was unable to follow through on a suitable warning to suffice. In the end, he simply remained a living, breathing statue, an abstract carving that if pictured in a dictionary, could have easily been defined as an example of the word 'petrified'. His wife's soft yet stern voice rang out repetitively within the confines of his fevered mind just as the injured soldier's mouth opened to scream.

"You should have left when I begged you to, honey," the voice chimed sweetly.

"Afraid you're *SOL* now, dear," it concluded.

Sergeant Ezop held his finger-less hands to his face just as the pear- shaped object with swirling sponge-cups for skin made contact with his tattered frame.

"G-get away, dammit! L-leave me b-be!" he whined before being swept up and away as easily as a dust-bunny beneath the wheels of an industrial strength vacuum.

The form never wavered or slowed as it curved back towards the rear of the compound with its ensnared prey stuck to its midsection like a struggling insect on freshly mounted flypaper.

Jimmy had seen the thing suck the soldier's head and shoulders inside its body, submerging him within the countless suction cups until only his flapping arms and limp, unmoving legs remained outside its genuflecting torso. As the thing glided back across the exercise yard, ignoring the two low-lying soldiers within its grasp, Jimmy saw the legs of the victim disappear also, sliding into the noticeably rounder midsection of the being as if being slowly digested. It reminded him of an old movie he had once seen where a man had been swallowed whole by a section of quicksand no larger than a manhole cover. He felt his gorge rise just as the spinning, levitating being floated out of sight and towards the same direction as the unearthly presence that had spawned it.

"W-wha...what...was..." he stammered, finally able to regain command of his lower extremities to back away while staring at the blank patch of stone where the soldier had lain just moments before.

The female private, her nametag reading 'KEMP' over her right shirt pocket, gripped his left arm and tugged as she jogged by, almost tipping Jimmy over onto his already raw backside.

"This ain't the time or place for sightseeing,

mister. Let's vacate the wide-open spaces 'fore another one of those things scouts around for additional morsels."

She released his arm just as he whirled around and joined her on the walkway, gradually picking up speed until he was right on her clicking boot-heels. He could hear the other soldier huffing and puffing a few feet behind, small animalistic grunts and groans escaping the young man's mouth with each strained step taken.

They cut across a narrow gravel path until they were hugging the side of the brick admin building, their shoulders periodically scraping the walls as they hurriedly proceeded.

Clearing the front edge of the building a minute later, Private Kemp's pace slowed considerably as she cut slightly to the right as if to possibly duck into the admin building's dark lobby if the need arose.

Jimmy ran into her extended left arm seconds later, and was subsequently barreled into by Private Bodine, who bounced harmlessly away, executing a rather clumsy tuck and roll upon impact with the smooth concrete.

"Nice. The Three Stooges run for their lives, part one. You okay, Lomax?" Private Kemp asked a bit mockingly without looking at her slowly rising comrade, who was busy brushing loose gravel and dust from his too baggy camouflage pants.

"Dead man walking, that's how I *am,* Sandy," he replied with utter disdain while angrily eyeballing Jimmy.

Jimmy returned his stare until both followed Private Kemp's gaze to the main gate. Their shoulders instantly dipped in unison.

"Locked up tighter than a politician's Swiss bank account, gents. Why am I not surprised?" Private Kemp said wearily, quickly turning her attention to the admin building's front doors, which were currently hanging from exactly one hinge on each side and looked to have been driven open by a runaway tank.

"Shouldn't we go check them? M-might just be closed and not locked," Jimmy asked between long, winded breaths.

She glanced at him sourly, like a parent preparing to scold a misbehaving child.

"If they're closed, man, they're *locked.* This is a maximum-security prison, not a park softball field."

Jimmy shrugged his sagging shoulders and winced from the throbbing pain that enveloped every fiber and nerve ending his bruised and beaten body possessed.

"Can't hurt to check it ou-..." he finally responded after a deep inhale of rank air.

"I tell ya what, big man, there's about forty yards of open space between you and the sally port there. Be my guest, just don't expect any tears on our part when one of those flying eating machines gulps you down like so much linguine, okay?" She blurted, taking an angry step forward. Her eyes were beyond simply bloodshot; they were red coals.

Jimmy stared down at his badly scratched bare feet. "Point taken, Sarge."

"Not quite. See the one silver stripe?" She said somewhat sadly, displaying her right shoulder as if showing off an old battle scar.

Jimmy nodded indifferently, wishing for the thousandth time in the past half-hour that he hadn't been so damned curious about the mystery smoke that had filled the woods around his campsite.

"*Private* Sandra Kemp, at your disservice. My unwilling and quite disheartened comrade is Private No Class Lomax Bodine, non-commissioned lunatic at large. You are?"

"Jimmy Rollins. I would say nice to meet you, but..."

Private Kemp cut him off with a stern nod towards the admin buildings wrecked entrance.

"What's say we continue the intros inside? I'm feeling more than a little vulnerable out here."

"Got'cha. Besides, I could really use a band aid right about now."

They exchanged smiles while trudging up the stone steps towards the ravaged doors.

"You look like you've been rode hard and stomped upon, man, no doubt," Private Kemp quipped before turning back around to address her fellow private, who continued to stare motionless at the gate, his mouth slightly agape.

"You coming, Lomax, or are ya waiting on an engraved invite? Can't feel too secure being that stupid *and* unarmed."

He jogged forward with a slumped gait, his youthful but strangely haggard face the very definition of downtrodden.

"We're just delaying the inevitable, that's all. They want us..." he ran by her, his doomed eyes meeting Private Kemp's own for the just the briefest of instants, but long enough to chill her very soul.

"...They'll *have* us."

She and Jimmy watched Private Bodine stroll between the wrecked doors and into the foyer beyond, then followed suit after giving the outside grounds a quick scan.

"Never mind Young Master Upbeat over there. He's playing the role of doomed warrior to the hilt, and I must admit scaring the ever-loving shit out of me in the bargain."

"You guys National Guard or what? Army Reserve?"

Private Kemp allowed Jimmy, who was roughly twice as thick around the waist as herself, to slide inside first.

"Dark Eagle Militia. Non-government affiliated in every sense of the word." The foyer was dimly lit, only a small number of the numerous emergency lights that hung from each corner of the spacious lobby actually working. Overturned desks and matching chairs, along with flipped and dislodged metal filing cabinets filled the room like the remnants from a rather severe storm.

Jimmy ducked into a nearby cubicle and sat down hard on one of the few remaining upright chairs, massaging his feet like someone who had just stepped out of a live fire-ant hill.

"Give me a minute. Have to catch my breath. Feel like I'm in the middle of at least my third stroke in the last fifteen minutes."

Private Kemp stood at the cubicle entrance, her shotgun balanced on her right shoulder.

"Where did Private Happy get off to? Dumb SOB is missing most of his marbles, I'm afraid. We found a pile…some bodies in the chow hall building a little while back. His senses have been pretty much AWOL since."

Jimmy leaned back until the chair whined its disapproval.

"Any idea what's going on here? I was conked over the noggin and dragged into this mess by two refuges from the set of 'Deliverance' who looked more dead than alive. I'm pretty damned lost. Did you *see* that thing that popped up from the ground out there?"

Private Kemp's squinted into the far West corner of the room, where the elevators and staircase were situated.

"I saw the incredible bulk alright, not to mention the half-man, half-squid thing it so calmly cut in half right before the man-eating eggs hatched and…' she halted to vigorously rub her forehead and face, '...can you believe what I just *said*? It's like something out of an old HP Lovelace book or something."

Jimmy leaned forward in the chair and laughed softly, his outstretched hands palming his head at the back of the scalp.

"I think you mean HP *Lovecraft*, and I can think of no better reference to what we just saw."

She didn't reply while shifting the weapon from her shoulder to chest level. "Hey, Bodine! You better sound off or risk getting your ear lobes blown onto the nearest wall!" She cried, her tone much milder than the relayed message.

Twin sets of heavy boot steps thumped loudly, filling the room from the direction of the stairway. Private Kemp crouched down instantly, the barrel of the shotgun held steady and pointed forward as the footsteps grew ever closer. Jimmy rolled to the floor and ducked his head behind the relatively tiny chair back.

"Sound off, dammit! I mean *NOW!"*

Private Bodine descended the steps in two quick leaps, his landing typically ungraceful as he barely avoided sailing headfirst over a fallen planter that blocked the bottom step.

"Don't fire, Sandy, it's just us chickens."

Blinking her eyes rapidly as if to clear away a particularly lifelike hallucination, it took Private Kemp a full five seconds of intense study to make a positive ID on the second figure present.

His uniform was coated in semi-dried blood, his hands wrapped individually in padded gauze that looked to be as thick as a big city telephone book. One arm was wrapped around an oblong object she deemed as strangely familiar but still unidentifiable in the shadows that held the majority of the room in check.

It wasn't until the initial set of marginally garbled words escaped his swollen lips that Private Sandy Kemp felt her hopes rise for the first time since entering the Briarston Correctional Facility.

"Hey there, Private Bad Ass. You as ready as I am to vacate these here fucked up premises?"

"Mac? Where...did you? I thought that Peterson..." she began; skipping forward between a line of downed office equipment so jumbled together it looked to have been welded into place.

The Corporal slung the object over his left shoulder, one she easily recognized as a chainsaw once they grew a mere five feet apart.

"He came damned close, him and that crazy ass guard. Chopped my fingers off for no other reason than they seemed to get their rocks off doing it. Can you believe that *warped* shit? I guess I can forget those piano lessons, huh?"

She started to pat his shoulder playfully, then paused once the blood-soaked gauze encircling his hands came into view. Knowing Ron McIntosh as she did, Private Kemp realized the last thing he desired was pity. Avoiding his direct gaze, she instead concentrated on the chainsaw blade propped over his shoulder like a garden rake.

"Strange time to cut firewood, Mac."

Balancing the engine end in the thick, muscled crook of his left elbow, Corporal McIntosh nodded apathetically.

"Veeerry droll, Private. Actually, once off the exercise grounds, I went searching for a vehicle behind the mess hall, truck or otherwise, to drive through that damned sally port. Found two Hum-V type trucks parked at the loading dock. Somebody had taken an axe blade to the engines. So, after a quick search of a small supply shack nearby, came up with this old Poulan brand wood slicer. Lady and gents, we're gonna saw our way outta this hellhole. Uh, I'm gonna need a little help pullin' the cord, though."

Kicking away a pile of loose paper from his left boot, Private Bodine stepped up next to the Corporal and placed a narrow arm around his massive shoulders.

"You were right in the middle of the shit out there, weren't you, Mac?"

"For certain, Bubba. The earthquake flipped over the gurney they had me strapped to, and I rolled away just before Peterson and those other freaky bastards met their maker the hard way. I've been shittin' it and getting it ever since. Must be the pain medication they loaded me up on."

"One of those…roving egg-things got Ezop. Sucked him up like so much carpet dust and swallowed him whole," Private Kemp said while looking at Jimmy, who was kneeling outside the cubicle with his head hung to the floor, a picture of exhaustion.

"Didn't really like the man, but he could've been a help in a shit-storm like this," Corporal McIntosh replied, pushing Private Bodine away with a nudge of his right elbow. The Private trudged away with a look of unbridled misery.

"Lomax and me almost butted heads on floor two. I came real close to planting this saw blade between his ears. Funny thing, I kept hearing noises behind me, and he ended up in front of me."

Jimmy joined them at the room's disjointed center a moment later.

"You getting your second wind, Jimmy Rollins?" Private Kemp asked, anything to keep from dwelling on the Corporal's gruesome wounds.

"I... guess. Thought for a minute that my ticker was gonna implode. I'm not exactly built for such antics, as you can well see. I'm ready if you people are."

"What's the plan, Mac? The gates are locked, and from what we've seen, my shotgun is about as useful as a bee-bee gun on an elephants ass," Private Kemp queried after softly patting Jimmy on the left shoulder.

The Corporal stepped past Jimmy indifferently, then side stepped a fallen computer console to reach the threshold of the small foyer.

"Like I said, Sandy, we're gonna gnaw our way through the fencing. Saw's gassed up and ready to rip…I hope. Not really sure it'll carve through that hard wire mesh, but I see no other option other than climbing, which is beyond my capability at the present time. Anyways, we'll catch up on old times later. I've got some serious pain creeping into my hands, so the morphine or whatever number they shoved into my veins must be wearing off. Pretty soon I won' be much used to ya."

"Come on, Lomax, we're leaving now," Private Kemp barked, noticing the Private's slumped form sitting atop a broken desktop at the far end of the room. "Yeah, by all means. We're off to meet the reaper," he mumbled while struggling to his feet.

For an instant, Private Kemp could have sworn she heard the sound of wings fluttering between herself and Private Bodine. It was a whizzing sound, like an industrial fan being kick started.

"You guys hear someth-..." she began.

Before her lips could complete the final syllable, the wooden handled axe completed its winding trajectory from the stairway it had been thrown so forcefully from.

***

"Hey, I c-could use a little help here, you guys."

Wilbo whirled towards the source of the voice, almost shoving his limping sister to the ground in the process.

"William, you m-mind not breaking my other

arm?" She said through gritted teeth, her good arm wrapped snugly around his neck and shoulders.

"Who the hell *was* that?" Wilbo asked, scanning the surrounding grounds and seeing nothing but unmoving carnage in each direction. It had been only a few scant minutes since they had witnessed a downed soldier being dragged away by an object that Kara had stated reminded her of a 'strobe light with a thousand mouths'. Needless to say, an unspoken agreement to take the low road to the nearest exit had been a no-brainer.

"I d-didn't hear anything. Let's get over to the n-nearest building before those…things come back," she mumbled.

They turned gingerly back towards the compound, Wilbo being extra cautious not to jar his sister's already tattered frame.

"Over here, folks. To your right..." one voice rang out.

"Actually, over here as well. To your left..." another chimed in exasperatingly.

Again, Wilbo paused and then turned them around, although exercising more caution than before. The compound lights shone into his eyes at an angle that made it difficult to focus, especially considering the throbbing headache at his temples.

Shading his eyes with his free hand, he pulled them near a portion of the former Warden's horribly mutilated form. He no longer felt the bulge at the back of his jeans, figuring the revolver once lodged there had been long since lost somewhere along the winding trek.

"Alright, this ain't the time for games. Speak up, damn it!" Wilbo blurted, trying but failing miserably to look away from the gruesome remains of their former captor.

"Down here, sport. You're looking right at me."

The air caught in Wilbo's throat like a chunk of insulation.

He stepped back as if poked with a cattle prod, then instantly braced to keep from dropping Kara.

"Wilbo, what's w-wrong with you? We can't help anyone e-else right now. Let's get go…"

Kara opened her eyes and her jaws locked. Shaking her head from side to side with as much vigor as her waning energy supply would allow, it did little to erase the reality of what she had hoped was a pain-induced hallucination.

The Warden/Thing's body had been sliced in half as neatly as if performed by maniacal magician equipped with a mammoth buzz saw.

They peered downward at what had been his left side, the face of which glared back at them with a single, wide eye that was fully aware and somehow gleaming with life. It looked as though his entire right side had melted *into* or melded with the ground, the split torso accompanied by a single arm, tentacle, and tree-trunk sized leg. Thick, dark bodily fluids lingered near the thing's upper body and scalp, the aroma from which caused Kara to immediately gag in revulsion.

"Give a guy a break, will you? Believe it or not, you need me as much as I need you," the thing's mouth croaked, it's tongue wriggling along the grass like a giant purple slug.

"I-I…h-how can you…you *gotta* be dead, man," Wilbo replied while sidestepping gradually to the left.

"Actually, that's neither here nor there, William. Right now, let's stick to the situation at hand..." the second voice spat, just a few feet to the twin's left.

A tentacle reached from the grass just as Wilbo leaned over to check the source and snagged Kara's left ankle, sending the twins reeling to the ground in a monkey pile of waving arms and twitching legs.

Wilbo tugged the appendage free and tossed it away with a disgusted grunt, his eyes as wide as plates. He then reached his arms beneath his sister's legs and lower back and heaved her upward.

It wasn't until he jogged a few steps to the left that he discovered the origin of the second, hauntingly familiar voice.

"Kinda hard to comprehend, ain't it, my man?" The other half of the Warden/Thing's severed face asked in a tone that was borderline cheery despite its obviously ragged state.

Although it lay on its partial back, the sliced portion of the head and torso thankfully faced away from the twins, giving it the illusion of being completely intact from their visual angle.

"H… h-ow can you… t-talk… how can either of y-you..." Wilbo whimpered, Kara's entire body trembling from his shaky hold.

The right half responded, causing Wilbo to cringe anew, again almost tossing his shocked speechless sibling onto the matted grass.

"You two may regard me as the enemy, and fittingly so after the way I so recklessly guided you to these rather frightening proceedings..."

"...but I guarantee this is not the case. We must

be allies if this very planet wants to live to see another sunrise…" The left side added.

"…am I being overly dramatic or have you two seen enough already to suspend your disbelief?" The right side concluded, the tone growing increasingly faint and harsh, as if a severe case of laryngitis was setting in.

Wilbo paused to gain a better grip on his sister, then sprinted forward in a mad rush, like a man escaping a burning room.

"…Listen to me, William! You'll die without my help, just as the rest of the population of this entire planet will suffer a similar fate without yours!" The left side bellowed, it's voice cracking like a static filled radio transmission.

"Stop, William."

His sister's voice was mechanical, almost robotic. He slowed immediately. "You *know* he's right. You feel it just as I do. We h-have to g-go back," she continued, only a bit more emotion coating the final words.

Wilbo stopped. He had barely made fifteen yards since the mad dash had begun.

"Yeah, ain't it a *bitch* though?" He asked before exhaling deeply and reversing his direction.

In the far distance, near the location of the cellblock building, a thousand tortured voices seemed to howl at once.

William would have literally pissed himself if not for the presence of his beloved sister pressed closely against his person.

***

Randolph P. Basham was considered, by both himself and all those unfortunate enough to fall victim to him throughout his twenty-six years, a certified bad ass specimen of the highest order. Six-foot four and two-hundred seventy pounds of rock-hard muscle (not a single shred of which wasn't naturally attained), sporting a Mohawk-do and a face mapped with scars of various lengths and widths, he played the part with gleeful relish.

Serving three life sentences for killing a trio of white supremacists in a bar room brawl some four years earlier, the 'Bash', as he was so respectfully referred to amongst his subordinates, was considered the one inmate residing within the walls of Briarston not to be trifled with in any form or fashion, be you fellow inmate or correctional staff.

He was the ordained king of the cellblocks almost upon his arrival, not only labeled such by his black peers, but the white and Hispanic population as well. Such an accomplishment wasn't handed out cheaply between the stone barricades of such an institution. Randolph had served three separate stints in administrative segregation in his first twelve months; two for assaulting fellow inmates and another for breaking the nose and ribs of a rookie correctional officer after a disagreement over TV time in the community break room. Randolph 'Bash' Basham could bench-press six hundred pounds and squat seven. He could break a man's jaw with a grazing blow from his stony knuckles. If the 'Bash' wanted pot, he got it, be it from the block supplier or a guard. If the 'Bash' wanted a bottle of wine or whiskey, his wish was their command. If the 'Bash' wanted to lay his pipe in a specific posterior that had caught his ever- roving eye (especially when new meat arrived in the compound), they would eventually bend over and satisfy his wish, either willingly or (painfully) otherwise.

Cowering against the rear wall of his eight by ten suite, complete with color TV, DVD player and Kenwood stereo straight from a Circuit City rack, the 'Bash' could delve up but a single, rather pathetic wish from his mortified brain.

He prayed his Mama would come and save him from the bad things that were eating his block mates.

The block population had been under lock down for several hours, at least half that time under total blackout conditions, and had become aware of the bizarre noises reverberating outside the cellblock walls, not to mention several series of earthquake-level tremors. Most had remained surprisingly calm throughout, though a shroud of apprehension was present within each cramped cell space, like the smell of sour sweat from the armpits of a thick wool shirt.

It wasn't until the lower cell block's eastern entrance door was bludgeoned from its metal hinges and the things squeezed through the narrow opening like maggots through an open wound that absolute fear took the reins in hand. It was the kind of fear that reverted grown men instantly back to their childhood in the single blink of an eye. Tears flowed freely and shallow cries rang out in hapless desperation.

The oval shapes spread out like a prepped military squad on training maneuvers, each choosing the next occupied cell that fell in line.

Compressing their shape until they were hardly more than an inch in diameter, they passed through the steel cell bars swiftly and with frightening ease. Once inside the cell, they simply reformed to their original shape and enveloped the whimpering, cringing inmates in an earthbound undertow. Upon departure, the shapes would again transform, sometimes dragging the only partially encased bodies through the bars with legs or arms hanging freely and at awkward angles, the grisly sounds of cracked and shattered bone replacing those of shrill cries as each floor was fallen upon by the gliding hordes.

They crisscrossed one another like worker ants within the narrow cellblocks, those full of cargo passing those as yet void of such in a well-organized formation that was strangely hypnotic to witness.

Randolph Basham threw a combination of wild, desperate punches at his own attacker just as it began to reshape itself from pencil thin (allowing entry through the bars) to original size, his oversized fists instantly penetrating through the putty-like flesh and sticking at the wrist. In a moment of frantic indecision, he had bypassed using the six inch-bladed shank taped beneath his bunk. One glance at the enemy invading his space quickly dismissed any chances that such a primitive weapon might prove useful.

As it shoved its bulk forward to begin the absorbing process, hundreds of concave suction cups puckering for their initial taste of human flesh, the 'Bash' could feel his hands burning as if being dunked in a vat of toxic waste. The bones contained within felt as if they were being held at close range within the blue flame of an acetylene torch. As his ludicrously huge arms began to slowly descend into the mushy quagmire, the skin peeled away from the bone and tendon with grisly precision.

Randolph Basham's yelping, whining prayer to his maker was cut abruptly short as his upper body was thrown forward in a viscous blur, snapping his neck like a dry twig beneath a fallen oak.

It took less than five minutes for the remainder of the inmate population of Briarston Correctional Facility to suffer a similar fate. Only a select few on cell floor number three were fortunate enough to complete their exasperated pleas to the heavens.

None had such prayers answered before the halls grew silent and unnaturally still.

***

The axe-blade had struck Private Bodine just below his left ribcage and above the hipbone, burying itself handle deep with a nauseating noise one might associate with sinking their boots into thick mud and pulling them out with a single tug.

By the time his already lifeless, rag-doll form disappeared behind the fallen partition of a nearby cubicle, all others had either dived or ducked to the floor as if avoiding a live fire bombardment.

"Sandy? You okay over there?" Corporal McIntosh screamed in a tone that was amazingly void of all apparent fear.

Upon witnessing the axe handle windmill towards her oblivious cohort, Private Kemp had reeled back and accidentally head-butted Jimmy just behind the right ear as he was in the process of ducking.

They toppled in opposite directions, each scrambling beneath separate pieces of scattered furniture for cover.

"S-still breathing, Ron. Where the hell did that come from? Stairwell?" She responded while pulling her dropped rifle back into position while remaining flat on her chest with her head against the cool tile floor.

There was a stilted pause, a dead moment in time comparable to the deafening silence that incurs between stormy thunderclaps, followed by the insertion of words voiced in a hollow, barely audible tone that caused everyone present to physically cringe.

"Damn right *stairwell,* missy. You stay cowerin' down right where you are, you hear? I'll be right there to end your misery for ya."

"W-who is that? Another one of your lunatic soldier buddies?" Jimmy asked while scooping up a metal letter opener from beneath a pile of spilled folders.

Private Kemp bristled, crawling forward until she was able to back against a large table used to house a large printer and copy machine. Fresh sweat matted her hair to her forehead and into the corners of her eyes.

"Nobody I know, man. Must be a local maniac. They seem to grow 'em around here on trees."

"Sandy, the bastard descends those stairs you make sure you fill his pores with USDA buckshot, you got it?" Corporal McIntosh yelled, sounding noticeably weaker than just moments before.

In the darkened space that had swallowed up Private Bodine following impact, a muffled gurgling noise could be heard every five seconds or so.

"You *do* that, Sandy! The bastard is gonna descend...right about..." Another pause ensued as the voice broke off like a radio with its electrical cord severed.

A loud, boisterous thumping filled the room as stairs were taken two and three at a time.

"...NOW!"

Private Kemp's head arose, clearing the bottom edge of the table, just as the shadowy blur leaped into the room as if shot from a canon barrel.

Just as quickly as it had appeared, like a levitating phantom from the edges of a particularly nasty nightmare, it was gone. She scanned every direction, including behind her, *multiple* times, the sparse emergency lighting providing little if any illumination in the rooms many cornered spaces.

"Ron? Where is he? You see anything?" She barked nervously while glancing over at Jimmy, who seemed to be contemplating whether or not his entire bulky frame could fit beneath a nearby desk.

"Chicken shit jackass is nearby, Sandy. Keep your guard up and your weapon steady."

Corporal McIntosh, his jaws clinched tight from the searing pain shooting through his hands, had cowered behind a rubber plant roughly the size of a Buick. The chainsaw was propped on his right shoulder, blade up. From a distance he looked like a space age lumberjack, preparing to ply his trade on the thin, rubber limbs obstructing his view. Hugging the saws circular base in search of a better grip, albeit a finger-less one, he smelled the putrid billowing of air just before feeling it brush the back of his shaved neck.

"Give you a hand, sailor? Better yet, a *finger?"* The voice whispered sardonically just inches from his left ear.

He whirled around while rising, swinging the chainsaw blade down viscously in the process, and connected with nothing but air and, eventually, a portion of the stucco-wood wall once his follow-through was complete, sending various sized chunks sailing into the distance like tree-bark shrapnel.

Executing an impromptu break-dance in order to regain his shaky balance, the Corporal was finally able to halt his own clumsy momentum at the center of the room, the chainsaw dropping from his loose grip and onto his left shin and foot.

Flinching from the fresh pain shooting up his arms like twin jolts of pure electricity, he reached over with his left foot to retrieve the saw, closing his eyes for only a single blink. When he re-opened them, he was face to face with a fleshless skull flashing a toothless grin.

"Ain't much to look at I know, but then, I *never* was," the thing smirked as its skeletal fingers wrapped around the Corporal's thick neck, the veins of which stood out like cable wire.

Private Sandra Kemp stood statuesque, as unmoving and stoic as a stone monument. She had seen the partially uniformed walking stick that still managed to speak like a living, breathing man leap from the shadows and begin strangling her cohort. A warning shout had hung in her throat a split-second before, but would have come far too late to alter the surrealistic, gregariously bizarre scene playing out a few dozen feet to her left.

The shotgun's barrel was pointed in the combatant's direction, wavering back and forth like a flag caught in a series of gusts from both east and west.

Peeking around the desk like a rodent hiding from a crouching feline, Jimmy felt his jaws unhinge in disbelief for at least the tenth time that evening. It was like a movie scene from one of those nineteen fifties dinosaur flicks, where the special effects were mostly Claymation figures that were embarrassingly cheap in both appearance and movement. He turned towards Private Kemp, who stood eerily motionless, as if frozen in suspended animation.

"Jesus, lady, shoot that damn thing before it k-kills 'im."

She blinked rapidly and slowly tucked the gun's stock against her right shoulder.

Corporal McIntosh began to laugh between hacking coughs as the piston-like fingers applied increased pressure to his windpipe.

The minute portion of his mind whose task it was to differentiate between fantasy and reality had permanently blown an inner fuse, resulting in the only workable reaction to such a scenario being hysterical ranting with just a touch of jocular lunacy tossed in for good measure.

In a different time, one in which he actually possessed working digits, he would have simply gripped the thing's wrists and torn the hands from his throat. As it was, he struggled to pound at the inner portion of the things tattered arms in order to loosen the steely grip, all the while howling like a Hyena on helium.

"W-who a-are y-you s-sup...supposed t-to be, man? And w-why t-the h-h- hell are y-you ch... choke...chokin' me?" He babbled while attempting to break the hold by jerking his upper body violently to one side, but to no apparent avail.

"Name's Settle, or at least was. I was put in charge of this here facility for the socially unfit a few hours back, thus the light show you may or may not have noticed. Turned 'em off once we hit lockdown, per instructions. Had to flip 'em back on for everybody to see the birthing of our master in full-bodied Technicolor. I've *always* been one to follow orders. See no reason to change just 'cause I've lost most of my outer shell, know what I mean? Naw...guess ya don't."

The Corporal slung his head forward, applying a viscous head-butt that landed flush on the creatures pointed chin, driving its head back only momentarily before it bounded back into position.

Its grin seemed impossibly wide, stretching the few remaining tendons of the jawline to the snapping point.

"Ouch. Nice try, jarhead. Now, be a good little GI Joe and relax for Doctor Settle. Dying ain't hard, son, and it don't have to be this painful. As the Doobie Brothers once sang, 'just listen to the doctor.'"

Corporal Ron McIntosh had rarely been bested in a lifetime of physical confrontations, most of which were brought about by his own cockiness fueled by chemical overindulgence of some type.

His arms, already enormously pumped, hung onto his bony captor's like Anaconda's over a clothesline. Still, as he felt his entire body lifted airborne and his booted feet dangle haplessly, the Corporal's frenzied laughter halted abruptly, replaced by a silent, desperate prayer of atonement.

Lashing out wildly in a final attempt to break loose before his neck eventually snapped from the constant pressure, the Corporal's boots made solid contact with his captor's ribcage, filling the room with the sharp retort of cracking, shattered bones. Regardless of the damage the kicks caused, they did little to relieve the ever-increasing pressure at his throat.

"Shhhh, go to sleep now, Sergeant Rock. I still have your comrades to dispose of before we all ride outta here on the master's all-powerful backside," the thing croaked gleefully, just before the top of its skull was blown apart like a rotted pumpkin struck by a swinging anvil.

The shotgun blast reverberated within the stone walls like a grenade detonation, the recoil sending Private Kemp staggering back into and almost over a set of sliding office chairs, her balance regained only after she had completely dropped the weapon to use her hands as twin windmill blades.

Corporal McIntosh immediately tumbled to the floor as the creature's grip was relinquished. Holding the palms of his mutilated hands against his bruised throat, his eyes coated in a layer of warm tears, he managed to look up only after sucking in a few much-needed breaths.

The former correctional officer turned walking archeology exhibit named Settle still stood upright, waving its rail thin arms around spastically, despite the fact that it no longer possessed a head above the nostril holes of its jagged skull. Its jaws clinched and relaxed repeatedly, a series of canine like grunts escaping its shredded throat.

Corporal McIntosh bull-rushed like a defensive lineman with a clear alley towards an opposing quarterback, his arms tucked tightly at his chest. His scream was that of a fatally injured warrior making a last-ditch effort to extract a measure of revenge before dying.

His left shoulder impacted just above the skeletal thing's right thigh, the sound of bone pulling away from tendon followed by an ear-splitting crack.

His two-hundred-plus pound frame landed atop the skeletal figure with the impact of a professional wrestler's best body-slam, sending fragments of breast and rib bone sailing away from its host in opposite directions.

By the time the Corporal rolled away and propped himself up on admittedly shaky knees, what remained of the horribly crushed form had grown completely still, its last movement a final, spastic shuddering of its mashed torso.

Jimmy was the first to reach him, tiptoeing past Settle as if expecting a hand to reach out and grab his ankle.

"You okay, McIntosh?" He asked timidly, placing his arm around the large man's wide shoulder.

The Corporal inhaled several times before attempting a reply. He managed the strength to do so just as Private Kemp strolled up, rubbing her right knee vigorously.

"Feel like I've been pureed, poured over a salad, and chewed like a shredded carrot. Thanks for askin' anyhow."

He looked from Jimmy to Private Kemp, smiling weakly between winces. "Good shot, Hawkeye. I recall your firing range prowess, girl. I must say I feel damn fortunate to only be without fingers at this moment. Sure beats the hell outta old headless over there."

He nodded towards the emaciated corpse, tiny strips of gray CO uniform sticking to portions of the frame as if glued into place.

"That dude sure got a healthy dose of whatever that giant worm is dishin' out, wouldn't you say?"

Jimmy nodded, unable to tear his eyes away from the blown-apart skull and the jaws that had clinched together a final time upon death.

"Can you stand, Sergeant?" Jimmy asked, obtaining a better grip on the other man's massively bulky upper arm.

"That's Corporal, chief, but thanks for the attempt at a battlefield promotion. It ain't like I don't deserve it, by god. Yeah, I can hop along with the best of 'em once I get on my feet."

Private Kemp stepped back to reload the shotgun, pulling shells from her front pants pocket. She then propped it on her left shoulder and stepped gingerly over to the spot where Private Bodine had last been seen. She paused to peer over a toppled cubicle, then sighed heavily before retracing her steps.

Standing with Jimmy's aid, Corporal McIntosh felt obligated to at least ask the fate of his young friend, despite the fact that it was more than likely a foregone conclusion. He had genuinely grown to like Lomax Bodine, despite their 'odd couple' differences.

"I take it he's.... beyond assistance."

She didn't meet his glare, choosing instead to observe Jimmy as he scooped up the chainsaw and began to carefully study it, like a pre-schooler with a new toy.

"*Way* beyond. The walking stick over there sure tossed a mean axe. Jesus, and I was just getting used to Lomax's constant state of depression," she finally replied, the last few words cracking with emotion.

There were a few moments of awkward silence as all three took turns scanning the ruins surrounding them, then they broke stride towards the front exit in almost perfect unison.

"Off to see the wizard," Private Kemp whispered to no one in particular. "Let's hope that saw turns the trick, 'cause I ain't searching this building for power switches. I'll dig to China with my bare feet first, Sandy," Corporal McIntosh barked, his limping stride and slumped gait giving him the look of a man suffering from extreme lower abdominal pain.

"I'm with you, Mcintire," Jimmy chimed in, cradling the chainsaw in both hands like a new-born.

"McIntosh, *Timmy,* McIntosh," the Corporal replied between pained breaths.

Jimmy laughed despite himself, stopping just short of playfully tapping the larger man on the back.

Private Kemp stepped out first, a silent prayer mumbled between her severely chapped lips.

Less than a fifty yards away, the locked sally port stood between them and the compound's main gate. From where they stood a moment later, just outside the admin buildings only entrance, the distance between the two seemed utterly endless, a wide, distant field filled with unknown pratfalls and lurking danger.

***

Peaking over his right shoulder, Wilbo shot his twin sister a worrisome look.

"You gonna make it, sis?" He asked while maneuvering the metal gurney past a large mound of what looked like burnt human intestines coiled like black snakes in the wheel's path.

"I seem to be getting my second wind. The thought of dying the way that solider did is quite the motivation, William," she replied in a tone filled with renewed vigor, despite being forced to shove the gurney forward with only one working arm.

The left portion of the Warden/Thing glared up at her with its single roving, unblinking eye.

"Then you might want to cut the chatter and increase the speed of this wobbling buggy, little lady. Time is definitely…"

"…at a premium," the right portion concluded from the gurney William was tasked to steer, it's partially severed vocal cords making it sound as if it were chewing on a handful of pebbles.

Wilbo paused as they neared the concrete walkway, took in several deep breaths, then spoke without actually looking at the disfigured monstrosity that hung half-on, half-off the slowly bending gurney, its sagging bulk threatening to collapse the table altogether.

"Why the gymnasium, Warden? We gonna challenge that thing to a little two-on-one?"

The right portion cackled, sending a fresh chill racing up the spines of both twins.

"Good one, William. You're a real card, you are. Especially considering that you and your lovely sibling are presently strolling atop a high wire directly over the churning, burning rivers of Hades itself."

As William resumed shoving the increasingly warped gurney forward past the edge of the mess hall building, he again looked back to check his sister's status.

She gave him a quick nod as the second gurney rolled onto the pavement, a flaccid tentacle hanging loose from one side, grotesquely swinging back and forth like a fleshy pendulum.

A loud blast, like that from a single shot rifle or similar weapon, caused the twins to flinch back simultaneously. Kara stared at her brother gravelly.

"Sounded like maybe the admin building. Some nasty shit going down, no doubt," Wilbo said solemnly, unconsciously picking up the pace, as his upper body seemed to surge with newfound energy.

"You missed your calling, William. You could have made a real splash as one of those telephone psychics," the right side remarked sourly.

"Tell me, one-eye, what really is going down here? Did the military crack open a hole to another dimension or is it simply some sort of chemical fart gone mad?" Wilbo smirked, keeping his eyes peeled for anyone or *thing* between themselves and the breezeway ahead.

"None of the above, I'm afraid. What we're witnessing this night is a grand scale production that has been centuries in the making," the right side responded, grunting as the gurney's front wheels crossed a deep groove in the stone.

"You of course have read stories of rogue angels within the storied annals of religious literature, yes?" The left side began as Kara slowed its forward progress a bit to avoid the same grooved dip her brother had ran across a moment earlier.

"Not exactly an expert on the bible, Cyclops. That was our mom's territory. Enlighten us."

The right side answered instead as its split twin began to hack and cough violently, almost tipping the gurney with its herky-jerky movements.

"There were rogue demons as well, you see. Not *all* evil entities conform to or play well within their own ranks, despite the general consensus. Garentu- Gormanite, I'll just refer to him as 'Gor' to save time and my rapidly deteriorating voice, was banished from the higher regiment of demons in a time before this planet was yet a gleam in your heavenly messiah's eyes."

The left side broke in after successfully dislodging a portion of neck bone that had hung at the base of its throat and spitting it over the side of the gurney. Kara felt her gorge rise at the sight, but managed to regain control by quickly turning away.

"There *is* a chain of command in such a place, believe it or not. Garentu- uh..Gor showed little patience for what he considered unnecessary trivialities. The one sin that even an upper regimen demon cannot commit is wilful termination of its own kind. Gor was known to dispatch of subordinates and peers alike with the same casual aplomb…"

The first gurney screeched to a sudden halt, causing the right side of the Warden/Thing to roll forward until the tip of his divided noggin hung from its top edge like a slab of sliced pork.

"…what's the frequency, Kenneth? You want to carry me piggyback the rest of the way? I warn ya, son, four hundred-plus pounds of dead weight can wear on you pretty damn quick."

Kara rolled to a much smoother stop a few feet behind, her brain working up a suitable query that would never be allowed to materialize.

"So Mr. Mega-worm is basically your run of the mill demon from hell? This is what you're telling us with a straight...make that a *half*-straight face?" Wilbo practically screamed, a thick vein throbbing at the center of his sweaty forehead.

"This ain't Ripley's Believe it or Not, my man. Yeah, that is *precisely* what I'm saying. Gor is no longer a demon in the spiritual sense, but a physical manifestation of such a being, thus, openly vulnerable to termination in a physical sense.

Now, how's about not dumping my innards and proceeding to the gym post-haste? I'd rather have a semblance of cover once big, bad and slimy comes calling here in a few."

"…I'll fill in the considerable blanks once we're inside, agreed?" The left side concluded harshly while glowering angrily at Kara.

Wilbo grabbed one of the creature's thickly

scaled ankles and tugged. The thing's head pulled back atop the gurney with a moist, squishy sound. He then jostled the table forward until executing a hard left towards the glass- covered breezeway separating the compound's second and third buildings.

"Damn right you're gonna fill in some blanks, Jackass. I'll be in Regis' seat and you'll be contestant number one. Won't be no 'phone a friend' or 'ask the audience' bullshit neither."

Kara followed closely behind, the throbbing in her one working arm close to matching the intensity of the broken one. Her side of the creature seemed to be observing her with morbid curiosity, as if *she* were the half-human, half-deep-sea fish abomination that lay split apart like a slab of pizza.

"You can beat it, girl. You and your twin hold the key, *yes* sir. You have all along. Without your presence, all this would be moot. Somebody knew to bring you here. Somebody on a higher plane was definitely clued in," it muttered in an outlandishly upbeat tone, its single stationary eye focused solely on her chalky white complexion.

"Shut up, whatever the hell you are. Just put a cork in it, o-okay?" She replied wearily, bracing for the sharp curve her brother had already cleared.

"Why, I'm your ally, Kara. I'm...your friend. In time, you'll come to know this as truth. It may be difficult in looking at me, but it wi-..."

"I said shut up, *Freak!* Y-your no friend of mine, damn it! That much I *can* feel as truth. Feel it in my broken, weary bones. Save the fairy tales for someone other than my brother and me. You may well be the *lesser* of two evils, and even that's iffy at this point."

The thing opened its bloodied maw to reply, but decided otherwise as the threshold of the breezeway drew near.

Kara halted the gurney just inches away from her brother's frozen pose.

He turned to her and flashed a pitiful grin that was the definition of uncertainty.

"This is it, huh sis? Our equivalent to the O.K. Corral. You feel it, too?" After a short pause, she nodded, meeting his badly bloodshot eyes with her own.

"Without a doubt, brother of mine. I think I've known since we were first making camp in these damned woods. Scary thing is not knowing exactly what to do, you know?"

"Definitely. If I was presently capable of crapping my drawers, the tanks a bit empty as we speak, now would be the time."

She scowled at the thing on the gurney ahead of her. Both sides had fallen conspicuously quiet, although their eyes remained open and roving about.

"Well, you ready to go play super-hero for real?" She asked with a pathetic smile of her own.

"I'm with you, Sis. You put on the Scarlet Witch's cowl, and I'll make like my man Logan and prep my Wolverine's claws."

Without uttering another word between them, the twins proceeded to shove the gurneys into the breezeway one at a time.

Determined in their efforts to secure a temporary safe haven, the fact that both halves of the Warden/Thing displayed equally gruesome smiles went completely unnoticed.

***

As each of its offspring returned triumphantly to the nesting place within its massive bosom, the being swelled with a power incarnate, one it had longed to embrace for centuries untold. No longer was it limited to the infrequent, normally woefully unsubstantial feedings provided by the mindless minions of the surface world. The periodic human shell or simple-minded animal creatures that had sustained it for decade upon decade while trapped within the stony walls of its self-contained dungeon had done little if any to prepare it for the bombardment of pure, raw energy relished within the previous ten minutes.

The elements of in-bred evil, the touch of hardly significant malice that lingered within the souls it had just consumed were the combustible fuel that fed the furnace within its suddenly reawakened existence. In its time of imprisonment, the purely good souls had been swallowed and digested through force of habit and ravishing hunger, but were the equivalent of a raw ground beef force fed to a strict vegetarian. Maintaining enough vitality to merely survive within such a solitary, restraining realm was obviously essential, but gaining the inner strength and concentrated raw power to escape towards the mission at hand was a vastly different state altogether. The essential food groups necessary for such a monumental task had finally been obtained within the frazzled souls at Briarston Correctional Facility. Souls reeking with heaping doses of malevolence manufactured not over time but at the inception of their miserable, ill-fated existence. Souls not unlike those housed within the surface-dwelling worshipers the being utilized so expertly in plotting his eventual escape. They all resided within the beings inner region, each one acting as a separate spark plug; tiny embers burning for all eternity and without aspirations for anything more elaborate than to serve their one true master.

The being understood this particular planet's importance to the ones who had forced its imprisonment. Its first order of revenge would be to consume the inhabitants, wiping the surface as clean as the day the cursed one had created it. With the immense, immeasurable power gained from such mass consumption, it would turn its sights to the realm from which it had been so cruelly dispatched. The ultimate goal, that being nothing less than confronting, challenging, and then terminating the higher commands, to eventually include the Dark Messiah as well, could very well become a reality if the planet fell as planned. It realized that the Dark Messiah would not fall easily, and even powers harnessed and honed to perfection would not guarantee victory in such an epic conflict.

The planet was merely one of many inhabited at the core by the higher realm of ancient ones, but was favored by the Dark Messiah as a personal favorite due to the credulous, small-minded inhabitants that had become ridiculously simple to use and manipulate through the centuries. The Dark Messiah loved nothing better than to play games with their kind, garnering the role of puppet master against the forces of the heavenly cursed one, who, for some unknown, inexplicable reason, protected this particularly pathetic creation with unmatched fervor.

It's bloated midsection now roughly the size of a Navy destroyer, the being lunged away from the cellblock building, utilizing the recently hatched trio of legs and feet that had emerged from its lower half during feeding. Individually, the feet were ten yards wide and perfectly flat, with nothing resembling toes apparent on their scaly surface. The legs were as thick as sequoias and the color of an ocean sunset. As it lurched off in the direction of the compounds main gate, perfectly square prints large enough for a half-dozen men to lay inside matted in both grass and shattered concrete, the being felt the manic thumping at its midsection. The black pit of its heart melted instantly with motherly joy, or at least as close as one such as it *could* fathom.

The magnitude of what they were about to become a part of and witness to had finally begun to dawn on each. Most would play willing participant, as was their true and only nature. Others would struggle and fight to no avail, the cursed ones more repugnant traits still apparent in their fading souls, refusing to let go and accept the inevitable. Still, the origin of their wilful demonstration planted a seed of doubt, however tiny, in the being' mind. There were still enemies nearby that must be eliminated. Enemies that might indeed pose a threat, again however minuscule, to the overall mission. It considered the Sentinel it had so effortlessly defeated as the source, but quickly dismissed such a possibility. That one's woefully weak presence was simply to guard and protect by reporting to superiors if escape was eminent. Sentinels weren't expected to even confront, much less defeat a greater, more malevolent being.

As it lunged it's way forward, unconsciously ripping away the front portion of the cellblock building with its mammoth, spiked tail in an explosion of shattered brick and bent metal, the being became aware of a new presence within the fenced-in compound.

A presence that had apparently allied itself with the Sentinel in a last-ditch effort to prevent the mass consumption of their pitiful planet.

The being threw its head back and howled in its version of a lunatic's guffaw, its outward arrogance disguising the slight pang of apprehension and fear that dug at its gut like the tip of a surgeon's razor-sharp scalpel.

***

Jimmy tossed the chainsaw aside in frustration, its broken chain swinging free like a discarded electric cord.

"Well, so much for that notion. Anyone for pole-vaulting?" He asked sourly, staring at the barely nicked section of barbed fence that had disabled the saw a second earlier.

"Looks like were pinned in for the duration, Jimbo. Its damned obvious somebody went to a whole lotta trouble to have it that way," Corporal McIntosh replied, kneeling down and hugging himself, his eyes glassy and unfocused from the flaring waves of pain that threatened to paralyze his arms.

Private Kemp gently laid a hand on his left shoulder. “You’re a hurting pup, aren’t ya, Mac?”

Staring into the pavement, he forced a smile without looking up.

“I could use a BC Powder, since you asked. Actually, a fifth of JD or a gallon of vodka might be preferable.”

Jimmy stood at the sally ports electronically locked gates and stared through to the semi-lit parking lot beyond.

From a distance he would have resembled a fat child, presumably on the verge of tears while peering into a locked playground.

The razor wire that topped off the fencing was three-tiered and at least two feet high, instantly eliminating any rational thoughts of climbing to escape.

“Sure didn’t leave us many options, did they?”

Private Kemp looked past him and towards the ditch where the militia’s weapons had been stashed before they entered the then wide-open gates of the compound. She laughed silently at the predicament they found themselves immersed in. No manmade weapon, including the one resting atop her left shoulder, was remotely effective within the blurred layers of such a bizarre, warped dimension. Even if each of them were parading around with grenade launchers, it would still prove haplessly inadequate when faced with such unworldly opposition.

She secretly pondered, while observing Jimmy assist the Corporal to his feet, why they had made such an effort to escape the prison grounds at all. Surely such an entity would catch up to them eventually, if it so desired, no matter how many miles they managed to cover on foot. The Private finally deduced that when faced with such surreal danger, the human mind would naturally switch over into autopilot mode, searching for a way to remain 'useful' and self-motivated to survive despite the massive wave of insanity threatening to engulf it from all sides.

"Back to cover, I take it?" Jimmy asked while attempting to hold the Corporal's substantial bulk upright. Beads of sweat the size of marbles stood out on both men's foreheads, despite the relatively cool night air, which had at least warmed a bit since the freak cold front of earlier.

Private Kemp nodded, flashing the unreachable parking lot one last forlorn look.

"I'm beginning to think Lomax was actually an *optimist,*" she blurted while positioning herself on the Corporal's opposite side and wrapping his immensely muscled forearm around her slim neck.

Forced to move forward at a snail's pace while practically dragging the Corporal, whose eyes flittered as if fighting off impending unconsciousness, it was Jimmy who first became aware of the building tremors beneath their feet.

"*Another* quake?" He blurted just as the first section of concrete leading to the admin building's entrance split neatly into two sections as if struck by an invisible bolt of lightning.

Private Kemp leaned hard to the left just as a jarring vibration that made the last seem almost non-existent split the ground on either side of the tightly packed trio, causing her to temporarily lose her grip on her groggy comrade. Corporal McIntosh seemed to snap to as one of his crutches was temporarily lost, his legs tensing instantly as his eyes grew wide with sudden awareness.

"Move it, Jimmy! W-we have to get inside before the ground swallows us whole!" Private Kemp screamed, taking the point only after insuring the Corporal was indeed able to proceed without her.

Jimmy was pulled forward before he could respond; the Corporal dragging him along as if their roles had been suddenly reversed and *he* were the injured party.

The intervals between quakes allowed them to keep their balance without falling, and it wasn't until they had reached the building's ravaged front entrance that the set pattern in which they fell became easily predictable at three to four second intervals.

Jimmy paused at the open entrance after the Corporal had jogged inside, grabbing the inside of Private Kemp's left elbow as she attempted to do the same.

"What the hell, man? This ain't no time for sightseeing...," she complained, jerking her arm away in frustration and dropping the rifle just inside the foyer in the process.

"Did you notice it?" He asked worriedly, peeking past the building's edge into the brightly lit wasteland that had become the exercise yard, now resembling some scarred, ancient battlefield.

"Notice what, man? Listen, get your ass inside before…"

His right hand arose mechanically, palm up in a halting gesture. "I... I think...it's *f-footsteps…*" he whispered.

Private Kemp's scowled as her eyes rolled back in comic wonder.

"My big old butt…there's *no way* it can be…I mean, *what* could possibly be large or heavy enough to…"

In the single blink of an eye, she witnessed Jimmy's expression transform from one of wall-eyed paranoia to sheer, unrelenting terror. His skin was a ghostly, bloodless shade of pale, his mouth locked in a silent scream that his shockingly wide and constantly twitching eyes echoed whole-heartedly. His raised hand pointed eastward, the lead finger convulsing madly.

Private Kemp started to reach for her weapon, but instead whirled around at the source of his dramatics. She instantly began to laugh without benefit of a smile, cackling madly through gritted teeth and purplish colored, pursed lips, the majority of the shrill noises trapped at the back of her throat as if her mouth were taped shut.

The gargantuan form that trampled towards them was approximately the size of a two-story office building, rampaging forth on mammoth, unbending legs and squared feet roughly the length and width of the room they were preparing to step into.

In the three to four second pause between steps, the being seemed burdened to work up the energy before executing each, its oval shaped body seemed to actually be growing bulkier and more defined, gradually losing the circular profile for more of a pumpkin-shaped outline. The stalk that held its enormous head aloft seemed shorter than earlier, the base of which throbbed and pulsated as if on the verge of a volcanic explosion.

"Holy…is that the same?…I…that c-can't be…just simply *cannot* b-be…," Jimmy babbled in a barely coherent ramble, his bottom lip dancing a spastic jig.

"Get inside, man, before it sniffs us out. Hell, it may already have," Private Kemp replied, placing her sweaty palms on Jimmy's chest shoving him back forcefully. For the faintest of moments, she considered reaching down for the shotgun, then just as quickly dismissed it with a humorless grunt.

"Might as well be hauling a BB gun around," she whispered before ducking inside the foyer, a fresh tremor assisting her momentum.

As they raced forward, dodging the scattered furniture and office equipment that littering the path towards the first-floor hallway, Jimmy began to rant aloud, a barrage of profanity-laced raves that was driven by equal parts panic and disbelief.

"…*SON OF A BITCH* piece of rat-turd fuck-face ass-wipe butt-licking dick- weed peter-pulling ball-sniffing *BASTARD!*…I try to escape the daily insanity and look what happens….I end up thigh deep in elephant dung…can you believe this *BULLSHIT*? I was trying to get away from it all and I end up in some alternate world Hell that makes a Turkish prison resemble Club Med…what the rolling *FUCK* is that all about? I ask you…give me a fucking *clue,* will you?"

Even as she kneeled to help the slumping Corporal McIntosh to his feet, Private Kemp was doubled over in a rollicking fit of laughter she had only previously experienced the likes of following the inhalation of some quality South of the Border wacky-weed.

Tears sprang freely from both eyes as she pushed the Corporal forward with both her arms lodged inside his armpits.

As they sprinted down the dimly hit hall, besieged by ground seizures that threatened to bring the surrounding walls crashing down around their ears, Jimmy's voice grew horse from his sermon-like tirade, his chest, shoulders and neck tensed to the point of paralysis.

"...sold the house, bought a tent...gonna live off the land with the peace and tranquility of Mother Nature as my guide towards a life filled with the simple pleasures and devoid of stress and strife...well, let me tell you...if this happy horse-shit is any indication, Mother Nature is one mean-spirited *BITCH* with a remarkably warped sense of humor..."

Her strength ebbing as the hysterical giggling spell continued, Private Kemp was unable to prevent the Corporal from bouncing off the suddenly curving walls like a human pinball.

"Cu-cut it out, man, you're k-killin' me..." she pleaded while bracing the Corporal upright, her laughter now mixed with sincere cries of pain.

"...my wife is probably sitting in the clouds howling her buns off at the colossal shit-pile I've managed to poke my feet into...bare feet at that...I've got splinters bigger than my pee-rod wedged in my heel...*SON...OF... A...BITCH!"*

"P-p-pee-rod? D-did you s-say...p-pee-rod?" She bawled, dangerously close to collapse as a new set of rib-throbbing guffaws ensued. Corporal

McIntosh, who wavered and lurched with each of the Private's similar movements, glared down at her with a comical look of disdain.

"Hell's Belles, S-Sandy, get a g-grip, will ya?" He managed to mumble just as the hallway imploded behind them.

***

"It's sniffing us out, folks. It considered flight, but couldn't help but to be naturally intrigued by the challenge you two provide. It yearns for a suitable test of combat before turning planet Earth into its personal lunch buffet."

Standing against the gym's far stone wall, his feet propped at the center of a wide, well-worn weight bench, Wilbo's pale face was void of emotion as he stared across at the Warden/Thing's left side.

"How do you know all this, hoss? I can't help but feel you have a bigger stake in the outcome than you're letting on."

Kara sat on the bench's edge, a large scattering of dumbbells and free weights making a semi-circle around her feet.

"You know he does, William, but why ask? He's not giving away any trade secrets, am I right, two-face?"

The gurney's had been shoved together, leaving the two sides mere inches apart and facing one another like matching poker cards.

The right side stared at Kara while the left seemed to concentrate exclusively on William.

"Y'know, the jokes concerning my rather

unfortunate condition are starting to wear considerably thin…" the right side said with a partial smirk, at least as much as the contorted face would allow.

"...think it's time I did something about it now that I've worked up enough stamina to do the job correctly..." the left side concluded, reaching over with both arm and tentacle towards its mutilated twin.

Not unlike spotlighted deer, William and Kara sat motionless, suddenly finding the simple task of blinking virtually impossible.

Appendages from each side, both human and inexplicably alien, fondled and embraced the other gently, almost lovingly, then began tugging and jerking until the bodies intertwined at the edge of each gurney.

The facial expressions were identical masks of unbridled agony as the bodies melded together like soggy oatmeal amiss a chorus of moist sucking sounds.

The grossly bloated body seemed to swell as if to burst as it's joining neared completion, eventually collapsing like an overcooked pastry just as each side of the face began to merge.

Instinctively and unaware of doing so, William placed a protective arm around his sister.

The two halves of the torn face pointed upward after the initial contact, magically sewn into one from the back of the skull forward, as if an invisible zipper was being tugged forward.

After a violent series of ticks and twinges, most of which originated from the upper body, forehead, eyes and lips, the Warden/Thing was again whole, smiling at the twins like he had just successfully executed a rather unique parlor trick.

"Ah, *much* better. I do concede, however, that more than a few internal organs seem to be missing or misplaced from their assigned locations."

As if to snap them from this latest state of shock, a string of intense tremors commenced, causing William and Kara to leap back in tandem. A well- stocked weight rack tumbled over to their left, sending various sized dumbbells rolling across the stone floor. William was forced to sidestep away from his twin just to avoid being nailed at the ankles by a set of forty-five-pound metal plates, his glasses sailing from his nose and into his tightly clutched left fist.

"Jesus Crow, what now?" He yelped, managing to finally regain a semblance of balance while repositioning his eyewear.

"Like I said, pal, he's sniffing you and Kara out like a bloodhound on a Coon's trail. You're a threat to the big boy, and believe you me, the Gor-ster don't take too well to threats, especially not at this early stage of the game."

Kara bounded forward like a charging bull, coming to a complete stop only when her frail chest made surprisingly solid contact with the Warden/Thing's, whose shocked expression might have been considered hilarious given other circumstances. A second quake, noticeably less severe, quickly passed.

"*Why* is it coming for us?" She screamed, the tip of her sharply pointed nose just inches from his pulpy, skinless version of the same. The Warden/Thing's grin was warped and hideous, like a reptile void of fangs.

"Answer me, *ASSHOLE*!"

Wilbo started forward, jumping the weight bench like an Olympic hurdler, just as his sister punched forward with both palms against the Warden/Thing's chest.

As if slung back by a cannon blast, the Warden/Thing sailed airborne, his head and back ricocheting off the tip a four-cornered Universal machine before landing in a heap atop a wide workout mat a full two-dozen feet from where the shove had impacted.

Wilbo stepped up next to his sister, although a bit cautiously, and stared into her fire-pit red eyes as if studying a total stranger.

"Did y-you do...that...or did he do it to himself?"

The question, along with a third, again less forceful, tremor seemed to awaken her much in the same manner as tossed ice water splashed against the face.

"I... I think I... did… I... think."

The Warden/Thing rolled to its feet, a moist, red outline of its torso and skull left as evidence of the less than gentle landing it had endured against the vinyl mat. He peered down at his stripped, blood-raw form as if to ensure all necessary parts were still intact, then calmly folded both his arms and tentacles across his chest and abdomen.

"Of course *she* did it, William. Think of any logical reason for me to throw myself across the room? Contrary to what you've witnessed on this night, I am not a big fan of physical pain. Your sister, like yourself, is harnessing newly created gifts from your…from the Messiah. Of course, it was more than likely preordained that each of you be awarded such majestic power on this night. No doubt you'll need every ounce of it by the time the new sun rises. That is, *if* it manages to rise at all."

A fresh quake, substantially more powerful, shook the room like dice within a gambler's palm. Remarkably, neither twin budged from where they so stoically stood, while the Warden/Thing was flung against a nearby squat-rack like a beach ball caught in a funnel cloud. Pulling himself up with an exhausted grunt, the left side of his head more gruesomely deformed than ever, he peered at the twins with nothing less than fatherly pride.

"See? You're both adjusting very quickly. It's unfortunate you don't have more time to...break in your new talents, however."

This time Wilbo lunged forward, wrapping his right hand tightly against the soggy warmth of the thing's vein-encased neck. Hoisting the creature, which dwarfed him by at least two hundred pounds in weight and two feet in height, airborne with frightening ease, Wilbo reared back his left hand as if preparing to throw a roundhouse punch.

"Speak now, Warden, or forever *lay* in pieces," he barked through a tightly wound snarl, just as the pointed spikes shot from his clinched fist like a trio of sharpened metal pistons.

Wilbo's eyes darted from his newly hatched claws, to his utterly shocked twin, then back to the hulking form swinging freely from his iron grip. He cocked his head to the side inquisitively and then winked playfully before pulling his thick-framed glasses free and pocketing them with the sudden realization that they were no longer needed.

"Wanna explain this little added feature, Skinhead?"

His already savaged vocal cords completely choked off, the Warden/Thing began swinging his arms and tentacles about as if instituting an impromptu game of charades.

As if to prevent any possible explanation, a shudder ensued strong enough to overturn the remaining Universal machines and flip a two-ton metal weight rack over onto its side like a discarded matchbox.

Just as rapidly, the room grew eerily quiet and motionless, the only additional noise that of the Warden/Thing's slumped form slapping against the mat as his neck was released.

"Okay…damn, I had no idea rabid irritability was a side effect of gaining superpowers. Give me a second to re-adjust my voice box, will you? Or at least what's left of it."

As Kara studied her own pale, thin arms as if just becoming aware of their existence, Wilbo did the same to the alloy spears protruding painlessly from his clinched fist.

"My…god. Are you feeling *this,* William?" She asked, her body shuddering as if in the throes of orgasm.

"Like intravenous Jack Black through my veins, sis."

Her brother looked to her briefly without a reply before returning his concentration to his newly hatched claws. The double take he executed a second later could have easily been labeled as planned or at the very least, choreographed.

"Holy Moses, Kara. Your hair…y-our arm," he managed to prattle just as another tremor struck, tearing a crack in the stone ceiling large enough to place a man's hand inside.

Blazing red and at least twice as thick as mere moments earlier, Kara's hair seemed to flow as if floating in clear crystal waters.

Her previously shattered arm held not a single blemish, much less the horrible swelling of just moments earlier.

"Just...like S-Storm...no, the Scarlet Witch. Sis, you even seem...taller," Wilbo finished as the shock waves subsided.

Even as he spoke, the brown pupils and black iris of his twin's eyes vanished, leaving glowing white orbs in their wake.

"My sister the X-Man. Now…*that's* definitely Storm," he said, grinning in child-like amazement.

"Look who's talking,' she replied with a broad smile of her own, 'check out your physique lately? Not to mention that suspicious growth on your right arm?"

The perfectly round shield was attached by small bands at his forearm and palm, it's glossy red, white and blue exterior displaying a lustrous shine that was meticulously flawless.

"Captain America's s-shield? Where did…how?" Wilbo murmured.

"What should we call you then, Captain Wolverine? It's your fantasy being played out, man. Comic book heroes come to life, all in a valiant attempt to...what else? Why, to save the world, of course," The Warden/Thing spewed forth in a haggard tone one might associate with a long-suffering throat cancer patient.

Not surprisingly, neither twin seemed willing or possibly even capable of listening, each focusing solely on the melodramatic physical alterations taking hold seemingly by the millisecond.

Wilbo's once visually toned but thin-framed physique now resembled that of a competitive body builder, cut muscle lining his appendages, chest and abdominal area as it carved from granite.

Even his neck, a childhood target of ridicule as such nicknames as 'giraffe-boy' and 'pencil-stalk' had been the rule until senior high school, was bulky to the point of deformed, although movement of the same seemed naturally fluid and not the least bit awkward.

Kara's exposed arms were finely toned, like those of a lifelong aerobics instructor, her legs lengthier and as defined as any Broadway dancer.

"I take it you two are *partial* to fantasy periodicals?" The Warden asked sardonically, his tentacles stretched to the breaking point as he hung to separate metal girders while awaiting the next quake.

Wilbo turned to him, displaying gritted teeth that had grown in both length and width. He now possessed dark, bushy sideburns and a thicker coif of hair that stood up at each corner of his forehead in twin cowlicks.

"What of it, carrot-boy?"

The ground shook ever harder, bits of broken tile raining down in an ivory shower. It was obvious to all three that whatever the source of the intermediate quakes, it wasn't long before formal introductions would be in order.

His tentacles relaxing their grip somewhat, the Warden/Thing held up his semi-normal hand's palms up in a gesture of peace.

"Whoa, William my boy. Whatever floats your boat, I say. Allowances from the man upstairs, no doubt, providing you the means to utilize such fictional powers in the upcoming rumble. Here's hoping these so-called heroes were top of the line bad asses. Not sure how much help yours truly can provide, other than in an advisory mode, that is. You saw how effortlessly I was dispatched of out on the yard. I can tell you this for absolute dead-certain, uh, sorry for the choice of words..."

Kara seemed to glide towards him without benefit of actually taking a step. "Spit it out, Octo-Man, before I give in to temptation and use your bothersome carcass for some hands-on training."

For an instant, barely a hiccup in time, the Warden/Thing's face twisted with rage, his entire body seeming to pulse, tensing as if to leap forward in full attack mode. Upon blinking almost in tandem, the twins discovered no such expression, just the same bland, openly sour disposition that had quickly grown so tiresome within the past half-hour.

"The powers you harness are from your own minds, so the potential there is only limited by your own short-sighted lack of imagination. In other words, kids, use 'em or lose 'em, permanently in this case."

"How do we...kill this *demon,* this *Ancient One*, as you called it? That thing we saw out there ain't going down under a flurry of punches or bolts of electricity, no matter how accurately placed, am I right?" Wilbo asked while glaring at his hugely muscled right biceps as if it were unquestionably someone else's.

"Wooden stakes? Silver bullets maybe?" Kara chimed in, almost whispering.

"Not quite. Terminating an ancient one is tricky at best, damned impossible at worst. This particular specimen has several centuries' worth of grudges to bear, and one massive hard-on swinging about to back up his anger. Gor, as with all of his type, does possess a nerve center, a *heart* if you will.

Make no mistake, it's an organ hidden away in the deepest pit of his rotted being, the canal leading to it filled with graphic images of excruciating agony not meant for viewing by mortal eyes. His outer hide can only be penetrated by the spiritually cleansed, while the inner walls contain toxic poisons that melt away human flesh like soggy pudding upon touch to all but the one preordained to do so. Only they may reach the decayed organ and rip it free, thereby ending Gor's impending reign upon the surface world."

The Warden's pit-like orbs dropped to the floor as his shoulders slumped like a weakened animal.

"I have no say in which of you is the chosen, nor do I have any idea which of you it may be. The higher power placing the chess pieces hasn't disclosed, and may not choose to until a fatally *incorrect* decision is already past. I'm good, but predicting fate isn't one of my specialties."

Looking back up, the Warden/Thing exchanged worrisome glances at each twin even as his tentacles visibly tensed for another quake.

"Needless to say, you may only get to choose once. Make it the correct one, if at all possible.

Otherwise, planet Earth is gonna be the equivalent of one hell of an oversized Big Mac, and Gor will be playing the part of a starved glutton with an appetite that goes beyond merely insatiable."

Kara, her puffy, dark crimson hair standing away from her scalp as if charged with static electricity, started to reply but was never given the chance.

Her brother had been tearing away what remained of his shirt, revealing a chest sculpted in sinewy muscle and layers of thick black hair, neither of which had resided there previously.

The twins whirled towards the gym's only entrance in perfect unison, just as the room itself seemed to peel apart all around them like a child's dollhouse beneath a wrecking ball.

The Warden/Thing flinched and held steady to the metal grids, the tiniest of smiles forming at the corners of what claimed to be his mouth, but what in reality was nothing more than a raw, pulped gash that looked to have been carved with a pitifully dull knife blade.

"Show time."

CHAPTER NINE
Caged Match

Early in his teen years, Ron McIntosh had been pulled to the side by his father's father to hear two complete sentences containing a total of twenty words. Twenty words that, at such a tender, carefree age, had sounded trite, melodramatic, even downright silly. His Grandpappy, long since dead of colon cancer, had simply stated, in a voice ravaged by time and literally thousands of smoked down to the filter cigarettes: "Ron, someday you'll be tested. You'll recognize it when the time arrives, but only God knows the outcome in advance." Almost two full decades later, sprinting past the overturned tables, chairs, and serving trays that littered the compound's mess hall floor, his horribly bloodied and mutilated hands throbbing like twin root canals, the question was no longer when such a test would arrive. The question was whether or not he was up to passing it. Regardless, a young man known for his short temper and lewd, crude ways had come to know religion in less time than a death row inmate being prepped for lethal injection.

Within the past two minutes, specifically since the walls and ceiling of the admin building had began to crumple like a tin beer can in a power lifter's palm behind them, the Corporal's psyche had been amazingly energized, as had his battle-weary legs.

Where exactly they were headed, or more importantly, what good such a haphazardly executed flight would accomplish, was draped entirely in mystery, though the source of the commotion was chillingly obvious. As concrete walls imploded and metal struts bent like heated licorice less than ten yards to their rear, none bothered to dwell on such trivialities. The only thing that mattered at such a moment was the ability to pick them up and put them down, post haste.

"Where…to...the y-yard again?" Jimmy screamed over the ruckus, his hands covering his scalp as if warding off attacking bats.

A metal chair shot over Private Kemp's head, a leg of which grazed her left shoulder, then narrowly missed sailing into the back of Corporal McIntosh's right knee.

"N-no! N-not into...a wide-open…s-space. Keep going! We'll…clear the breeze…way and go from there..." she replied between gasps, then quickly following the Corporal through a wide hall that led past the kitchen and into an extremely cramped supply room. The emergency lighting provided was sporadic at best, but adequate for their meager needs.

Just as she sailed past a neck-high rack filled with bulky flour, sugar, and powdered egg bags, Private Kemp felt the tiled floor swell and crack beneath her boots. She dived forward headfirst, barely catching a glimpse of Corporal McIntosh's flexing buttocks as he exited into the breezeway just a few feet ahead.

She slid into the mess hall's metal exit door just as it was halfway towards closing, her lower back absorbing the brunt of the impact.

Scrambling like a fish trapped atop a sand dune, Private Kemp got to one knee just as Jimmy swan-dived over an overturned bread-rack and directly into a milk gurney that had rolled into the pathway. The floor had buckled and split apart like a parched desert landscape just beyond the narrow entrance, making it resemble a concrete anthill and jostling loose even the bolted-down objects inside the room like tossed confetti.

Jimmy first smashed into the bottle-heavy gurney and then held onto it like a lifejacket in rushing floodwaters. Several dozen glass bottles burst like detonated grenades upon impact with the floor and adjoining metal racks, instantly painting the majority of the room in various shaped spatters of moist ivory.

Peering up at Private Kemp through eyelashes coated in milk, Jimmy slipped and fell twice before his bare feet found a plastic wrapped loaf of bread to brace upon, all the while being pulled along by the right forearm.

"G-Got milk?" He managed to quip hysterically, despite the tiny shards of glass digging deeper into his feet with each clumsy step.

Giggling despite herself, Private Kemp practically threw him through the exit door, then leapt inside the breezeway without looking back.

"You're a tried and true idiot, Jimmy R, a rare bird indeed."

The breezeway glass was cracked but not quite shattered as they shambled through, eyeing the gymnasium entrance that Corporal McIntosh held open so generously.

Just as Private Kemp galloped inside a moment later, the mess hall exit door creased.

As the gym entrance slammed shut, the mess

hall building as a whole ceased to exist.

***

"Doesn't company always happen to drop in at the most inopportune time?" The Warden/Thing croaked while carefully studying the three individuals as they jogged frantically forward.

The twins reeled back in similar battle stances, dropping their guard a bit once they got a closer look at the infiltrators.

Private Kemp's slow jaunt forward halted abruptly once her sights fell upon the Warden/Thing, his tentacles hooked around the grids giving the initial impression of a man tied up against his will.

"What the…w-who...what are you supposed to be?" She managed, swinging her left arm up to block Jimmy's charging momentum. Wiping smears of warm milk from his eyes and face, Jimmy kneeled down and began to huff and groan like an ancient freight train climbing a steep grade.

"Who...what's going on *now*?" He spat between long inhales and even lengthier exhales.

A few feet to his rear, Corporal McIntosh stood with his arms across his chest, his own gaze frozen on Kara's sinuous red hair, which seem to pulsate with a life all its own.

"Why, we're castoffs from an H.R. Puff 'n Stuff revival, can't ya tell?" The Warden/Thing replied sourly.

Wilbo stepped forward, the luminous shield still held at his chest in a guarded position.

"It's behind you, ain't it?"

Still focusing exclusively on Kara, the Corporal answered as if entranced. "Obviously."

Private Kemp, her palms resting on her kneecaps as she panted heavily, managed a sarcastic guffaw while continuing to keep both eyes peeled on the Warden/Thing.

"Damn *right* it is, pal, and it ain't in the best of moods at the moment. Any ideas before we're all mashed flatter than I-HOP pancakes?"

The Warden/Things tentacles suddenly retracted, wrapping themselves around his midsection until he looked as if he were sporting a partially deflated inner tube.

"Haven't you noticed? The shakes have ceased for the moment. Besides, where exactly would you go?"

They all looked around silently, eyes pointed towards the walls and ceilings, then seemed to blow out a collective sigh of cautious relief.

"It has to be right outside the damn door. Why would it pause now?" Wilbo asked angrily, the arm possessing the claws pumped to enormous proportions.

"Why, I do believe ol' Gor might just be feeling a few butterflies about what he's about to face. It's power meter isn't even a quarter pegged yet, and won't be until it's absorbed at least half a dozen states or maybe even the majority of the East Coast. Gor's hesitance is natural for a being that's suffered through eons of entrapment and isn't exactly in a rush to return to such a state."

Kara motioned towards Private Kemp, who was still wheezing a bit as she rose into a straight pose.

"You three get behind us and stay there."

Wilbo interrupted, although Kara seemed to welcome the intrusion.

"No matter what happens, do not make a break for greener pastures, mainly cause their ain't any, but also because..."

"…if you do, we won't be able to protect you," Kara concluded, flashing her brother an apologetic smile.

He simply nodded in mild bewilderment and inhaled deeply, like a cliff diver preparing to leap.

Private Sandra Kemp, Jimmy Rollins, and Corporal Ron McIntosh adhered to the command, both out of sheer exhaustion and a lack of motivation to question the order. All three stepped gingerly past droves of scattered free weights and capsized Universal and Nautilus machines until they stood in shaky formation behind the twins.

"I take you two are tasked to save the day, as it were?" Jimmy queried timidly, still wiping milk film from his bare arms and chest.

The Warden/Thing replied before either twin even tried.

The silence within the walls was deafening, a stark contrast to the frenzied hour that had proceeded it.

"As it were. Three Stooges, meet the Super Twins. Hey, wasn't that an old black and white flick?" He growled sarcastically, his flesh-free dome showing just a flash of bone at the tip of his bare skull.

"Clamp your pie-hole, squid-boy, that is unless you have additional wisdom to pass on about how we're supposed to come out of this with our collective rear ends intact?" Kara snapped, waiving her arms out in front of her in a tight circle as if waxing a car.

The Warden/Thing faced the gym entrance, the ruin that represented his face uncharacteristically without expression.

"If I get any flashes, you'll be the first to know, my dear heroine."

A tentacle rose into the air and suspended midway, pointing in the twin's general direction. The Warden/Thing's tone was flat and weary, but somehow chillingly foreboding at the same time.

"It will show you things. Things you won't want to accept. Things pulled from your subconscious that are better left buried. Pay no heed, or you'll leave yourself open. Leave yourself open, the cause is instantly lost, as will be your eternal souls. It is a creature whose physical appearance is inherently intimidating, but whose power is overwhelmingly mental. Keep your mind as honed as your bodies, or suffer the consequences."

Again, utter silence wallowed within the dead air like slowly drifting waves of fog.

"Damn. I think I liked you better as a smart-ass," Private Kemp quipped, pitifully unable to halt the shaking of her hands before finally sticking them in her pants pockets.

Five sets of lungs sucked in a fresh supply of oxygen almost in perfect harmony, just as all five sets forced out the same in a unified scream a moment later, just as the gym's entrance wall disintegrated in an explosion of wood, metal and stone.

Originally intending to crash through the

compound's gates and towards the nearest populated area, the being had again felt the presence of a species far superior to those he had previously ingested. Pangs of fear both shocked and angered it to the degree that nothing less than an immediate confrontation would suffice before the planet-wide sweep could ensue.

It easily detected the feeble creatures within the first structure and gave chase, although it was obvious from inception that these were not the ones posing the mysterious yet undeniable threat. Figuring they could possibly lead to the empowered ones, the being trailed them through the covered hiding places that such paltry creatures dwelled within, effortlessly flattening each structure with every descending step.

Towering over the smallest of such abodes, the last of which that remained erect other than that which it had so fitfully fed from minutes earlier, the being first hesitated before growing utterly immobile. A wave of sheer electric current, one it had never previously experienced, lit up each fiber and living cell within its physical core. Not since the banishment sequence all those infinite centuries ago had it witnessed such an overwhelming aura of unrestrained power. The Dark Messiah and his hierarchy had utilized the element of surprise quite effectively, instigating an attack plan that instantaneously weakened and disabled all previously set defense systems. The being had expected such retribution, but not a punishment so shamelessly cruel and indifferent, especially to one created of their own ilk. The Dark Messiah had clearly seen him as a viable threat to the kingdom, and meant the banishment to be of permanent status. Little had even the King known what riches of decay and incomprehensible potential for evil lay at the core of such a barren, desolate planet, one which would feed and cultivate the being's eventual escape.

One the being would surely relish snatching from his former King's grasp, savoring each step in the annihilation process, until the time when a showdown for the Kingdom of Darkness itself would ensue.

It hesitated a moment longer, its massive bulk pressed gently against the structures cool stone entranceway, then flung its head back and released a warrior's roar that, even for fifty miles in the distance, sounded every bit like twin 747's impacting in the pitch-dark skies. It was finally ready to commence upon the task that it was created to perform, that being to annihilate with extreme prejudice.

***

Large chunks of shattered stone and fragmented wood bounced, rolled and sailed towards them as if hauled forward by the base of a twister.

Just as an iron rod the length of an Olympic javelin was milliseconds from ending his twin's life, Wilbo's outstretched arm flew forward in a streaky blur.

The bar clanged off the shield and ricocheted harmlessly over the group, all of whom lay curled behind the twins in varied ducking poses as the glut of the debris grew closer.

Legions of splintered wood and shattered stone descended upon them almost immediately, almost as if dropped from a low flying aircraft.

Instinctively, Wilbo quickly positioned the shield over his sister's head like a makeshift umbrella, although the expected barrage never transpired.

Private Kemp had caught a brief glimpse of the carnage headed their way, just before ducking her head beneath her folded arms.

As she cautiously peered up from between the narrow break provided by her crossed forearms, it was as if someone had pressed a universal pause button.

Kara stood with her arms spread wide and her palms up, her eyes glowing with snow-white radiance. Wilbo backed away a step with his mouth agape, taking in his sister's accomplishment with shocked amazement.

Jimmy rolled onto his back but refused to totally accept the message his eyes were transmitting.

Corporal McIntosh scrambled to one knee, scanned the space above their heads and smiled broadly, shaking his head in dumfounded disbelief.

No less than four feet above them and on all sides, countless tons of debris floated in the air like balloons on a string. The sheer volume of what had been wall, ceiling and floor encircled them like a hastily built mud cabin strung together by invisible binding.

"Did *you*...do that, sis?" Wilbo asked, looking straight up at a jagged, boulder-sized rock hanging directly overhead.

The beams of white light shooting from her eyes subsiding to a tiny glimmer, Kara spoke in a voice only partially her own. It was deep, husky, and laced with a newly discovered confidence that both thrilled and slightly frightened her twin.

"Yes, William, just as you blocked that iron spear like it was no more than a brittle twig."

Without warning, she swung her hands inward in a fierce clapping motion. All but Jimmy, who had again ducked his face away, witnessed the debris scatter and crash into the far corners of the room, leaving only a thick cloud of dark brown dust in its wake. Wiping her hands together calmly, Kara turned to check the others, unaware that she had accomplished this without benefit of taking a single step, or that she floated a full six inches off the ground while doing so.

"Everybody intact?" She asked, her voice less husky but still eerily alien. Private Kemp was helping Jimmy to his feet, her arms wrapped around his rotund waistline. The dust drifted among them like concert fog, making it impossible to see past a distance of more than two feet.

"Y-yeah, s-still here. What was that, some kind of. Force-field or something?" Private Kemp asked, turning her attention to the Corporal, who leaned next to her a moment later.

"Uh, something like that. I guess. We've got company, folks. Stay close to William or me at all times, understand?"

Madly waving through the smoke cloud engulfing his face, Jimmy grunted cynically.

"Pretty lady, color me super-glued to your backside."

"Where's Octo-Warden?" Wilbo asked, attempting to peer through the soupy fog in the direction where the Warden/Thing had last been standing.

The voice bellowed through the mist, causing Jimmy to cringe back as if pinched.

"Right over here, Superman. Other than a severed tentacle and one major-league migraine, I'm hunky-dory. Carry on; I'm right behind you taking notes. I think you just might have *other* pressing issues at hand."

Wilbo fronted his sister, still unable to pick up anything beyond the fog surrounding them. A cool draft of air scooped a large section of the cloud away just as he turned to face his sister. Miraculously, just enough emergency lighting remained operable within the rear of the room to assist in the gradual clearing.

"It's in here, Sis. Dead ahead and big as a Navy Destroyer."

Her eyes lit up once again, cutting twin beams into the fading haze. "We can take it, William. We…have no choice."

Nodding amiably, Wilbo flexed his recently hatched muscles and sighed. "Well, *Witch-Storm*, let's do the deed, then."

She grinned through perfectly white, exquisitely even teeth, the braces completely dissolved.

"After you, *Captain X-Man.*"

Huddling together as if bound to one another, Private Kemp, Jimmy and the Corporal exchanged weary, worrisome glances as they followed helplessly behind.

"Are we damned sure these are the good guys, Sandy? I mean, did you see chick's *eyes*? The dude she keeps calling her brother looks like a muscle-bound badger," the Corporal whispered, leaning down until his parched lips were just inches from the Privates left ear.

The Private leaned over to reply just as she felt the tentacle gently wrap itself around her waist and squeeze. The Warden/Thing hugged the trio snugly with its one remaining Octo-appendage, keeping a two-step distance to their rear. The chalky dust that clung to its sticky-moist face gave it the look of a long dead, mostly decomposed corpse come to life. They trudged forward as one in a grotesque imitation of the 'Yellow Brick Road' scene from The Wizard of Oz.

"Worry-warts. Of course they're the good guys. Would *I* hang with them otherwise?" The Warden/Thing cackled. Private Kemp shuddered, barely suppressing a piercing scream.

After only a few dozen steps, Kara froze in mid-stride. Wilbo instantly tensed and parked the shield over his sister's upper body.

Collectively, they held their breath, a virtual symphony of startled gasps. The open-air space that had been the Gym's ceiling revealed a star-filled sky that held the occasional drift of white vapor.

As if to replace what it had so effortlessly demolished, the creature sat motionless less than a dozen yards in the distance, it's immense bulkiness filling the landscape like a mountain come to life.

Wilbo reared his head back without turning, whispering as if not to wake a slumbering giant.

"Damn it…we're supposed to fight *that* with

nothing more than a few magic tricks, a metal shield, and a fistful of claws? Please tell me you've got a howitzer loaded with a nuke warhead tucked away somewhere, smart guy…"

The Warden/Thing stuck his disfigured skull between the shoulders of Private Kemp and Jimmy Rollins, causing each to flinch back. "Settle down, Bubba. It not only detects fear, but feeds off it. The majority of this battle will be *mental,* my boy, not physical. Better suck it up or it'll suck you up, in the literal sense."

Kara took a tentative step forward, her arms crossed at her chest in an upside-down V shape.

"Let's go, William. There's no running from this, no matter how tempting the notion. It's no accident we were brought to Red Bridge. You know it…I know it…God surely knows it."

Jogging stiffly forward while using muscles he hadn't previously possessed, Wilbo overtook his sister, fronting her like a presidential bodyguard on a crowded inter-city street.

"I gotta admit, sis, I've never felt stronger or as hyped for anything before. You're right as rain. If it ain't now, it's undeniably *never.*"

Behind them, the Warden/Thing again leaned forward, this time balancing his gore-covered chin atop the Corporal's thickly muscled shoulder.

"Don'cha just love a showdown? Now, If I were a betting man…"

"I take it back. You *were* easier to take as a doomsayer. Now, do us a colossal favor and clam the fuck up, okay?" Private Kemp interrupted without a trace of humor.

Despite her bravado, she felt a fearful tingling

rocket up her lower spine, as they grew steadily closer to the abomination that lay ahead. She felt like a hapless pawn within her own never-ending nightmare, unable to either wake up or even minutely alter the eventual outcome. A rush of sentimentality that she never knew existed within herself suddenly shot forward in a cascading rush, and Private Sandra Layne Kemp came to the realization that she had never missed her mother more than at that very moment.

"Mama misses you *too,* sweetie-pie," the Warden/Thing cackled. On the verge of fainting, Private Kemp didn't dare reply.

***

The being's neck and head began to swivel gradually from side to side, a low humming noise reverberating from seemingly every fiber of its scaly torso. A torso which subsequently began to bulge and pulsate, the hundreds of human- sized appendages vibrating frantically until their frenzied movements were twitching, hazy blurs.

"What's going down, Warden? What's it up to?" Wilbo asked, although in more of a curious than fearful tone.

The Warden/Thing cleared its ravaged throat and coughed, sounding like a fast-fading victim of double pneumonia.

"Can't read its mind, Bubba. Scanning those brain waves are beyond my capacity, *unlike* reading your species. Whatever it's planning, you can bet the farm it has nothing to do with a peace treaty."

"Forget him, William. He's no help at this

stage. Concentrate solely on the demon," Kara said, her pace slowing just as her pupils grew a brighter shade of pure ivory.

"Check, sis."

Private Kemp scanned the portions of the mostly leveled building for a possible escape route, despite the pitifully low odds of such an event ever occurring. She suddenly wondered why they had so sheepishly accepted the notion of being sitting ducks amid such a cataclysmic scenario, despite the lack of logical alternatives.

As the creature's humming grew louder, each member of the group felt the vibration within their chest cavities. Private Kemp leaned towards the Corporal while keeping her head pointing straight ahead.

"If it suddenly goes to shit, Mac, haul your carcass to the back of the room. There's gotta be an exit back there. If we can find a way into the woods behind the compound, we can st-..."

"Ain't gonna happen, San. Like the incredible melting man behind us said, it's all decided right here and now," Corporal McIntosh replied sternly, looking down at her with eyes mirrored in resignation.

Jimmy chimed in from her left just before the humming noises ceased as if a fuse had blown.

"Afraid so, Private Sandy. Hate to s-say it, but we've got to have faith in these two, uh, specially endowed folks."

As the noise cut off and all eyes were again focused front and center, the spastically wiggling limbs began instantly popping free from the being's outer layer like kernels of freshly heated popcorn, chunks of alien flesh accompanying each upon landing like milky afterbirth.

Kara halted progress with her legs spread wide and her arms raised high above her head with fingers splayed.

Her brother backed to her side, his clawed hand reared back while the shielded arm served as a blockade for his twin's front side.

It wasn't until a dozen or more of the forms bounced away from the group as if pulled back by invisible bunji cords that their implausible identifies became horrifically apparent.

The Force-field that Kara had conjured was similar to the one which had deflected the debris, though inexplicably a bit more pliable, allowing the assailants to sink within its borders before being violently flung back.

As the alien offspring began to cautiously congregate and subsequently encircle the perimeters of the transparent field like campers around a blazing campfire, the thick film of ivory mucus gradually fell from their heads and bodies in moist, chunky layers.

They stared into the circle of inhabitants like anxious shoppers through the glass walls of a store display, their mouths slack and drooling, their eyes blank and distant. The circle grew tighter as the bodies multiplied, until the few trapped within its oval contents were shrouded in shadow. The mammoth birth seemed to have tired the being, its enormous bulk utterly motionless in the background. Even its constantly shifting neck and head had frozen in mid-swing once the birthing had been complete.

Wilbo saw the strain in his sister's face; her eyes illuminating like lit Roman Candles as the corners of her mouth began to twitch. "How long can you keep 'em off, sis?"

When she didn't respond immediately, Wilbo turned away to avoid further distracting her. His arms were steel bands; his legs like wound copper cords awaiting sweet release. Obvious danger aside, he could hardly contain the side of him that ached to try out his newly found, rage-infused powers on the nearest available target.

"N-not real s-sure, William. I…don't think they're going a-away anytime soon, however. My arms feel like lead pipes."

Her voice had weakened significantly since blocking the debris. Wilbo was about to suggest she release the field to allow him to wade into the fray when Private Kemp's shrieking announcement aborted such thoughts of reckless valor.

"…Peterson…that's the Major..." she yelled, pointing to her left with a single shaky digit.

Corporal McIntosh echoed the findings in a barely audible whisper, one laced with comical skepticism.

"Sure as my mom was a devout Southern Baptist. But I watched that crazy bastard get cut off at the knees…literally."

The man was being shoved forward into the elastic field, the imprint of his face a bit warped, as if he were wearing a nylon stocking over his head. He was no longer sporting the camouflaged fatigues of earlier, but a green-colored dress uniform, complete with a plastic nametag over his left shirt pocket and a three- tiered stack of ribbons over the right.

The black beret pulled so snugly across his forehead displayed a circular metal insignia that read 'U.S. Army' in metallic groove.

Unlike the melting monstrosity that had been so easily dispatched on the compound exercise grounds earlier that evening, this version of David Peterson looked unnaturally healthy, significantly younger somehow.

When the Major's lips parted and his voice rang out, it was with the same gravelly, cocky tone infamous to all militia members who had served within his command.

"Kemp and McIntosh, sitting in a tree…*K I S S I N G*…first came love, then came marriage, and here comes Major Peterson with a baby carriage. Tell me, Sandy, is the kid gonna be born *with* or *without* fingers?"

The Major's arms were pinned by the bodies swarming around him, two of which became instantly recognizable to Jimmy once his boggling eyes focused on their strained but gruesomely smiling mugs.

"Hiya, Pork Chop. How's it hanging?" Buck Lomax the Third asked with a wink, his voice slightly muted as if speaking through a glass cage.

"Darned if he don't look surprised to see us, Buck," J.C. Carlyle added, the palms of his hands held high and flat against the invisible barricade. He looked a bit like a referee signaling a touchdown.

"What's the matter, tub-a-guts, ya never seen nobody reborn before?" Buck concluded, straining to free his own wriggling limbs from the forces holding them captives on both sides.

"Look at…look at their legs," Jimmy managed, nodding in Buck's general direction.

From the waist down, all the bodies displayed an identical deformity. The legs were spindly and scaled and were held aloft by flat, arch-less feet containing a trio of webbed toes.

They stood like half-drawn cartoon caricatures from a Chuck Jones feature, half human and half amphibian.

"Don't listen to 'em, folks. Whoever you think they are, they're *not*," the Warden/Thing said between hacking coughs.

A wad of greenish phlegm landed on Private Kemp's right shoulder, then dribbled to the ground like water from a duck's back. The Warden/Thing grinned at her apologetically before continuing.

"Once dissolved, Gor can utilize absorbed memories to create a cloned being that walks and talks just like the real thing. It's simply going for the subtraction by distraction method. Kinda sad, actually, but it just tells ya how little respect a high echelon demon has for your kind."

Private Kemp elbowed Jimmy in the ribs, breaking the almost hypnotic hold the man's old advisories had created.

"You heard him, Jimbo. Don't look or listen to it." The Warden/Thing giggled mischievously.

"It's not you three I'm worried about. It's the Mutant twins that better keep their ducks in a row, so to speak."

Her face wearing a mask of fresh sweat that ran in thick beads down her forehead and onto her neck, Kara spoke to her brother in a pained whisper.

"Did you see...?"

Wilbo stared at the rubble-strewn ground, the shield now held over his own face as if to avert bright sunlight.

"I... saw…s-see them, Kara. Three-o'clock."

"I... *thought* it was, although I only had a brief glance. Don't...stare at them. It's weird, but I can feel myself getting physically weaker when I do."

"N-no problem. But...can we make them g-go away, somehow?" He asked sadly, still staring almost straight down.

"Ignore them, dammit! You're doing exactly what it wants by acknowledging its creations," the Warden/Thing barked angrily before another coughing spell arose.

Unable to resist, Wilbo kept his head down but peered over to his left. Their white-haired father sported a red Dockers sports shirt, his bushy gray eyebrows setting off the blue in his ancient eyes.

Beside him, her frail, chalky arms wrapped around his shoulders in a lover's embrace, their mother's displayed perfectly square dentures in a broad, wide smile that looked a tad predatory in nature.

"Let us in, Kara. Mama and Papa just want to give you both a great, big hug," the thing posing as their mother gently cooed, her thinning, brownish dyed hair glistening unnaturally underneath the dim light bathing her face.

Lifting his head, Wilbo turned to the imposter and growled, baring his own teeth in animalistic rage.

"Yeah, I'll just bet you do. No dice, demon. If it comes down to it, I'll gut you both without a second's hesitation and send you back to the fiery pit you crawled from."

Turning back to his sister, a small tear ran down his rugged, unshaven jaw.

"They're really… gone, Kara. He couldn't display them otherwise, right?"

"At l-least now the mystery is over. He must have had someone on the surface lure them into a trap or…murder them as a sacrifice of some kind," she replied wearily, the fingers on both her hands slowly curling.

Buck the Third waived his arms about like a marooned man attempting to flag down a passing plane.

"You mean the geezer's over there? Why, me and my true-blue pal and confidant J.C. performed the happy deed. Faked car trouble and waited for the first kind soul to stop and render us aid. Your pappy there put up quite the scrap, if I 'member correctly. Mom wasn't much trouble after the machete blade split her skull, though. The master wasn't as picky in those days…a semi-warm body was sufficient, regardless of how old or worn it might have been."

J.C. grinned happily at Buck the Third in an expression of sincere admiration.

"Sure as hell wasn't the first nor last, huh Buck old buddy?" Buck stared directly at Kara and winked playfully.

"Naw, there were many, but none quite as memorable, J.C. old hooter. Tyin' the old man to that elm tree was a real chore, but once we broke out the straight razors and commenced to skinnin'…"

"*Fuck* off, pal. You ain't nothing but a figment

of your own imagination," Wilbo interrupted, waiving them both off with his clawed hand while stepping directly in front of his sister.

"It's not so bad, son, really. In...*there*, I mean. At least we'll be together again," the thing imitating their father pleaded; his skeletal, scaly legs far too thin for the overly swollen torso they supported.

Ignoring the repulsive being he no longer viewed as anything but, Wilbo continued to stare down his twin.

"Drop the screen, Kara. This can't end in a standoff. Do your best to protect the others. I can handle this crowd."

After a quiet pause, Kara dropped her hands and instantly stepped back as the field collapsed. For just an instant, she whirled to face Private Kemp head on, almost tripping into the exhausted, badly leaning frame of Corporal McIntosh.

"Get behind me and don't move if you want to live."

The Warden/Thing cringed back at the brief glance she fired towards him, her eyes like twin spotlights centered into his own.

"You better at least *attempt* to aid in this little skirmish, or I swear I'll scatter your worthless hide from here to the same pit *that* thing sprang from."

She turned back with her slim, muscled arms curled behind her as if she were handcuffed, then shot them forward in a double-jab motion just as the wriggling forms fell upon them like swarming flies onto a dung pile.

Just as the bodies fell forward, temporarily off-balance due to the restraint being so abruptly lifted, Wilbo leapt to the left and pummeled the thing which had called itself his mother, crunching its skull with the flat of the shield. Stepping back with jungle-cat quickness, he easily ducked the attempt his father-imitator made at placing him in a makeshift bear hug, then lunged forward with his newly formed claws slashing wildly.

The first blow caught the imposter just beneath the chin, severing its head with the ease of a straight razor through tissue paper. Greenish liquid spurted from the diced stump as the headless body wondered about aimlessly for a full five seconds before tumbling forward in a lifeless heap.

Several sets of strangely soft, moist hands gripped his shoulders, chest and upper thighs as he watched the severed head melt away into a yellow puddle of bubbling goo atop the stone floor.

Behind them, the being shrieked as if gunshot, its head lolling hard to the left even as its torso remained stationary.

Kara's air punch sent a half-dozen of the previously charging forms airborne as from a grenade detonation, a few of which landing without previously vital portions of their anatomy, left behind from the primal force of the blow.

To her left, the Warden/Thing held a squirming body in each lower tentacle; one a tall, lean young man who looked to have been no older than eighteen, the other an older, heavyset black woman whose eyes bulged like saucers from the pressure being applied to her throat.

A third form, this one a bald, elderly man wearing suspenders and a bloodstained tee shirt, which read 'Old Fart' across his narrow chest, sprinted forward in a bull rush towards the

Warden/Thing's blind side. Just as it bowed to possibly ram his back with its skull, the first tentacle swung around with the speed of an alligator's tail, using the ensnared body of the younger man to ram the attacker. Their heads merged together like two overripe melons, bursting into a single yellow slush oddly void of tendon or bone. The Warden/Thing instantly released the no longer struggling body of the young man, then casually tossed the hefty black female against a far stone wall. Her entire body seemed to come unhinged like a tossed water balloon upon contact, initially sticking to then dribbling down the concrete wall like a descending slug.

"Pitiful, Gor old man. Downright disgraceful. Centuries of pent-up rage, and *that's* all you've got?"

The Warden/Thing leaned back, comfortably propped by using the tentacles as makeshift lean-tos, and studied the non-stop mayhem taking place at the room's center.

Wilbo stood directly to his left, furiously mowing down adversaries by the handful with sweeping blows from both the shield and the bared claws, both of which were soaked in yellowish fluid. The young man's arms and legs were a blur of frenzied motion, although each fatal blow was delivered with the unmistakable precision of a veteran warrior.

To his right, the Warden/Thing found Kara's performance even more impressive, considering she was tasked with the double-duty of both Sentinel and combatant. Her left arm was held aloft and bent at the elbow in the classic driver's 'stop' gesture, while her right executed a series of punches and jabs that seemed to initiate several varied marital arts techniques.

The small bubble field her left hand had created and fought to maintain held Jimmy, Private Kemp and the Corporal within its oval perimeter even as hordes of the being's spawn clawed and scratched relentlessly to get at them.

The series of stylishly performed punches never got closer than a half dozen feet from any of the intended targets, but nonetheless sent each flailing backward with brutal efficiency, periodically two or three at a time.

Admittedly impressed and astounded by both the fighting prowess and grit each twin displayed, the Warden/Thing then looked towards the slowly swaying behemoth in the background and began taunting it mercilessly.

"They're making mincemeat outta your babies, old ancient one! Maybe you should have stayed safely tucked away in your hole, huh, big boy? Did ya also notice they ain't exactly *begging* for my help? You have to admit, pal, when it comes to *our* kind, the Cursed Messiah doesn't spare any expense on firepower."

The being rolled and heaved it's massive torso in apparent rage, a large section of brick wall sheared away like soggy cardboard.

"Maybe you ain't the bad ass you make yourself out to be! You figured the souls of the wicked lodged inside that cellblock would at least guarantee unstoppable momentum in taking this weakened burg, didn't ya? Think again, ugly! The Cursed one from above saw ya coming even before *our* boss did, and left these two as a waiting party for your little coming out shin-dig!"

Lurching forward, the being bent its head as if to charge, then re-arose and bucked out its blimp-sized chest in a gesture the Warden/Thing first passed off as simple defiance.

"Did I touch a nerve, Gor old pal? Touchy, touchy. This from a former upper-crust spawn who supposedly wore the tag of 'next in line as Council Head for the Nether Regions of Gunther?' Such potential for unlimited dark rule in your youth, now relegated to fighting for your very existence against creatures you barely deem worthy to feed upon. Such a shame, really, when such powers are first abused and then misused…"

The Warden/Thing's rambling monologue halted abruptly just as the being's chest split open in a relatively narrow but perfectly lined horizontal smile that quickly widened, revealing a dark chasm large enough to drive a semi-truck into.

"More parlor tricks, man? Isn't this beneath an entity that once proclaimed itself the 'true ruler of the Black Core?"

A greenish rope erupted from the murky gap so rapidly that the Warden/Thing's attempt to dodge its trajectory never had the opportunity to materialize. Like a frog's extended tongue ensnaring a fly in mid-air, the tar-like goop enveloped the Warden/Thing's upper body and carted him airborne. His lower tentacles flapped madly in search of an object to hang onto as he sailed up and over the battle scene towards the object of his taunts.

As he was heaved closer to the chest opening,

the Warden/Thing observed a second appendage emerge from the same wound. Unlike the tubular goo enslaving him, it was solidly defined and coated in a scaly armor, and shaped like a fisherman's hook. As he was being levitated directly towards it, the Warden/Thing watched in wry amusement as the egg sac at the end of the arm opened like a blooming flower soaked in spring sunlight. The flesh parted and peeled back in flaps just as the lobster-like pinchers appeared.

"Go on with your bad self then! This ain't nothing but a rotting shell to me anyway! You're doing me a *favor*, you bloated, overrated maggot...I'll give you the worst case of indigestion you could imagine, buddy-boy! You haven't seen the last of -…"

Working in tandem like dance partners in a meticulously choreographed program, the glue-stick limb held the Warden/Thing prone while the hook-arm looped around and slid the razor-edged pinchers over his bare skull and around what remained of his ruined neck.

"…me, big shot! When you least expect it, I'll be on your ass like white on rice…"

The blades folded over each other in a flash, snipping the Warden/Thing's head from its body with the ease of a pruning shear over a brittle shrub branch.

The glue arm dropped the body instantly and swept downward to catch the severed skull. As soon as its prize was in tow, it retracted back into the wound from which it had come, along with the pincher-arm, like dual fishing lines back onto a set of graphite rods.

The wound itself closed immediately and without evidence that it had ever existed, just as the Warden/Thing's lifeless, headless husk toppled onto the stone below like a truckload of gutted livestock, the tentacles wriggling like electrocuted snakes.

Wilbo had seen the impromptu decapitation take place just as he had flayed open the midsection of a plump young woman who had been attempting to throttle him from behind. He had been in the process of front-kicking another assailant, this one a skinny middle-aged man with thick black framed glasses and rather large ears, when the Warden/Thing had taken flight and narrowly missed kicking him in the side of the head.

As the Warden/Thing's glutted remains smacked the concrete just a few yards to his north, Wilbo had turned towards Kara with a pained sneer.

"Looks like big mouth finally got his, sis. How you doing over there?"

While awaiting her reply, he managed to sidekick one assailant into a pile of smoking rubble while mashing another's face into jelly with a backhand blow from the shield.

His twin's facial expression was calm even as the flesh of her face grew a frightening shade of crimson from the constant strain.

"Just tiring of the games, brother of mine. Time for round one to end."

Both her hands arose through the wide-open space where the ceiling had once been and seemed to reach into the hazy sky, then clinched and came together forcefully at the thumbs.

Their safe-haven bubble dissipated, Jimmy was the first to be fallen upon. The thing claiming to be

Buck Lomax the Third wrapped its steely strong arms around his chest and pulled him down from behind, its putrid breath moistening his ear as it spoke.

"Settle down, fat thing. Deep down, you know you like it. Hey, J.C., come get ya some, dude!"

The left side of his face pinched against a mound of jagged rubble and his lungs dangerously low on oxygen, Jimmy felt himself slowly sinking into unconsciousness even as his body twisted and thrashed.

"I'm with ya, Buck. Hold that sow steady and I'll give 'im a good greasing. Make 'im squeal like that chubby guy in Deliverance, will ya?" J. C's voice chimed in from somewhere in the distance, Jimmy only able to note the passing of several various sized webbed feet within his very limited, increasingly blurred line of sight.

The whispering at his ear was so clear it seemed to be actually originating from inside his own mind. As his own futile struggles began to finally subside, Jimmy wondered seriously if that just might be the case after all.

"Chunky butt, I've had this perpetual boner I can't seem to rid myself of. Seems the master's original 'seed plotting' plan was a bit short-sighted, but you know, I can't say I regret he targeted me for 'stud duty'. Me and J.C. have been two rapin', hell-raisin' fools the last five or six years, man. Too bad the last bare behind I'm gonna see and pillage is that hairy hump of yours."

The J.C. imposter burst into machine gun laughter from what seemed to Jimmy to be miles away.

"Beggars can't be choosers, Buck old buddy. Let's just enjoy the moment, what do ya say?"

From a distant plain in a dark, dusky landscape, Jimmy felt several sets of hands begin to peel away his trousers.

As if spiritually re-charged, the last fiber of energy he possessed bubbled to the surface of his subconscious like volcanic lava, the scream that emerged that of a caged, cornered animal baring its teeth in final defiance of its eventual fate.

"Get *OFF OF ME*, you red-neck rump-wranglers!" He bellowed, rolling to his left and using his bulk to pin the Buck clone onto its back while kicking out with both feet and landing with a soft thud onto J. C's pudding textured midsection.

"Daaamn, t-there's life in them thar rolls after all," the Buck clone spat as Jimmy rolled hard to the left, halted, then executed an equally hard tumble to the right, finally managing to shake his attacker free.

As he rose unevenly to his naked, bloodied feet, Jimmy scooped up a nearby fifteen-pound barbell with his left hand and a ten-pounder with his right.

The J.C. clone rambled straight towards him sporting a comically perverted grin, his slender alien legs bending *backward* at the knee joints, ala a flamingo.

"I like it when they play hard to get, don't you, Buck?"

Buck the Third responded with a loud grunt as he leaped forward from the right of Jimmy, his own set of amphibian-like appendages acting like steel springs from a crouched position.

No further than five yards to Jimmy's left,

Private Kemp's left boot buried itself into the gummy quagmire serving as Major David Peterson's groin. Shaking his head in mock sympathy, the Major raised an index finger and shook it mockingly from side to side.

"Such unexpected hostility towards your former mentor, my dear Sandy? You and I never quite reached the warm and fuzzy point in our relationship, did we?"

Sandy backed off and quickly assumed a defensive posture; her left fist in a blocking stance while her right was tucked tightly against her side.

"You ain't Peterson, jackass, but even so, you look enough like 'im to make me want to plant a grenade up your buns and pull the pin with a claw hammer."

The Major leaned back, crossing the perfectly creased sleeves of his dress uniform across the legion of medals lined across his chest.

Correctional Officer Jerrod Dickenson, his own shirt looking recently pressed and possibly over-starched, stepped up, propping his left arm on the Major's right shoulder.

"Old friend of yours, David?"

Peterson picked his pearly white teeth with his left pinky.

"I wouldn't say friend, Jerrod. More like a worthless, shiftless, pimple- assed drunken whore with absolutely no respect whatsoever for her elders."

Jerrod Dickenson's glazed eyes sparkled as he sized up Private Kemp like a livestock judge at a county fair.

"If you have a little OJT session in mind for

her, Major, I'd be honored to assist."

Major Peterson winked at the CO without actually looking at him. "Let us proceed, Jerrod, but not before…"

The Major pulled the shiny object from his front pocket and waived it back and forth in front of his own sadistic smirk. CO Dickenson began to cackle wildly as the Major gleefully cut the air with the gleaming blades of the surgical sheers.

"We can do her up just like we did her lover-boy over there, Major, make them a matching set of GI gargoyles."

Private Kemp backed away until she found herself leaning against a cool stone wall, then began digging frantically into the pockets of her fatigue pants. She pulled the tiny Taser free and fired it in a straight line at the Major's forehead just as he broke into a clumsy sprint towards her.

A dozen yards to her left, Wilbo judo flipped a middle-aged man wearing a ridiculously thick wool coat; into and practically through a nearby Nautilus squat machine, not noticing until seconds later that he still clutched the majority of the man's left arm in his right fist.

A young male clone stepped up and was promptly backhanded by the flat of his shield, instantly turning the teen's face to yellow puree.

An elderly woman was next, wobbling up to Wilbo on scaly, stick legs and waiving a straight razor dangerously near his right ear. Ducking as the blade whizzed overhead, he planted the full length of his claws into her minuscule midsection, lifted her tiny frame airborne, and tossed her into the nearby rubble like so much bagged trash.

Turning to his sister while finally in-between assailants, Wilbo had thought himself to be shockproof at that particular point. A single extended glance at the young woman he had once shared the same womb with quickly proved that point to be a fictional one.

Kara's entire frame glowed yellow with the occasional flash of blue, as if encircled in a perimeter of fire that left her flesh magically untouched, her crimson coif pointing skyward as if caught in a draft of pure static. Her hands were still aimed into the clouds and clinched tight, but were no longer joined at the thumbs.

Her mouth was agape, apparently screaming a silent command only the clouds above could comprehend.

"Sis, a-are you…alri-..." Wilbo managed while stepping purposely towards her. A fresh group of clones, perhaps as many as twenty, descended upon them both just as the sky above began to crackle and spark like a fourth of July fireworks display.

***

The being shuddered internally as each of its combat spores met their demise. The pains were of small consequence, no more than insignificant spasms, really, but were substantial enough in number to cause serious concerns. The two creatures it had viewed as nothing more than merely bothersome enigmas within the framework of the task at hand possessed unexpectedly formidable powers. The being studied their combat prowess with more than just a passing interest while leisurely ingesting and attempting, mostly in vain, to digest and alter the Other's mindset. The Other, a shape-shifting Sentinel no doubt stationed upon the grounds eons earlier by the Dark Messiah, had sensed their power and wisely recruited them into a clash it knew it could not possibly win alone.

As the battle below drew to a startling conclusion, the being's frustration began to upsurge into a rage of volcanic proportions, due to its spores combat ineffectiveness and its own failures in being unable to alter the Other for useable purposes.

Feeling the earlier surge of energy gained with the cellblock absorption begin to noticeably wane; the being focused its many varied faculties on ending the debacle without further drainage.

Within the vast arsenal of weapons at its disposal, the single most effective when dealing with a lower species was the transference of brain matter.

The whole of the being fell into a self-inflicted trance, its entire enormous form as motionless as an ancient mountain ridge.

The creation and subsequent release of the fleshy electrode appendages tasked for such a procedure were in the final stages of completion just as the skies erupted overhead like multiple supernovas.

***

Jimmy waited for the Buck Clone to get within touching distance before chunking the larger of the two barbells like a pitcher tossing his best fastball towards home plate. Home plate, in this case, turned out to be the bridge of the charging clone's nose, which was shattered like pine kindling beneath an anvil upon contact. Buck the Clone groaned as he staggered away in a shambling lurch, jagged pieces of teeth and thick, mucus-like fluids running through the fingers he placed over the wounds.

About the same time the weight had made contact, J. C's clone had attempted to swing around from the rear and tackle Jimmy below the knees. Displaying an agility and fluidity of movement he never knew previously existed, Jimmy had timed his leap perfectly, jerking his lower legs upward into a mid-air squat just as the clone had dived forward. Landing with a resounding thump, Jimmy planted his knees in the Clone's lower back and pinned him to the stone flooring. He raised the smaller barbell overhead, preparing to crush the clone's skull, his entire body tingling with both fear and the instinctual exhilaration of completing the kill.

"Mess with the bull, asswipe, you will eventually get the horns…" Jimmy exclaimed passionately as the barbell began its trajectory downward.

The very air around them seemed to fill with crackling static just milliseconds before everything changed.

***

Giggling hysterically, although utterly unaware of doing so, Private Kemp leap-frogged the slumping form of the Dickenson clone, discarding the Taser before landing awkwardly onto a loose pile of smoking rubble.

The taser's probe had punctured the former CO's left eyeball, the Taser wire hanging from the seeping pupil like severed fishing line. She doubted the electric charge produced had effected the clone, figuring the nervous system of such a creature was more than likely immune or possibly incapable of transmitting the surges. Regardless, the probe's penetration had allowed her to dodge his initial lunge, which in retrospect was more than she could have ever hoped for. The cloned CO wobbled off into the distance, tugging at the hanging wire while his eye spurted and leaked porous amounts of fluid onto his lower jaw, neck and chest.

"Slippery bitch, aren't you?" The Major Peterson duplicate spat angrily, stepping aggressively towards her with the surgical snips in one hand and a short-bladed combat knife in the other.

Once again, in lieu of having no other options available, Private Kemp implemented a fighting stance and held her ground, all the while regretting she seemingly wasn't going to be allowed time for even the briefest of prayers before her short life was extinguished.

"Come and get me, Major Crap for brains."

As he grew closer, the Major clone began crisscrossing the blades in a circular slashing motion. Private Kemp leaned her head and chest back, careful to keep her hands out of striking distance while kicking out with her right boot.

The heel struck the clone's darkly tinged shin right below the backward bend at its knee, sliding harmlessly off of the slimy textured skin.

Falling forward from her own momentum, Private Kemp felt a burning sting just above her left biceps as the knife blade cut through her uniform shirt, then allowed herself to tumble forward in order to avoid further damage. Her combat roll ended at the edge of a large black weight bench with her legs slid between thick steel braces. Struggling to pull herself upright, she glanced up just as the Major knelt down with the tip of the snips balanced on the side of her throat.

"Time to say goodbye, Private. Can't *honestly* say I'm not gonna enjoy this…"

Closing her eyes tightly as if to ward off the excruciating pain about to come, Private Kemp never saw the perfectly implemented body-block that sent the Major's imitation sailing away from her as if struck by a monstrous tidal wave.

Corporal McIntosh used every ounce of body weight and centrifugal force he could muster while plastering the Major clone onto a pile of jagged brick and splintered wood.

Grinning as much from pain-induced delirium as victorious glee, the Corporal wrenched the surgical snips from the fallen clone's shaking hand with a vicious slap from his left stub, then began using both his elbows to pummel and pound the imitation unmercifully. Private Kemp got to her feet unsteadily and momentarily checked her arm wound, which didn't seem to be as severe as it felt, the bleeding already beginning to subside.

Using his bloody stubs as clubs, the Corporal was quickly transforming the Major's face to yellow-tinted ground beef, all the while displaying a broad smile that was the definition of derangement.

"...wish it was the *real* Major I was pounding the shit out of...but since his rank ass is no longer available, you'll fill in just fine."

The room caught fire just after Corporal McIntosh had begun mashing the Major's already pulped head further into the concrete with his size thirteen boots.

***

Wilbo crouched down with the shield pressed atop his head just as the bolts rained down.

Kara stood just a few feet away, her entire body bathed in flame but seemingly unscathed as her flexing hands magically invited the storm to descend.

The streaking bolts fell like a meteor barrage, at first landing at random within the closed confines of the room, then apparently locked on specific targets held therein.

The remaining clones were individually and systematically singed into heaping piles of brown ash without a solitary drop of wetness left in their wake.

Private Kemp had pulled Corporal McIntosh away just a split-second before the Major's imitation was torched by a bolt that disintegrated his upper body like tissue paper thrown into a lit crematorium.

Jimmy had ducked away just as Buck and J. C's clones were sheered away by the same bolt, a narrow beam that had halved them at the waist like a swinging pendulum blade.

Once the final clone was charred, Kara swept

her arms over just slightly to the left, the center of the being's head visible between the sparse space provided between her radiant hands.

As Jimmy joined Private Kemp and the Corporal in taking refuge just to her left, Wilbo staggered up next to them, the shield now held casually at his side.

"Watch this, folks. My sister is gonna fry big, bad and ugly over there like bacon on a grill," he said, pointing towards the being with his clawed hand, which still dripped with alien goo.

The frequency and intensity of the lightning bolts seem to increase ten-fold as they struck the being relentlessly and without pause.

Each pre-emptive strike burned a circular hole deep into the being's flesh roughly the size of a manhole cover, wounds which almost immediately closed upon impact without leaving evidence of even the tiniest scar.

The being's upper body hardly moved throughout the assault, although his lizard-like tail end wriggled and rocked, dismantling whatever lay within its wide reach like a baseball bat waived inside a cramped China shop.

"Keep beltin' him, lady! Drive that ugly SOB back into the ground where it came from!" Corporal McIntosh screamed, enthusiastically patting Private Kemp on the shoulder as if all were witnessing a particularly exciting sporting event.

Only her twin brother was aware of the incomprehensible strain Kara's mind and body was undertaking to administer such an all-out assault from the skies above.

He stepped behind her, gingerly reaching

within the luminous glow engulfing her frame in order to help brace her already sagging form.

To his relief, the flames held no heat on his skin, just a mild tingling sensation at his fingertips.

"Cut it off for a sec, sis, before you pass out. I won't be worth a good damn without you. Take a break before I lose you for good."

To their left, Corporal McIntosh had stumbled ahead of the pack like a drunken hockey fan at rink side, waiving his mutilated hands high into the air and dancing a joyful jig in response to the low, rattling moan the being had begun to emit as the salvo continued.

"How do ya like that, worm-boy? How does it feel to get your unworldly ass kicked by a couple of puny earthlings? If I had fingers I'd shoot ya the bird with both hands, ya miserable chunk of rat sh-…"

His lips had been suspended in mid-word as the projectile sailed forward with the speed of a bullet fired from a high-powered rifle.

Both Jimmy and Private Kemp caught only the briefest glimpses at the object, which had held the shape of a circular saw blade and the height and width of a tractor-trailer tire.

Corporal McIntosh's arms had clapped together one final time before his body was utterly unhinged in a crimson glut, a wide smear of bodily fluids, roughly half a combat boot and a sparse spattering of ripped uniform left as the only evidence he had ever actually existed within their midst. The fleshy projectile swayed to the left after impact, eventually crashing through the far gym wall, leaving behind a horizontal outline that looked to have been painted on.

"H-holy…M-Mac?" Private Kemp whispered between rapidly blinking eyes suddenly brimming with warm tears. Jimmy grabbed her around the shoulders just as she began to wander aimlessly towards the last space her comrade and infrequent lover had or would ever again occupy.

"He's… gone, Sandy. We…you can't help him now."

After a short-lived, half-hearted struggle against the arms that held her, Private Kemp sank into his waiting arms like a sobbing child to a trusted adult.

They crouched as one behind the twins, Jimmy's mouth trembling in silent prayer.

At precisely the same moment that Kara's arms fell in complete exhaustion and the last remaining torrent of bolts rained down, a similar object to the one which had disemboweled the Corporal rocketed forth directly towards her as if fired close range from a giant crossbow.

Wilbo had a split-second to brace his back and legs while raising the shield to his sister's face.

His felt his shoulder pull free from its socket with a sickening popping sound upon impact, his upper body twisting at an impossibly warped angle as he was jarred from his feet.

Rising from the nearby rubble pile he had been tossed so forcefully onto, Wilbo gripped his injured arm and pulled upward, grimacing only slightly as the joint clicked back into place.

It wasn't until he re-joined his sister a moment later that he realized something new had been involuntarily added to his arsenal.

"T-thank you, William. I'm pretty sure whatever that thing was, it would have caused me considerable pain."

Wilbo continued to stare blank-eyed at the wooden-handled mini-sledge hammer gripped in his right hand. The metal hammer was darkly tinted, and held numerous scars from past usage, some of which looked actually carved within its frame. It was at that same time that they both noticed his fist was also mysteriously claw-free.

Her shoulders badly slumped; Kara regarded the object of his concentration with guarded surprise.

"What's th-…oh, I get it. Where are my claws? What do I use this for, help rebuild the compound maybe?"

Her brother glared at her in confusion.

"William, I'm surprised at you. Founding member of the Avengers, remember? Blond locks? Funny hat with wings?"

As he carefully re-examined the hammer, the answer finally sank in. Despite her obvious fatigue, Kara couldn't help but marvel at her brother's child-like excitement.

"Aw man! *Thor,* God of Thunder! Oh, *hell* yeah!" He exclaimed cheerily. "Now I can inflict some serious damage!"

The being shifted forward in a spastic lurch, causing each of them to cringe back a step.

Stringy tubing that resembled cable cord fell in thick groves from its underbelly and hung just a few feet from the stone floor surface.

"What are...those things?" Kara asked weakly in between long, labored breaths.

Her brother replied while checking the two slumped forms behind them and flashing each a reassuring nod.

"Looks like overcooked linguine to me, sis. How long before you're recharged?"

"A year, maybe two. Honestly, I really *don't* know. I feel like I could sleep at least that long."

A low, vaguely muffled plopping sound caught their attention, a sound not unlike thick soup bubbling to a boil.

The goo-coated head that emerged from the left side of the being's upper torso looked so misplaced, so utterly *ridiculous*, that Wilbo couldn't help but laugh aloud at its outlandish presence.

"Go ahead and bust a gut, wise guy, get your jollies while you're still breathing!" It screamed in anger before whipping viscously back and forth to clear away the sticky slime.

"Where ya been, Warden? Performing your own personal gut and bowel exam on old ugly there? We figured the next time we saw you would be in a big old brown chunk of *stool*."

The being seemed totally oblivious to the growling growth protruding just a few feet from the tip of what it utilized as a chin, its total concentration seemingly centered on the ever-growing number of tubular ropes emerging from its lower half.

"Stow it, funny man. Shove a sock in it and listen up before the demon takes notice and sucks me back in like so much Italian meatball. You see the dangling ropes below? The ones that seem to be individually sniffing out the ground they hang so precariously over?"

As the twins shifted their attention back to the being, it seemed at least a few hundred additional feelers had fallen free, all of which now swung and swayed from their master's lower half in flowing waves.

"Of course we've noticed 'em. We haven't exactly had time to set up a research team to investigate. What exactly are their purpose in this little nightmare anyhow?" Wilbo asked, his sister now leaning into the bulk of his shoulder and chest.

The Warden/Thing started to speak, paused to gag before spitting a stream of black, oily textured liquid towards the floor, then calmly resumed.

"Their *purpose*, old great God of Thunder, is to first fatally alter and then end all life on the planet. Each one of those stringy looking tubes is packed with poison, a poison unlike any this world has ever seen nor ever could imagine. Just *one* of those things planted into the earth's rich soil would suffice to take out this state in a matter of days. Five of 'em would take out the southeast. As many as old Gor is displaying as we speak…your looking at the entire damn *continent* within a week's time."

Kara stumbled forward, still shaking the cobwebs free as Wilbo reached over to brace her.

"What kind of poison could be that powerful?" The Warden/Thing sighed irritably.

"Lady witch, I ain't got time for scientific graphs or charts, and you wouldn't be able to decipher 'em if I did. Remember the black plague that swept Europe all those centuries ago? Let's just say it's like a mild *head cold* in comparison. A minuscule dose of the stuff turned certain townspeople and Briarston Correctional officers into walking piles of mush over the last several years.

It…seemed to feed off the wicked more intently, at least that was Gor's intention initially. He used certain individuals that were found to be morally bankrupt and mentally weak in his rebirthing scheme. Take my word for it; this batch of disease won't be so picky. It'll sweep over towns and cities like a dark cloak. Once the demon plants those stalks, it sweeps through the underbelly and into water supplies, eventually blowing through the air in a fine mist of toxin so stout it'll pretty much melt people's eyebrows upon contact."

Ensuring his sister could stand alone, Wilbo charged forward a step, his teeth bared, waiving the hammer about like a protest sign.

"Fine, the world turns into a true melting pot the hard way unless we stop 'im, we *get* that part. Now tell us exactly *how* we're supposed to accomplish this, Warden! With a hammer and a few magic tricks maybe? I seriously have my doubts, pal!"

The being seemed to snap from its self-imposed daze just as the feelers stopped multiplying from its torso, its head again beginning to rock gently from side to side. The Warden/Thing grimaced and then released a muted scream, his eyes rolling back into his head and then closing tightly.

"The son of a…its yankin' m-me back I-in…listen...closely…I...won't get another chance...to repeat this… Kara…go for its heart… you alone…p-possess the….inner...s-strength…the…spiritual...qual-qualities…to…implode the bas-bastard's black heart….William will...have to…distract...to give...you...the ch-chance... K- Kara…get in-inside the organ… use...what...your…messiah has given you…good luck…guys….I..I…won't b-be…back…I'm...afraid h-he's…r-r- really…pi-piss-pissed...at…m-me...this...time…"

The head twisted and turned as if the body underneath was being shifted and tugged upon, the Warden/Thing's face contorted wildly just before the top of his skull exploded in a soupy splash of bone fragments and thick, dark liquid. Tiny strips of brain tissue rained down around the twins like portions of soggy oatmeal as they ducked away disgustedly. What remained of the Warden/Thing's head, basically just a nose, mouth and chin, was then pulled back inside the torso, submerging gradually like a submarine periscope beneath calm seawaters.

The being wedged itself a bit closer, effortlessly ripping up sections of stone flooring and metal framework, and seemed to be sizing up the twins as its head cocked to one side.

Wilbo turned and sternly addressed Jimmy, who still held Private Kemp to his chest.

"Listen, man, you two are on your own for a few minutes, hopefully no longer. Find a cubbyhole somewhere and quick. I don't think old gruesome there is gonna be worried about your whereabouts from here on out, but then again… that's just a guess, and I make a nasty habit out of being wrong. Don't sweat it though…we'll keep 'im plenty busy in the meantime."

His eyes huge and aware, Jimmy felt instant relief, a sense of protective security, in just a quick study of the intense resolve present in the young man's eyes. Never a man of religion, Jimmy Rollins nonetheless understood there was a special presence surrounding the two siblings. A presence that would steadfastly refuse to accept defeat as an option in such a potentially grim scenario, despite the overwhelming odds it faced.

Turning back to his sister, Wilbo watched her pupils reappear within the glowing ivory of her eyes for the briefest of moments, just long enough to read the anxiety held there.

"How, sis? How are you gonna…?"

White flame flew from her sockets as a broad, wide smile surfaced. As she placed her left hand on her twin sibling's shoulder, Wilbo felt a tingling sensation sprint down his spine.

"I think I know, William. Keep it occupied the best you can…and be careful, brother of mine."

He returned her smile while fighting off the building warmness around the corners of his eyes.

"You got it, Kara. Do what you have to do, sis, then get the hell out of there, you hear?"

Kara nodded, hugging him to her and giving his right cheek a swift kiss. "Affirmative. Inflict as much pain as possible, you Norse God you."

As if to acknowledge the impending clash, the being immediately extracted two wriggling attachments, each similarly armed with similarly dangerous accessories. The first was as thick as a telephone pole and approximately ten to fifteen yards in length, its bulb-shaped end riddled with hundreds of jagged spears, some as thin as syringe needles while others held the thickness of a shovel handle.

The second arm had been utilized earlier that evening on the exercise yard, its painfully spindly appearance only increasing the foreboding presence of the baseball-mitt shaped hand it braced.

Each arm seemed to waive and float in limbo, as if awaiting an attack command.

"*YOU WAITED ALL THIS TIME JUST TO DIE, GRUESOME*!" Kara screamed, the sheer anger in her tone causing her twin to flinch back involuntarily.

Wilbo looked down to see that his sister's feet floated a full six to eight inches from the stone floor. Just as she hovered slowly upward, like a balloon with a cut string, Jimmy and Private Kemp broke into a scrambling sprint towards the rear of the gym.

Wilbo heard their thumping steps, but ignored them in lieu of viewing his sister's impromptu flight towards the heart of the beast.

"Where exactly are we g-going, Rollins?" Private Kemp blurted while stepping around an overturned, dust-coated abdominal machine, then staring ahead at the white painted sign that read '*restroom*' a few dozen feet ahead.

"Time to drain the old *pee-rod*, I take it?"

Jimmy leaped a fallen stationary bike, then looked over at her with a wry smirk. If nothing else, he was thankful she had at least partially snapped out of her earlier funk.

"Lady, my pants have been soiled numerous times already. Such mundane practices as using a urinal is passé as far as this man's concerned."

They crashed through the surprisingly wide entrance door a second later, each donning parallel masks of unbridled delirium on their badly drained faces.

Ducking next to adjoining toilet stalls, they eyed each other worriedly while sucking in fresh servings of oxygen.

Outside the thin, wood-framed walls of the community bathroom, a low rumbling noise was growing consistently louder.

“My money’s on the brother-sister act, Sandy. They’re like...mutants or something. Besides, good always finds a way to boot evils backside, right?”

Private Kemp looked down at her own grime-layered boots and nodded apathetically.

“I don’t gamble, Jimbo. If I did, I’m with you. I always had a thing for underdogs. I guess it’s ‘cause I’ve always belonged in that particular category myself. Besides, those two look like they jumped off a comic-book cover, and comic book heroes rarely go down for the count.”

Despite his earlier reservations concerning such practices, Jimmy Rollins lowered his head and began to pray.

CHAPTER TEN
White Hunter, Darkest Heart

Wilbo barreled ahead, peeking over the shield's top edge, the hammer cocked back in his other arm, all the while keeping an eye trained on Kara, who glided almost directly above him.

The being's spear-arm stretched out in a straight line, then swung down like a wrecking ball. Kara ascended just a bit higher until she was even with the being's head, then swayed a few feet to the left, effortlessly avoiding the potentially fatal blow.

Forty feet below, Wilbo leaped to his right and bounded off a heaping pile of mangled metal and crushed stone, using the shield to buffer the impact. The spear-arm ripped into the open flooring just a few feet to his left, easily burrowing through the stone tile.

Jogging a few steps to build his momentum, he heaved the hammer like a shot put towards the being's midsection just as his twin altered her positioning above its suddenly swaying head. Kara looked like an Olympic high diver in free- fall, her hands cupped together and pointed out, her legs and feet pinned together as one.

As the hammer struck the being just below its neck stalk with the force of a speeding tractor-trailer, Kara's flight speed hit overdrive, as if a hidden turbo- drive had been initiated.

The handle of the hammer slapped Wilbo's open palm just as he halted at the shockingly wide base of the being's lower torso. He had known somehow of the weapon's boomerang qualities, despite its cumbersome weight. Without waste of movement, he swung it forward with the might of an ancient blacksmith pounding heated steel, driving it into the beast's soft underbelly with every ounce of energy he possessed.

The being's second line of defense, the mitt-shaped appendage, sailed across in a tight arc in an attempt to block Kara from her intended target. Somehow sensing this, she waited until it's opened pinchers were mere feet away and hooking directly towards her upper body, before curling into a fetal position, the outline of which was bathed in swirling blue flames.

Wilbo continued to relentlessly pound away at the wall of thick, scaly flesh, each thundering blow of the hammer's edge actually jarring the entire colossal form back several inches.

Entranced within his own maniacal rage, he hardly had time to raise the shield upright before the spear-arm impacted.

The collision tossed him airborne, his body executing several spinning loops before he miraculously landed on the heels of his feet at least ten yards from the original point of contact.

Still a bit dazed from the jarring blow, Wilbo looked up at the precise moment that his twin's body was being enveloped by the mitt-hand like a pesky fly within a clinched fist.

"KARA!" He growled while rearing back to toss the hammer, hoping to clip the being's upper arm in hopes of freeing her.

Just as the hammer sailed away in a blur from his right hand, the trio of razor-edged claws again sprang forth from the same with a loud 'thwacking' noise.

Wilbo bounded forth in a series of leaps that covered at least a dozen feet each, his thighs and calves bloated with newly formed muscle. From a distance, he resembled a prehistoric species considerably more animal than human.

The mitt closed around Kara's curled frame and squeezed with thick, serrated digits that were almost sword-like, and that actually sliced into one another upon interlocking.

The being used its giant cinder-block legs for balance, twisting until the thrown hammer vanished within the flapping folds at the center of its neck stalk, then began to back slowly away from the gymnasium building. The mitt-hand was held high into the clear Mississippi sky, as if encasing a fragile artifact within its grasp.

As it's gargantuan frame begin to ponderously attempt a complete turn, Wilbo leapt onto the torso, using several of the hanging tubes for handholds. He continued to climb the scaly frame, departing the tubular growths for the higher placed deformities jutting out from the being's upper body. Legions of arms, legs, and unidentified bones, more than likely from both animal and human hosts, protruded from the slimy surface of the being's skin like swarms of wriggling parasites.

Glancing upward while swinging from one hand by what looked like a human foot and ankle, Wilbo noticed a strange, fluorescent glow surrounding the mitt-glove. A glow that was growing increasingly bright as the being continued its turn.

Hanging from the shielded arm, Wilbo began to

frantically slash the alien flesh, opening gapping gashes that were strangely fluid-free.

The being continued its tedious U-turn, its dinosaur-like tail battering another large portion of the gymnasium into rubble.

Flailing away like a man attempting to carve his way through a wall of whale-blubber, Wilbo felt the haplessness begin to overwhelm him in waves of somber futility. He knew Kara had been the key to victory, however slim the chances, and even though his heart still felt her presence nearby, his mind had mentally thrown in the proverbial towel once she had vanished within the beast's grip.

Still, his aching, badly fatigued arm refused to drop, ripping and tearing away layer after layer of scaly tissue, despite the realization that it was nothing more than a valiant effort in an ultimately losing battle.

The being wailed like a howling banshee, freezing Wilbo in mid-slash. He momentarily considered his slicing claws might possibly had severed a vital nerve center of some kind, then peered upward and grinned happily upon visualizing the true reason for the beast's pained cries.

The mitt-hand had blown apart as if an atom bomb had detonated within its steely grip, leaving behind a saw-toothed, shredded stump that quickly fell away as the attached arm collapsed in a downward arc.

Kara still occupied the space that had imprisoned her, floating with her arms and legs spread impossibly wide, as if she were attempting to create a 'snow-angel' in mid-air. The multi-colored flames engulfing her skin were nova- bright, and Wilbo suddenly understood the origin of the glow around the hand just before it was so violently disintegrated.

"Get the bastard, sis! Go for the JUGULAR!" He yelled, wildly pumping his clawed fist.

As if on cue, she rocketed forward, again stretched into an arrow-straight pose.

Wilbo was suddenly tossed roughly to one side, barely maintaining his grip on the large femur bone he had been clinging to, as the being finally completed its strenuous about-face turn with one final lunge.

Despite the fact that he was suspended at least fifty feet from the matted grass below, Wilbo was forced to relinquish his grip just seconds later as the spear-arm lumbered directly into his path.

***

"The noise is growing fainter, you notice that?" Jimmy asked, leaning against a bathroom stall with his arms crossed over his chest.

"You think it's over?" Private Kemp replied more timidly than she had intended, staring into a badly cracked mirror that was only partially intact. The fear that had paralyzed her upon viewing the appallingly abrupt death of Corporal Ron McIntosh had been slowly replaced by a gnawing dread. A dread fueled by lurid visions of hell on earth. Hell on earth defined as a flesh-melting plague that inflicted symptoms of homicidal rage within its victims before peeling them like ripe grapes. Her chest felt far too tight, as if banded down by tie-down straps that were being systematically tightened as the seconds ticked by.

"I…I don't know. Maybe that explosion a second ago means the Calvary has finally arrived. You would have thought all the noise in the past hour would have brought out the Navy, Army, Marines and maybe a few armed Girl Scout troops to boot."

Private Kemp nodded apathetically, her slack expression the definition of downtrodden.

"Maybe, but do you really think man-made weapons of *any* kind can stop that damned thing, Jimmy?"

Jimmy found no suitable response, and instead began diligently chewing his grime-coated fingernails.

A new, infinitely louder scream filled their ears a moment later, causing each of them to release an unexpected shriek of their own.

Jimmy's eyes were saucers. Private Kemp stood stiffly, then glared at him with stark uncertainty.

"Wanna take a look?"

Shrugging his shoulders weakly, Jimmy stepped tentatively towards the door.

"Why not? Nothing to lose but our souls."

Sighing deeply, Private Kemp grunted in mock dismay. "Nice choice of words, Buck-o."

***

Like a flaming arrow, Kara had pierced the being's lone eye, bursting the greenish orb within like a syringe penetrating an overfilled water balloon and instantly halting its forward movement in the process.

Thrashing its head in a frenzied series of jerks, a loud series of pops ensued from the base of its twisted neck, the skin of which visibly swelled from the object rapidly trailing south through its relatively slender passageway.

Flapping his arms as if to sustain flight, Wilbo had barely avoided being clipped in the side by the edge of the spear-arm as it had whooshed by. He heard the being's anguished cries as his fall commenced, and instantly felt a surge of pride despite his predicament. Although clueless to the reasons why, Wilbo instinctively raised his clawed hand over his head as he descended towards a pile of mangled metal that had once been a rowing machine, stretching his fingers out as if awaiting a handshake.

The hammer handle entered his palm at an upward trajectory just as his shoe tips were inches from what surely would have been a fatal landing, jolting him back into airspace just as his grip intensified.

"Bout time you showed up," Wilbo mumbled as the feeling of weightlessness overwhelmed his finely tuned senses.

While navigating a tight circle of flight that would eventually lead him directly into the being's path, Wilbo became aware of two distinct details. The first was the ragged hole that the enchanted hammer had created upon departing the being's chest on its erstwhile rescue mission, a squared, gashing wound that had already begun to sew itself closed. The second was the unmistakable outline of his sister's body beneath the creature's skin at the base of its neck, a rapidly descending bulge that instantly reminded him of footage he had seen of Anaconda's devouring their prey.

The swelling vanished into the thick trunk as Wilbo circled around to the front of the being's skull, where his sister's point of entry became all too apparent.

The eye was already beginning to regenerate as Wilbo hovered a dozen or so feet overhead, the left corner of the socket pulsating with a generous build- up of greenish-black fluid.

Releasing the glimmering shield from the forearm straps and gripping it like an oversized Frisbee, all the while still holding the hammer aloft like a flaming torch, Wilbo twisted his upper body to the left like a discus thrower. He uncoiled in a weaving jerk, the shield a red, white and blue blur hardly perceptible to the naked eye.

Upon impact just above the eye socket, it's swiftly spinning edges carved a foot deep groove, like a whirling buzz-saw blade through rotted plywood. The shield then spun away and reversed direction, discarding bits of torn flesh and scaled tissue before floating gently back into Wilbo's waiting grip.

"Need a haircut with that *shave*, gruesome?" He yelled, dipping lower until he floated directly across from the hastily reconstructing orb.

As he observed the flaps of the slashing wound begin to immediately reseal above the eye, Wilbo hoped he could buy his sister the precious time she needed. Even with the combined powers of fictional Avengers and X-men at his disposal, he was relegated to playing the role of a pesky fly buzzing about a bull elephant's ears.

Dodging quickly to the left, he easily avoided the lumbering spear-arm as it whizzed by. The being glared at him momentarily with its rebuilt eye, then just as quickly refocused on the compound entrance.

Just as its forward progress resumed with a lurching roll that shaved away the left side of the admin building in a mass wave of smoldering rubble, Wilbo went into a free-fall in a desperate attempt to somehow block it from ground level.

He never saw the lashing tail swing around like a scaly funnel cloud until it was far too late to avoid the carnage it wrought.

***

The creature was inside it, searching. The being could feel the alien heat source within its infinite canals, tunneling and probing for the prize it so intensely sought. The mystifying powers the creature had displayed in so easily disposing of the memory extensions had indeed shocked the being, although nothing akin to fear had even been remotely felt until it had actually entered the bodily realm. The being realized the target of the hunt. The Other had passed the word to the lone organism on the entire planet capable of not only pinpointing the targets location, but executing extraction of same.

The being of course had a built-in defense system against such an attempt, but would take no chances in the event of inexplicable failure. It would plant the black roots as soon as a viable distance was gained outside the fenced walls of its rebirth. It would have preferred to institute the initial laying of the diseased groundwork near one of the populated areas to ensure a more fertile, solid foundation, but realized the constraints of time would now forbid such cautionary measures.

Subsequently, the roots would be jarringly ineffective if seeds were sewn too near the compound on damned grounds already ripe with the decaying veins of centuries past.

Over roughly a ten-mile radius on or around the Briarston Correctional Facility, literally hundreds of tunnels had sprouted forth, some no wider than dental floss and others large enough to drive a Greyhound bus through.

The being had been able to mentally construct each through pent-up rage and frustration. Unfortunately, such grounds were useless upon its escape, as unfertile as sand dunes to a cotton farmer.

It sought fresher land to lie upon and plunge the infectious seeds of fatal contamination into.

As it lumbered forth with recharged vision and renewed vigor in completing the task at hand, it did well to block out the uneasy throbbing within its midsection. It would first terminate the bothersome creature flying about its topside, then find a suitable place to release its birth right, cautiously optimistic that the internal problem could be alleviated after the fact. As each earth- shaking, pondering step brought it ever closer to that unknown landscape where an entire planet would first begin the process of slowly disintegrating, the being felt an inner twinge. A twinge it hadn't experienced since the day of banishment that preceded infinite imprisonment.

A twinge created and cultivated by a five-letter word it knew no true definition of.

Dread.

***

Kara swam through the maze of endless, curved tunnels that she knew would ultimately lead her to the being's nerve center. The aura her skin emitted had turned a lighter shade of purple since gaining entry, providing her ample illumination within the pitch-black caverns.

Several of the circular, slick-coated pathways had led into wider, cave-like entrances, each with several exits to choose from. She had felt a bit like a lost traveler standing at a four-way stop and unsure of which highway to take.

Kara had quickly decided to allow her instincts to choose the correct passage, and had been infinitely grateful that she could literally glide forward without having to physically touch the tunnels gooey linings. As a child, she had developed a phobia concerning all things slimy, and even as an adult had found it extremely difficult to touch raw meat or fish without openly cringing. She couldn't help but reveal a grim, irony-laced smile while passing from one curved channel to the next inside an acutely alien intestinal tract like some otherworldly miner. The force behind her mystifying powers had obviously deleted the 'squeamish' factor from her psyche, along with a large majority of the brain tissue that controlled one's inner fear.

She wasn't sure how far she had descended since penetrating the being's eye, or how much time had expired, but knew somehow that she was drawing close to the intended target. Sliding through the end of a narrow valve-like space that led into a wide, almost perfectly square cavern, Kara's scalp began to tingle as if electrically charged. The enclosure's walls were significantly darker than the earlier tunnels, creating a feeling of foreboding that Kara could almost feel as a physical presence. Unlike the other circular clearings she had passed through, this one was box-shaped and featured only a single exit to her right, one, which held a circumference roughly the size of her head.

Taking a deep breath within the sheltered confines of her body's force field, Kara's initial movement towards the octagon-shaped hole halted abruptly as the shadows surrounding her suddenly came alive with frenzied movement.

***

The tail had whipped forth like an uncoiled spring, shoving several tons worth of rock-filled dirt and matted clay towards Wilbo in a gargantuan wave he was unable to avoid. With just enough time to cover his head and face with the shield, he was first battered and then swallowed whole by the shifting mountain of rubble, finally vanishing altogether as the tail's forward progress ultimately ceased, reversing its direction with noticeably less velocity.

Unable to breath, his mouth and nostrils packed with grass, dirt and chunks of gravel, Wilbo nonetheless felt no panic. Utterly paralyzed, as if he had been dipped in fast-drying cement, he felt the hammer begin to tremor and convulse within his right palm.

Despite knowing he had mere minutes remaining before being overcome by suffocation, Wilbo felt a surreal calmness he instantly attributed to the outside force that had guided his every move since first entering the compound.

Hardly able to even maintain his strained grip on the hammer's handle upon being leveled by the wall of debris, he felt it grow undeniably stronger while being gradually tugged to the surface.

***

After disposing of the weaker pestilence, the being built up speed as it neared the compound's main gate area. It was extremely aware and no less anxious of the other creature's location within its main core. It could feel its natural defenses surround and defend, but found shaking the uneasiness surrounding the battle's eventual outcome virtually impossible. It yearned to break free of the contaminated grounds beneath it, choosing a suitable location, and plunging the roots downward into the soil like a thousand throbbing erections into virgin flesh.

The razor-wired top portion of the perimeter fence only reached the midway point on the being's torso as it blasted through, plowing over the sally port's guard shack like a speeding freight car over a dollhouse.

It had barely reached the edge of the

compound's parking lot when a series of wrenching spasms assaulted every fiber of its existence. The being tilted forward like a punch-drunk fighter, then managed to straighten, slinging fifty yards of compound fencing and several concrete-based signs into the night sky in the process.

Its body quivered as if in the throngs of an epileptic fit of nuclear proportions, its single eye swirling in a kaleidoscope of crimson and lavender.

The being was no longer able to command its own movements, frozen solidly in place as the clash within it began in earnest. A battle that the being now understood was eons from being a sure victory, nor merely a mundane formality within it's personal tour of destruction.

The invading creature had been given power, but also something infinitely more dangerous. It had been handed an indomitable *spirit* that simply refused to accept defeat.

The being shuddered, then fell motionless as the wait began.

***

A mere nine miles down highway sixty-eight, passing a large metal road sign declaring 'BRIARSTON CORRECTIONAL FACILITY NEXT EXIT– Do Not Pick up Hitchhikers!' A convoy of seventeen State Trooper and county police vehicles lined the otherwise deserted roadway in a chain of flashing lights and wailing sirens.

Reports as far away as Morgantown, a tiny hamlet fourteen miles east of the compound, had reported explosions, ground tremors, putrid smells and smoke-filled skies near the outskirts of Red Bridge. Red Bridge itself had not been heard from, the power and phone lines having been mysteriously severed hours earlier.

***

Nearing the ragged edge of what had been the north corner of the gymnasium, Private Kemp peeked around a badly bent iron frame, once part of a Nautilus squat machine, and into the well-lit yard beyond.

"Can you see it?" Jimmy whispered from the floor behind her, attempting in vain to pull on a pair of ill-fitting boots over his raw, bloodied feet.

"Oh yeah, big bastard just totaled the sally port. We can blow this hellhole, for whatever *good* that's gonna do us."

Tossing the scared, dusty boot away in disgust, Jimmy stood and peered sheepishly over her shoulder.

"Any sign of the X-twins?" "Neither hide nor mutated hair."

Jimmy side stepped around her, careful to avoid a spattering of glass shards, and scanned the space that just moments earlier had been the compound's locked entryway.

"Damn. Looks like it took most of the fence with it. For some strange reason, I felt better when that thing was locked *inside* with us. Crazy thought, I know, but..."

Private Kemp clapped him on the shoulder while keeping her eyes glued to the motionless being.

“Same here, Jimbo. There’s something about the thought of that thing rambling free about the countryside that just don’t feel right, you know?”

“Yeah. Can you imagine the body count that thing can generate in a populated area? I’m sure it drools at the very thought.”

“It ain’t moving, Jimmy. *Why* isn’t it moving?”

Jimmy shrugged, then reached down to pick a splinter from the tip of his right big toe.

“Contemplating its next conquest, maybe? Can’t decide whether to turn right or left at Albuquerque? Your guess is as good as min...”

Suddenly grinning like a lunatic, Private Kemp turned to him and practically beamed, her voice crackling with hope.

“Maybe it has something to do with the twins. Maybe, just maybe, they ain’t quite done with his worthless hide. Jimmy, there’s something going on here me and you ain’t seeing. That much I *know* for sure.”

His face flushed with newfound color, Jimmy rubbed his hands together excitingly.

“I get the same vibe. I’m also picking up a separate frequency that’s telling me that you and I have a vital part to play before this little tragedy ends.”

“You and me both, Jimbo,” Private Kemp replied, her expression no longer dull and subjugated as she scanned the smoking rubble piled between them and what remained of the mess hall building.

“What’s say we stretch our legs a bit?”

Nodding agreeably, Jimmy didn’t even have to

ask the destination.

"I saw the chapel sign in the admin building's lobby. Probably a small conference room in the rear, if it wasn't totally demolished already."

"Rest assured, *Brother* Rollins, we'll find what we need," she said in a playfully stern tone as they began to exit the ravaged structure, resembling battered survivors roaming an apocalyptic wasteland.

***

Once, when she had been a rather sickly child of five, Kara had fallen from the top row of rod iron monkey bars while on the preschool playground. Her left thigh had scraped a jagged section of rusty metal on the four-foot fall to the hard dirt surface, ripping a frighteningly deep eight-inch-long gash in her leg which had required stitches, the scar of which was still present over two decades later.

Until the broken arm she had suffered (and seen magically healed sometime later) earlier in the evening during the Warden/Thing's rampaging departure from the admin building, she had always considered that childhood playground injury the worst physical pain she had ever endured.

That particular memory would forever be defined in astonishingly different terms if discussed within the contents of her future life, possibly utilizing such phrases as 'hardly a scratch' or 'an insignificant scrape.' It was a flea-sized blood-blister in comparison to the internal and external agony she now classified as such. Every bone, every muscle, every single *vein* within her possession pulsated and pounded as if individually assaulted.

Kara wanted to scream, to stretch her jaws to the breaking point and release a piercing howl that would serve as a fitting testimony to her immeasurable grief. Such measures of primal relief were not to be, as even the muscles of her face were haplessly paralyzed beneath the unyielding grasp of unbridled agony.

The shadows had come to life around her, encasing her within their grisly, spidery web before she could even attempt a counter assault.

Each form floated about her frozen form like gliding Stingrays, their nylon-textured web flowing freely like sewing thread from a spool, each line proceeded by a tiny, hooked end that punctured Kara's skin and held there as a means of leverage.

Her legs were pinned as one, the anklebones grinding together as the webbing continued to tighten. She felt the air forced from her lungs, the building ache at her chest cavity as the pressure increased.

The murky waves continued to circle her like vultures hovering over a fresh kill, each line of netting melding with the last as the hellish cocoon grew thicker and higher.

The top-half was only inches from overlapping her shoulders and reaching her lower neck, the end result of which Kara refused to contemplate as her frantic struggles intensified.

Blurred images began to form within the shadowy flesh whirling near her head and face as she concentrated on stretching out her tightly bound fingers. Her clenched fists were pinned to her outside thighs, and Kara felt as if her entire body was nearing a living mummification mode that would translate to a torturously slow death unless she found a way to free her hands. She tried to ignore the swirling images that filled her vision, but closing her eyes did little to prevent their intrusion.

Faces emerged from the dark membranes, like the heads of mannequins mounted on a hunter's trophy wall. Kara knew each face from her past, although the majority of the names escaped her.

There was old Mr. Lumley, her second (third?) grade teacher who had frequently referred to her as 'young ms. Retardation' whenever she failed a test or could not answer a question in class, and who had seemed to revel in devilish glee on such occasions.

Her old teacher looked the same as she remembered, fat-cheeked and balding on top, his kind, toothy grin filled with dark, nasty secrets better left undiscovered.

Beside him was Mrs. Olanda Pole, who had babysat Kara and William several times when both were just short of their ninth birthdays, her bony, emasculated face nothing more than an ebony shaded skull. A rail thin, middle- aged black woman who spoke softly but had a notoriously short fuse, William had always referred to her as 'Bean Pole,' referring to her overly scrawny, pitifully unhealthy look. Kara had experienced many a nightmare on the nights following Mrs. Pole's visits to their home. Visions of being chased through a never-ending cornfield, the stalks of which reached high into the black sky above, an army of sprinting skeletons on her trail. An army led by the naked form of Mrs. Olanda Pole, whose eyes were pit-red, her spider-like arms reaching out for the back of Kara's best white dress. Mrs. Pole was never re-hired after the day she whipped the twins with a wooden switch, leaving bloody whip marks on the backs of their thighs, all for accidentally tossing a foam rubber ball onto the kitchen table.

Kara's mom had seriously considered legal action, but inside made it her mission to black ball the woman all over town as an 'unstable individual prone to physical acts of child abuse.' The last they had heard, Olanda Pole was forced to move away to find similar work elsewhere.

Thrashing her head from side to side, Kara hoped to somehow extract the woman's predatory expression from her mind.

Her fingers began to tingle, and a searing heat began to build like coal embers struck by a passing breeze.

Despite her continued attempts to shut out the visions by tightly clamping her eyelids, a new series of faces flashed brightly into place, like slides from a projector tray.

There was John McGinley, the glue-inhaling thug who had tried unsuccessfully to rape her in high school, his bloated cheeks and wide set eyes imitated perfectly, as if taken from the class yearbook.

Above him set the head of Marcy Brookens, a former co-worker of Kara's who had once confided that she was a lesbian, proclaiming her love for Kara over a sandwich and cup of coffee while they flipped through paperbacks in a local bookstore. Marcy's sad, dark eyes mirrored the look she had displayed upon Kara's rejection. The homely young woman, barely twenty years old, had committed suicide a few days later, swallowing a handful of pain pills and chasing them with pure grain alcohol. Kara had never forgiven herself for the girl's passing, despite knowing that her rejection had been nothing short of kind.

Marcy smiled at her weakly, revealing sharp-pointed teeth like that of a Piranha.

Upon opening her eyes as if electrically jolted, Kara watched the heads vanish as one, dropping from the shadows folds like handfuls of sand.

At the same time, she felt the initial strand of webbing wrap snugly around the base of her throat like copper wiring. Kara felt her hands react just as narrow beams of laser light shot from her eyes.

The dense webbing at her sides began to smolder and smoke before falling away in thick chunks at her ankles just as the shadows recoiled from the beams of light cutting into them like flames from an acetylene torch. Kara heard the hooked lead lines begin to snap and pop free like cut guitar strings. As her hands rose slowly from her sides, the webbing split neatly apart and fell away like separate sections of thick blanket.

A moment later, standing alone and facing the chambers lone pathway entrance, Kara shuddered at how dangerously close she had come to falling beneath the being's hallucinatory spell. Studying her arms and torso, not a single cut nor slash mark was evident from the hooks she had felt penetrate her flesh upon the shadow's assault.

The being had delved deep into her memory banks for the worst of the lot, creating a virtual Night Gallery of malevolent images in an attempt to lull her into a fatal trance.

She drew two conclusions from such an endeavor. Number one; the black heart she sought was *very* near. Number two; the being was more than likely out of offensive options. Her billowy red locks flowing freely about her face, Kara felt her power surge as if magically re-charged at the thought.

Kneeling to enter the cramped cavern, she silently prayed that such renewed confidence wasn't just another cleverly planted trap within the dismal caverns of a demon's core.

***

Plowing through the top layer of rubble with the hammer's tip leading the way, Wilbo began spitting out large brown chunks of matted clay, wiping the dirt and grime from his eyes with his free hand.

Landing on strained, weary legs, it took him a half-minute to get his bearings before he noticed the being's mammoth still form posed just outside the demolished main gate area.

He had taken only a few short steps forward, initially planning on allowing the hammer to again lift him airborne for a fresh assault, when the inspiration emerged like a lightning bolt from a clear, blue sky.

Placing his arms slackly by his side, he allowed the shield and hammer to fall from his open palms, as the ghoulish smile grew wider on his clay-stained face.

"Now why didn't I think of *him* before?" He

whispered huskily as his body painlessly expanded to meet the skyline.

"Always did like Giant-Man. Now I can stand eye to orb with the ugly som'bitch and duke it out with 'im, man to blob."

His thundering steps jarring the landscape like mini-quakes, Wilbo stepped up to and then around the frozen being, actually towering *over* the motionless form as he cocked back his massive right fist.

"*Now* give me some lip, one-eye. Let's see how bad you really are now that you're picking on someone your own damn size," Wilbo barked wildly.

***

Pulling the wooden-handled, silver-coated cross from the splintered rubble, Private Kemp turned to Jimmy and held it aloft like a ragged battlefield flag.

"Told ya we'd find it, Jimbo. What's meant to be is meant to be."

Stepping up next to her, Jimmy observed the foot-high symbol with dumbstruck awe.

"That's the ticket alright. I just wonder when and why, that's all."

Exiting the roofless building that held only a single standing wall amidst the surrounding wreckage, Private Kemp held the cross at her chest like a protective talisman.

"When faced with the ultimate evil, my man, you must counter with the ultimate good."

Jimmy followed close behind as they steadily

picked up the pace, the looming shadows of two giant figures standing just a few hundred feet in the distance.

***

Kara entered the space horizontally, the tip of her well-coifed head leading the way. By the time she found adequate room to stand vertically, the scene, which filled her shimmering sight caused an involuntary shriek to vault from her tightly pursed lips.

The main target of her assault lay spread before her, hissing like a startled nest of rattlers. It was the color of freshly poured tar, round vessels as thick as a man's waist engulfed its bulbous core from all sides, like the hardened roots of an ancient sequoia. The organ itself was pear-shaped, its tip no larger than a human finger, while the base was as thick as a hippopotamus' backside. Scales as large as half-dollars coated every section of its pulsating skin, and a lengthy, vulva-shaped opening was present at the organ's center.

Kara took a cautious step forward, and the organ's palpitations instantly intensified. Kara was tempted to cover her ears from the thundering onslaught that followed, a savage, pounding barrage that made her think of being trapped inside a tin can during a raging thunderstorm.

Ensuring the force field around her body was set at full protective mode, she took another half step forward and then lurched back as the vulva-gash flayed opened in a grisly vertical smile.

The milky goo it spat forth coated the field in a

fine mist, then dribbled away harmlessly as Kara moved forward.

She looked down and observed the liquid eating through the being's own entrails like concentrated acid, hundreds of tiny puncture wounds opening up and almost instantaneously closing up again.

Kara halted once she got to within touching distance of the throbbing organ, its connected arteries bloating to the point of eruption as she leaned forward with one outstretched hand.

"To all things, both pure and unnaturally impure, …comes an ending," she said aloud without realizing it, her fingers suddenly balling into a gnarled fist and punching forward in a viscous blurred streak of light.

***

It began as a low moan, the origin of which Wilbo was unable to pinpoint until the pitch increased and the tone mutated into something undoubtedly distinctive and altogether alien to the limits of human hearing.

Within seconds, a shrieking akin to a million wailing Klaxon horns filled the night air in blaring waves.

Instinctively covering his face with his colossal hands, Wilbo stumbled back; accidentally ripping away another forty feet of compound fencing in the process, the razor-wire slashing yard long scrapes onto his enormous calves.

Just a few hundred feet to his south, Private Kemp dropped the cross and covered her ears with both hands, falling instantly to her knees. Jimmy joined her in a similar pose, rolling onto his side with his mouth agape, screaming in silent agony at the rolling wave of reverberating thunder assaulting them.

***

Three miles to their west, several police cruisers skidded to a halt almost in perfect unison, miraculously avoiding colliding with one another as windshields shattered and windows exploded as if struck by falling meteors.

Thirteen miles to the east of the compound, several residents of Morgantown, Mississippi reported noticing a shrill humming sound, followed by shattered windows within their homes, complete loss of TV and radio reception, and bizarre behavior from the family pets.

Kara twisted her neck as far to the right as her muscles and tendons would allow, her arms buried elbow-deep in the moist quagmire of the being's life source. Her closed fists had penetrated a space just above the vulva shaped orifice, which continued to spit forth glutinous streams of creamy gunk onto the force field protecting Kara's legs and feet. The sharp-edged scales coating the organ broke away like an Armadillo's armor beneath her ferocious assault, revealing a soft underbelly that held the texture of undercooked tofu.

The blazing heat her hands generated acted as twin lasers upon contact, easily piercing the organ's outer layers. Kara uncurled her fingers once submerged past the wrists, and instantly began tearing and ripping at the core like a frantic archaeologist digging around the edges of a great find. Before the immense heat melted them away, she could feel the fat, circular arteries within her grasp. They were smooth and slick, with an exterior as tough as a triple- treaded tracker tire.

What could have been veins, but felt to Kara like strands of coiled fishing line, snapped noisily away from the arteries at the slightest touch of her fingers.

Once she heard the beast wailing in obvious anguish, Kara no longer avoided visual contact with the carnage being inflicted by her own hands. Facing forward, she discovered her entire being now floating entirely within the mangled core. The luminescent glow around her body lit up the misty haziness around her, allowing an intimate view of the inner workings of a demon's nucleus. A single crimson-shaded lode faced her amidst the ripped tissue and severed veins. It was as wide as her waist and spread from her feet into an enormous pod that loomed overhead.

The throbbing, goo-coated stratum seemed to inhale as she glided forward, as if aware of her intentions.

Kara stood posed, resembling a boxer sizing up a formidable opponent. Just as she crossed her arms over in a 'V' shape with the palms facing in towards her, the sagging pod split open in the center as if slashed, dumping its contents as if stricken by a severe case of projectile diarrhea. Kara could easily identify body parts, both human and animal, within the blackish muck piling up around her protective aura. Ignoring the seemingly never-ending onslaught of gore, she concentrated every ounce of freshly regenerated power into the tips of her fingers, which began to tremor and spasm from the effects of electrical overload. Kara's arms felt strangely lighter as her hands grew overwhelmingly heavy. With only her neck and head uncovered by the grisly pile of skeletal remains spat upon her by the pod, which hung like a loose tent blowing in a stiff breeze, Kara threw her head back and moaned in orgasmic ecstasy. The vein seemed to deflate as if inhaling a final, desperate breath.

The rays of blue flame shot from Kara's hands in circular sonic waves, instantly transforming the entire core into a volcanic inferno.

***

Wilbo lay prone on his stomach with his hands over his ears, his upper body draped in wired fencing. He had been unable to maintain his Goliath height due to the being's shrill squealing, shrinking back to original size to find himself pinned down by the same coiled metal he had so effortlessly trampled over just moments before.

He looked up from between layers of fencing just in time to see the being's body unhinge, it's midsection blown apart in a rush of red and blue flame.

***

While Private Kemp had kept her head planted in the loose soil of the yard, Jimmy had also witnessed the annihilation, leaning on his elbows with fingers planted in both ears.

"Mercy…" he had managed to mumble with childish awe.

In many ways, it reminded Wilbo of the morning of nine-eleven, two thousand one, when he awoke to the news of the terrorist attacks and first viewed the collapse of the twin towers.

The being's upper body past the mid-way point tilted back severely and began to descend, the stalk-neck and head swaying back and forth, no longer able to navigate a proper course of direction.

The skin of its belly that hadn't already been blasted or burned through ripped free like wet tissue paper as the upper half toppled over like an ancient pine.

As it landed with a thunderous thud, the stalk-neck snapping loudly and then lolling over, the surrounding grounds quaked one final time in a series of shuddering tremors, followed by a single aftershock which paled in comparison with those experienced earlier that evening.

The bottom half stood erect on the flat-bottomed, pillar-like legs, resembling a recently lit Olympic torch as multi-colored flames shot from its obliterated surface. The tubular ropes all swayed to one side and hung there, as if individually attempting to avoid the heat from above. Huddled together like twisted cable cord, the tip of the ropes hung suspended just a few inches from the low-cut grass.

Like a thousand outstretched fingers, they strained and stretched as one to make contact with the surface.

The being's head rolled about the grass and adjoining paved lot like a snake in search of a tunnel, its single eye glossy and glazed, like a beached fish on the verge of expiration.

It took Wilbo a full two minutes to wriggle and fight his way free of the wire, some of which had entangled his ankles in a complicated knot a veteran Boy Scout would have struggled to loosen.

By the time he wearily arose and took his first step towards the massacre, the being's head had ceased all movement, managing only a final spastic twitch before falling motionless.

He jogged forward, forced to trudge through the yellowish ooze that coated the surrounding grounds near the being's lower half.

"Kara…Kara? *KARA*!"

Nearing the detached top half, Wilbo frantically leaped over the top edge of the spear-hand, barely giving it a glance in his frenzied state.

Thick waves of white smoke poured from the being's severed upper half, forcing Wilbo back as he stared into the gaping abyss through tightly squinting eyes.

"Kara? Damn it..." he managed between coughs, waiving the smoke away from his face with both hands. His heartbeat thundered in his chest, feeling as though it might violently exit between the breastbone at any given moment, a breastbone he hadn't bothered to notice was now back to it's original, pre- compound entry size.

The billowing smoke began to subside just as the torso collapsed as if deflated, the scaly outer flesh growing visibly moist, like melting candle wax.

Again, Wilbo ran forward into the choking fumes, cupping his hands over his mouth while simultaneously pinching his nostrils shut.

"KARA! Can you…hear me? Kara…"

The being's upper portion began to rapidly liquefy, the skin first bubbling and subsequently dissolving into a molten mix that was almost instantly swallowed up by the earth beneath it.

Wilbo sprinted backwards from the flow of squalid slime that splashed at his feet, still screaming his sister's name in a haggard tone laced with panic.

He barely avoided backing into the lower half's hanging tubes, ducking hard to his left as one of them leapt at him like an uncoiled cobra and lightly brushed the back of his neck.

Less than thirty seconds later, the grounds fronting him held only the outline of where the being had crash-landed, the matted grass beneath completely evaporated and emitting a foggy mist where the top half had lain.

Wilbo stepped up and stood in the center of the grooved outline, his shoes sinking into the sticky, warm wetness almost to the anklebone.

The jolt of agony welling within his chest threatened to cut off his oxygen supply as his breathing grew increasingly labored. All his life, he had felt his twin's presence within him, no matter the distance between them. There was a true sense of security in such a physiological connection, one that only siblings of the same birth could ever comprehend. The connection between himself and Kara had been disconnected the moment that the being had met its fiery demise. Wilbo opened his mouth to roar as the building fury rose to the center of his throat and begged for release.

Before the first ragged note could be launched, the moist, softened ground to his left cracked and split apart as if giving birth.

***

Jimmy bent to assist Private Kemp, who winced in pain as she arose, waiving him off impatiently.

"Leave me…h-here for a minute, Jimbo. I... need to find my second...wind. Think I fractured a rib on that last f-fall. Feels like somebody's sticking me with an ice-pick every time I inhale."

His face beet-red, Jimmy left her balanced on one knee, gingerly cradling her right side just below the rib cage.

"Take five, Sandy," he replied, turning to scan the scene ahead, which was surrealistically tranquil in comparison to just moments before.

"Looks like the worst is over. I see one of the twins scouting the grounds. The big bad beastie got halved like a loaf of bread. I wonder how they managed to g..."

The cross was shoved in front of his face, causing him to cringe back a step.

"Take the damn cross, Jimmy. It ain't over yet. You know that as well as I do. You'll also know *when* to use it," she barked, her breathing harsh and inconsistent.

Grasping the handle at the bottom, Jimmy cradled the symbol like a brittle, ancient artifact.

"You…you're right. Stay right here and try to catch your breath. I'll be back for you regardless of what happens."

Private Kemp nodded, then quickly cocked her head to the right, rolling her eyes to the sky.

"You hear sirens, Jimbo?"

Pausing in mid-movement, Jimmy shook his head in mock disbelief and sighed deeply as the shrill whining noises in the near distance became more evident.

"Always there when you need 'em, huh?" Private Kemp stared gravely ahead.

"We really don't want to be here to try and *explain* all this, Jimbo, if you get my drift."

Breaking into a sprint, Jimmy's only reply was a muffled grunt.

She hit the nail squarely on the noggin there. Five minutes into the story, the Feds will break out a loaded syringe and call ahead for reservations at the nearest banana farm. Spending the rest of my born days sedated to the gills, forced to repeat the bizarre tale of the earth's impending doom involving correctional officer zombies, a compound full of missing inmates and mountain- sized demons from the earth's core is not in this boy's plans.

With the cross clutched snugly to his chest, Jimmy had reached the paved edge of the employee parking lot just as the ground had opened up like a blooming flower at Wilbo's feet.

***

Wilbo fell backwards, landing on his backside with his hands submerged to the wrists in the warm goop layering the being's final resting place.

The egg-shaped orb popped from the earth like a new-born hatchling, floating a few feet off the ground before vanishing in a single blink like a burned-out bulb, unceremoniously dumping its contents to the surface like an oversized bag of potatoes.

His face a mixed map of utter confusion and unparalleled joy, Wilbo jumped to his feet and sprawled forward, almost trampling his fallen sister in the process.

"Kara? A-are you…how do you…? How *did* you?" He babbled, pulling her frail frame to his.

The long-flowing red locks were gone, as were the glowing eyes and overly toned physique, leaving behind a pale, thin young woman teetering on the edge of total exhaustion.

"Not enough…gas in the t-tank for all those…questions, dear brother of mine. Let's just say…chalk one up for the g-good guys."

Wilbo kissed her gently on her sweat-coated forehead, then placed one arm beneath her knees and the other around her back. Lifting her airborne, Wilbo shuddered at how light his sister felt. Studying the skeletal outline of her face as he walked back towards the compound, he estimated her weight loss conservatively at eight to ten pounds; all since entering the Briarston compound a scant few hours earlier. He noticed that Kara's braces had not reappeared with the loss of her power, just as his eyesight hadn't reverted back to blurry status without his glasses once his physique had shrunken back to normal size. Gifts for a job well done, he quickly deduced, from a source occupying the highest plane imaginable.

He first heard the sirens just as he stepped onto the concrete parking lot. "Day late and a hundred grand short, as per usual," he moaned in disdain, looking directly at the lumbering form jogging towards him.

He didn't recognize the object tucked against Jimmy's chest until they were only a few dozen feet apart. Kneeling to give his wobbly legs a respite, Wilbo saw Jimmy's eyes grow wide as he sprinted up to and then by his crouched frame.

"Not over! *NOT OVER YET*!" Jimmy was screaming, pointing the cross straight ahead like an infantryman's rifle.

Wilbo whirled around and saw two things happening at once, either of which did little to sooth his shattered nerves.

The stilted legs of the being's lower half had sunk into the soft earth, allowing the suddenly spread out tubular tentacles to dip low enough to penetrate the surface.

Viewed from a distance, the smothering mass resembled a giant mushroom plant secured to the ground by hundreds of perfectly spaced tie-down straps.

The second, equally terrifying vision filling Wilbo's red-rimmed eyes was the shambling heap of inhumanity that had crawled to the surface from the center of where the top-half had disintegrated, just a few feet to the left from where Kara had previously resurfaced.

It wobbled forth on multiple sets of legs, some human and still others seemingly insect in origin, all of which were equally disproportionate and deformed, like some mutated centipede.

The head it displayed sat atop the squat, rotund torso without benefit of a neck, although Wilbo was too far away to identify any specific facial features.

Wilbo carefully laid Kara on a relatively soft pile of loose soil that had been relocated onto the parking pavement, then stood and studied her slumbering form before turning away.

"You've done all the man upstairs could have asked of you, sis. If you do happen to speak to him in the next few minutes, put in a good word for me, hear? We're definitely gonna need it."

Dashing forward, his knees popping like M-80's, Wilbo observed Jimmy near the tubes, all of which wriggled like a nest of partially submerged snakes. The upper portion of each narrow cylinder, nearest to the being's scorched skin, was obscenely bloated, and neither Jimmy nor Wilbo needed a scientific explanation of what was coming down the pike.

The roots were prepping to dump their poisonous load, a task they obviously required no living host to assist in completing.

Wilbo caught up to Jimmy just moments after he had slid to a halt, barely avoiding tripping into the first row of pulsating cylinders.

"Stay the hell away from those, man! Back up!" Wilbo yelled, gripping Jimmy's shoulders and pulling him back a step.

"You know what they are! We can't just stand here and let them spew that toxic soup of theirs into the soil!" Jimmy replied angrily, easily breaking Wilbo's grip with a violent shrug.

"Eyes *right,* man!" Wilbo screamed, whirling Jimmy around in frustration as the shuffling horror closed in from their immediate right. He prayed for the magical powers of earlier to return to his severely weakened frame, fearing his weary knees might buckle beneath him any moment.

"Hiya, Chuckles. How hangs it?" The thing croaked; its horrid features fully bathed in the dim light reverberating from the compound's remaining lights.

Wilbo's arms went limp at his sides, his mouth hanging open like a panting hound.

"Warden? Is…that *you* in... there?"

Instinctively, Jimmy held the cross out in front of his face in a blocking stance, as if warding off an impending vampire attack.

"Well, it ain't Uncle Bubba Clinton. In need of some spiritual advice, my sons?" The Warden/Thing hissed from lips that resembled thick black slugs, one of which hung loosely on his chalky-pale chin. The face he possessed was a grisly montage of several recent victims.

It held Major David Peterson's stone-blue eyes, the prominent nose that once belonged to CO Jerrod Dickenson, and the oily scalp and overly long, pimple-riddled forehead of one Buck Lomax the Third.

"W-what the? Stay a-away, dammit… or I... we'll…" Jimmy babbled, the cross shaking uncontrollably within his sweaty grasp.

"Do what, pal? Pound that cheaply painted piece of carved elm into my chest 'til I die? I ain't Count Dracula and you sure as hell don't qualify as Victor Van Helsing. You two listen up and listen good..."

Behind them, a sound not unlike rushing creek waters ensued, generating an equal portion of both chills and instantly formed gray hair for both Jimmy and Wilbo as they both reeled around to check the source.

The tubes were depositing their loads in unison, resembling probing insect antenna, the infrequent sucking sounds rapidly intensifying to a deafening volume.

Jimmy and Wilbo each held a similar expression of disgust before the ringing echoes of the Warden/Thing's roars refocused their shell-shocked attention.

"Over here, gents. You might wanna hear this, unless you want to end up looking like me and feeling a hell of a lot worse."

***

Private Kemp attempted to rise and fell back into a shaky crouch, realizing for certain that something inside her wasn't just severely strained, but badly shattered.

She observed the two men and the freakish beast that addressed them, although she couldn't make out the words being spoken due to the resounding clamor of rushing waters overlapping them.

She understood the scenario as it was displayed to her like a stage drama with an audience of one left behind to critique it.

Liquid seeds of plague were being injected in a final attempt at some measure of retribution by an ancient evil already expired.

Two mortal men stood in its way, only one of which held the secret to preventing the faithful planting from inflicting irreparable damage to all mankind. She also knew the identity of the creature performing the impromptu 'sermon on the mount' as precious time slowly, painstakingly slipped away.

She tried to holler out, to share the vital information that had been mystically implanted, but discovered that without a healthy set of lungs to initiate such a process, one's vocal cords could be easily relegated to mute status.

Falling back with her legs pinned underneath her, Private Sandra Kemp could do little else but groan in utter dismay.

She couldn't help but dwell on the possibility that the gods of fickle fate had already deemed her nothing more than a hapless spectator to the eventual outcome.

The stark fear that accompanied such a grim possibility helped raise the question of why such a decision had been preordained, and exactly what, if *anything,* did it mean in terms of the future ahead.

***

"The crop is in the ground, men, as you can plainly see. Not the choice spot old Gor was hoping for, no doubt, but better than nothing, regardless. Despite your sister's valiant efforts, William, plan B has been set into motion. The wad of doom has been shot, so to speak," the Warden/Thing announced, the single peg arm he possessed at the center of his plump, tick-like body gesturing frantically.

"Admittedly, I'm one tough SOB to terminate, kind of like a queen roach, but mankind as a whole is gonna have its world rocked to the roots, forgive the pun, unless one of you wises up in the next minute or so. That is, before the plague juice hits a main vein and tunnels it's way to the nearest medium-sized city."

Wobbling forward like some futuristic bug from an H.G. Wells novel, the Warden/Thing's mini-hand pointed towards the hanging tubes.

"I'm not equipped to spell it out for you, as Gor has seen fit to wipe clean the portion of my mind that held such information. I can only provide…moral support. What I do know is, whatever action is to be taken…you've got less than a minute to initiate.

Remember, gents, to properly wipe out a plague, you've got to sever the roots."

Jimmy and Wilbo traded confused, exasperated glances, then looked back to the Warden/Thing like stage actors awaiting their cues.

"Damn it to hell, Jimmy, what are you holding in those over-fed mitts of yours? Figure it out, man, it ain't exactly brain surgery, you just have to have faith. If the faith wanes, the rot's gonna spread like a wildfire in a vast field of dry grass," The Warden/Thing croaked, clumsily stumbling forward and past the two men.

"Faith? What faith? Faith *Hill? Faith* in God and Country? Man, I'm sick of your damn riddles. Just for a welcome change of pace, how about saying what you mean?" Wilbo growled, clutching the sides of his head as if experiencing a horrific migraine.

The Warden/Thing lurched back as one of its hind legs snapped in half like splintered kindling. For a brief moment while regaining its shaky balance, it focused on the cowering form of Private Kemp a few hundred feet to their east, its eyes narrowing suspiciously.

"I can't explain what I don't know, William. I'm as much in the dark as you two. Concentrate and it will come to you."

His eyes widening in sudden realization, Jimmy held the cross out from his chest and seemed to intensely study its very construction.

Another of the Warden/Thing's back legs collapsed with a loud crack, sending the disproportionate body tilting backwards in a bundled roll.

"Awww, shiiittt..." it spat in droll disbelief as all balance was haplessly lost. William reached ahead tentatively in a feeble attempt to grab the Warden/Thing's midget-sized hand, but pulled back in lieu of being jerked forward by the weighty torso.

The Warden/Thing landed on its beach ball shaped backside, the back of its head lightly brushing against one of the sunken tubes.

William started forward as if to assist, but was quickly cut off as Jimmy blocked his path.

"William, I... *know*."

"Know what? Get outta my way, will ya? Old pumpkin head needs a hand or two..."

Lifting the cross until it was eye-level to Wilbo, Jimmy's tone was uncharacteristically stern.

"Leave it. It's served its purpose here. I need your help, William. We have to work together on this. I can't do it alone."

Reaching up to grasp the cross's narrow top edge, Wilbo started to vehemently protest, his lips curled in anger.

He began to blink rapidly while focusing on the cross, gingerly caressing it's sharply honed edges as if he were checking the sharpness of a blade.

Exhaling as if he had just completed a ten-K sprint, Wilbo reached over and firmly patted Jimmy on the right shoulder.

"I'm with you, man. Let's do this before the feeling fades away."

Both men walked briskly to the left, keeping a close vigil on the forest of tubes to their right as they trailed around it, leaving the Warden/Thing to wriggle and squirm on the ground like an overturned tick.

"That's it, men! Go for it! *Do the deed*! Perform the coup de grace! Bury this ugly sucker once and for all! *GO GO GO!!!"* The Warden/Thing barked cheerily, struggling mightily to roll to its side just before one of the tubes tore free from the earth, rearing back like a striking viper. It attached itself to the tip of the Warden/Thing's scalp like a vacuum hose to thick, shag carpet.

"Damn…here we go agaaaaaiiiinnnnnnnnnn…." it screeched as its skull's contents were sucked dry, the face imploding like a punctured balloon. Within seconds, the entire torso collapsed in a similarly grisly fashion, subsequently drawn into the tube-like chunky soup through a straw. After completing its erstwhile feeding, the hollow-ended probe replanted itself within the same tunnel it had earlier occupied.

***

Private Kemp watched Jimmy and William jog around the left side of the being's remains, keeping a safe distance between themselves and the obviously ravenous tubes, one of which had just made liquid puree out of the latest incarnation of the Warden. The sirens were growing clearer, less garbled. She deduced they were within four or five miles of the compound, at the very least.

Leaning forward on her bruised and battered kneecaps, she limited her breathing to tight, short inhalations and equally cautious exhales. Turning to take inventory of what little remained standing inside the torn perimeter fencing of Briarston Correctional facility, she nodded nervously while whispering through lips chalked with dried spittle.

"You're the *man* now, Jimbo. Do that voodoo that you do so well."

As the two men vanished from her line of sight, blocked by the being's remaining bulk, she felt a nauseating twinge within her gut.

Faded whispers filled her senses from the compound's trampled, still grounds, murmuring mostly incoherent, incomplete sentences that hardly qualified as gibberish. Private Kemp refused to turn around or in any way acknowledge their presence. She had never been a believer of such phenomenon. Never bought into the idea of tortured spirits, furry creatures with outsized feet roaming mountainsides or alien crafts kidnapping farmers for fun and profit. Despite the outlandish, surreal side-show she had witnessed within its perimeter, her ransacked mind steadfastly refused to buy into the hypnotic chant of Briarston's ghostly choir singing at her back.

Her focus unwavering, the jumbled voices

eventually, mercifully, began to fade away like a foggy mist within the morning sun's blaring rays.

***

Jimmy skidded to a stop in mid-stride, causing Wilbo to jump around him to avoid climbing his back.

They stood at least thirty yards to the east of where the being had taken root, just to the left of a fairly deep drainage ditch that trailed off into the nearby woods, not far from the exact spot where the militia had exited from earlier that evening.

"This far enough?"

Jimmy bent down and placed the palm of his right hand atop the grass nearest the ditch.

"Might as well be marked with a big old 'X', my friend. You ready?"

"Ready and ever-steady, Freddie. After what I've seen tonight, I could preach a yearlong tent revival without taking a single pee break. Go ahead and do the honors."

Jimmy shoved the broken, jagged lower end of the cross into the soft grass until it stood up like a grave marker, then quickly got to his feet and backed away, gesturing for Wilbo to step forward to complete the ritual.

Balancing his shoes on either side of the cross, Wilbo used his body weight to submerge it ever deeper, until the base of the cross was just inches from the ground.

Both men fell to their knees and secured handholds onto the cross before peering into the sky in silent meditation, their eyes clinched tightly shut.

The night seemed to stick in pause mode, the stiff breeze that had blown so steadily all evening shut off like a fan with its plug pulled, the only sound the constant blaring of sirens from the nearby hills.

Jimmy and Wilbo sat motionless, their heads cocked to the sky as their knuckles turned a light shade of blue from the constant pressure being applied to the wooden symbol they leaned upon.

The flash of white that blanketed the landscape a moment later was all consuming, like the flash from a camera bulb the size of Texas.

Pencil thin trails of ivory light shot from the buried portion of the cross, traveling in a perfectly horizontal line towards the tube-stalks, then split into a dozen similar tracks as it drew to within a dozen yards of them. The veins of light scattered into every direction, even crisscrossing one another at several intervals, meticulously working their way towards the tubes like swirling waves of penicillin coursing through a grassy bloodstream that would eventually lead to the main core of infection.

Jimmy gritted his teeth as if receiving a mild shock from his grip on the cross, which shone like a lighthouse beacon from between his spread fingers.

"I know it's a temptation, but don't open your eyes. It'll blind you instantly." Wilbo turned his head in Jimmy's direction, his broad smile a bit gruesome within the luminous glow.

"I was about to tell you the same thing, my man. How much longer, do you think?"

"We'll *know* when to let go, I think."

***

From where she lay flat on her back, her hands tucked over her eyes like twin blindfolds, Private Kemp fought the urge to scream aloud. The engulfing wave of light had thrown her back, landing with her left arm pinned against her already throbbing rig cage.

Despite the cover her hands provided, her sheltered pupils were still bathed in the light that had assaulted them.

The sickening vibes within her midsection had yet to subside, and her legs had begun to tremor as if on the verge of paralysis.

She was beginning to seriously ponder the notion that possibly Lomax, Ezop, Mac and all the others *had* been the lucky ones, after all.

Just then, a final torch ignited, one that seemed to burn like a candle lit from both ends, the cornucopia of blue, orange, and green colors within its weaving flame piercing the flesh of her hands and eyelids like an X-ray's beams.

***

Once the rotted veins of plague had been significantly purged, the spider- web trails of ivory light again congregated as one and enveloped both the tubes and their master's lower half in a massive surge; swallowing all in its path in a mountain of insatiable flame.

The tubes burned like torched linguine, then fell away in thick strips of black ash. The being's remains melted away amidst the blue and green flames, settling into a lofty pile of leafy cinders that was strangely smokeless.

Just as quickly as it had emerged, the prevailing light vanished, leaving the prevailing darkness to settle back onto the surrounding terrain.

Jimmy inhaled deeply, then slowly opened his eyes like a man testing his sight after laser vision surgery.

As he scanned the minute carnage left in wake of such traumatic turmoil, Wilbo followed his lead, both releasing the cross at almost the exact same time.

"Is that all that's left? A tall pile of soot, some scattered ashes, and the crater it dug on the way out?" He asked sardonically, failing to conceal the excitement in his tone.

"Afraid so, William. The light must have followed the root's drainage course, performed a little 'Roto-Rooter' service, cleaning up the mess, then wiped out the source," Jimmy replied as they both stood up and surveyed the scene as a whole, then looked to the cross a final time.

"We had just enough faith as a team to pull it off, pal. The man upstairs knows a winning team when he fields it."

Jimmy beamed, reaching down to tap the plain wooden symbol like a man petting the family dog.

"No arguments there, William. No doubt we were all placed in the woods surrounding these damned grounds for a reason. You and your twin were the key elements. The rest of us were supporting cast, at best."

Cocking his head to the side but still staring at the charred remnants ahead of them, Wilbo frowned deeply as the siren's irritating drone seemed to be closing in around the compound.

"Let's grab Kara and your militia pal and vamoose, Jimmy. They're libel to toss us in the nearest padded cell just for general purposes, much less buy a minute of our story. Hell, would you?"

Jogging back towards the compound, no other words were necessary.

A line of headlights two across and twenty-five deep neared what had been the entrance to Briarston just under seven minutes later, the sound of squealing brakes gradually replacing those of shrieking sirens.

Carrying his sister on his back in a piggyback style, Wilbo shot Jimmy a playful wink.

"Meet you back at town at dawn's early light, man. The ham and eggs are on me."

Huffing wildly while attempting to get a better grip beneath Private Kemp's shoulders, Jimmy paused in front of a recently fallen elm. The group was only a few dozen yards from the edge of the perimeter road leading to Briarston, having missed the stunned authorities arrival by less than a minute as they had ducked into the nearby woods.

"You got it. Remember, when they search the woods and find your camp, you heard loud noises and smelled some funky scents, but that's *all.* We stick to the story, right?"

Wilbo grinned, his eyes drooping like a man who had gone weeks without benefit of either sleep or sufficient nourishment.

"Damn tootin', my man. Nothing but name, rank and serial number from this boy. They'll be looking for the inmates, won't they?"

Scanning the pitch-black forest for the correct

path back to his campsite, Jimmy glanced down at the slumbering Private in his arms and then back up to Wilbo with a harried expression.

"Oh yeah. They'll scour these woods like blue tick hounds on the scent of a bleeding raccoon. I still think the worst thing we could do is attempt to vacate the area while it's still hot. Make us look damned suspicious."

Wilbo re-positioned his own sleeping passenger atop his back, then nodded agreeably.

"No doubt. So we meet at the diner at first light?"

"Biscuits and gravy, plus a heaping helping of aspirin. I'm hoping Sandy has a civilian set of clothes to change into. If not, I'll have to leave her at a drop- off point somewhere along the way. Can't have those militia colors showing in these parts...not now."

"What if you don't show? What if *we* don't?" Wilbo asked before slowly stepping towards a beaten down path a few feet to their right.

Heading towards a similar path in a westerly direction, Jimmy paused thoughtfully.

"Grab your sausage biscuit to go and get out of town as fast as you possibly can without raising eyebrows."

"Should we even meet at all? At least in this town?"

"We have to be...*certain* that things are at least back to semi-normal within the city limits, William. Not a choice really, but a command from a higher source, I think. You feel the same, right?"

Wilbo sighed heavily, sounding and resembling a man at least twenty years his senior.

"Yeah, I do. Just wanted to make sure you were on the same psychic wavelength. But…*how* will we know if things are hunky-dory in Red Bridge or not, Jimmy? How will we know if things are any different at all, and if they're still rotten, what exactly are we four to do about it?"

Before shambling off with an unsteady gait, Jimmy smiled at a young man he had just recently made the acquaintance of, but felt as though he had known since birth.

"We'll *know*, William. The man above will surely give us a sign in either case."

Lumbering off in another direction, Wilbo couldn't help but inject a final blurb, one meant to be humorous, but instead conjured up a sense of foreboding that neither man could shake for the rest of the short night ahead.

"Oh, I'm sure he will. I just hope it *ain't* in the form of a pissed off devil worm roughly the size of Delaware."

***

The remaining four-plus hours of darkness spilled by in a mercifully silent blur for the four survivors of what would become internationally known as the *Briarston Incident,* only the slightest hint of sourness drifting through the air left as evidence of something being dreadfully amiss within the adjacent vicinity.

***

Her head throbbing relentlessly, former militia

Private and future civilian Sandra Kemp slid into the padded booth next to Jimmy and flashed a forced, pained smile at the two people sitting across from them.

She hardly recognized the two haggard looking individuals, only vaguely recalling them in their earlier, bulked up incarnations. The young male smiled at her kindly as he sipped steaming black coffee from a Styrofoam cup. The female, her hair matted to her head as if coated with congealed grease, fully concentrated on the plate of runny eggs sitting before her. Sandy thought the girl looked seriously ill, and possibly on the verge of heaving her cookies at any moment.

Jimmy reached over and shook the male twin's hand vigorously, neither speaking but both obviously aware of the exclusive kinship present within the cramped booth.

The two men made small talk while each took turns carefully scanning the semi-filled booths and solid oak counter that made up "Harry's Burger's and Fixings."

Whatever served as the 'morning rush' in Red Bridge had mostly filed out already as the large 'Coca-Cola' clock on a far wall read eight-ten AM. Only three of the eight available booths were presently occupied by separate couples, plus three older, possibly long-since retired, gray-haired men sitting at the counter, each nursing cups of freshly poured Java.

The balding, beer-bellied man who greeted them a moment later with pad in hand did so with cheery indifference, displaying a brief smile that was less than sincere.

Sandra ordered black coffee and a Danish roll, while Jimmy ordered the full breakfast special, to include eggs, pancakes, and hash browns.

The man strolled away with a grunt and a nod, eyeballing the older men at the counter as he entered the kitchen area. The frail, gaunt-faced men subsequently turned and stared at the newest arrivals with a look of unnerving suspicion, one normally associated with strangers passing through small, rural towns.

They both turned away just as Sandra leaned over to whisper in Jimmy's ear concerning her growing feelings of unease, prompting her to instead remain silent.

She watched Kara fork the soggy plate of eggs without actually putting any near her mouth, and found her own initial hunger wane.

Jimmy and Wilbo continued to trade small talk, most of which Sandy instantly recognized as nothing more than an elaborate front.

She didn't know about her cohorts, but the gnawing fear of something being terribly wrong within the confines of the small establishment refused to fade from her gut.

Tapping her fingers atop the table nervously, she was bordering on interrupting the two men's rambling bull session when she noticed the eatery's balding waiter (cook? owner?) emerge from the kitchen with a small tray filled with steaming cups and saucers.

As the chubby man reached around to place her coffee and Danish onto the table in front of her, Sandra's nostrils were suddenly filled with a sharp, sour odor. It wasn't exactly BO, nor did it seem associated with the food being served. She was still mulling over the somehow familiar smell while observing the man place Jimmy's dishes next to her own. The man's fingernails were a dark shade of purple, the fingers themselves coated in a yellowish ooze that stuck to the plates and saucers, leaving behind a gooey residue in the shape of his prints. Jimmy seemed oblivious while concentrating on the food itself, while Wilbo's attention was focused on the two elderly gentlemen at the counter.

Elbowing Jimmy gently in the side, Sandy looked up at the waiter and felt her breath cut off as if she had been physically struck in the pit of her stomach.

The bald man's smile was laced with malice, but displayed not a single tooth. His gums were colored the same shade of purplish/yellow as his fingers, and oozed a gluey textured liquid that seeped onto his chin in stringy, narrow trails.

As the man stood there, the rubbery ooze literally dripping from his chin onto Jimmy's hash browns, Sandy kicked forward with her right foot in a desperate attempt to awaken the half-snoozing Kara to what was transpiring.

Jimmy began to casually shovel down heaping spoonfuls of egg and sausage, somehow ignoring the elbow smacking forcefully against his rib cage.

Feeling the presence of probing eyes all around her but unable to speak or even grunt aloud, Sandy reached down and scooped up the still warm Danish roll, then proceeded to toss it across the table. It landed with a soft, hardly audible plop just below Wilbo's right breast shirt pocket. He looked down at his icing stained shirt in comic dismay, then up at

Sandy with the same unbelieving expression.

Feeling as though a large block of ice was hung at the base of her throat, Sandy leaped up from the booth and eyed the eatery's front glass door. It wasn't until then that she noticed her own stark nakedness. Her belly was grotesquely bloated, leaving only the tips of her toes visible as she glared down in utter shock.

When her head again arose, Sandy felt her face grow instantly flushed, as if a potentially fatal heat stroke was only moments away.

The bald man's head had split open like a ripe melon struck with a machete blade, a tubular spike protruding from where his mouth had once been. The man's puffy midsection hung on the edge of the table as he leaned forward and injected the sharp end of the spike into Jimmy's forehead, blowing out the back of his head in a wide spray of scalp-bone and brain tissue.

The two elderly men held Kara down on the tile floor, each of them taking turns stabbing her in the chest and abdomen with the large metal forks they held. Although her eyes remained open, Sandy could tell Kara was long past seeing or feeling what was happening to her.

Three other people, a middle-aged couple and a younger man wearing a faded "Ole Miss Rebels" ballcap, had pulled Wilbo from his seat and had thrown him atop the counter, the couple holding his hands and feet down while the younger man straddled his chest.

Sandy saw the younger man's chest open up like a blooming flower petal, the rib cage spreading wide with a loud crunching sound as shards of clothing flew away like discarded confetti.

Just before an intense throbbing pain forced her to stare down at her own mutated abdomen, Sandy observed something crawl from the man's chest cavity as if emerging from a dark, dank cave. The crimson-coated form fell upon Wilbo's jerking, wriggling body like a starving lioness upon a downed Wildebeest, ripping away large portions of flesh from his neck and jaw line in a flurry of fierce, tearing bites. The assailant's head rose just high enough for Sandy to recognize before painful contractions forced her attention elsewhere.

The blood-sopped face had once belonged to a friend of hers. A friend, occasional drinking buddy and subsequent lover named Ron McIntosh.

Falling to her knees, her insides feeling as if someone were churning them with a blender, Sandy cradled her swollen belly and released a silent cry of pure agony.

As if watching from a high distance, she saw the skin of her belly stretch and tear, the strangely bloodless wound opening just far enough for the human head to pop through. Despite the thick rolls of intestine covering the majority of its skull and forehead, Sandy had little difficulty recognizing her new-born's face. She rediscovered the ability to scream just as Major David Peterson's lips parted to address his motherly host.

"I'm coming for...you, Private. It won't be…long…now…"

***

Jimmy wrapped his arms around her sweat-soaked shoulders and shook her awake just as her screams reached a piercing crescendo.

"A dream, honey. Let it go…it's just a dream," he whispered in her ear, hugging her shaking form next to his own.

As was usually the case, it took her a full five minutes of tender consoling from her husband to sufficiently calm her down. Sandy left Jimmy to slumber as she departed their bedroom for the kitchen. As was the ritual when the dreams came, normally at least a monthly occurrence, but of late more often or not weekly, she sat at the kitchen table and dwelled on the grisly specifics while her tea slowly brewed on the nearby stove.

It had been over three years since the Briarston incident, but instead of fading into the past where it so acutely belonged, the images of that nightmarish evening seemed to be gaining unwarranted clarity, adding new, increasingly ghoulish chapters in the battle for Sandra Kemp's sanity.

Minutes later, while stirring honey into her steaming cup, Sandra pondered a viable solution for at least the millionth time within the past thirty-eight months. She had considered psychotherapy, but both her and Jimmy feared the possible repercussions if such a common treatment method as hypnosis was used. They understood and accepted without question the fact that certain secrets had no choice but be tucked away inside their coffins on the day of eternal passing, despite the inner turmoil that grew within them like a cancerous growth from carrying such a burden.

Their son William, age two and a half, and infant daughter, Kara, barely six months of age, would never know the true site of their parents first meeting. Jimmy and Sandra would always maintain it was while on a Disney Cruise for singles. They couldn't bear the thought of their own children thinking them insane if the truth was unveiled. Over time, Sandra had even tried convincing herself that such a bizarre night had never transpired, the annual Christmas card received from William or the occasional letter from Kara instantly blowing that particular ruse sky high.

She couldn't help but smile whenever she thought of the twins, even now, with the storm clouds building on the distant horizon in foreboding hordes.

William was married and living in Little Rock, heading his own construction company. Kara had wed just a few months earlier and had given birth to a baby daughter just a week before. She ran a prosperous catering business from her home in Mobile.

Jimmy referred to them as *'The Marvel Twins'*, referring of course to the popular comic book company. In the infrequent phone calls he made to William, she always called him 'Captain Thor' with only a hint of humor attached.

The Briarston complex had been the site of a yearlong investigation that revealed little of how over one hundred people (most of which were convicted felons) could literally vanish without a trace from a compound that looked to have been carpet-bombed. The tunnels that had riddled the landscape in and around the complex had, mysteriously, never been mentioned at by federal authorities or the news media, which had turned the sleepy burg of Red Bridge into a town overflowing with myth and legend within a matter of days following the event.

One theatrical and two TV films had been produced concerning the enigma that would forever remain unsolved, each able to do little more than speculate on what had actually transpired. Law enforcement officials waited impatiently for news involving one of the missing convicts to appear in hopes of gaining clues towards solving the ultimate mystery. Months passed in wake of the event, and it became painfully obvious that no such episode would be forthcoming.

Much like the construction techniques used to build the ancient pyramids or the whereabouts of the Loch Ness Monster, the facts concerning the Briarston Incident were destined to remain forever cloaked in obscurity.

***

The four survivors had indeed met in Harry's diner that next morning at nine AM sharp, having driven through countless roadblocks along the way, answering questions concerning what they had heard or seen the previous night and forced to show ID's in the process.

Sandra had worn her fatigue pants, all but the calves of which had been covered by a lengthy button up shirt that Jimmy had provided, and a pair of oversized Reebok tennis shoes in lieu of her combat boots.

Each had consumed a hearty breakfast, and downed two full pots of coffee between them, all the while gauging the local area for unsavory vibes. After an hour and a half spent within the diner and an additional two strolling about town like sightseeing tourists, it was decided there were none to be had.

They congregated at Wilbo's truck, shook hands and agreed to never speak of what they had seen or experienced.

Kara had hugged Sandy long and hard, although the words spoken between them were few.

They also agreed to keep in contact with one another in case of possible side effects from what they had been exposed to on the prison grounds.

Approximately seven hours after facing down an entity most of their species would never believe existed, much less have the courage to combat for the fate of the planet; four people casually departed the city limits of Red Bridge, Mississippi in opposite directions.

***

After splashing tap water into her empty teacup, Sandy returned to the bedroom and lay next to her astonishingly slim husband, who had dropped over eighty pounds in the last year alone, and close to one hundred since the day they had first met.

She dreamed of William and Kara, each donning comic book hero garb, to include black cowls and matching capes that hung to the backs of their ankles. William and Kara raised their hands to wave at Sandy, who seemed to be growing farther away from them as the dreamscape altered. The purple tint covering their fingers was only half as frightening as their dark, toothless grins.

EPILOGUE

April 13th, 2007

Feeling the need to pee only minutes after finishing her tea, Sandy tiptoed from the kitchen to the hallway bathroom, careful not to step too lively past the open door of her young son's room. She was doubtful he would stir even amidst the loudest of screams, but simply didn't want to chance it. Not now, when the time was drawing so near.

She urinated quickly and turned to view her own waste as it swirled within the bowl. It was even darker than the night before, when the first traces of crimson had become evident. Her chest suddenly burned with indigestion, and she fell to her knees and heaved violently. Large chunks of undigested food floated atop the swiftly rising water, along with thick wads of blackish tissue she figured to be portions of her stomach's inner lining.

Sandra stood wearily, sighed deeply after wiping her mouth, and walked back towards the spacious living room at the front of the house.

Picking up the phone as if entranced, she dialed the number from memory. It was a call she had hoped would never transpire, but one that had to be completed. After all, they had all *promised.*

After just a few moments of pause, she began to speak in an eerily mechanical yet completely rational tone.

"Kara?…Sandy. There's…no doubt now. Evidence is…much too strong. It must have…gestated in us all this time. Might be a different strain. There's always a chance it isn't contagious, but there's no doubt that it's part of our family's bloodlines.

Did…you? William's on his way there now? Is he bringing William Jr.? And his wife? G-good. Did William say his own symptoms were passing? Damn. None of us could be that lucky, I guess. Couldn't have just been a group head cold, you know? Kara sweetie, you know what you…what *we* must do. The men…are weak. They'd never accept…never allow…" she paused, breathing deeply and letting the tears run freely down her red, swollen cheeks.

"Make sure you make it as…painless as possible, and I'll do the… same."

The tears coated her face and ran down her neck in thick, ropy lines. "…good luck, Kara. I…love you guys. J-Jimmy does…Jimmy does too.

Yes…. Kara? We…did good, you know? In the grand scheme… we… we did damn *good.* The world owes us, Kara, a-although they'll never realize it. Yes… g-goodbye."

Sandra Kemp stood within the living room for another full minute, holding the silent phone aloft as she studied the Spanish-styled living room she and Jimmy had designed themselves only two years back. After a quick trip to the bathroom, where the sounds of rattling pills and splashed water quickly came and went, she paused to glare at her own haggard reflection in the toothpaste stained mirror which hung over the sink.

She then walked to the hall supply closet in a robotic shamble, reached inside and gently pulled a hard-plastic gas container from the tall boxes it had been stored behind, and strolled casually over to grasp a butane lighter from the oak mantel above the fireplace.

The tranquilizer she had laced her family's dinner with hours before had done the trick, as all slept peacefully within their respective rooms.

As she began to calmly pour a thick stream onto the kitchen floor, backing away as if laying a line of gunpowder, Sandra's blurred, shell-shocked thoughts turned to her husband. A husband who had begun mysteriously losing his teeth a few days earlier; just as Kara's daughter had begun to spit up yellowish, putrid smelling liquid after each meal; and just as William's young son had developed a scaly rash on his forehead that the doctors could not seem to diagnose. Worst of all, Sandra's own young daughter had displayed purple-tinted fingernails within the past forty-eight hours.

As the pungent liquid splashed on the thick carpet leading to the children's rooms, Sandra thought back to the phone call she had received from Kara less than a month before. Kara's voice had been shrill and filled with panic, unlike previous calls through the years.

She had mentioned a man who had come to the door of her home/business. A man wearing a uniform that had seemed hauntingly familiar, like those donned by correctional officers in the state of Mississippi. The man had tipped his cap politely and spoken six simple words before casually turning from her and hastily strolling away while whistling an old rock tune it had taken her days to properly identify. The song had been 'Don't Fear the Reaper'. The words: *"All of you carry the seed."*

Kara had said she ran out onto the street that fronted her home just seconds after the man had turned the corner, but that he had vanished from the area in a manner befitting a ghostly sentinel whose message had been successfully communicated.

Hours later, Kara had noticed the tingling at her fingers, and the bluish color beneath her nails.

Kara's husband was out of town on business, thus providing the perfect opportunity for mission success. He would survive his wife and child, as would only one other amongst a trio of families destined to endure great tragedy on the same faithful night. William's wife was unable to accompany her husband and young son on their visit to Kara's home due to job obligations. Again, fate had written the perfect script for the night's dreaded outcome.

Pouring the remainder of the gasoline atop her slumbering husbands still form and then around the bed frame itself, Sandra paused before lying next to him with the butane lighter clutched at her chest. The room smelled heavily of natural gas from the kitchen oven, the door of which lay wide open like the feeding jaws of a Great White. The handful of Quaaludes she had ingested were beginning to take their toll as her eyelids began to flutter uncontrollably.

She thanked the one above for at least giving them the last four years to spend as families, living each day with a true appreciation for the joys around them.

She then cursed the same entity for allowing such unbridled happiness to be so ruthlessly torn asunder, as if utterly meaningless.

Kissing Jimmy lightly on his exposed forehead, Sandra held the lighter to her fuel-soaked thigh and gently ignited the flame just as soothing darkness enveloped her senses.

To halt a plague, someone they had all known once said, you must first *sever* the roots.

THE END

www.ingramcontent.com/pod-product-compliance
Lightning Source LLC
LaVergne TN
LVHW030907080826
845145LV00010B/2792

* 9 7 8 1 7 8 6 9 5 3 9 7 1 *